THE DAY SHE DIED

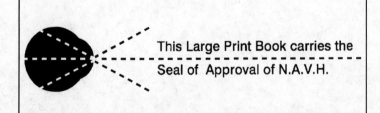

This Large Print Book carries the
Seal of Approval of N.A.V.H.

THE DAY SHE DIED

CATRIONA MCPHERSON

THORNDIKE PRESS

A part of Gale, Cengage Learning

GALE
CENGAGE Learning·

Farmington Hills, Mich • San Francisco • New York • Waterville, Maine
Meriden, Conn • Mason, Ohio • Chicago

LIBRARY OF CONGRESS CATALOGING-IN-PUBLICATION DATA

McPherson, Catriona, 1965–
    The day she died / by Catriona McPherson.
      pages ; cm. — (Thorndike Press large print mystery)
    ISBN 978-1-4104-7101-7 (hardcover) — ISBN 1-4104-7101-2 (hardcover)
    1. Family secrets—Fiction. 2. Fathers and daughters—Fiction. 3. Abusive parents—Fiction. 4. Child rearing—Fiction. 5. Large type books. I. Title.
PR6113.C586D39 2014b
823'.92—dc23   2014014730

Published in 2014 by arrangement with Midnight Ink, an imprint of Llewellyn Publication, Woodbury, MN 55125-2989 (USA)

Printed in Mexico
1 2 3 4 5 6 7 18 17 16 15 14

A12006534284

For Brian and Bogusia,
with love, thanks, and
a crack of the whip.

PROLOGUE

Inside

She could stand up straight. There was room enough for that. But when she raised her hands above her head, they hit the ceiling. She could reach them out to the sides too. There was room enough for that. But just a step or so either way and her fingertips touched the walls. And all she could see was absolute perfect nothing. Never before in her life had it been so dark. If she kept her eyes wide until they ran with tears, there was nothing. If she closed them, waited, and opened them slowly . . . nothing. She held her hand in front of her face, but she only knew it was there from her breath hitting her palm.

Quiet too. No sound at all. Blood in her ears, air in her nose. She cleared her gummy throat and spoke. "Hello?" But the sound didn't leave her mouth. Seemed to hang like fog at her lips and settle back into her. "Hey!" she called out. "Is anybody there?"

7

She waited, listening, and then she must have slept again, because when she woke the second time — twitching awake — the taste in her mouth was worse than before and she was clear of whatever she'd been under. She scrambled up and put her hands out, feeling her way around the walls for the door, round and round until she was dizzy, finding nothing.

That was when she shouted for the first time. "Help! Help me!" She bellowed it into the dark, only stopping when her throat was raw. Then she quieted again, slowing her breaths, in through the nose and out through the mouth, like yoga.

Hatch, *she told herself,* trapdoor. Must be. Just got to find it. Find it and open it and leave. Laugh about it later. And don't, whatever you do, think about the memory just starting to uncurl from where it was hiding inside.

Kidnapped, *she thought.* Captured. *Adventure words.* Incarcerated, detained against her will. *Police words. And don't think about those other words, from stories, not from life. Stupid words.* Bricked up, buried ali—

Stop. Find the hatch and open it. Climb out and walk away.

She put her hands on the ceiling and felt her way towards the middle. Her leg banged against something on the floor. She crouched. Plastic. And something else. Cardboard. The cardboard thing moved and the plastic thing stayed still. A light box and a heavy . . . a tray of bottles, shrink-wrapped, full. Twelve of them. And the box? She shook it. Packets of something inside. That's when she noticed her knee was jammed against a third object, there on the floor. Cold and solid, this one. She knew what it was. Even before she touched the china of the bowl and the wood of the seat, she knew what it was, and she started to cry.

ONE

Tuesday, 4 October

It was already a hell of a day. That much was clear when I found myself curled in a corner, in a cupboard, feet tucked in, arms wrapped round my shins, head buried between my knees so I could squeeze it hard, hurt it enough on the outside to make the inside hurting go away. My breathing was good and loud, from how your legs make a kind of cup if you sit that way, like an echo chamber, but I still heard Dot's soft knock on the cupboard door.

"Jessie?" she said in that kind way she's got.

It had to happen sometime. So, okay, it had happened today. Now what? (A) I could walk out and never come back. Wouldn't be the first time. (B) I could tell her everything. (C) I could make a joke of it. Wouldn't be the first time I'd done that either. I was an old hand. Had my spiel polished like a double-glazing salesman. And laughing at yourself first before anyone else gets the chance to? That's nearly as good as squeezing your head between your knees. Works every time.

They do laugh too. No one laughs at claustrophobia. Or agoraphobia either. Or blood and needles. But try pteronophobia and see what you get. First it's the lip twitch and then, even if they listen to the story right to the end (of the bit I'm willing to tell), when my granny came and found me, even if they nod and murmur, eventually they get that look and start laughing. Smiling anyway. So I play along.

"Sodom and Gomorrah," I say. "I know what you mean."

Because that was just the same.

There was much wickedness, so God sent in the boys — angels actually — to sort it out. And they went to stay at the house of Lot, who was a righteous man. And the not-so-righteous got wind of it and came to see what was up. "We know you're in there" kind of thing, "come out here where we can get a look at you." But Lot — hell of a host he was — was all, "don't bug the angels, whatever you do. Here, take my daughters; knock yourselves out." So then the angels start to get a hustle on, no surprise, asking

Lot to gather his family together — wife and kids, all that — and hit the road. And they said, "Don't look back."

But here's the thing: they didn't say why not. And so Lot's wife looked back (who wouldn't have?) and blammo! Pillar of salt, which, if the angels had mentioned it, might have helped her not do it in the first place, but there you go. And so Lot and his daughters end up camping and they get him plastered and then they sleep with him, and they both get knocked up and then the whole plot goes back to Abraham again, where it started anyway.

"And the moral of the story is," I said to Dot once I was out of the cupboard and back in the tearoom at work that day, "God hates fags. He doesn't mind dads pimping out their daughters or daughters seducing their dads, but he reckoned the angry mob banging on Lot's door had a twinkle in their eye. And since the mob were men and so were the angels, there it is. God hates fags. Couldn't be clearer, really."

"Well," said Dot. "There was Leviticus too."

"Oh, right! Leviticus!" I said. "Tell the truth, Dot. Who would you rather be stuck in a lift with? That angry mob from Sodom and Gomorrah or creepy Leviticus?"

She shuddered.

"Hah! I knew it. 'What's that blouse made of, little girl? What's in your sandwich today? When's your period due?' Total psycho."

"Stop it," Dot said. "How can you sit there and talk about being stuck in a lift after what you've just said to me?"

"That's my whole point," I told her. "I'm not claustrophobic. It's like Sodom and Gomorrah all over again: the take-home message isn't what you'd think it would be. And I wish I was because tight spaces are pretty easy to avoid. Unless you need a pet scan, and then it's not your biggest worry. But me? Walking down the street, going in people's houses, watching things on telly . . . it's rough."

"But you seem fine," Dot said.

"Yeah," I answered. "I know I do."

So when we went back to work again after lunch, she opened the bin bags and poked around to see they were safe before she turned them over to me for checking. I do the checking because I'm the boss. The manager, or maybe just the supervisor. Really, it's because I'm an employee, in all four days a week the Project's open, and the others are volunteers. So strictly speaking, Dot should have opened the bags if I asked her, even *told* her, without the story at all. But it's not that kind of place.

And while I was busy sorting, checking the labels, checking the pockets, colour-coding the washing loads, writing up the dry-cleaning (only if they're worth it, even with the discount), I was wondering how long it would take her to come and ask me.

An hour and twenty minutes. She appeared at the door of the wee room by the toilets where the washer and dryer are and leaned against the jamb.

"You came to us from the RSPB," she said.

"Guilty," I said. "Shoot me."

"How could you work in the charity shop of the Royal Society for the Protection of *Birds* of all things if you're —"

"I couldn't!" I squeaked. "Not in the shop. My God. I was in the office. Totally separate building."

"But even so . . ." Dot said.

"Yeah, even so," I agreed. "I lasted a year, though."

"Why?" she asked me. "Why did you put yourself through it?"

Her face was puckered up with concern. Well, she's sixty-three, so her face was puckered anyway, but the way she was looking at me, almost like she would cry in a minute? It floored me. Shouldn't have, really. Dot rakes through manky clothes fifteen hours a week for no pay and deals with our lippy clients too. Dot organised five separate jumble sales for JM Barrie House and didn't even swear when it went tits up in the end. She's got to have a caring streak a mile wide running through her.

"Atonement," I said. First time I'd said anything like it to anyone.

"Atonement?"

I'd floored her back. Was I really going to tell her the rest of it? How something doesn't need to be true for you to be sorry it happened? How you can know from a thousand hours of therapy that you didn't do something, and still it's the worst thing you've ever done?

"It's not the birds' fault, you know," I went for in the end.

"You were atoning to the *birds*?" she said, and the middle of her face unpuckered as the edges creased up. "You're a funny wee bunny, Jessie, you know that?" She shook her head, laughed a soft laugh, and then squeezed past me to fill the kettle for our tea. "Quite entertaining, mind you," she called over the sound of the tap. I just kept stuffing in my load of dark mixed-fibre easy-care.

So my point is basically this. The day I met Gus, the day she died, the day I grew a family like I'd planted magic beans, was the day I told Dot at work about my pteronophobia and told her quite a lot really, when you get right down to it, about where it came from too. *It was the very same day.*

Maybe I ended up where I ended up, did what I did, because I was already down the rabbit hole, through the looking glass. Maybe it's not totally my fault that I tripped and went over the rainbow.

Two

So Dot struck out for the top of the town to catch the Thornhill bus back to Drew and the bungalow and the corgi, and I peeled off at the bottom of the High Street for the five items or less queue in Marks and Sparks food hall.

"Morry's is actually closer," Dot said, like she always did. "Never mind cheaper."

"It's not my road home," I said, like I always did too.

"You youngsters," said Dot. "My mother fed a family of eight on a foreman's wages and saved enough —"

"— for skiing every winter and a second home in Tuscany, I know."

She made as if to cuff me, then looked at her watch and started walking again. "Be good," she called over her shoulder. "See you Friday."

So Steve was on tomorrow. Okay. Dot's a bit dittery, which means a lot of extra work voiding the forms she mucks up, but she brings scones from Gregg's and apples from her garden, whereas Steve makes his own deodorant from baking soda and — I'm sure of this — nicks the stock if he sees something he fancies. He says he's an anarchist, but the Project isn't exactly a multinational. And the worst of it is that he's about five foot five, and we've never got enough stuff for short men. We get loads of donations from tall people, but it's a hundred percent Hobbits that come in the front door. Break your heart to think, in this day and age, rich people are still bigger than the rest of us, like in Dickens's time or Henry the Eighth or something, but there it is. The war, Dot said once when I asked her, and then smoking and then microwaves. Triple whammy.

And I swear to God, it was right then, halfway up the soft drinks and groceries aisle, when I was thinking about work and how all our clients are basically Borrowers, that I saw him, pushing his daughter along in the trolley, like neither one of them had a care in this world.

It wasn't the first time I'd clapped eyes on him. It was actually the fourth. When I recognised him, my throat got a sudden lump in it, like the thing people call their

19

heart leaping. It's hard to say why. I mean, he's tall and broad, but he's got that kind of sandpapery skin that sometimes goes with red hair. Except not as bad as that sounds, really. I smiled. He looked straight at me and then away, and the smile died without me having to kill it. I never remember, never bloody learn, even though the only reason I shop in Marky's, spending a fortune, is so I don't run into them all every day. It's the worst thing about my job, to be honest — apart from the obvious, which goes without saying. I hate seeing people's faces fall when they spot me, seeing them whip their heads away and pretend I don't exist. Must be the same for prostitutes, only they get better money.

Kids are different. Sometimes they dance right up to you and twirl, show off their outfits. They don't know the Project isn't a shop like any other one. Father Tommy's dead right there.

"Children are too easy, Jessica," he says. "Show me a pretty little girl in a wheelchair and I'll show you ten people who want to run marathons to get her a better one. Show me a smelly alcoholic in his seventies, cursing at the top of his lungs and throwing his fists about, and I'll show you someone St. Vincent's will get all to itself."

20

Which is why he took such a lot of persuading to get involved in that Barrie House
project, because a children's respite home
with a magical garden attached is definitely
at the pretty-kid-in-a-wheelchair end of
things.

"*Practical* Christianity is my game, Jessie,"
he told me. "Not fairies and wishing wells."

But Father Tommy's favourites are easy
too. Proper tramps that just want a warm
coat and thick boots. They're a dying breed,
with their long beards and purple faces and
their country accents. Irish tinkers, Dot calls
them, no matter how many times Steve asks
her not to. And then she spreads her hands
and lifts her eyebrows and asks how it can
be racist if it's true.

Mostly our clients aren't pretty little girls
or quaint old Irish tinkers. They're either
reeling from some disaster or worn out from
years of them. Either way they're pissed off,
and there's no one but me, Dot, and Steve
for them to nark at. Especially the parents,
like this guy. And of course, here he was
again. I'd pass him on every aisle in the
place unless I did a Uey.

Strictly speaking, mind you, he wasn't a
client at all. And it wasn't the Project I knew
him from, not really. And anyway, he'd
decided to pretend I was invisible. He was

bending over the wee girl standing up in the belly of the trolley, blowing raspberries on her neck, making her giggle. I sneaked a good look as they passed me. I'd have remembered that dress and sandals coming in: bright coral corduroy pinafore, the nap still velvety, sandals with not a single scuff on them.

On the other hand, it was even worse than usual, because there *was* a time I thought we might be pals. Or — be honest, Jessie — there was a time when he was a wee tiny bit friendly to me like anyone might be, and I thought we might be . . . Anyway, I was wrong. Turns out it was wishful thinking.

Now eggs, cakes, and baking. He was on his phone, she was sitting down, fat legs braced under her, tugging open a bag of figs. Figs! Not many of our clients give their kids M&S figs for a snack. Not in a world with Pringles. Except that made me sound like Dot, saying they were poor managers, was all. "They're not poor managers," I tell her. "They're just plain poor." And then Steve (who's taken every social science course the Open University ever invented) says that expression's inappropriate. *Inappropriate* is Steve's second favourite word, after *unprofessional*. Everything he doesn't like is one or the other. Never *cruel* or *rot-*

ten or *clueless* or *mean.* We've had run-ins about it, proper set-tos, because I reckon it's better to try to be funny and kind and make mistakes than to be a sodding appropriate professional robot all the time.

The first time I'd ever met this bloke was a prime example. It had been months ago, maybe even a year ago, and he'd been dressed different then — a polo shirt and trousers like a uniform, ponytail under a baseball cap. He'd been standing in front of the Disney princesses birthday cakes in Morrison's, just staring. I'd noticed him because usually it was women who stood in front of cakes and stared. Then I'd seen him again at the Kiplings, with a sponge sandwich in his hands, a chocolate one, and he was gripping it so hard his knuckles were white and his chest was moving up and down so that the untucked polo shirt hem lifted and fell underneath his wee bit of a belly. He put it back on the shelf just as I passed him and, when I turned at the aisle-end, gawping over my shoulder, I saw him heading back to the bakery section. I couldn't help myself. Inappropriate, unprofessional. I followed him.

It wasn't until I was right at his side that I noticed what he was doing, and by then it was too late to back away. And in my defence, Lauren, that I'd been talking to about stuff, had just the day before told me that I should . . . Oh God, I don't know. Typical Lauren guff. Own my past, feel the sadness, bring what I was missing into my life whatever way I could. I liked her a lot, but I didn't always listen. Anyway, I steamed in.

"Excuse me?" I said. "Can I help you?"

He stuffed the handful of notes and coins back in his trouser pocket and turned, frowning. "Eh?" His voice was a bark.

"Are you all right?"

"I'm fine," he said. He picked up one of the cakes without looking. "How?"

"I don't mean to butt in . . ." Liar.

"I'm just —" He put the cake back on the shelf. "Cannae believe how much they are. Size of them too."

"Can I get it?" I asked.

He blinked, drew his chin back into his neck. "Why should —"

"Please? I haven't got a wee girl. I've never bought a Disney cake. Goan let me buy it for yours."

He stared at me for such a long time that my heart started to pump, and I wondered if he could see my shirt going up and down like I could see his. I remember wondering if he was drunk. I also remember thinking

I'd never seen anyone look so angry who wasn't actually shouting and, between work and my childhood, I've seen a lot of angry people. *Random acts of effing kindness my arse,* I remember thinking. Steve was right after all.

"Sorry," I said. I saw his hands clench into fists at his sides and I took a careful step backwards. "I didn't mean to offend you. Sorry I barged in."

"Right," he said. "You're sorry." For a minute I thought he was going to say that playground thing, *you will be.* Moving slowly, I backed away.

He sounded angry now too, standing in the middle of the aisle, growling into his phone, the wee girl chewing a fig, solemn eyes fixed on him.

"Becky, for Christ's sake," he was saying.

Becky. Of course he had someone. He was just a friendly guy and the rest of it was my imagination. Not that there was much "rest of it" anyway. Only just that a couple of weeks after the cakes, he'd come to the Project one afternoon when I was on my own, and he'd just kind of stood there.

"Have you got a form?" I'd asked him. "Are you just looking? We're not actually a charity shop, not really. You need a form if . . ." He was shaking his head, sort of smiling. "So, you'd be better off up at Cancer Relief, actually."

"I'm not after clothes," he'd said, and he'd smiled wider.

But clothes was all we had, so what was he doing here? And that was the moment I thought I knew what the smiling was. He wasn't here to buy stuff; he had come to see me, talk to me, maybe ask me something. I smiled back at him and, without another word, he opened the door and was gone. I puzzled over it for a minute or two and then put him out of my mind.

Good thing too, since it turned out there was this Becky, whoever she was, that he was talking to now.

"It's not forever, Becks," he was saying. "It'll stop again."

I wasn't listening, but I had to squeeze right past. I don't think he even noticed me. *It's not forever.* I was at the fridges. Pomegranate and raspberry juice. No drinking tonight. I'd put myself back together right as rain after the bit in the cupboard, but it had cost me. I was drained, kind of heavy and soft, like a birthday balloon three days after the party, and one glass of wine would be one too many. I'd put pomegranate juice in a stem glass and pretend. "It's not forever," I said to myself. What would that

26

be then? Sounded like a duff job, or staying on your friend's couch. But "It'll stop again" sounded like . . . what? Noisy neighbours? Hay fever? I put on a wee spurt to catch some more of it on the next aisle.

At first I thought he'd gone. The trolley was crossways between the shelves with the wee girl standing up in it, holding onto the side, looking over. She was probably four-ish, I thought, not big enough to climb out but plenty big enough to try. And she had the look of a climber to me. Standing four-square with her hands clamped on the rim. As I watched, she pushed up the sleeves of her jumper, all but spat on her palms. So even though her dad was a bampot and he hated folk sticking their noses in, I scooted forward, letting my trolley carry me, and that's when I saw him. Sitting on the bottom shelf in a space where someone had taken a jumbo pack of kitchen roll away, his head in his hands.

He'd been sitting like that the third time I'd seen him too.

My flat's right opposite the library on Catherine Street, and public libraries are total nutter magnets. (Steve would go daft if he heard me say it, but nobody ever asks what I mean.) They're always open, always warm, and they can't turn anybody away, so it stands to reason if you're the sort that couldn't get past a bouncer or maybe you'd have a security guy follow you round Safeway, the public library's the place you'll go. And if you smoke, then the bench outside the public library's the place you're going to go for a break.

Mind you, he wasn't smoking the day I saw him there. He was just sitting, with his head in his hands, staring down at the ground. I watched him a while — I was doing nothing better — until he stood up and went back inside. Then I decided to go over and change my DVDs.

Another mystery solved. He'd only been waiting for his photocopying to get done. A great big pile of it from the reference desk where they keep the papers and all the history of the town and that. He'd maybe just been thinking, with his head in hands that way.

I was pretty sure he wasn't just thinking now, though, sitting there on the space on the bottom shelf.

"Dad?" said the girl. "Daddy?"

"Hey." I hunkered down beside him. "I'm sorry for sticking my — Are you okay? Your wee one's worried about you." His hair had fallen forward over his face and arms and it made a solid barrier; that crinkly hair's like armour if you brush it down. I turned and smiled up at the wee girl. She scowled back at me. She had a great face for scowling, her eyes, nose, and mouth bunched together, plenty of cheek and jaw all around, and her own halo of red hair fluffed out in a cloud all around her Alice-band. I can take or leave pretty wee girls, but plain wee girls melt me; I was one myself. Still am.

"I don't think your Daddy's feeling too good," I said. I gave her one last smile — like dropping a stone down a well — and looked around for help. There was no one. Because what kind of moron buys kitchen roll and cleaning stuff in Marks and Spencers? He was moving. I turned back and got ready to leg it if he looked like going for me.

"She's gone," he whispered. "She's left me."

"Your girlfriend?" I whispered back. I'd assumed he was a divorce case that night with the cakes, assumed he was going round to see his kid at the mum's, not wanting to turn up empty-handed. "Could take your wee one back to her —" He needed to get over himself and stop spooking his daughter was what I was thinking.

"My wife," he whispered. "Ruby's mum. She's gone."

"Oh," I said. Big help.

"Dad?"

"Can you call someone?" I asked him. He lifted one of his feet and his phone was under it, smashed and flattened. "Here," I said, rummaging. "Use mine."

"I don't know any numbers."

"God, I know," I said. "Everybody's on speed dial. If you —" *If you stamp on your phone you've had it,* was what I was going to say.

"I've got to go," he said, pulling himself up, holding onto the shelf. But he swayed, and his ruddy face went grey in streaks under his eyes.

"Yeah," I said. "Go out and get some fresh air. Do you actually need any of this stuff?" I nodded at the bags of apples and bread rolls around the wee girl's feet. He nodded. "Do you need anything else?" He just stared at me. "Milk? Tea? Bog roll?"

"Nappies," he said, and I flicked a glance at the kid in the trolley. I was usually great at guessing ages. "Pull-ups, I mean. Twenty-four to — Oh my God!" And his feet went out from under him again. He sat down like a load of washing someone had dropped there, right down on the floor.

"Okay," I said. Too bad if I offended him. I twisted the cap off the posh juice. "Have a

30

slug of this, it's pure sugar. Are you in a car? Yeah? Well, you can't drive. Take the wee one outside — Ruby, is it? — and I'll get your shopping and meet you. I'll drive you home." I lifted Ruby out of the trolley, setting her down on her feet, waiting for her hands to let go of my arms, once she was steady. "What kind of car is it?"

"Skoda," he mumbled, standing again.

"Go," I told him. "I'll get this. For real this time."

"What?" His eyes were blank in his blank face.

"Doesn't matter."

He didn't remember me. No clue. Not from the cakes day, or the time he'd been in the Project, or even the day I'd been skulking about the library when he was getting those copies done, and I thought for sure he'd clocked me that time. He must have looked away like that, quick and sure, because . . . because he doesn't smile back at strange women who smile at him in Marks and Spencer's food hall? Because he's a happily married man? Not anymore he wasn't, from the sound of things. Or maybe his wife was the jealous type? Only it looked like she'd set him free.

I stood and watched as he walked away. He was bent over to one side a bit so he could steer his daughter with a hand on her back, and it made him look kind of broken, like he kind of was.

There was no sign of them at the back door. I scanned the street both ways, looking for a Skoda, wishing I'd asked what colour instead of what kind. But there was no one sitting in any of the parked cars. Maybe he'd hoofed it; maybe these apples and nappies were mine to keep now. I almost went back inside to get a refund — good old Marks — and go out through the front and home. Then I wondered. Irish Street, the back street, was all offices and permits. He'd never have parked right here. He'd be down in the proper car park at the Whitesands, like everyone else. Because, even while I was standing there, I could see that this time of day, half-past five, everybody was headed down there. Like Irish Street was draining out through the side alleys, people all pouring the same way down to the river.

Worth a try, I told myself. *Last thing he needs is another let-down now.* So I hoisted the shopping bags off the wall and joined the stream. Funny thing, though. You'd think at half-past five folk would be tired — plodding back to their cars — but I was getting passed, people hurrying nearly, and there was a bit of a thrum going. At the bottom of the street, they all crossed the wide road, edged around the rows of parked cars, and made for the railings. I followed them with my eyes, and there he was. His car — a battered hatchback, no hubcaps, paint dulled down to a matte finish with age — was right by the edge, and he was leaning against the door, facing the water. *Staring* down into the water, in fact, so I hurried, scuffling over the four lanes with the bags hitting my calves, swept up in all the crowd hurrying with me.

Ruby was strapped into a booster seat, still holding the bag of figs — shoplifted without me noticing — but not eating, and he was looking straight down into the water, like I said. He was the only one, though. The folk who'd hurried down the alleys were staring at the far bank and taking pictures with their phones. On the other side of the river, a police van and an ambulance were parked on the grass, half a dozen guys in high-vis jackets milling about.

"What's going on?" I asked him.

"Divers," he told me. As he said it, two heads popped up like seals from the rolling grey of the river, and the high-vis jackets lined up at the fence to look over. The crowd on this side made a noise all together like they'd been practising.

"Poor buggers," I said. "It'd take more than a wetsuit and mask before I'd jump in the Nith. Has somebody hoyed a dead dog off the bridge again?"

He shrugged. I put the bags in the boot and got in behind the wheel. He slid in to the passenger side.

"Seatbelt," I said. He didn't move. "Seriously, when you see me reversing out of this space, you'll wish you had." But his lips didn't so much as twitch. "What's your address?"

"That's a lot of cops for a dead dog," he said.

I looked in the mirror. "What's your address, hunny-bunny?" Fingers crossed it wasn't too far.

"Fifteen stroke three Caul View, Dumfries," she said, triumphant.

"Clever cookie," I told her. Caul View was just across the river. Five minutes away, even in Dumfries's excuse for a rush hour, as long as the road wasn't closed for the divers. In fact, if the dead dog had been lobbed in off a balcony instead of the bridge this time, a Caul View balcony was a contender.

As I had that thought, I felt a wee cold trickle of something down inside. Why

34

would that be? Maybe it came from the way he was staring at the cops and divers. And what he'd said too. *That's a lot of cops for a dead dog.* Just for a minute I was glad we weren't alone, him and me. I caught Ruby's eye again and smiled.

"Caul View, eh?"

"Only but we moved," she said. "To the seaside."

"Right," I answered. "Okay. Listen, sweetie, what's your daddy's name?" He was still sitting like a carved rock beside me.

"Daddy," she said. I remembered thinking that about my dad too.

"Okay, Daddy," I said, tapping him on his knee. I started the engine and put the car in gear. "Where am I going? Eh? Say Becky's not finished packing yet? Where will we go to find her?"

"Bypass," he said, at last. "A75 to Stranraer."

"Right," I said again, thinking I'd already shelled out for Marks and Spencer's pull-up nappies and, even if I felt like a pig for asking, I'd need him to chip in for my taxi back. The chances of getting a bus after dark were exactly nil.

I'd no idea how long it would be before the next time I went home.

THREE

And how weird is it that I enjoyed the journey? He never said another word for twenty miles and Ruby went into a car trance, thumb in her mouth and eyes glazed, but I like driving and I don't get to do it much. I hadn't been out of Dumfries for weeks, hadn't been west since spring, and I could feel the town lifting off me in big grey flakes, like that kiddy-on microscope film from the washing powder advert, that shows the dirt floating away.

Dumfries and Galloway; there's a clue in the two separate names. Flat grey plains by the sea, flat grey moors up above them, and wee grey towns from when Scotland had mines, just the spot for a free clothing project. In Dumfriesshire, they'll put a car park on the banks of the river instead of picnic tables and, if a beautiful old house is falling down, they'll give it a shove to help.

And it is a beautiful house, even without

the magic garden, but it was the garden that swung it. JM Barrie came to visit there — a family with a sister and little brothers and a big smelly dog — and he sat in the garden and wrote *Peter Pan.* Right here in Dumfries, while the brothers played at pirates. So of course it should be a children's centre, but it took a shed load of people donating and protesting before the council gave in. And even then someone on the committee took on cowboys to save a quid, and they nicked the lead off the roof or something (Father Tommy knows the story but he won't tell me) and vanished. Nicking the lead off the roof of a children's respite centre. That was Dumfriesshire for you.

But Galloway? Out of the world and into Galloway, as my granny used to say. Can't fling a stick without hitting an artist's studio, or a cheese-makers' commune, or a stone barn that's been turned into a theatre. Cottages painted like ice cream, harbours full of sailing boats, folk eating scallops. In Galloway, if you get more than six miles from a handmade candle, an alarm goes off and a beeswax SWAT team copters one out to you. I'd have moved there from Caul View too. We even had to stop for dairy cows crossing the road. Pain in the neck it must be if you did it every day, but it made me happy.

Only, when we'd got past Castle Douglas, a road sign said Stranraer 45 Miles and I thought I'd better check.

"Uh, how far are we actually going?"

"Gatehouse," he said. "Sandsea." Then silence for another ten miles, as we drove into the sea-light, towards the sinking sun, until I heard, "Next turn."

The "next turn" was onto a farm track between two fields. And not even a good one — grass up the middle and deep ruts from tractors so that the belly of the Skoda scraped along. I winced and clenched myself up off my seat is if that would help us, but the man didn't seem to notice. He didn't move in all the time it took to cross the fields in that flat milky light from the water, not until we'd passed under some trees and came to the farmyard itself, the usual dilapidated war zone, with its pallet gates and string hinges, piles of tractor tyres and oil drums. Then he jerked right forward, craning out of the windscreen and either side, gripping the dashboard, holding his breath. I slowed.

"Keep going, keep going," he said. "There's no one here."

"Is this your place?" I asked him, but he motioned me to drive on. The track went right past the yard, through an open gate, and then the trees closed around it again. I fumbled for the lights, got the windscreen wipers first, and then there were two patches of yellow ahead of us. All of a sudden, like always, the dark was darker.

"Stockman's Cottage," he said. "Over the fields." Then he twisted in his seat and looked behind. "Definitely no one there."

"So . . . no point asking if someone saw her leave?" I guessed, wondering what was getting to him. He didn't answer. And between the dark and the woods and the way he was jumping around, I was really starting to wish I was at home in my flat with my juice in a wineglass after all. Then the trees cleared and the land unfolded, and suddenly we were right on the bay — wet sand gleaming in the last of the sunlight, the stink of seaweed, and the line of the far hills looking as sharp as a knife edge against the pink of the sky.

"Bear left," he said. Right into the blaze of the setting sun, blinding us, filling the car with flames.

"I can't see a goddamn thing, by the way," I told him, and I slowed to a crawl. His hair looked like his head was on fire and the stubble on his cheeks was like gold glitter scattered there. Then we drew into the

39

shadow of a rowan tree (like they always have beside houses here, to keep the witches away), and the world was grey again, proper twilight, the last sliver of sun winking out, snuffed for the night.

"Where's Mummy's car?" said Ruby. "Where have they gone?"

We were parked at the back of a cottage; not the colour of ice cream this one, it was a farmworker's place for sure. Grey walls, metal window frames painted dark red like a railway station, pebbled glass in the bathroom window, and a lean-to porch against the back door.

"Can you come in with me?" he said. He hadn't turned — he was sitting staring straight ahead at the house — but he had to be talking to me. He couldn't be asking his daughter. His hands were gripping his knees, patches of red and white all up and down his fingers from the pressure.

"Of course," I said. I hate going into strangers' houses, people who don't know about —. Well, usually I've got my excuse ready before they even ask, but this was different. The state of him for one thing, plus what else was I going to do miles from anywhere with it nearly dark now? He fumbled the door open and hauled himself out. Ruby was unbuckling herself, scrambling down.

"I'll get the kettle on and you can call a friend on your landline," I said as I followed him, making it clear that I'd stick to the kitchen. Kitchens were usually fine. "I'll even stay till they come if you want me to." I felt sick and my heart was banging inside my ribs, making me think of my granny with her carpet beater — *bam bam bam* — but my voice sounded fine. I'm a star turn at sounding like I'm a-okay in much worse states than this one.

He stepped over a low fence into a garden, lifted Ruby over, and kept her riding on his arm as he disappeared round the corner to the front. I followed him. The path was red brick and the edges were bricks sticking up like saw teeth. Two patches of grass and two flower beds against the house. Blue front door and a window on either side, like a drawing. And beyond the garden gate, a few feet of that dead short grass from sheep eating it and then rocks and the beach and the sea — just a ribbon of light in the distance and the slow sound of low tide and the feel of the breeze with a hint of salt in. I looked at him standing there with the kid on his arm, picking over his keys.

This "Becky" must be mad leaving here. Walking away from everyone's dream life.

Stark raving bonkers.

He was struggling with the keys like a drunk, so I took them out of his hands and opened up for him. The wee girl wriggled down and burst into the house shouting.

"Mummy! Mummy?"

From one of the rooms came a sound. I couldn't have said what it was, but beside me, on the doorstep, he swayed again.

"No way," he said. "She'd never." And he took the length of the hallway in three strides, his hair flapping and his heavy boots booming on the thin carpet runner, then he shoved a door open and stood on the threshold. I edged up behind him and peered over his shoulder, standing on my tiptoes.

The blinds were closed, but I could see a double bed — sheets and blankets, flat foam pillows, no cushions, thank God — and beyond it a cot wedged in, in front of a tiled fireplace. And in the cot was a baby. A toddler, a boy by the look of him, standing up in footy pyjamas, holding on to the bars. He lifted his arms and squealed.

"Daddeeee!"

The man sat down hard on the edge of the bed and put a hand through the cot bars. The baby grabbed on, wrapping his whole fat little fist round one finger and tugging. He started bouncing up and down, his nappy — pull-ups, twenty-four months — rustling, saying "Da-ddy, Da-ddy" over and over in time with each bounce.

"She left him," said the man, looking up at me. "She locked him in and left him. What if something had happened to me? How long . . ."

I sat down too then, right down on a stranger's bed, and I could feel the stale close air of a stranger's bedroom pressing in, the private smell of sleep and worn clothes.

"It's okay," I said. "He's fine." He really was too. In fact, the boy was in the best shape out of the three of us, actually, but he'd picked up enough of the feelings in the room to stop bouncing. He was standing still now with the end of the man's finger in his mouth, looking at him with the same big dark eyes as his sister.

"Are *you* all right?" The man stretched out his other hand and touched my bare arm where I'd pushed my sleeves up for driving.

"Me?" I said. Yelped, really. "Don't worry about me! Time like this. God!" And now I put a hand on him. It was a shock to feel him burning through his padded shirt, damp with sweat.

"You need . . ." I said. What? He needed his wife back, was what he needed. Nothing that I could give him anyway. "Jeez, you're roasting."

"I'm . . . When she phoned," he started. He had lowered his head and he was mumbling again. "All I could think was she'd left me. She'd left *me.* Didn't even think of trying not to scare Ruby and I forgot —" His throat closed. He cleared it and spoke again. "Until you asked about the nappies. I forgot —" He was trembling.

"You'd had a shock," I said. "Don't beat yourself up."

"I forgot him!" He was whispering. "What kind of dad am I?"

"A brilliant one," I said. "You remembered the nappies. And you nearly broke the door down getting in here."

I was trying to help, but what the hell did I know about any of this? Well, truth was, a bit more than I'd want to tell him. Luckily he wasn't paying attention. He stood, stooped over the cot, and swiped the baby up into his arms. Buried his face into the fat little neck and blew raspberries, just like he had with the girl. The baby kicked against his chest, squealing. I could smell the sour stink of his nappy, overdue for changing.

44

"A brilliant dad?" he said, but he looked hopeful, like he just needed to hear it maybe one more time.

"For sure." I tried to sound as definite as could be. "Or she wouldn't have left them with you, would she?" Which didn't come out the way I meant it, but he was okay. He nearly smiled.

"Roobs!" he shouted. "What are you doing so quiet through there, you wee monkey?" And he turned and left the room, clomped through the house, still shouting. I could hear her giggling somewhere.

Maybe it was just a fight. Maybe she'd gone round to a friend's to give him a scare, bring him to his senses, stop him . . . coming in late or putting his boots on the couch. (Except he'd been wheeling a trolley round M&S, buying figs for the kid.) Or maybe the poor cow was happier in Caul View near her mum or her pals and had just had enough of the cottage — taken off, back by bedtime. (Except she had her own car, so how bad could it be?) Storm in a teacup. Someone needed to get her told about leaving the baby alone, right enough, but there was no harm done, so —

I'd been letting my eyes drift over the cosy mess of the bedroom, being quite brave really, now I knew the big dangers were

45

behind me. The floor was littered with toys and clothes — but boys' toys, quite safe. The dressing-table top was crowded with bottles and brushes and a row of Playmobil knights in armour ready for battle. I didn't think much of them and looked away. Something was propped against the mirror. Something that didn't belong. I stepped closer and read. It wasn't in an envelope, wasn't even folded.

I'm sorry, it said. *I can't go through it again. I can't go on.*

FOUR

"Hi!" he shouted as I slipped into the room. I let my breath go. There wasn't a kitchen door off the hall. Two bedrooms on one side, bathroom at the back, and just one door opposite. So I knew the kitchen had to be off the living room, no other way to get there. I'd told myself they weren't the type for those big Ikea couches. I was right; the three-piece suite was black and grey vinyl with red furry cushions. Only, a suite that old-fashioned made me think of a vase of bulrushes dyed different colours, and that made me think of pampas grass, and from pampas grass it wasn't too far to —

So I sprang to the kitchen door — Jessica Constable: super hero — and slipped through and he shouted "Hi" right at me.

Pretty overwhelming, actually, because the kitchen was small. And his grin was too broad, like his voice was too loud. And his eyes were too wide. What big pain you're in,

Grandmamma. It was about to get worse too.

"Can I have a word?" I said. I had the note behind my back.

"PB&J for dinner!" he shouted. "Yeay!"

"Yeay!" shouted the kids. They were sitting at either end of a tiny table squeezed between the door and the larder — it was that kind of kitchen: no work space at all, but a table crammed in — the boy in a high chair and Ruby kneeling up on a stool, feet tucked under. The baby had a sippy cup, nearly empty, hanging from his mouth, the spout held in his teeth.

"And ice cream!" the man said.

"Yeay!" shouted the baby, letting the cup drop. He started banging his hands flat on the tray of his chair. But it had gone too far for Ruby now. She spoke up in a smaller voice.

"Is Mummy coming back?"

He didn't answer, was still grinning that awful grin.

"Can I just have a quick word?" I said.

When he followed me back through, I closed the door on the kids and put the note in his hands.

"I'm really sorry," I said. "It was on the dressing table. And her purse was behind it. I mean — I didn't look, but this is her purse, right?" I handed it over, fat, bulging with cards and receipts. A right mum purse. He unzipped it and I caught sight of a photograph in the plastic bit you put your travel card in if you live in a city. Two babies.

"She didn't take anything," he said, flicking though the compartments. Then he put it down and read the note again.

"I think you should call the police," I told him.

He walked backwards, staring at the paper, until he bumped up against a sideboard — dark wood, but no carvings — and he leaned there.

"Where's your phone?" I asked him.

"No," he said, jerking his head up. "She didn't mean it. She'll come home."

"Cos she can't have had much of a head start, can she? They could look for her car."

He was shaking his head. He had twisted his hair into a rope — maybe for hygiene, making the sandwiches — but it shook loose again now and he swiped at it. "Listen," he said. "If I call the police and tell them this and they find her, they'll take her to hospital."

"But it sounds like that's where she needs to be —"

"And she'll never forgive me. It'll all be ten times worse. If they find out she left the baby, she might get charged."

"Not if she's ill. If her doctor says she's ill."

"She won't see a doctor. I've tried. Look, it's not the first —"

"Daddeee!" A wail from the kitchen. "We're hungreee! Where's Mummeee?"

And then the little one started up too.

"Mummeeeeeee!" A peal of sound that rang in your teeth.

"Look," I said. "I see this at work all the time. People just drowning because they think if they tell, it'll jump up and bite them. It doesn't. There's help. No matter what's wrong. There's always help."

"At work?" he said. "Wheesht, kids! One minute! What do you do, like? Are you a social worker?"

"No! God, no. This is just — just a friendly word."

"Kids, shut up!" he shouted again. Then he smiled, as best he could. "Thanks," he said. "It's just a friend I'm needing." The next smile was a bit better. "So what's the name of this new friend then?"

"Never mind that now," I said. "You need to call the cops and get them looking."

"I'm Gus King," he said. "And Ruby and Dillon King are the backing singers."

I laughed a bit — he deserved it for trying

— but I wanted to shake him.

He looked at the note again, out the front window, at his watch, back at me. "You really think I should phone?"

"I really do. Right now." *Inappropriate, unprofessional.* What you're supposed to say is, *it's your decision, I'll support you but it's up to you.* "Where's your phone?" I asked and then followed him through to the hall.

The phone was on a kind of hallstand thing, wrought iron and glass, half-hidden under coats and bobble hats. He looked up the number in the book — I'd have just called 999 — and dialled, then tidied the coat rack while he waited, pulling sleeves the right way out, balling up gloves and tucking them into a drawer. Then his eyes opened wide and he swung away.

"Yeah, hi, hiya," he said. "Em, it's my wife. She's left in her car and there's a note and I'm worried about her." He looked back at me as if to ask if he'd said it right. I nodded and gave him a tight smile. "Hello? Oh, uh-huh. License number, yeah. It's, em, SD02 ZJY. A Micra. Dark green. I — I don't know. I just got back in ten minutes ago. Me and my kids." He gave me a hard stare, daring me to disagree. "I had both the kids out with me and we all got back and she was gone. Becky King. Yeah, Rebecca. King,

51

yeah. She left a note, saying she couldn't go on." I reached out and touched his arm, squeezed it a little. "It's the Stockman's Cottage at Cally Mains, Sandsea. Gatehouse, yeah. No, no, it's okay. No, it's fine." He glanced at me again. "I've got a friend with me." And he dropped the phone back down as if it was burning him, turned, put both his hands against the wall, and let his head hang down.

"Gus?"

"Jesus," he said.

"What did they say?"

He stood up and stared at me. "They're sending somebody round," he said. "Jesus. I thought they'd tell me not to worry. Twenty-four hours and all that. Check with her friends . . ."

"You could do," I said. "Check with her family. Her friends."

"No family," he said. "Well, her dad. But . . ." He shook his head. I knew the type. Saw plenty of dads like that at work. Or heard about them anyway.

"Friends?" I asked. He walked back through to the living room and dropped down onto one of the vinyl chairs. They were the kind that the cushion squirts out if you move too fast and he looked miserable, balancing there on the edge of it, feet braced. Those big Ikea couches, at least you can plop into them after a shock.

"Her best friend was Ros," he said. "But she's away back home to Poland. She only broke the news a couple of weeks ago."

"That can't have helped," I said. I sat down too, right on the edge of the sofa, on one of the furry cushions, still not sure. But it squeaked like horsehair, so I shoved myself back a bit.

"It didn't," said Gus. "But I know Becky. She'll come back."

"But . . . do you mind me asking?" I said. A bit late. "It wasn't *just* her friend leaving, was it? What couldn't she go through again?"

"Depression," he said.

"Right," I said. "Christ. Yeah. Well. I've never had it. I'd rather have pretty much anything else, though."

He nodded. "Me too," he said. Then he looked at me. "Makes a change to hear somebody take it seriously."

That was a nice thing to say. He didn't half notice wee things for someone who'd just had something truly enormous happen. So I said no more, in case he thought I was milking it.

After a minute, he cocked his head towards the kitchen. The kids were laughing, squealing a bit. Someone was kicking their chair.

"Yeah," he said. "Post-natal depression. Ruby was bad. Dillon was worse. And she told me this morning she was pregnant again. Did the test and everything."

I remembered what he had said on the phone. *It's not forever. It'll stop.* And her note. *I can't go through it again. I can't go on.*

"Oh, Jesus," I said. He looked up and nodded really slow. "But —" He stopped nodding as soon as I spoke again.

"But what?" he asked me. He looked like he'd been turned to stone.

"She won't *have* to go through it," I said. "She can stop it. If you agree."

"Think I want to see her in that state a third time?" He was instantly angry. Zero to sixty in a heartbeat.

"So she'll do that. She won't just end it all. She won't just leave you lot."

"I hope you're right," he said and put his head back in his hands, like the flash of anger had never happened.

"Of course I am," I told him. "She'd never leave them."

"She left Dillon," he said, his voice muffled.

And the truth was, I *did* think that was funny. It's easy to overreact to stuff that pushes your buttons, and if anything I go the other road to make sure. But a mum leaving her baby was a kicker, no two ways there. And if she'd never done that before and she'd never left a note before, I could see why he was scared. But nothing about this whole stupid mess made sense. What was he even doing in Marks in Dumfries on his own with Ruby on this day of all days? After that news? How could he hear her cry for help and then hang up and smash his phone? Why the hell were they having a third kid anyway, with their boy and girl already? He was talking again. *God's sake, Jessie, at least listen, eh?*

"It's not just the depression," he was saying and he sat up again, leaned his head against the lace mat on the back of his chair, and looked at me from under his lashes. It should have been a creepy look, really. Sly, kind of. But he just looked wiped, as if he'd been drugged and could hardly stay conscious. "It's more than that. It's everything. Everything's crap."

I couldn't help flicking a glance around the room then. "Looks okay to me," I said.

"It's not though," he said. "Happy Families and all that. We weren't. We're not."

"Well, not today maybe," I said.

"Oh, me and the kids are fine," he went

on. "Me and Becky . . . Look, come on back through. They're doing murder in there."

The shouting started as soon as he opened the door, noise breaking over us.

"We're starving, Dad!"

"P B a J! P B a J!"

"Can I have syrup instead of jam, but?"

"Jam but, jam but!"

He high-fived Ruby on his way back to the breadboard and kissed the baby. He put a hand down on both their heads and tousled their hair, making a noise like a machine churning, messing her strawberry curls, his blond silk.

"Say hello to Jess, kids," he said. "She's staying for tea, seeing Mummy's gone out."

But he'd only got as far as spreading marg on the bread when a car door slammed outside. I watched the blood drain out of his face. Becky? Then a second door slammed, and two sets of feet walked up the brick path to the door. Even the kids fell silent, listening to the two sets of feet in heavy shoes, slow deliberate steps. Police. And a crackle from one of their radios made it true, and then Gus was edging round the children's chairs, gripping them tight, hauling himself along like he was climbing a cliff face. I followed him through the living room and out into the hall, watched as he opened the door.

"Mr. King?" said one of the coppers.

A woman and a man, and the way they stood there said it all.

"Aye?" said Gus.

"You're the husband of Rebecca King?"

"That was quick," he said. "Where did you come from?"

"Quick?" said the woman, frowning. Then she smoothed her expression. "Can we come inside, Mr. King?"

"Have you found her?"

"So you did know your wife was missing?" said the man.

His partner scowled. "Can we step inside, Mr. King?"

"I phoned Castle Douglas," said Gus. "How did you get here so fast?"

"If we could just come in."

"What do you want?" He was holding the door so hard that the hinge creaked. "If you're not from CD, what are you doing here?"

"Gus?" I said softly. What was wrong with him? Was this denial? From the kitchen, the kids started whining. The woman copper looked past him and caught my eye.

"I'll just go and see to them," I said and backed away.

I couldn't hear anything over the din of

sorting out who stole what and who kicked who and where was their dinner, their daddy, their mummy (Oh God), but I felt him fall. Felt it right through my feet and up to my teeth when Gus King heard the news and hit the floor.

FIVE

The woman copper was looking at me like something stuck to her shoe.

"You should try and find someone else," I said. "I really don't know Gus all that well."

"You know him well enough to call him Gus," she said, which was weird. Cops might *Mr.* and *Mrs.* everyone they meet, but normal people don't.

"Yeah, the kids don't know me at all and . . ."

She waited.

"I'm not that great with children actually. They need someone who knows what they're doing tonight of all —"

"We don't want to be bothering Mr. King about babysitters just now," she said. "He's got enough on his plate." The man copper had gone back outside to use his radio and not frighten the kids, and Gus had gone into the bathroom. The woman and me were sitting in the uncomfortable chairs in the living room. I could tell she had her legs braced to stop the cushion scooting out from under her. The kids had got their ice cream and were quiet in the kitchen with a story on the tape recorder.

"Of course," I said. "I'm sorry." She didn't answer or smile, but she maybe unfroze a wee tiny bit. "What happened?" I asked. "Are you allowed to tell me?"

"She drove her car off the road this afternoon. The B797, godforsaken spot, halfway between nowhere and nowhere else."

"Sanquhar and Abington?"

"Exactly."

I knew it well. Abington services was where Dumfriesshire air-kissed the M74, and every divorced dad who'd left the sticks and moved to Glasgow dropped his kids there or picked them up again at least a few times. Hellish dump it was too. As well as the bored dads and miserable kids, there were always a few dodgy blokes selling cars for cash, and a few even dodgier blokes having meetings without any cars at all to explain the cash. And the road to get there from here was only one banjo backing track from a horror film. The copper was talking.

"A turn and a drop, God knows how many feet down to the water. And the crash barrier might as well be crocheted."

"I know where you mean," I told her. I would have sworn her ears pricked up, but they couldn't have really. It was probably just her eyebrows, those dead dark ones that make the rest of your face look peeled. "Used to meet my dad at Abington," I explained.

She sat back, and her torn face straightened itself a bit. She nearly smiled. "Aye, me too," she said. "If you know what *she* was doing there, you should tell me. Mr. King couldn't think, state he's in."

I didn't speak. But there's no fooling a cop. Or there wasn't this one.

"I'm right," she said, and she wriggled forward until her knees were nearly touching mine. "You know something."

The letter was still on the sideboard; I could see it from the corner of my eye. I could hear it humming. I couldn't help the glance I flicked at it.

"If you know something, you need to tell me," said the copper, twisting round in her chair. "We're having a very bad day today, you know. Between this and the river."

"The river?" I said. "The Nith at Whitesands? What happened there?"

"God knows where it happened," she said. "Whitesands is just where it bobbed to the surface again." She shuddered. "So tell me what you know about Mrs. King." It was odd the way she didn't ask any actual questions. It worked, though. I nodded at the sideboard and then looked away. Which was when Gus came back.

"Oh Jess," he said. The copper had risen and picked it up, stood there reading. "It's not how it seems," he told her.

"We'd better make a start then, Mr. King," the copper said.

"Is there really no one else I could call for you?" I asked Gus. The copper made a sound with her teeth like a beer bottle top coming off.

"Try Ros," he said. "Her number's on the — Oh God Jesus, what am I — Look." He came over and held both of my hands in his, looked really hard into my eyes. "Just please stay, eh?"

"Okay then," said the copper. "Let's go." I followed them through to the hall.

"Don't bother about their teeth for once," said Gus, "but a bath'll help them get sleepy. Thanks, eh?"

And they were gone, leaving me standing there on the thin carpet strip that ran up the middle of the hall from the front mat to the bathroom door. An hour ago I'd been headed home to a bottle of wine — who

was I kidding with that pomegranate juice?
— and a box set, and now here I was all
alone in a stranger's house with sole charge
of two little kids. Jesus, I could be *anyone*. I
could be an axe murderer. Lightning could
hit the same wee house twice on the same
miserable day.

Could, but wouldn't. I took my coat off
— finally — and jammed it onto the hat
stand. I took my shoes off too and lined
them up at the end of the row. Work boots,
trainers, a pair of pretendy Uggs, Ruby's
wellies, Dillon's wellies, scuffed Start-Rites,
old jellies, and now mine. All in a row.

"Do you like bananas?" I asked them, going
back into the kitchen again. The ice cream
in the bowls hadn't gone down much. Well,
what did I know about toddlers' portions?

"Uh-huh," said Ruby.

"And do you like sugar?"

A big yes from the baby.

"Do you like fried bread and butter?" No
answer to that one; they were too young to
know that fried anything is a winner.

"So how do you fancy fried banana and
sugar pieces? You can't just eat ice cream or
you'll wake up in the middle of the night
with your tummies rumbling and your
daddy'll think it's monsters and be scared."

Ruby kind of smiled and glanced at Dillon, and I wondered if maybe you shouldn't speak about monsters to kids when they were all alone with a stranger.

"I'll make one and cut it in half to see if you like it," I said.

"Can we watch the telly?" said Ruby.

"Doy Dory Doo!" Dillon put in.

"Can we go and watch Doy Dory Doo?" said Ruby, giggling.

I thought about the red and grey flecked carpet and the vinyl suite, and how much harm could banana do it? So I nodded. Ruby hopped down from the stool and the baby held up his arms and screamed, kept screaming until I worked out how to undo the straps and lifted him down.

And then finally, when they were settled side by side on the couch and Ruby had popped the tape in — *Toy Story 2* — I just gave in. I put on a cotton apron that was hanging from the window latch by the fridge. I put the radio on to the news and let my daydreams take me where they wanted to, loading up a tray with plates and cups, wiping the ice cream off the high chair tray, trying to make a bit of space to turn round, looking for a pan in the big larder cupboard to fry the sandwiches in. I found a black iron one, thick with what Steve at work calls seasoning and everyone else calls grease, and so heavy I had to lift it with both hands.

It was a funny old place, this, for a young family. The black pan, the apron, the walnut-veneered bedroom suite with the old painted cot crammed in. Except for the Playmobil knights, everything in that bedroom looked straight out of the fifties, and the kitchen was just the same. Painted wooden cupboards with those black handles from before plastic and a china sink with a curtain across the underneath. Waxed paper, see-through with oil, on the shelves, mustard and cress growing in saucers on the windowsill. Outside, in the light from the kitchen window, I could see a washing line, one of those coat hangers with a dress on for pegs, lines of veg with milk bottle tops swinging above to keep the birds off.

"Dig for bloody Victory," I whispered. Except for the video player and the Fisher Price tape machine — still burbling on with *The Big Friendly Giant* — this place was like a museum. I pressed a slice of bread into the hot oil, laid long slices of sugared banana on top and pressed another slice over them. If Gus hadn't had a mobile phone, I'd think they were those retro-freaks who pay bid on eBay for faded —

It wasn't until I blinked and saw myself in the window that I realised I was standing there, spatula up in the air, like a statue. He'd been speaking to Becky on the phone when we were all in Marky's. Then we came back here, hardly started making the tea, and the cops arrived. Two cops saying she'd gone to the middle of nowhere and crashed and they'd found her, ID'd her car, got the address, and come to find him.

It wasn't Becky. It couldn't be.

I flipped the sandwich and pressed it down again.

How could they make a mistake like that, though? If someone stole her car and crashed it, they'd have their own bag and purse and that. And why would a girl steal a car?

I slid the sandwich onto the spatula again and then chuted it onto a plate, cut it in half, and poured the milk. The plates were white glass with yellow flowers, like I hadn't seen since I used to visit my granny.

But that woman copper had said she drove off the road *this afternoon*. How late was the end of the afternoon? Five. Definitely. Then it was evening, or teatime anyway. So it wasn't Becky. It couldn't be.

Through in the living room, both kids were slack and dreamy on the couch, slewing sideways to see past me when I blocked the screen. I put the tray down on the coffee table between a stack of library picture books and a fruit bowl full of Lego.

"Here you go," I said, dishing out the plates. "If you like it I'll make some more. If not, PB and J it is. You decide." I turned to get their milk and Dillon screamed, the loudest scream yet. I knocked the tray, toppling the cups, sending milk all over the library books and dripping off the table onto the floor. I whipped round. He was sitting straight up yelling holy murder, his mouth wide open, tears just beginning to trickle down his cheeks.

"Dillon! Dilly baby," said Ruby. Her plate slid off her lap and the sandwich disappeared into the couch.

"Foo-foo," said Dillon.

"Burny, burny," said Ruby.

"Foo-foo."

"He's blowing," Ruby said. "To cool it down. You should of blowed it, Dilbert."

"Oh Jesus!" I snatched the plate away from him, pressed my finger on the greasy bread, and pulled it away again, hissing. "Oh God!" I knelt down in front of the couch and turned up Dillon's hands. One was bright red and shining with butter. "Oh baby boy, I'm so sorry." I hoisted him, squirming, into my arms, bumped against the table, and heard one of the milk cups smash as it hit the floor. "Oh God! Okay, we'll go to the kitchen —"

"Doy Dory Doo!" said Dillon, really howling.

"Where's Daddy gone?" said Ruby. "I want Mummy." She was starting to whimper.

"Mummeeee!" Dillon squealed in my ear. I held him tighter.

"I've lost my sammidge," Ruby shouted, holding her empty plate out to show me.

"Down!" screamed Dillon, wriggling and pressing his hands hard against me to shove me away. I held him tighter still.

"Ruby," I said, over the noise of them both. "Just sit really still on the couch and watch your film and don't stand on the floor. Eat Dillon's sandwich."

"Noooo!" screamed Dillon. He turned the tips of his fingers in, digging his nails into the skin of my neck.

"I'll be back before you know it," I said to Ruby.

"Down! Down!" shouted Dillon, bucking and kicking. But Ruby was sorted. She took a big bite of his sandwich with her eyes fixed on his face to see how he liked *that* and then she turned to the telly again.

"One minute, I'll be back again," I said. "Unless Mummy gets here first, eh?"

And she'll come home to find a total stranger burning her kids and spreading broken glass about. I could feel tears beginning to gather at the base of my throat. *Useless bitch. Useless bitch.* I effing well told that copper I couldn't do this. If Becky tore a strip off me, I'd give her her arse in her hands. At least *I* didn't leave them, I'd say. At least *I* didn't get pregnant and then just walk. *Useless bitch.* I sort of limped into the kitchen, trying to keep a good hold of Dillon as he twisted and yelled. I even remembered to shut the door so Ruby could hear the telly, but his screams had turned to moans now and his sobs had turned to sighs, just about as deep as mine. I kissed the top of his head.

"I'm sorry," I said, sitting him down on the edge of the china sink and running the tap until it was stone cold. "I'm really really sorry." Which had to help. I remembered Caroline with the couch asking me if anyone had ever said sorry, and me being amazed. Adults didn't apologise to kids where I came from. It was working with Dillon. He was hardly sobbing at all now. "Put your wee hand under there for me, eh? Oh, you're a good big brave clever boy." I stretched his hand over to the tap, and he slipped down a bit into the plastic bowl half full of water, his knees coming up under his chin.

"Bet bum," he said. "Ouch."

"You can't say ouch for a wet bum," I told him.

"Ouch handy," he said.

"That's true." I took it out of the stream of water for a minute to kiss it and then put it back under again.

"Kiss it better," he said and he rested his head against my chest. A flood of feeling filled me up from the pit of my bowels into my throat, and right then I thought something unforgiveable. I'll never tell a soul what I thought, what I wished for.

"Mummy'll be home soon," I told him, trying to wash it away.

Six

I hadn't heard a car, but then the bath water was running and the thunder of it in the old enamel bath could have covered a jet landing. The whole place was an echo chamber, shiny lino tiles on the floor, glossy painted walls, and nothing more than a bathmat, thin from washing, to muffle the sound.

I was trying to make up for the fiasco their tea had turned into — cold water in first, top it up with hot, test it with my elbow, the pair of them told to stay out of the way, backs against the other wall, until I was sure it was warm enough not to give them a chill, cool enough not to give them a scald. Dillon's hand was still pink, but that might have been from holding it under the tap so long.

"Okay," I said. "Kit off. In you pop." They stared at me, four big brown eyes the colour of treacle toffees, but before I could ask them again, there was a soft knock on the kitchen door.

They turned and looked out of the bath-room window, cracked at the top to let the steam curl out. It had to be Becky. If her keys were in her car at the bottom of the drop on that godforsaken road, that must be her knocking, really mouselike, embar-rassed now by taking off that way.

"Wait here," I said to the kids. Then, flash-ing on the wee one trying to climb into the bath and banging his head, I changed my mind. "Let's go and see who it is, eh? I bet it's a nice surprise." I took their hands and led them to the kitchen. I opened the door and got ready to start explaining. It wasn't Becky. Thank God for the chain, because it was a stranger — a young guy, dressed rough, a good couple of days from a wash or shave. He rushed right up and put his face to the crack.

"Jess," he hissed. "Wait. Jess. Sorry." His lips looked cracked and sore and his eyes were wild, darting back and forward.

"Do I know you?" I could tell that the kids had moved back at the sound of his voice.

"Jess," he whispered. "Hello."

"Who are you?"

"Jess, hello." He looked over his shoulder, then he pressed himself even closer in to the door like he was trying to wriggle through the gap. "I need speak, Jess?" he breathed. *Yes,* he meant. Foreign accent. And he was talking in a foreign language now. The same phrase over and over again. *Jaroslawa? Jaroslawa?* I looked behind me at the kids. He went back to English again. "I see he is gone. Becky is gone? Jess? You alone?"

"I'm not alone," I said. (Stranger At Your Door 101.) "Gus is right here. And Becky . . ."

One of the children had come up and was tugging at my jeans. Ruby.

"Missus?" she said. "Lady?"

"Jess," he said. "Becky, please? My name is Kazek. Kazek, jess? You open?" He snaked his hand around the edge of the door towards the chain. "He is gone."

"Wait a minute, Ruby," I said, without looking.

"Friend, Kazek," he said. He had his fingers on the edge of the door, holding on hard. "Where is gone? *Jaroslawa?* You tell Kazek."

"Missus, Missus," Ruby said, tugging harder.

"He's not gone, pal," I said. "He's right here." Then I called over my shoulder. "Gus? Can you come here a minute?" The stranger shifted, wondering, and as soon as

I saw him loosen his grip a bit on the door, I booted it, dead hard. He let go. I slammed it shut and turned the lock. What the hell was that about? I could hear his feet on the path as he scurried away.

"Missus?" Ruby said again. "Dillon's crying, by the way." And right enough, he was. Standing with his head against his high chair, big silent tears running down his face. *Stupid, useless evil bitch.*

"Baby boy," I said. "What a rubbish night you're having."

"Who was that man?" Ruby demanded.

"I don't know," I told her, hunkering down beside Dillon and stroking his back. "Don't worry. He's gone now. Come on and get in your bath and get nice and clean for Mummy, eh?"

The bubbles cheered them both up. I'd put in far too much and the foam was stiff and crackling, up to their skinny little shoulders and wisping off when they blew at it. When I was sure they were safe — Ruby telling me cross her heart and pull her pigtails that Mummy left them in the bath together all the time — I went to pick up broken glass and mop milk in the living room, peel fried banana off of furry cushions. Everything back on track again. Until I thought about the bath getting cold and the question of pyjamas and all the blood left my head and I sat down hard, shaking.

It took me three big breaths to get up again, get into the hall, and put my hand on the door of the other bedroom. I gripped it until the sweat nearly popped it out of my grasp, but I couldn't turn it. Just . . . no. I couldn't make myself push down and open that door. No way.

I stumbled back to the kitchen again and saw my salvation. There was one of those old wooden pulleys with the cast-iron ends and the rope round a cleat, kids' clothes draped over it, including a Mulan nightie and snuggle socks. I stretched up and snatched them down. Dillon could go back in the same PJs again with a fresh nappy out of the packet in the bathroom.

And they could tuck up on the couch, one at each end with a blanket, put the film back on. They'd love that.

And so they did. Nearly as much as they loved not getting their teeth brushed and the bowl of M&Ms I gave each of them as I bedded them down and tucked the throw round them.

"D'you want to pick up where you left off or go back to the start?" But they were glazed-over already. I clicked and tiptoed away and was sitting in the kitchen, dishes done, worktops wiped, when I heard a car rumbling up the track and stopping.

I was ready for Becky, praying for Gus — and Gus it was. With the same two cops again, all solemn and pale. I took the chain off the back door, undid the deadlock, and they filed in.

"D'you want a cup of tea?" Gus said. He leaned against the sink and rubbed his face with both his hands.

"We'll need to be getting along, Mr. King." The woman copper turned to me. "You're staying." It wasn't a question, but I answered it anyway.

"I can't," I said. "In fact, I was wondering if you would give me a lift back as far as Castle Douglas if you're going that way." She gave me the chewing gum stuck to the shoe look again, and I bit my tongue.

"So, Mr. King," said the other one, all business, no time for this mooning around. "Someone will call round tomorrow to take your statement and in the meantime, you've got my card and it's got my direct line. There's a voice-mail on that. So . . . have a dram and get some rest." He nodded to me, put his hat on, and left. The woman gave Gus one of those syrupy looks, head on one side, frowning and smiling together, and followed.

Looked like I was springing for a taxi then. But I'd give it a few minutes. He needed a bit of a shoulder, it looked like to me.

"Pretty grim, was it?" I asked him.

"Feels like a dream," said Gus. He came and sat down. For a minute I thought he was going to put his hand out for mine.

"Did you look through a window or were you right in the room?" I said. "What a horrible thing to have to do either way. No news at this end, by the way."

"News?" he said. "What do you mean?" He'd gone very still and suddenly the house seemed extra quiet, the night outside extra dark.

"No word from Becky," I said. "Someone did come round, but I didn't let him in."

"I don't understand," said Gus.

"I worked it out," I told him. "Not long after you left. I would have called if I'd known your number and your phone wasn't smashed." I was babbling. "I could have called the cops, I suppose, and got patched through. But what with the kids and then this guy turned up."

"Worked what out?" he said, cutting right through my voice, his so loud in the tiny kitchen I thought I could hear it booming back off the walls.

"That it wasn't Becky," I said. "It couldn't be."

"Jess, what are you talking about?" he said. "What guy? It *was* Becky. It *is* Becky. My wife's dead. She's gone. She did it." He put his hands round his shoulders and started rocking, not back and forward but side-to-side. I'd never seen anyone do that before; it looked like Stevie Wonder's sit-down dancing.

I didn't mean to be cold, looking at him instead of going to comfort him, but I just couldn't get my head to take it in.

"Was she —" I began. He moaned very softly. "This woman," I said. "Was she really messed up? Her face? She was, right? Gus, it might have been her car and I know about the note, but it can't have been Becky."

"Why are you doing this?" he said. "What's wrong with you?" His voice had risen, and I flashed back to that day with the cakes, how scared I'd been, how fast I'd backed away.

"You're upset," I said. "Of course you are. But listen: you were talking to Becky on the phone at quarter-past five. What time did this woman die?"

"Three o'clock," said Gus. "Give or take, they said. But it's Becky. Her face was fine. It was a message. I told you that before."

"What?" It was like he had changed midstream but without changing his tone, like I'd flipped over the telly channel and found the same actor in a different role.

"I told you in the car, didn't I?" He was looking at me very closely now and I thought that if he started swaying his head from side to side, he'd be expecting me to start swaying too. "It was voice-mail," he went on. "Becky sent me a voice-mail message. I was listening to it when you saw me." I said nothing. He hadn't been listening, he'd been talking. I'd heard him. *It's not forever,* he'd said. And: *It'll stop again.* I heard him talking to her, walking up and down the aisles of the food hall. And he hadn't said *anything* to me in the car.

"Sounds crazy, eh?" he said. I nodded. "She left a lot of messages. Long ones. I got in the habit of talking back to them. Kept me sane when she was . . ."

"Right," I said. I hadn't known my shoulders were hunched until I dropped them. "That makes sense then. You didn't tell me though, you know. In the car."

"I thought I did." It was on the tip of my tongue to tell him I was sure he hadn't, and then it struck me what I was doing: I was arguing with him. *Arguing,* for God's sake.

At a time like this. What *was* wrong with me?

"I'm so, so sorry, Gus," I said. "I'm so sorry. I just don't know what to say." I knew what I *couldn't* say; I couldn't segue straight to *call me a taxi.* "Have you eaten anything?" I asked him instead.

"I'd puke."

"Or how about that dram?"

"I'd definitely puke," he said. "I just want to go through and kiss the kids and then . . . if you didn't mind, I'd really love to just sit for a bit. Sit by the fire."

"Of course," I said. "Call someone. I'll get out of your way."

"I meant with you. Talk, maybe."

And again, I could hardly say no. "Except the kids are tucked up on the couch," I said. "Sorry. I let them doze off with *Toy Story.*"

"Best thing," he said. "Good thinking. I'll lift them through now. Once they're off, they're like sacks of spuds — you could roll them along the beach and they'd never know."

"I'll put the kettle on."

"Now, you're talking," said Gus, pausing in the door. "A good cup of tea. Milk and two sugars." Not a drinker then. Just got that red skin from being Scottish, poor bastard.

80

I stood at the sink a long while with the kettle under the tap before I turned it on, staring at my reflection in the dark window. It all made sense. She phoned him a lot, he spoke back to her messages, he thought he'd told me, he hadn't. I made a mistake, he got confused, we sorted it out. It all made perfect sense. Tied up tight. So why did I feel like every time I turned my back on it, a bit of it slithered free again? I shook my head.

Crazy night. It was up to me to be the together one.

I gave the fireplace a good look, waiting for him to come back, once the tea was made, and if it had been coal and firelighters, I'd have got a good blaze going to cheer things up — no fireplace at all is fine, but cold ash is like death in your living room, even at the best of times. Here, though, there was a basket of twigs and a basket of logs and no box of Zip in sight, so I just swept up the worst of the spilled ash with the wee broom from the brass set and sat down.

It was the first thing Gus did when he came through anyway, on auto. He knelt, screwed up paper, dumped a load of sticks on top, three logs balanced together like a teepee, set a match to it, and sat back into his armchair to lift his tea. There was a curl of smoke, a snap, and the flames started to flicker.

"Scouts?" I said.

He smiled, took a long draught of his tea, sat back with his head against the chair cover.

"Been doing it every day since I was twelve," he said. "Getting sticks up the track, sawing lengths, splitting them, stacking them, lighting them, raking the ashes, spreading them under the rhubarb. Drove Becky nuts. She wanted a gas heating system. I wish . . ."

"Twelve?" I said.

"I grew up here. Teenage years anyway. It's my grandpa's house. He left it to me. I thought it would be perfect for the kids, but Becky missed the town. I wish . . ." he said again.

"So your Grandpa brought you up, did he?" Normally the kind of subject that's best avoided but compared with Becky, I took it.

"Divorce," he said. "Dad took off. Me and my mum and my brother came to stay with Dave. She met a new guy, moved in with him, took my brother. I stayed here. Moved out when we got married. Came back after he died." He looked around himself at the fire brasses, the pipe rack on the mantelpiece, the print of highland cattle standing in a loch above it. That explained the walnut veneer and the Bakelite handles.

"You called your grandpa Dave?" I said, like I was competing against my personal best for dumb stuff to come out with.

"He was a dude," said Gus. "Not what you'd think. He totally got my work. Supported me."

"What do you do?" I said, hoping he wasn't a strip-o-gram or a bailiff or something.

"I'm a sculptor," he said. I must have looked surprised. "What?"

"Nothing," I said. "You just seem dead . . . normal. Sorry."

"I only wear my lavender smock and my velvet tammy when I'm in the studio," he said.

"Right," I said, letting him laugh at me.

"And Ruby and Dillon are really called —" he broke off, couldn't think what to say.

"Iolanthe and . . ."

"Tarquin!" he said. "Becky wanted to call him Porter." I raised my eyebrows. "Her maiden name." He finished his tea and set the cup down. "What am I going to tell him?"

I thought it over. "Same as Ruby," I said. "Even if he doesn't really get it. You need to tell them straight and answer all their questions. There's books . . ."

He was nodding, but his bottom lip had started to tremble. A tear fell, then another and then, for the first time, he really started to cry. Great big painful sobs. I went over, sat on the arm of his chair, and rubbed his back hard with the flat of my hand.

The flames were dying down by the time he stopped. Gulping and coughing, he sat up, leaned back, and let his head fall against the chair mat again. We were pressed close down our two sides.

"If there's anything at all I can do," I said. That useless thing folk say.

"There is," he told me. "You can stay."

Shit! What was I going to say now? *Oh sorry, I didn't mean it?*

"Please, Jess," he said. "It would mean a lot to me."

I could hardly answer, *try again with something smaller.* "Of course," I went for. "I can bunk down on the couch."

"No," he said. "I couldn't ask you to do that. I put Ruby in my bed. You can have hers."

I was on my feet before I knew it.

"I can't!" I said. "I mean, I'm fine on the couch, honest. In case she wakes up and wants to go back to her own room."

84

"You're kidding!" he said. "She'd never sleep in her own bed if she had her way." He peered at me. "What's wrong, Jess?"

"Nothing," I said. "Absolutely nothing. And even if there was, think I'd bother you about it now? Look, I really should get a taxi. I'll call you tomorrow if you give me your number, but I really should go."

"Tell me what's wrong," he said. "Jesus, you're shaking. What's got you this scared, eh?"

SEVEN

Which is how come I wound up telling my troubles to a guy I'd just met, who'd hours before ID'd his wife's body after she'd killed herself after years of depression, which makes me the biggest spoilt selfish evil bitch that ever drew in breath to whine with.

"Take your time," he said.

"You really don't need me dumping my crap —"

"I'm asking what's scaring you," he said. "Throw me a bone and tell me, eh?"

So I focussed on a spot in the distance and after two deep breaths, I said it very calmly.

"Feathers." It took ten weeks of counselling (well, seven years of counselling and then the ten weeks that worked) to learn to do that without gagging.

He tried not to look surprised, but he failed.

"Pteronophobia," I said. "I'm sorry. I

know it's nuts. I know it's nothing. I'm sorry."

"Pteronophobia," Gus said slowly, trying it out in his mouth. "Is that why you wanted to stay in the kitchen? When we got here?"

All the breath left my body like someone had punched my guts. Never before, not once, had anyone ever done anything except laugh or tell me they preferred foam pillows too.

"Yeah," I said. "Pillows, duvets, cushions. Those big Ikea couches you get. None of the worst stuff is ever in the kitchen."

"Is this place okay?" he said, twisting in his seat to look around. "I've never even thought about it."

"Of course you haven't," I said, "because you're not insane. This place is fine. I wasn't too keen on the Playmobil knights. Plumes, you know. And I checked that there wasn't carving on the sideboard."

"God, that must seem sick to you. Carving . . . them . . . onto furniture."

"Just a bit," I said, still reeling.

"But listen. Ruby's duvet's micro-whatsit, like ours, and her pillow's foam. You'll be fine."

"Has she got a Barbie?" I said. "Fairy costume? Anything like that?"

"I can't think," said Gus. "I'll go and check."

"You shouldn't have to bother," I said. The guilt was killing me, like it always does but worse. He was off, though. I listened to him quietly open a door and close it again. Waited. He came back into the hall, went out the front door. I could hear his boots on the path. Two minutes later he was back in the room.

"It's fine," he said. "Come on, I'll come with you and show you. It's all okay."

"Where did you go?" I asked. He hesitated. "It's all right. You can tell me."

"Novelty pen," he said. "It's in the wheeliebin, wrapped in a bag. I didn't want to walk through here with it."

I gave him a long hard look. I was used to indifference and ridicule. This was freaking me. "Does someone else you know have this?" I asked.

"No," he said. "Why? Is it common?"

"Hardly. Just . . . nothing. You're . . . good with people."

"Look who's talking," he said. I had no idea what he meant. I had done nothing but boss him around, try to crap out, upset him with my brilliant wrong deductions, and burn his children.

"You were going to tell me how to break

it to the kids," he said. Was I? He had some recall for the state he was in. I couldn't have told you what we were talking about before the . . . *feathers* . . . with a gun to my head.

"How far had I got?" I asked him.

"Tell them straight and answer their questions. Mummy loved you both very much but —"

"No!" I said. "God no. That's what my dad always said to me after he left. Don't tell them that whatever you do."

He put his head on one side and kind of crinkled up his face, looking at me. After a bit he nodded. "My dad said that too," he told me. "Once. In a letter. Well, a card. He wasn't that touchy-feely, as it goes."

"It made me want to scream." I had screamed once, in Abington Services actually. " 'I love you more than life, Jessie. I'd die for you, Jessie. I didn't leave you, Jessie. I left your mum.' I always wanted to say, 'I live in Dumfries, Dad, and you live in Glasgow. How'd you manage that without leaving me? And I don't need you to die. I need you to stay until I'm more than seven.' " I took a deep breath. "Sorry." But he was still nodding, a bit faster now.

"No, you're right," he said.

"I am, as it happens."

"I totally agree. I don't think it's okay for

people to leave. Married people. Dads." His face clouded. "Mums."

"Here's what to say," I told him, thinking Steve would die if he could hear me. "You should tell them that Mummy loved them as much as she could, but she wasn't very good at loving people." He was nodding again, so I said a bit more. "That she was ill in the bit where the love comes from. That way they won't think loving means leaving. And they won't be as fucked up as —"

"You and me," he finished for me. "You're totally right."

"You're totally not fucked up," I said. But he was thinking, not really listening. I wondered whether to chance my arm all the way. In case I never saw them again after tonight, I'd better.

"You know what they will ask and I've got no idea how to answer?" I said. His head jerked up. "Why you were having another baby if it made her so low she'd do this instead."

He relaxed a little, but then groaned and shook his head. "You don't know the half," he said. "After Ruby, I said no more, like I told you. Rubber raincoats." I blushed and hoped the low light — one lamp and the logs burning — would hide it. "Until one night she jumped me. I'll let you off with

90

the details . . . but eight months later, Dillon appeared."

"Weird," I said. "You'd think she'd be really caref— *Eight* months?"

"Nine pounds five ounces," said Gus. "Straight blond hair. I'm a ginge and Becky's dark. You tell me."

"Lots of kids start blond," I said. "But . . . yeah."

"And as for this one, she pounced again about three weeks ago," he said. "And she did the test today. If they do a post-mortem, I'm thinking seven weeks."

"So Dillon . . ."

He bent over and pressed his head to his knees, like he'd suddenly got cramp out of nowhere. "I forgot him," he said. "Wee man, waiting in his cot. Oh Christ."

I stood to come over and sit close to him again, but he waved me back. "I can't cry anymore," he said. "I'm too tired."

"It's been some day," I agreed. This morning I hadn't known him beyond a face to smile at and wish I hadn't. I might have thought I'd known him, from thinking daft things months back, but he was a stranger, really. And now here I was, in his house, talking like his best friend, rubbing his back while he cried. What the hell had happened?

"All in one day," he said, but of course he

91

didn't mean me. "Pregnant, leaving, missing, dead." He was frowning into the embers, and he might have said he was too tired to cry but I could see he wasn't too tired to think. His eyes were darting back and forth like he was doing sums in his head or something. "I can't believe how quickly they found her. On that road. She should have lain for weeks."

Something low down inside me shifted at the thought of it.

"Could have, you mean?" I said.

He nodded absently, then blinked. "What did I say?"

I shook my head, no way I was starting to nitpick again about this now. I didn't understand why talking to him made me so persnickety. "How come she didn't?" I asked instead.

He heaved a sigh that was half a groan, like the first note of a bagpipe striking up, a creepy sound. "A hill walker," he said. "His dog slipped its lead and went down the bank. I need to try to get in touch with him and say . . . thank you, I suppose. For getting it all over quickly."

"Better this way?"

"All in one day," he said again. "Even if it leaves you too tired to cry." He looked up at me and gave an exhausted smile, all the quick darting looks totally gone. "I'll make a note to cry tomorrow."

"Safe bet," I said. "Why don't you go through to your bed? You know where I'll be if you need me."

I used the bathroom first. Brushed my teeth with my finger, washed my face with my hands, and dried it with Ruby's bath towel. I took some baby lotion for moisturiser and slipped into Ruby's room.

The bed was short, but so am I. I switched off her Ariel lamp and watched the shadows jump as the moonlight took over. I had just closed my eyes when I heard him leave the bathroom and then a knock came at the door.

"Jess?" he said. "I just thought of something."

"What is it? Come in. Don't wake the wee ones."

He put his head round the door. "We're right on the beach here," he said. "There's gulls everywhere, oyster catchers, ducks come down the estuary. Flipping geese sometimes, this time of year."

"I'm fine with birds," I said. Now he'd laugh. Surely.

"Oh," he said. "That's good. Good! I'll just nip out first light and check for sand-castles. You know, sometimes kids decorate the turrets . . . well, you know. Night-night."

"Night-night," I said.

"And Jess?" I waited. "Thanks. Thank you."

I put my hands behind my head and lay thinking. If it wasn't for the note, if the cops knew about Dillon and the new baby, they'd be asking Gus where he was at three o'clock for sure. Or if her car *had* lain there unnoticed for days and they'd never pinned down the time. But they'd have searched for her after he called, when he found the note. Except he'd never have called if I hadn't made him. And it was a chance in a million that I'd got involved. And heard him talking to her. Like an alibi. Except it was a voice-mail message.

I turned over on my side. Who does that? Talking to a voice-mail message like it's a person.

I curled up tighter and closed my eyes again. Who won't go in a wee girl's room in case she's got Marabou Barbie?

Don't beat yourself up, I told myself, just like Lauren coached me. *You drove him home. You stayed with the kids. Even if it was because you couldn't get away. You helped him get ready to tell them. You agreed to stay the night, for God's sake. With a complete stranger. And the last thing he said was thank you.* I ran over it again in my head, feeling a little smile start at the memory. *And Jess? Thanks. Thank you.* In the morning I'd tell him it was Jessie, or Jessica for Sunday best. No one except my mother called me Jess. Had I said Jess when I introduced myself? I'd never. Had he just shortened it without thinking? I sat up on my elbows. Something was bothering me. Something was making my heart beat faster. What had I forgotten?

My eyes popped wide open. Of course! That creepy guy that I thought knew my name. I'd never managed to tell Gus he'd been here. What had he said his name was? Started with K. Maybe a C. He'd said he was a friend, but he seemed pretty keen to be sure Gus was out. Maybe he was just Becky's friend. Maybe he was even Becky's *special* friend. No point upsetting Gus about him, in that case. Not when I couldn't even remember his name. Ka-something. Ka-zakhstan, was all I could think of. Kalashnikov, Cossack, kazoo . . .

EIGHT

Wednesday, 5 October

I woke to the sound of Ruby wailing like a siren and knew he had told them. That was my first thought as soon as I heard the noise. There was no, *Where am I?* No piecing together the strange room and memories filling in. It was as though I belonged there.

I threw back the covers, pulled on my jeans, and, in my bare feet, went through to the kitchen to try to help. She was like a rag doll in his arms, legs hanging down, arms flopped over his shoulders, head buried in his neck, bellowing. Dillon was in his high chair eating Cheerios off his finger ends, watching his sister.

"Here's Jess," he said. "Look, Roobs, here's Jess come to give you a cuddle."

"Nooooo!" she screamed. "Mum-meeeeeee!"

"Okay, okay, you're all right," said Gus.

She lifted her head and looked at him.

"It's okay?" she asked.

"It's all going to be okay."

"Mummy's coming home?"

"Mummy's not coming home, darling. Mummy died. Mummy's gone to live in heaven with Grandpa."

She twisted in his arms and started yelling again. "No! Stop saying it. Mummy doesn't even like Grandpa! Mummy lives here. I want Mummeeee. Now! Now! Now!" She was bucking like Dillon had the night before, but she was bigger, had to be turning him black and blue the way she was laying in to him, but he just rocked her until she was calm. Then he sat down with her still in his lap. He was in boxers and a t-shirt and his arms and legs looked cold, his big ugly feet purple and his toes white. Poor circulation.

"Can I do anything?" I said.

"Coffee'd be good," said Gus. "Want some hot chocolate, Roobs?"

"Lot-lit," said Dillon.

"Coming up," I said and started looking for the fixings.

"D'you want to go to nursery today, darling?" Gus was saying. "Or d'you want to stay at home with me?"

"And Mummy?"

"Just me, sweetie pie."

97

"Nursery," said Ruby. "I'm telling Miss Colquhoun what you said. I'm telling on you."

"I'll phone Miss Colquhoun," said Gus. "Come on and we'll get you dressed then. Your chocolate'll be ready by the time you are."

"Lot-lit," said Dillon.

"He'll be lucky to get out of his jammies today," said Gus, looking over Ruby's head towards me.

"I'll dress him, if you like," I said. I thought that's what he was hinting. But he screwed his face up and gave me the kind of look people get when they're going to ask something big and they know they shouldn't. It's the same look when someone's going to pop a cork on a bottle of Cava.

"I was going to ask you if you'd run Ruby into school," he said.

"Where's school?" I asked.

"Dumfries," he said. "I thought, if you're going in anyway. To work." Ruby turned her head and looked at me. Her face was swollen and blotched — you could see where she got her complexion, could see how tough a time she'd have in her teenage years. I smiled at her, but she didn't so much as twitch a muscle at me. Who could blame her? How could she deal with strangers on a day like today?

"I don't think —"

"I said I'd stay in for the cops," said Gus. "I don't really want a big meeting." He jerked his head towards her. "Different with Dillon, but . . ."

"Won't you need your car?" I asked. I thought a frown flashed across his face, but it cleared before I was sure.

"I've got the van," he said. "At the workshop. I'd really appreciate it. That's okay, Ruby, eh no? If Jess takes you to school? I'll tell her the secret word so she can pick you up again too."

It was the worst idea I'd ever heard. Ruby and me agreed on that. She slid out of his lap and left the room, giving me a wide berth on her way.

"How come she still goes to school in Dumfries?" I asked. It was getting on for an hour's drive away.

"Just nursery," said Gus. "She calls it school to feel like a big girl. We didn't want too many changes all together, you know."

Sounded crazy to me. Far better to have her with her new friends at her new house. And it was October. She must have been away from this Miss Colquhoun all summer anyway.

"What about family?" I asked him. "Wouldn't Ruby be better with someone she knows today? I'm really not that good with children."

"Mum never came to my wedding," he said. "Why should she rally round now?"

"Your dad?"

"Wouldn't know me if we passed on the street." The kettle was boiling, and I got up to make the coffee and watch the milk in the pan

"What about your brother?" I asked. "Where's he?" Silence. I turned round. Gus was staring at me.

"Who told you about my brother?" he said. Dillon had gone very still, with his hand spread like star, a Cheerio on every finger.

"You did," I said. "Last night, remember?"

"Right," said Gus. "Did I? He's a bit of a . . ."

"Black sheep?" I said.

He smiled, easy again. "I was going to say wild card," he said.

"Baa-baa back seep," said Dillon.

"Anyway, he's in Bangkok."

"Sounds pretty wild, right enough," I said. "Is this the kind that's sweet already, or will I put some sugar in?"

"Tugar in!" said Dillon.

"Sugar in mine too!" Ruby was back. Her face was still tear-stained, but she was dressed. Leggings, a velvet dress, and a sparkly shrug. She had her hairbrush in her hand and a bobble with tinsel ribbons hanging from it.

"Can you do my hair?" she said to me. "Dad's rubbish. Do it nice for when Mummy gets home and sees me."

I sat down without a word, and she backed herself in between my knees. Gus got up and went to the cooker. I don't know why, but I stretched out one of my bare feet and touched his leg. I was right. He was frozen and, at my touch, goose bumps sprang up on his skin, so that the red hair stood out like soft focus, or radioactive. He stopped with the milk pan poised above the cups.

"Thanks," he said.

"How will I get the car back to you?" I asked, but he gave me a look that was so hurt, so totally miserable that I didn't say any more. I was taking her to school and it looked like I was bringing her home again.

Very gently, starting with the ends, minding out for knots, I brushed Ruby's hair. But no matter how depressed Becky had been, she hadn't neglected her children: it was hardly tuggy at all and it smelled of Johnson's Baby. It shone like sheets of copper when the brush pulled it straight and then bounced back into coils when I let it go. If it was right enough that Gus had no family, then the kids would end up with a babysitter anyway while he got himself sorted. If they were going to have to put up with a stranger, I reasoned, it might as well be me. And nothing would happen. Probably. We'd all be okay.

He offered me a loan of clean clothes. He couldn't have been thinking clearly. I managed to turn him down without letting on how creepy it was that he'd even imagined I'd wear them. I'd bend a rule and take something from work, for once. The underwear's always new; we use the money we get from selling the brand name stuff on eBay and hit Primark for them. One of my favourite bits of the job, as it goes, shopping with somebody else's money. Shame I'm always buying men's socks and kids' undies.

For now, I dressed in yesterday's and soon we were ready to go. I was standing at the coat rack when he opened the front door and I turned to the light.

"Wow," I said. Ruby ran out, Dillon toddling after her in his pyjamas. It was a perfect autumn day, clear blue sky, crisp white clouds. And the tide was almost in, the bay sparkling, the beach ruffled with waves. I walked down the path and out across the turf. The dry sand was white and a breeze sent it sheeting across the darker strip down where it was wet still. It was a stiff enough breeze to be shifting the shells too, sprays of tiny blue, pink, and gold ones at the high tide line, and it shivered the little plants tucked into the cracks in the rocks. Big rough grey rocks splotched with green and orange.

"What are those stains?" I asked, pointing.

"Lichen," he said.

"It's beautiful. Is that chives?" I pointed at the rippling little plants.

He laughed. "It's called thrift."

"It's lovely," I said.

"You're easily pleased."

I turned. "Don't you think so?" He was gazing far out across the water. "I'd think . . . for an artist —"

His face clouded. I was getting used to the way it did that and I waited, but this time it didn't clear. He didn't smile, didn't look at me.

"I don't do nice wee pictures of the seaside," he said.

"I didn't mean to insult you," I said, feeling myself colouring. How many times had

I blushed since I'd met him yesterday? And how long had it been before that? I'm not a blusher. He was standing with his eyes closed and his face turned up as if the sun would warm it, but the sun was behind him.

"Becky wanted me to churn stuff out and tout it round the craft shops," he said, eventually, still with his eyes closed. "Present from Galloway. Said what was the point of living out here if I didn't paint it. Boats in the harbour, roses round the door." At last, he opened his eyes. "Jesus, I'm the biggest bastard that ever lived to be moaning about her." He threw the dregs of his coffee away, making a dark splash that spoiled the green and orange on the nearest rock. None of it splashed on me, though.

Then he cupped his hand to his mouth. "Roobs, come on, darling! And Dillyboy, get out of the water with your socks on, you numpty. Come on."

"Yeah, you're a total bastard, right enough," I said. "I'll pick her up at four then. Steve won't mind if I leave early. See you getting on for five. Text me a shopping list if you need anything."

"You're saving my life, Jess," he said.

"Jessie," I told him. He blinked. "Now, *that's* a bastard," I said. "Picking nits at a time like this."

"Jessie," he said. "A time like this, yeah." He gave me a look. If he had just been a guy, and we'd just been standing on a beach somewhere, I'd have known what kind of look it was, no question. But with his kids there, not to mention his wife in the morgue, it couldn't have been. Sick of me even to think so.

I dropped Ruby off at the nursery wing of Townhead Primary and stopped at the door to have a word with the famous Miss Colquhoun, a nice girl with a worried face and holes all over her lips and nose where she must wear rings when she wasn't working.

"I'm picking Ruby up this afternoon," I told her. "Her dad told me the password. And I think I should give you my number in case she needs to leave early."

"Trouble?" she asked.

"He hasn't called you yet?" I turned and watched Ruby in the playground. She had put her backpack down and was tearing in to some game with three other girls who all looked like they knew what they were doing.

"Big trouble," I said. "Becky — Mrs. King — was in a car crash yesterday." Miss Colquhoun's hands flew up to her face. I could see the very edges of her full-sleeve tattoos peeking out from her cuffs.

"Is she okay?" she said. "Is she in the hospital?"

"She's not okay," I told her. "She didn't survive." I watched her chew on that and translate it into the bald fact I didn't want to say.

"She died?"

I nodded. "She died."

Miss Colquhoun swung round to look at the girls playing. "Does Ruby know?"

"Well," I said, "Gus told her."

"Gus?" said Miss Colquhoun. "That's her dad? We do Mister and Missus here with the parents."

"But I'm not sure it went in," I added.

She nodded, but she looked pained. "I'll need to tell the head teacher," she said. "I'm not sure Ruby should be here."

"There's going to be cops and all that today," I said. "Gus reckoned Ruby'd be better off not at the house."

"Police?" said Miss Colquhoun. "Like, was it a hit-and-run? Drunk driver? Why police?"

"I . . . no. Just — She drove off that bad road to Wanlockhead. It was an accident. Tragedy, really." I wasn't going to say the word.

"Oh my God," said Miss Colquhoun.

There were tears shining in her eyes. "I heard that on *West Sound* last night. That was Becky King? They said it might have been suicide, though. Two in one day, they said. Made a big special feature of it."

"Two? Oh yeah, those divers."

"Evil bastards, making up stories. Oh my *God*!"

The bell rang, blocking out all sounds, sending the kids wheeling back to their schoolbags and then jostling to the door.

"She was so happy!" said Miss Colquhoun, over the rabble. "Out at that cottage, by the sea. Making her garden, fixing the place up. She was a really lovely person, you know. So much to live for and such a great mum."

I nodded, turning my lips down at the corners, mirroring her look, agreeing. Of course Becky King would suddenly be a wonderful mum, devoted and blissfully happy, so much to live for. Or maybe she had talked a good game while she was alive and had the teachers fooled. It wouldn't be the first time.

"What time d'you call this?" said Dot, "as my friend Irene would say." She always does that. If she gets nippy, it's in Irene's name. Dot herself — this is the idea — wouldn't say boo.

"I know, I know," I said. I dumped my bag and started up the computer before I even took my coat off or went through to the scullery to check the scone situation. "But I've had a very unusual time since I left here yesterday." And it seemed more unusual than ever now that I was back in my real life again. Like a dream. I jumped at a sound coming from the back room. The bosses — Father Tommy and Sister Avril: they who can sign cheques — usually stayed in the office up at St. Vince's and left us alone as long as we filled in our sheets on time.

"Is Monsignature here?" I asked.

Monsignature was one of Dot's best near-misses, and a better name for a priest with a chequebook I couldn't imagine.

"Steve's doing the bags," said Dot and fluttered a hand at her neck. "We got a wee bit muddled." In other words, Dot turned up for Steve's shift. "I'm meeting my friend Irene for lunch, so there was no point me traipsing home and back. I'll just stay. How d'you mean, unusual?"

"Did you hear on the radio that a car went off the road at Wanlockhead?" I asked her, deleting all the junk mail from the inbox.

"I did," said Dot. "That's a terrible road.

108

Makes me as carsick as anything."

"Well, it was a friend of mine," I said. "Or the wife of a friend of mine anyway. I was with him."

"You were in the car?" said Dot on a rising shriek. "Oh dear. Oh Jessie pet. Steve! Jessie's been in a car crash."

"Dot, no!" I said. "You've picked up the wrong —"

"What's up?" said Steve, coming through from the back with the water cup for our iron in his hand.

"Did they keep you in? You shouldn't be at work straight out of the hospital, Jessie."

"I was with my friend Gus when he heard that his wife had been killed," I said, very slowly and loudly, the way you need to when Dot's really birling.

"Is that who the police were fishing out the Nith at the Whitesands?" she said, clutching me.

"Why were you in the hospital?" said Steve.

"I wasn't. I had to babysit their kids while he went to identify the body, and then I stayed the night in case . . ."

"Oh dear goodness me," said Dot, which was quite strong language for her. "A local lass was this? What was the name?"

"King," I said. "Local, I think. Gus King.

109

Don't know her own name." Although Gus had said it, hadn't he? She'd wanted to give it to Dillon. I tried to remember, and Dot started clacking through her mental rolodex for Kings, but it was Steve who came through.

"Gus King?" he said. "Our age?" I nodded. "Big guy with red hair? Artist."

"That's him," I said.

"I didn't know you knew him," said Steve.

Until that moment, I hadn't realised I'd lied. I'd said "a friend" because . . . because over the course of the night and morning it had started to seem that way.

Many times since, I've thought back to that moment. That fork in the road. If I had put that lie back in my mouth right then, if I'd said: *Hang on. Rewind. I didn't actually know him this time yesterday.* If I'd tried to explain it to Dot and Steve, I'd have failed. And failing to get them to understand, I'd have started to question it myself. And then I'd have climbed back up the cliff I was falling down, stepped away from the edge, and got clear. And what would have happened then? Who would have lived, and who'd have died? I've wondered many times and I'll never know.

"So you know him too?" was what I said.

"I know his brother," said Steve.

"Is he another artist?" said Dot. "Talented family."

"No, the other one's a headcase," Steve said. "Or he was when he was wee." That explained the language, then. It was a throwback to Steve's childhood, when people were *headcases* instead of *Mental Health Service users.*

"Were you at school with him?" I said. "Gus doesn't say much — makes you wonder."

"Cubs," said Steve. "And the less said, the better."

"Whae's this?" We hadn't noticed a client coming in. It was one of our repeat customers — Buckfast Eric. He was a harmless alcoholic who could always rely on Father Tommy when his overcoat got the usual "organic stains."

"Honest to God, Eric," I said. "If you'd have a bag of chips and a pint of milk before you started, you'd keep it down."

"It's not that this time, ye cheeky besom," Eric said. "I fell over in the park and sat in dog's dirt."

Dot shuddered.

"Nice," I said. "Just gets us in the mood for our coffee."

"You're very kind," said Eric, settling himself down on the shoe-trying-on chair.

"And who are we bitching up today, pardon my French, ladies."

"Gavin King," said Steve. "Jessie knows his brother. Stayed out Heathall way. His dad worked at Hunter's."

"Oh, *I* know who you mean *now,*" said Dot. "But they moved years ago. I think it was" — she lowered her voice — "divorce. Very sad. And he got a transfer, and she wasn't far at his back and went to Lancashire. Somewhere on the coast. And so this is her daughter-in-law, is it? And children too?" She went clucking off to make the coffee.

"But Gus isn't like the rest of them," I said. "He's a sculptor."

"A sculptor," said Eric. "A right sculptor — marble and a chisel — or does he put stale bread in a old toilet and sell it for millions?"

"You're a Philistine, Eric," I said. Going by what had been said about seaside scenes, though, I reckoned he'd got Gus's number.

"I might well be, but I'd rather be a Philistine with no shite on me. So if you can show me what you have in a 40/32 trouser, I'd be very grateful."

Steve and I both recoiled.

"Are you telling me you've got kak on those breeks you're wearing now?" I said.

"Get up off our chair then, you manky old toe rag. God almighty!"

"Jessie!" said Steve. "Your tone is completely inappropriate and unprofessional."

"Our Lord himself washed the feet of the poor," said Dot, coming back with the coffee tray.

"He wouldn't have touched Eric's," I said.

Steve glared, but Eric only said, "You're not wrong, Jessie hen. I've an infected toenail that would turn the milk."

In other words, it was a pretty typical morning. Dot with her shift wrong, Steve bugging me, Eric being Eric. And the comfort of it all stopped me thinking. I nicked some undies from stock and changed in the toilets, and only for a little sliver of a second did I look at myself in the mirror and ask the questions that were rumbling away deep down inside. How did I get so far into something that was nothing to do with me? Why did I lie to Dot and Steve? How would I phrase it when I went back tonight, my kind but firm good-bye? Then the phone rang and I went to answer it, expecting Father Tommy or a donor or the usual. But it was Miss Colquhoun from Townhead Primary telling me to come right away.

Ruby had lasted through the morning song and chosen a jigsaw for her quiet time, but then she'd had a pretty nuclear meltdown, going by Miss Colquhoun's account, when one of the other kids said her mummy was dead like a ghost and the worms would eat her.

"I never dreamed any of them would know!" Miss Colquhoun said to me when I got there. "Think I'd have wised up by now, eh? They're four, for f—"

"—uck's sake," I filled in, since she was a primary school teacher and she was at work and couldn't.

"What the hell are the parents thinking?"

"Who'll win *Strictly* this go-round?" I said. "It never occurred to me either, and my bar's set pretty low."

"Oh God no!" said Miss Colquhoun. "Look, here's the secretary coming with Ruby now. She's wet her pants and she's quite upset about it, just so's you know. But it was one of our Guardian Angels that said it — all muesli and first names, ken the type? Mummy treats them like they're forty-five."

"Oh, them!" I said. Ruby was plodding

along beside the secretary, still in her velvet dress and shrug, but with bare legs now. "Hello, Rubylicious," I called out to her. "I missed you. I'm glad I didn't need to wait till four to see you again. And I bet Daddy's missing you too."

"Bye-bye, special sweetheart!" said Miss Colquhoun, giving Ruby a huge hug that would get her sacked if you believed the *Daily Mail.* "I'll see you very soon. I'll maybe come and see you at home at the weekend, eh? Bring you a present." I caught her eye, pretty sure this wasn't in the guidelines. "Couldn't care less," she said quietly to me. "Couldn't give a stuff."

"What are you talking about?" said Ruby, grizzling.

"Boring grown-up stuff," I said. "No need for you to worry, hunny-bunny. Let's go and get some nice treats to take home for Dillon."

"And me," Ruby said. "Can I get a comic?"

"Only if you let me buy you some sweeties too."

I pretended not to hear as I walked away, but I knew the secretary and the teacher were asking each other who I was and saying Gus was lucky I was around. I took Ruby's sticky little hand in mine and tried to think what I could get Gus in Tesco that would feel as good as a comic and sweeties but wasn't drink and that I could afford and wouldn't seem weird when I'd only known him a day.

And maybe that explains why I got sucked back in again and totally forgot my plan to say take care, all the best, and good-bye.

Maybe.

NINE

The farmyard wasn't deserted this time. Two quad bikes sat there with their motors going, a collie on the back of each, plunging about and barking their heads off but so well-trained they wouldn't shift off the bikes until somebody told them. There was a car, a big muddy 4×4, pulled off the track with its back doors open. In the yard itself, three men were strong-arming pallets into place to funnel sheep from one shed to another. One of them, in a waxed jacket, ignored me, but the two in Gore-Tex trousers and padded tartan shirts stopped what they were doing and turned to stare. A vet and two workers, I thought. None too friendly. One of them strolled over and stood in front of my car, making me stop whether I liked it or not.

I rolled down the window, working the handle round.

He frowned at me. "Is this the car fae the

cattleman's hoose?" he said. "Who're you?"

"I'm a friend of the family," I said. "Have you heard?"

"Heard whit?" he said. "Was that you yesterday an' all? This is no' the way."

"Mrs. King has been" — I checked Ruby out of the corner of my eye; she wasn't listening — "killed in a car accident."

He was the type of guy that would rather die himself than show surprise, a real hard man (and to think he helped lambs into the world), but he started back a bit at that. "Aye, well," he said, not exactly overflowing with sympathy. "If there's gonny be loads of folk comin' you'll have tae get them tellt. Girthon turn." He jerked his head. "Through the site."

I had no idea what that meant, but I'd ask Gus. No point trying to get this one's knuckles off the ground to give proper directions. I just wound the window back up again and went on my way.

At the cottage, Gus was sitting on a bench under the front bedroom window with Dillon on his knee, both of them staring at the sea. The baby was wrapped in a blanket — one of those old army-issue things, scratchy as hell, but he looked happy enough, sucking on some toy. Gus was wearing a suit that could have given the army blanket a good run. It was green with a kind of orange fuzz about it, brown leather buttons. I know clothes, and this suit was prewar. He had on a shirt with no collar, but when I took a close look at what Dillon was sucking, there was the collar there. Gus shuffled along the bench, gouging out pits in the gravel with his work boots.

"I'm going to have to buy a suit," he said. "This was Dave's."

"It's . . ." I said.

"It fits okay," he said, "but it's like fancy dress. Hi Ruby-two-shoes," he went on. "Miss Colquhoun phoned and told me you were coming."

Ruby said nothing. She sidled up to him, wriggled between his knees, and put her head down on Dillon's blanket. He patted her hair with the collar and then went back to sucking it again.

"Okay, then . . ." I said.

Gus looked up at me. "Can you just sit here beside us for a wee bit?" he said.

"Of course." I dropped down beside him and looked out at the sea, looking for whatever he was finding there. It was hard to stay quiet. I wanted to ask about Becky, about the police, the Girthon turn and the site. I wanted to get dry knickers for Ruby, thinking she must be cold. I wanted to help. Instead, I counted the rocks between us and the tide. Tried to name the flowers in the two beds along the fence. Red-hot pokers. Daisies. Although they might just as easily be chrysanthemums or dahlias or even asters. And an edging of those red, white, and blue things. Lobelia, salvia, and . . . the white ones.

"What are those white flowers called?" I said.

Gus shook his head.

So maybe Becky did the garden. Depressed and miserable and planting flowers? It didn't go together. Unless having her garden looking good was part of pretending she was happy. But there was a vegetable patch with rows of cabbages — or they might be sprouts or kale or even cauliflowers — and who plants cabbages if they're down already? Or cooks them, or eats them, or makes their kids eat them? I'd say if life was getting away from you, everything to do with cabbages would be near the first thing to go.

"Alice," said Ruby.

She was right. Alyssum, lobelia, and salvia. They were like the father, son, and holy ghost of my granny's garden.

"So the cops have been back," Gus said

after another silence. I flicked a glance at the kids. "The Fiscal's going to review the case tomorrow. Decide whether he wants a full post-mortem. If not, should be free to have a cremation by early next week."

"If *not*?" I said.

"What's them things you said?" said Ruby, screwing round to look at him.

"Nothing," said Gus. "Just Daddy's work."

I supposed you got good at hiding stuff in plain sight, with children around. Talking over their heads, making sure they missed what you didn't want them to catch, but it still seemed wrong to me.

"Can I get a ice-pop?" said Ruby.

Dillon stirred himself inside the blanket. "Ice-pop," he said, breaking out of its folds.

"For ten pink shells," said Gus. Ruby marched down towards the beach, toes turned out, tummy pushed out, a right wee swagger about her. Dillon pattered along at her back.

"That'll take them a good while," Gus said, and we sat in silence again until I couldn't take it anymore.

"How could there not be a post-mortem?" I said.

"Depends whether the Fiscal thinks it's needed," said Gus.

"Really?"

"Everybody's seen too much *CSI*," Gus said. "Nobody knows how it works in Scotland."

"But you know?"

"I'm going to push for the full PM, obviously," said Gus. "If they'll listen to me."

"Did the cops tell you anything?"

"The engine was off," he said. "She had her seatbelt on. She died of head trauma. I told them it was an accident. Again. If it was deliberate, the engine would have been on, and she'd have taken her seatbelt off, eh? That's what I told them."

"And what did they say?"

"Said suicides nearly always leave their belts on. That woman one — Gail — said she'd heard of someone before, driving off a cliff and switching off the engine. Scared of burning to death if they survived the fall."

I didn't know what to say to that, just shook my head.

"But I don't want suicide on the books. On the record. I want them to keep investigating until they find someone that saw something, or find someone she spoke to, or . . . I'd rather have anything on the record other than that."

I nodded again. Pretty useless even if he was looking at me, which he wasn't. But what was there to say? Then a thought struck me.

"Hey Gus, did you ask the farm guys?"

He shook his head. "We never see much of them unless they're moving sheep in this field right here."

"Only I was just coming through the yard there and one of them told me I should go a different way. He asked if it was me driving through yesterday. Maybe it was Becky."

"She doesn't go that way," he said. Then he leapt to his feet, making me jump. "But she might if she didn't want anyone else to see her! To stop her!" He turned to look at the children, squatting at the high-tide line, poking through the shells with their fingers. "Will you mind the kids? I need to go and ask at the farm if they saw her. What time she left. Maybe someone even spoke to her."

I could see why it had got to him. Any bit of something to explain anything was going to seem important, state he was in, but he wasn't thinking clearly.

"Yeah, sure but, Gus?" I said. "They might have meant us last night, eh? *We* came that way."

He stared at me, then rubbed his face. "Yeah, we did. Yeah, I remember. You missed the turn. But . . ." he shook his head. "No. If the guy said *yesterday,* not *last night* . . ."

"Worth checking," I agreed, because he

was like a catapult ready to go. "And while you're there, ask them if there are any foreigners working on the farm. Shearers or pickers or that."

Because who he really did need to speak to was Mr. Panic from last night, the one that might be Becky's boyfriend.

"Foreigners?" he said. "The only foreigner here was Ros. If there'd been a few more, she might have stayed." Then he strode off round the side of the cottage and I heard the car engine start. The children looked up; I waved to them.

"I've got six, Jessie," Ruby called.

"One, two, three, ten!"

"Cool," I called back. "Keep looking." I could see Ruby's little pink bottom sticking down under the hem of her dress from the way she was crouched down, and I wanted to ask if she was warm enough, or go and get her some pants to put on, but I didn't want to remind her of why she was bare-arsed in the first place, upset her again.

I missed the turn, I thought to myself. He hadn't said that. He'd sat there like a stone and then said "next left." I stood up and walked to the far fence, saw what I hadn't seen before — a double track coming through the gorse. Another way to the cottage. I glanced at the kids, stepped over the fence, and followed it.

So much for poor Becky's isolation and loneliness! Just round the rocks from the cove where the cottage sat, a sandy beach stretched for a mile or so, and the slopes of the field above it were carved into plots, and on the plots were hulking great static caravans, all painted the same sage green, each with its big end window facing the sea. The site, like the guy said.

And it wasn't just a site either; she couldn't have been lonely even in the winter because in the prime spots right along the edge of the beach there was a row of bunga-lows and cabins, some nearly as rough as Stockman's Cottage, some over-the-top swanky. Not all inhabited, true. Not in October. But at least three of them had cars parked in their drives, and one had a wash-ing hung out — beach towels and wetsuits — and there was a man working on an upturned kayak in the garden.

"Jessie? Jessie, where are you?" Ruby's voice sounded farther away than I thought I'd come.

"Right here," I said, picking my way back through the gorse as fast as I could.

"Jessieeeeeee!" she squealed. The sound of it gripped at my guts. I got the same squeal as Mummy and Daddy now.

"Jessieeeeeeeee!" Dillon sounded like someone stretching the neck of a balloon. It meant even less from him; he was just copying.

"I'm here, I'm here, I'm right here," I said, crunching down onto the pebbles beside them. Ruby held up her cupped hands, showing me enough pink shells to call it ten any day. Dillon held out his two fists and I let him drop his haul into my palms.

Two pink shells, three blue shells, a twig with a piece of seaweed wrapped round it, and what I should have known to expect. *Stupid bitch.* What any little boy would pick up on the beach. Right there, right on my hand, touching my skin. *Useless bitch.* Quite a small one, curled and soft, white-ish with just a bit of sandy colour near the tip, right there on my hand, touching my skin. *Stupid, useless, evil bitch.* I dropped my arms to my sides and let it fall, feeling my hand pulsing where it had touched me.

Dillon stared at ground where his treasure had dropped, and his face screwed up and turned dark. I stood still and stared at him, did nothing. But I didn't run. I didn't look for a corner, didn't curl up, didn't squeeze my head. I just stood there trying to get my breathing back to normal, staring at him as his eyes filled with tears and he cranked up for a good loud howl. It had just broken when Gus shouted from the garden.

"What's up?" he said. "Jess?"

"Jessie," I muttered under my breath.

"Jessie threw Dillon's shells away," said Ruby in the thrilled bossy voice of every four-year-old girl. "*And* she burnt him."

Gus jumped over the rocks and landed on the beach beside us. I cringed at the sound of his feet striking the ground.

"Jess?" he said, gently.

"Jessie," I told him. I was still standing straight, but I needed to wrap my arms round my body and press them in tight. "I gave Dillon his sandwich too hot last night. I had to run his hand under the tap. I'm sorry. I should have told you." Gus brushed it off with a shake of his head, kept up his close, unpeeling stare. "You're like a ghost," he said. He looked at the pebbles around my feet and his eyes flared. He kicked loose grit and shells, covering it.

"It was only a wee one," I said. "I'm sorr—"

"Tsst!" said Gus. He squatted and took one of Dillon's hands in his, one of Ruby's too.

"Listen, kids," he said. "This is very important. Jessie . . ."

"No," I moaned. "It's not them, it's me."

". . . is allergic to feathers. Feathers are very bad for Jessie."

"Like peanuts," said Ruby. "Like Kieran."

"Much, much worse than peanuts," Gus said. "Dilbert? No feathers. Got it?"

Of course he hadn't got it. The poor kid. He was sniffling, still staring at the ground.

"Now say sorry to Jessie," Gus said.

"No!" Louder this time. "He's wee and I'm big. It's me who should — I should — If I can't — it's crazy anyway. Dillon?" I dropped down beside him. Closer to it. Right down where it was hiding under the scuffed-up sand. But I made myself think *Dillon, Dillon, Dillon. He's two. I have to.* I took his hand, the one that might have held it tight for ages, but I made myself not think that either.

"Dillon," I said. "I'm sorry, honey. Look, there's one of your blue shells. And there's your stick with the seaweed."

"Pink sells," said Dillon, with a catch in his throat.

"Beautiful pink shells," I said. "I love them."

"Take them up to the house then," said Gus. "Ice-pops all round." Ruby and Dillon looked from him to me and then at each other, and then they took off. I sank back onto my heels. *Useless bitch, useless bitch, stupid evil useless bitch.*

"What are you saying?" Gus said.

"Nothing." At least not out loud. At least, I didn't mean to. *Useless bitch* was just another little trick, like the head squeeze. And it was helping. I was talking myself down again. I had made Dillon cry. But I hadn't hurt him, and I hadn't run away. He'd get an ice-pop and forget all about it.

"D'you find anything out?" I asked Gus, and that worked too. He forgot all about me.

"She left about three o'clock," he said. "Through the yard. Nobody saw her, but a couple of them heard the car. And one of the shepherds saw it on the track."

"So Dillon wasn't on his own that long, really," I said. "Especially not if he was sleeping." That was the kind of thing Caroline with the couch used to say. So reasonable, so understanding, never judgmental. It meant there was nothing to brace against, and half an hour with her left you spinning. But Gus was fine with it. He only nodded.

"That's good to know, right enough," he said. "But taking the quiet way out, avoiding running into people . . . it definitely looks like suicide."

"I suppose," I agreed. "But it's the note that does it."

129

"I've thought of something to tell them about the note," Gus said. "Listen to this: she ran away."

"Without her purse?"

"Just listen. No, not running away like that. She snapped and drove off. But then she cooled down, came to her senses, and she was coming back again; only while she was turning the car, it went off the road."

"Snapped," I echoed. He nodded. "Because she was scared maybe."

"Scared, depressed, desperate —"

"No," I cut him off. "I mean really scared."

"Why the hell would I tell them that," he said evenly. "They'd end up thinking it was me that scared her."

"I was thinking about the foreign guy," I said. "He scared *me.* And if he doesn't work on the farm, why's he hanging around? He might know something."

"It's a caravan site, Jessie. There's always folk hanging around. Did he actually talk to you?"

"Gus, he did more than that. I tried to tell you last night. He came to the door when you were out. In a hell of a state. Looking for Becky."

And again he had turned to stone.

"Gus?"

"Someone came to the door?"

"Yeah, but only because he knew you were out. He must have been watching the place. So here's what I'm thinking." He had sort of jolted halfway through what I had said. It was hard to make sense of what floored him and what he could take in his stride. "I'm thinking he was the guy. He's Becky's boyfr— well, he's the guy, right? And so he must know something. And he might easily have frightened her into running away."

"No," he said. He put his hands up to either side of his head, and I could tell he was pressing hard from the way his hands were shaking, like he wanted to burst his own skull open to stop his brain from having to let it in. I knew all about that, knew better than to stop him too. "No," he said again. "She didn't run away with another man, and she didn't run away and kill herself. It didn't happen. I don't care who he is, and I don't want you to talk about him."

It was like he'd forgotten there was anything else apart from getting the story straight and not hurting the kids. Like he'd completely forgotten the quite important bit of what actually happened. Then I caught myself. Right. Like, who's never done that? When you know damn well what happened but you just can't let it be true? As if to show me I was right, he let his hands drop and then he let his face fall, mouth open, eyes half-closed.

"Oh Christ," he said. "What's the point? A note, leaving her purse, depression, leaving the baby. No way it's ever going down as anything except suicide, is there?"

"They don't know she left the baby," I reminded him. "But no." I put out a hand and squeezed his arm. "*I'll* tell the cops I think it was an accident," I said. "If they ask me."

"Thanks," he said. He was smoothing the pebbles and shells with the toe of his boot. My heart picked up a pace thinking what he might uncover, and I looked away.

"Can I ask you something?" I said. His face did that thing, the sudden cloud, or as if a membrane had come down over it, like a veil. "Why didn't you tell me to go out the right way this morning?"

The cloud thickened. His face looked carved from wood. "I'm sorry the farm guys gave you grief," he said. "They're kind of bolshy."

"I'm not . . . You've misund— I'm not giving you a hard time," I said. "I'm really just asking. You didn't tell me I'd missed my turn last night and you didn't tell me to go a different way this morning. Seems weird, that's all."

"I didn't want to criticise you," he said. "When you were being so good to us all."

"Criticise," I repeated. Trying to see it from wherever he was looking.

"Aye, tell you you'd missed the turn."

"Why the hell would I think that was criticising?"

He said nothing.

"Gus?"

"Becky did," he said at last, "and you shouldn't speak ill . . ."

"Gus," I said. "Listen. I know old habits die hard, but you don't need to walk on your eyelashes round me."

He kept his head down. "I know," he said. "It's just a habit. I could tell right away it was different with you." Then he looked up, and the blaze in his eyes was enough to make my breath catch.

I thought the same thing again as I had before. If he was just a guy and we were just here on a beach. Then I got hold of myself. *You need to turn the key in that lock and throw it away, Jessie,* I told myself. *You can watch and see where it lands, but you need to throw it a good bit off and leave it there.*

He stood and went inside the cottage. I

followed him. In the kitchen Ruby had dragged a chair to the door of the fridge to reach the freezer bit on the top. Gus sank down onto it.

"You don't really think it might have been an accident, do you?" he said. "You think it's cut and dried, same as the cops will."

"Not quite," I said. "I think there's something . . . off. I wonder if she told her friend anything that would help. What was her name?"

"Ros," said Gus. "Something off like what?"

I shrugged.

"Cos I'd give anything to not have the kids think she left them," Gus said. I smiled at him. What I was thinking was if he was on *Columbo,* at least you'd know he hadn't killed her. Killers on *Columbo* are always tying themselves in knots to make everyone think it's anything but murder. And getting angry with Columbo, and not looking upset enough. Think they'd learn.

He was certainly upset. He looked worse than I'd seen him yet.

"So," I said. "What sort of sculpture do you do? Where's your studio?"

And he grinned like a kid that's been given a puppy. Pure delight. Not the least wee bit like the guy I'd been looking at five seconds

134

ago, never mind someone whose wife had died yesterday.

"Once the kids are in bed for their nap," he said. "After their dinner. The monitor reaches fine to the workshop."

It looked like I was invited for lunch then. Good thing Dot mucked her shift up. I was free to stay.

And I wanted to too. Because something really *was* off. And I like things making sense, me. As well as that, though, life was bigger here. Louder, brighter colours. Jesus Christ, I had had one of them in my hand touching my skin, and any other day I would be in my bed, *stupid bitch*ing it, squeezing my skull, waiting for it to fade away. Here, it wasn't even the biggest thing that had happened, not compared with Ruby's morning at school and Dillon crying and Gus's sadness and what the cops might say.

TEN

It was evening before we got to the studio. I had heard people say that the day just disappears when there's kids, and I never bought it — thought they needed to get a grip and how could a person call the shots who was so small you could just pick them up and put them where you wanted them to be? That Wednesday afternoon was boot camp. Ruby needed a bath. Gus wanted a long walk. Dillon wouldn't go in his pushchair. The milk in the couch was starting to stink. Three times I filled a basin with hot soapy water and it cooled, unused. Dillon's nappy. Ruby was hungry. Gus came back and needed quiet to make some calls. They both got wet in tide pools when we were staying out the way. Ruby didn't like what clothes were clean. Gus wanted to find some paperwork he needed for the undertakers. Dillon was hungry but only for sweeties, not for food. Ruby wanted to walk to the shop on the caravan site. Dillon wouldn't go in his pushchair. Gus had a headache and wanted a bath. There was no hot water. Go to the shop in the car. Ruby wouldn't go in her car seat. Dillon wouldn't be left behind.

"I'll just take your pushchair in case you get tired," I said.

"Noooooo!" he squealed.

"He wants a carry," said Ruby, making trouble.

"No," Dillon sobbed. "Walk. Pomise. Pomise, Jessie."

"Will he walk?" I asked. Gus was standing heating up pans of water on the cooker-top, wrapped in a towel. I was trying not to look at him. Topless men never seem to think they're as naked as I think they are.

"No chance," said Gus. "Dillberry, why don't you have a bath with Daddy and let the girls go shopping?"

"Not much good for your headache," I said. "I'll carry him. He's only a baby. I'm a big strong girl."

But God almighty it was a long way. We were hardly on the sand before he was lifting his arms and smiling up at me, batting his lashes. I hoisted him onto one hip. It seemed okay. Twenty paces later, it felt like I was carrying a bag of rocks. I shifted him

137

to the other side. Ten paces later, I put him down.

"Nooooo," he moaned, as if I'd dropped him in a pit in the woods and left him there.

"How about a kelly-coad?" I said. Dillon sniffed and stared. "A piggy-back."

"His legs are too short," said Ruby.

"Noooo," said Dillon.

"High-shoulders?" That did the trick, but there's a reason it's always men you see with kids on their necks. It kills your back and it doesn't make them weigh any less. By the time we were at the end of the beach, going up the track to the shop and shower block, my legs felt rubbery enough to make me worry I would slip and drop him. And my arms had pins and needles from holding onto his feet, so putting him down didn't feel that possible either. There was no one around to ask for help. Just the blank gaze of all those caravans with their net curtains drawn across their single eyes.

Ruby ran ahead over the car park and leapt at the door handle. She bounced back. Tried again. Turned to me.

The lights were off inside. Just the drinks fridge glowing.

"I think it's closed, honey," I said.

Ruby stuck her bottom lip out and glared at me. "It is not closed, you stupid!" she said. "It's open when Mummy comes."

And right enough, the hours said *Wednesday 10 to 5,* and it was just on four now. Four o'clock on an October afternoon, with two grumpy kids and a stiff neck, and a sore ear from the cold wind and the other one set to catch it all the way back. I banged hard on the door and shouted.

"Shop!" Ruby giggled at that.

"Hello?" I called.

Over at the house, a door walloped open and a woman in a toweling kaftan, bright yellow, no excuse for it, stood scowling in the doorway with her hands on her hips.

"We're shut!" she shouted.

"How come?" I shouted back. "It's nowhere near five."

"We're short-handed," she said, and made to close the door.

"You might have put a sign up!" I said. "In emergency, call at house or something."

"What emergency?" she said. "There's a shop at Gatehouse."

"Aw, come on," I said. "I've lugged this pair right along the beach promising sweeties. Two minutes, eh?"

"You're not the only one having a bad day, hen," said the woman and slammed the door.

"Shop!" shouted Ruby. Dillon joined in.

"Shop! Shop!"

"I'll make pancakes," I said. "Come on. And Dillon, pal, you'll have to walk for a wee bit because my neck is killing me."

We were a sorry procession that trailed back down to the beach. Ruby was whining, Dillon was whining. I nearly joined in. I held them by the hand, one on each side, and dragged them along. It looked even farther this way, the outcrop of rock tiny at the end of the sands. And it had started raining too; sore, cold rain lashing across our faces. The beach was deserted. One of the houses had a light on — the one with the kayaks — but it was the light that people leave on when they're out: one lamp in the front window, not the kitchen strip lights, not a reading light by an armchair, just the light that tells burglars the place is empty.

We trudged on.

"Wanna carry," said Dillon.

"You've *had* a carry," said Ruby. "I want a carry."

I said nothing.

"Jessie, I want a carry," she said again.

I was staring along the beach at someone approaching. A tall someone with flapping hair pushing an empty buggy.

"Here's Daddy," I said, pointing.

"Good," said Ruby. "You're rubbish." She

140

sat down on the sand, getting her second wet bum of the day. Dillon sat down and leaned against her. I ripped the hood off of my borrowed kagoul, put it Velcro side down on the sand, and sat down too. Gus broke into a run and, as he drew near, I could hear him making *nee-naw* siren sounds.

"The shop was shut, Dad," Ruby said.

"We'll go to Gatehouse," said Gus. "Buggy, Dillon. No discussion. Cuddy-back, Roobs."

"What a waste of a hot bath," I said, shuffling, ready to get up. Gus put out his hands and hauled me to my feet. "You'll be in a muck sweat again." He kissed my forehead before I had time to dodge it, and I felt the kiss, the ghost of it, for the rest of the day. It was like when you scoop for a dog and your hand's got that radio-active feel till you wash it. Except good, not manky, but otherwise the same.

I turned away from the endless whipping wind coming off the sea, sheltering myself while I velcroed my hood back on (and to get my face to stop smiling in case I embarrassed him), and that's when I saw a shadow just flitting between two of the caravans. I wiped my wet hair out of my eyes and looked harder.

It was him. I was sure it was. His hair was

even wilder than the night before, and I could see the black on the bottom half of his face from here. He was standing pressed hard against the wall of the caravan now, peering round the corner, like the pink panther, or whoever it is, because Steve's always telling me how the pink panther isn't the pink panther at all, like Frankenstein.

"What is it?" asked Gus. The guy had ducked out of view as soon as Gus turned to face him.

He'd told me he didn't want to know. "Nothing," I said.

"You've had a hell of day, haven't you?"

"Coming in in fourth place," I said. He lifted Ruby onto his shoulders, clamped one arm across her feet, and nodded at me to take the handles of the buggy. Why couldn't he push it one-handed, I was grumpy enough to think, before I found out.

He needed his other arm to put round me.

So it was pitch black and getting on for nine o'clock before he dropped the baby monitor into his jacket pocket and took me to the studio. It was in a dip in the field right by the headland, on the side away from the caravan site. Gus's torchlight bobbed over the dark grass, and then he raised it to show me where we were heading. I couldn't

142

remember seeing so much as the top of the roof during the day, but there it was: a long stone building with grey slates, two sets of double doors, windows painted the same dark red as the cottage, a Bedford van parked alongside.

"Does the monitor really stretch all this —" I said. "Sorry. As if you'd — so what is this place? What was it, I mean."

I felt Gus shrug beside me. We were walking close together, coats just brushing.

"Just a bothy kind of thing. A cow byre. Dave used it for a workshop as long as I can remember, and I just gradually took it over."

"And how come they don't still use it for the cows?" I said. I knew solid buildings with roofs intact were never going spare on a farm.

"It's not theirs," said Gus. We had arrived at the big double doors and he gave me the torch to hold while he opened the padlock. "Dave bought the cottage and this building for peanuts back in the sixties. He bought a right of way through the farmyard too, but they mump on till it's not worth the hassle, so we come through the site."

"*They* don't mump on, the site folk?" I asked. "I met one today that won't win any awards from the tourist board!"

"Oh, they wish we'd go away too," said Gus. "They'd buy us out, change the name to Bayview, and charge a thousand pounds a week in the season."

"You'd never get a grand for Stockman's Cottage right enough!" I said. He hauled open the doors and paused with his hand on the light switch. I could smell a shifting cocktail of unfamiliar smells — oily, sharp, earthy.

"Becky always wanted to change the name," he said. "Listen, Jessie. This — my work — it's . . . What I mean is, if you think it's crap —"

"Tell you straight?"

"No!" He sounded just like Dillon. "Keep your gob shut." I laughed. "My br— well, folk that don't get it come out with stuff you wouldn't believe. And it usually starts with 'I have to say . . .' And I always think, 'No, you don't.'"

I laughed again. "You're dead right," I said. "No more than you 'have to say' your mum's cakes are like bricks or your friend's kids are ugly." I shot him a look, wondering if he'd think I meant Ruby. I didn't. She was growing on me — stroppy, gobby wee madam. She'd go far in this world, and I'd be happy for her.

"Right," said Gus. He switched on the

144

light. I took a good long look around and got ready to be polite if it killed me. It was a single room, taking up half of the building. Sacks of concrete. Shovels. Planks. Scaffolding. Rolls of roofing lead. The usual power tools you'd see in any workshop, the usual orange extension cables. Shelves of boxes, labelled in code. And lamps. Loads and loads of lamps. Standard lamps, desk lights, bedside lamps, angle poise. Whole ones and parts of ones, boxes of bulbs. The edges of the room were stacked high with total junk, as far as I could tell. It smelled pretty lousy too.

"So this is . . . the workshop side?" I said, looking towards the other end of the byre.

"Yeah," said Gus. "I use the other side to store finished pieces." I must have sniffed, maybe my nose even wrinkled. "I know. There's a grate over a pipe from when it used to be a byre. God knows how it can smell when there hasn't been a beast in here for years, but it really does honk sometimes."

"So, what are you working on just now?"

He walked ahead of me and set the monitor down on a tool bench. "Just finishing something off," he said.

I waited to see if he'd show it to me. "And then what?" I asked, when it seemed he wasn't going to.

"Lamps," he said. "Well, lights. You know. Bulbs. Lamps, mostly."

I couldn't help remembering what Buck-fast Eric had said.

"What are you going to do with them?"

"Hard to say." He was sliding cardboard boxes out from the shelves, looking at their contents, and sliding them back in again. He pulled out a tangled string of fairy lights and started straightening them. "What would you do with them?" He was really asking me too. The truth was I'd wire them to plugs and use them to help me see things inside my house when the sun went down.

"Okay," I said. "Could you . . . put them all in the . . . space with a ton of plug boards and a ton of bulbs and leave it up to the people who came to see it, what to do with them?"

I thought he would laugh. I'd have laughed. Gus, though, looked suddenly miserable.

"I haven't got a *space*," he said. "I've got one thing ready to sell. If it sells I might get asked to . . . But I don't know if I can make myself sell it."

"Is it here?" I asked. "Can I see it?"

"It's next door," Gus said. "Wait and I'll bring it through."

He left me and — it must have been habit — as he went out, he clicked the lights off. I blurted something out, but he was gone.

It was cloudy outside, no moon, and so the room was black as ink around me. I picked my way towards the open door, feeling ahead for obstacles, guessing where to go from the sound of the sea. I stepped out onto the grass and felt the empty air above me.

"Gus?" I said. There was no light from the other room, but one of its doors was slightly open. "Gus?" I said, louder. The door banged shut.

It could have been the wind. Except the doors this side didn't move an inch. Had he just shut me out? Why would he do that? If he had one thing finished and he'd gone to get it anyway, what did it matter whether I saw the half-done stuff too?

I stood there, useless, doing nothing. Should I walk back to the house and wait for him there? Should I follow him through the door, banged in my face or not? Or stop being so touchy. I could find the light switch and wait in the workshop side. That's the thing about therapy. Everything ends up meaning something huge. Nothing stays small like things really are. So in the end I picked my way back to where he had left me and stood there in the dark, waiting.

A minute later he reappeared, clicked the light back on, and smiled at me.

"Okay," he said. "Here goes." He turned and pulled something into the room. It was on wheels and was hidden under a dust-sheet. "Ready?" I nodded. He swept the sheet aside and stood back. I stared.

It was a pram. One of those old navy-blue monsters with the painted sides and the big wheels. A double pram, both of its hoods pulled right up so it was almost round. Gus beckoned me forward.

"I can see it fine from here," I told him, and my voice sounded strained even to me.

"You need to look inside," he said.

"What's in there?" I asked. "Nothing . . . bad?"

But he didn't know what I meant. Why would he? So I stepped close and looked into the gap.

Except it wasn't a gap. There was some kind of substance there, not quite see-through, not quite not. I touched it.

"Resin," said Gus. And then something caught my eye. Behind the strip of resin, inside the belly of the pram, a light had gleamed, just for a second. It wasn't a flash, it was a gleam. Slow, measured, as if some creature had opened its eye and then lazily closed it again. I turned as another gleam lit the other side. In its light I thought I saw movement, but it was too far away to be inside where I was looking. I waited. And waited. And just as I was raising my head, a stronger, brighter steadier light shone for a half a second. I missed it. All I knew was that there was more in there than there could be.

"What it's called?" I asked.

"Pram," Gus said. "What do you think of it?"

"It's hellish," I said. "In the good way. It's creepy as hell."

I hadn't offended him. He was trying not to beam, but it was breaking through. So I decided to mention it, while he was smiling.

"Do you know you put the light off when you left me in here?" I asked. I gave him a chance to say sorry, but he just waited. "If I'd have known your sculptures were this creepy, I'd have legged it!"

"The new one's not creepy," he said, like that was the only thing he'd heard. "But it's big. It's next door." He was grinning now. "You want to see more? You like it?"

"I really do." I really did. "Why did you put the light off, though?"

"Well, it's not ready. But I'll tell you about it, if you promise not to tell other people."

He dropped the dustsheet back over the pram. He hadn't turned anything off first; I didn't like thinking about those lazy gleams carrying on in the dark with no one to see them.

He moved to the light switch again.

"Yeah," I said. "That one."

"Don't forget the monitor," he said, nodding to where he'd set it down.

"I get it," I said. "Fair enough." And it felt good to see the puzzled look spread over his face. He didn't ask what I meant. Guys never do. Because they don't want to admit they don't know already. And that's another thing therapy makes you forget: guys are just guys. And they hate making mistakes, so if you ask them why they did something daft, they'll pretend they can't hear you. Nothing sinister, nothing deep. Just guys.

In silence, we stepped outside and I waited while he closed the padlock and switched the torch on. We were halfway back when he started talking again.

"It's Dave's house," he said. "A replica. About three-quarters size. Life-size would have been great, but it wouldn't fit in the byre. I've got the breezeblocks done, skimmed the front, done the doors and windows, done the roof. Can't decide about the porch."

"What's inside?" I was thinking about the pram again.

"Wrap-around video screen. Plays a video of the rooms. With sound."

"Empty rooms?" I said.

"Yeah."

"I thought you said it wasn't creepy."

"It's not. Well, the breathing is till you get used to it. Dave shot the film and he had a cold. He kind of whistled under his breath a bit too."

We were back at the garden fence. I looked at the cottage, the orange light over the door, the net curtains turned see-through by the lights on inside. There was a replica of this place inside a barn in the next field. A dead man whistling. Not exactly stale bread in a bog, but not exactly the Mona Lisa.

"How will you move it?" I said. I could see the gleam of his teeth when he smiled.

"Thanks," he said, and then he laughed at my confusion. "You think I'll need to move it. When someone buys it or asks to show it somewhere."

He opened the front door to the sound of Dillon sobbing, dry cracked sobs as if he'd been crying for hours.

"Daddeeeeee!" he shouted.

"What the hell?" said Gus, charging to

151

the bedroom. "Did you switch that bloody monitor off when you were touching it?" He slammed the door behind him.

Shame and rage flooded me, both together, so strong I was almost reeling. Then together they ebbed away.

Did I? What did I know about baby monitors? Did I turn it off without knowing? Like he did with the light? Except I was a grown-up and Dillon was a baby. I could have turned the light back on but Dillon just had to cry and cry, just like yesterday, and had no way of knowing why nobody came. How I could do that to a little kid? What was wrong with me?

So I went to the kitchen, *stupid bitch,* to see if there was anything left to tidy up after I'd tidied up earlier when he was bathing them. The table was clear, dishes draining, cloth wrung out and hung to dry on the edge of the sink. I had already washed out some clothes for myself, spun them, and hung them up on the pulley to dry. I could sweep the floor if I could find a broom. Or I could clean out the fridge, check the dates, write a shopping list. I sure as hell couldn't go through and sit down and see what was on the telly and just be sitting there like the Queen of Sheba when Gus came back. Imagine switching off the monitor after

152

what they'd already been through. Except I didn't. I knew I hadn't, and there was one right there on the windowsill, nearly the same design, and there was no way I could have switched it off without noticing.

Maybe the batteries were dead. Finally, something I could do: I could look for new batteries. I slipped the compartment cover off the monitor on the windowsill so I knew what I needed and then eyed the kitchen, wondering which drawer was the Sellotape, cracker prize, spare key, dry biro, and battery store. There had to be one. I found it on the third go, right after tea towels and Clingfilm. All of the above, and hair bobbles and dummies too. And mid-rummage I found the other thing that always ends up there with the foreign coins and chargers for old phones you've flung out. Photographs. Real photo-booth photographs of two girls, one sitting on the other's lap, both mugging and gurning and giving it duck-face for the camera. Gus only had a brother. It was too new a picture to be his mum. So this had to be Becky. One of these dark-haired girls was lying in the mortuary in Dumfries right now, waiting for them to cut her open. I couldn't take my eyes off their shining faces, both of them. Which one was she, and who was the other one? Her sister?

They looked enough the same.

"What's that?" said Gus. I hadn't heard him come in. I almost put the photo strip behind my back like a kid would. *Look over there!* And then hide it in the biscuit tin. Something about this guy unhinged me.

"Photos," I said. "I was looking for batteries for the thingy. In case that was why we didn't hear it, you know? Was Becky a twin, Gus?"

"Becky?" He was giving me his turned-to-stone face again. "What photos?"

"Sorry," I said. "I was thinking about Pram, I suppose." He crossed the room and took the pictures out of my hand. "How's Dillon?" I said.

He stared at the photographs. "Fine. Just dropped his Spongie. And Ruby wouldn't get it for him. She can be a right wee besom." He turned the pictures over, looking for dates and captions, I guessed. "I bought the pram at a boot sale." He took his wallet out of his pocket, folded the strip in half, and slid it in. "Good thinking about the batteries, by the way." He went to the fridge and opened it. Sighed. Slammed it closed again. "Do you like red wine? How do you fancy a glass of red wine sitting outside looking at the sea?"

Maybe that was as close as he was going

to get to saying sorry. Maybe he didn't remember that he had shouted and sworn at me.

"Okay."

"Getting frostbite," said Gus. "Should have included that, I suppose."

"If Dillon didn't suck that blanket away to nothing, I'll take it." He smiled. "So who is it? In the pictures. With Becky."

Gus put his hand on the pocket where his wallet was and shook his head, like a dog just out of water.

"God! I was so . . . I was looking at Becky. I'd never seen those ones before. That was Ros. Her that left. Becky's pal."

"They could have been sisters," I said.

"Except then she wouldn't have left and maybe Becky would still be here," he said. He took a breath as if to say more but let it go. Took another that went the same way.

"Is this a cure for hiccups?" I asked. Gus's laugh was like fresh air, like a cold splash of water.

"I want to tell you something," he said. "But I'm bricking it. Come out and sit with me." Maybe he was one of those guys who think saying sorry is the biggest deal on the planet. That would suck. But at least he was trying to say it anyway.

I was glad of the blanket, even over my

coat. The wind was stiff and salty, making me lick my lips, making the cold wine taste sweeter than my first sip had in the kitchen, and I drank half the glass as we sat there in silence, listening to the dead leaves of the rowan clattering on the bricks of the path as the wind stirred them, listening to the slack sound of low tide sloshing in the distance, listening to the quiet murmur of *The Big Friendly Giant* on the Fisher Price soothing Dillon to sleep again. It was so long before he spoke that I jumped at the sound.

"I didn't love her," Gus said. "There."

"Okay," I said. "Things were pretty tough, I know."

"Ever," he said. "She was — I love the kids and I loved the idea of a family. Making a family. But I didn't love Becky. I didn't even like her very much. And the cops and the undertakers' guys and the folk at the hospital last night are all treating me like I'm heartbroken."

"I heard you on the phone," I said. "Trying to talk her down. I saw the state you were in. I see you trying to stop the cops finding out bad stuff about her."

"I don't want the kids hurt, that's all *that* is. But I didn't love her, Jessie. I'm not sorry she's gone."

"You're in shock," I said.

"I would never have left her," he said. "But all I feel now is free."

"Okay," I said again, needing to stop him. I couldn't bear it. That dark-eyed girl, whichever one of them she was, cold and dead and her kids not even old enough so they'd remember her. "You're telling me how you feel. I shouldn't be arguing. I'm sorry."

"Have I got a free pass to say anything then?" he said. "Get out of jail?"

I couldn't speak. What more could there be?

"When Ruby was born," Gus said, "I felt love like I never even imagined before. No way to explain it. Same with Dillon."

"Yeah?" I said.

"Yeah," said Gus. "Bugger all to do with genes. Manky wee space alien screaming his head off in a hospital blanket. *Bang!* It was just like someone hit the on-button." He took a big drink of his wine, and his throat made a dry, sore noise as he swallowed it. "I thought it was only kids that could do that to you."

I drank every drop of wine in my glass, right down to the specks of black stuff.

"Do you understand what I'm saying?" he said.

"You mean . . . you sort of did love Becky,

just not as much?" I asked. "Is that it?"

"No," he said.

I closed my eyes and listened to the sea, to the wind, to the leaves, to *The Big Friendly Giant,* to the buzz of the bulb in the orange light above the door. Kept them closed so that I wouldn't see the world rushing away from me and have to hold on. Anytime I've ever been up high looking down, I've wanted to jump. Or maybe push someone. How can you not? And that's what I felt like then. Like I could fall off the shore into the water. Could pull him over with me, drown the pair of us.

"I think you know what I mean," he said even quieter than before.

He was sitting close enough so I could feel the heat of his body. Except how could the heat of his body jump over two inches of cold October air so I could feel it? It wasn't that after all. It was just every hair on my arm and my leg all down that side of me, standing up on its own wee goose-pimple mountain, trying to grow long enough to touch him. It was the blood in my brain washing up against that side of my skull trying to float my head over to his shoulder. It was the earth underneath that foot nearest his foot, tilting, hoping to slide my ankle over to twine under his.

"Gus," I said at last. "Here's what I'm going to do. I'm going home, and maybe after Christmas or something, give me a call and we can go out for a drink." Go out for a drink and never spend another day apart until we die in our bed on the same night when we've just turned ninety-nine.

"I've got no one, Jessie," he said. "I'll never make it to Christmas alone."

And who did I have? Dot and Steve. Father Tommy and Sister Avril. My brother that screened my calls and pretended he didn't. My chocolate teapot of a mum. How did I end up with no pals? When did that happen?

"I need a friend," he said, mind-reading me.

"Friends," I agreed. I didn't need any more than that. If I could just see him, feel the ground tilting under my feet, feel all my hairs standing up on end, feel my blood course over to whichever bit of me was nearest him instead of going round and round me like it used to do before he was there, I could wait. I'd rather wait. I'd rather build my reserves for the next bit, in case — like it felt it might — it just plain killed me. Like a frog in a blender. One wild whirl and then gone.

But he stretched his arm up and back and

around me and pulled me along the bench. Made me think of those things for shoving chips about in a casino, like you see in films. Or a window-washer's blade pulling suds off the glass, like you see everywhere. And when he put his mouth close to me to whisper, his breath was hot, sour with the wine.

"I lied about the friends thing," he said.

It wasn't really that comfortable, the way he was holding me, but I didn't want to hurt his feelings.

"You need to sleep," I told him.

"If I put Ruby and Dillon in her room and promise not to lay a finger on you, will you sleep next to me?" he said.

"If you promise," I said. And he did.

But that was a lie too.

ELEVEN

Thursday, 6 October

By six o'clock the next morning, when I woke up in the grey light of near-dawn, it all seemed like a dream.

It had started when he put his hand out, feeling for mine, on top of the covers. I'd been lying as far away from him as I could get, but I reached out and grasped his fingers, making my heart rattle high up inside me, really fast, kind of scary.

He took my hand to his lips and kissed my knuckles.

"I don't want to have to go to a church," he said. For one wild moment I thought he meant a wedding. "Or take whatever minister they dish out at the crem."

"Was Becky religious?"

"Dunno. We never talked about it. Are you?"

"They tried," I said. "It didn't take."

"I don't think I could sit through God's

161

plan and everlasting life and all that. Couldn't make the kids sit through it."

"Oh! Are you taking —" I caught my tongue, but not in time.

"Would you?" he said. "Would you not?"

"I really wouldn't," I said. "They're too young."

"Will you watch them for me then?" he said. "Whenever it ends up being?"

"Course," I could hardly say no. "And I'll look up the humanists. That's the ones you're after."

"Cool," said Gus.

"You won't be offending anyone, will you?" I said. "Cos you could pick a good bit: *let not your heart be troubled.* That bit. *In my father's house are many mansions. If it were not so I would have told you.*"

"Christ, they really did try, didn't they?" He turned on his side to look at me. "Don't tell me you know the whole thing off by heart."

I laughed. "Just the sound bites."

"But you're not a big fan?"

"*For God so loved the world,*" I said, "*that he gave his only begotten son, that whosoever believeth in him should not perish, but have everlasting life.*"

Gus let go of my hand to prop his head up. "That's exactly what I *didn't* want," he

162

said. "That's what I just said."

"I'm agreeing," I told him. I shuffled round and propped myself up too, even though sitting like that gives me pins and needles in my arm. "That's why I'm not a fan, is what I'm saying." He shook his head. "Okay," I said, "*For God so loved the world,* right? Pretend you've never heard any of it and try to finish the sentence. *'For God so loved the world that . . .'* I waited. "Well?"

"He . . ." said Gus, "cured all the diseases and banned evil?"

"Exactly." I lay back down. "How long would it take you come up with the right answer? From our studio audience of one hundred, zero people chose *gave his only begotten son.* Might as well say, *God so loved the world that he painted butterflies on all the wheeliebins, that whosoever saw the butterflies should not perish.* Makes as much sense."

"Well, sacrificing your only —"

"Makes you a shit dad not a great god. And it's not like he couldn't have had another one if he'd wanted to. Only you're not supposed to focus on that bit."

"So what . . . was it nuns, or something?" said Gus. He had put his hand flat on my belly.

"God no. Nuns would have been great.

163

Nuns would have been a party. These were Brethren. My dad skipped off. Couldn't stand it. Brother swallowed it whole. I just wound them up. Wound her up. My mother."

"Likes of how?" said Gus. He had curled his hand round my side and was using me as leverage to pull himself closer.

"Didn't take much," I said. "When she told me Jesus died for my sins, I'd say 'Aye, for three days, big whoop!' That kind of thing."

"You know who you remind me of?" said Gus. He was hanging right over me. A bit of hair was tickling one of my cheeks.

"No," I said, thinking *please God, not Becky.*

"Roobs," he said, and he leaned down and kissed me quite hard, for quite a long time, with his lips open, until I had to breathe out through my nose and it made that sort of whistling sound. And it was so weird that he would tell me I made him think of his four-year-old daughter and then kiss me like that, that it sort of overshadowed how weird it was that, lying there in him and Becky's bed, he would kiss me at all. And I'd been wrong about needing to get ready. I think I was so electric already just with the thought of it that when he touched me, I went too

164

far, nearly numb.

"So what do they think of you working for St. Vincey's now?" he asked, when he broke off. "Or aren't Brethren funny that way?"

"Brethren are funny every way," I said. "But they — she — gave up on me years ago."

He shifted until he was lying on top of me, a smooth move that should have been awkward. He should have grunted and had to sort his arms and legs out. Something anyway. But he did it in one gliding move, like a snake.

"All the more for me," he said and, when he kissed me this time, there was a rhythm to it, pushing against me and pulling away, and the rest of his body moved to the same pulse, and I kept thinking about how a snake moves through grass until I joined in and then I was part of it too, and it didn't feel weird anymore.

Of course, he had pyjamas on, and I had kept the new knickers I'd filched from work on under the long t-shirt I'd borrowed from him, so it wasn't all undulation. There was a bit of wriggling and buttons and that. And then it turned out, of course, that the condoms were on my side, in a drawer, so that was awkward. And after we got all *that* sorted out, it was actually kind of crap, to be perfectly honest. Pretty basic, completely silent, and nothing to distract me from what I was doing. So between that and the conversation we'd just been having, my mother appeared for the first time in years. Just her face, just behind his shoulder, looking at me like it was all she could do not to retch. And as soon as I'd had that thought, retching was all I could think about, so I held my breath and gritted my teeth, and if he had kept going, I think I would have got up in the morning and left, never seen them again.

But he stopped.

"What?" he said, pulling right up until his arms were straight and looking down at me.

"Ghosts," I told him. "Sorry."

He drew carefully away from me, shifted over until he was just to the side and lay down with one arm and one leg still over my body.

"Did some guy hurt you, Jessie?" he said. "Is the . . . can I say the word?"

"Feathers?"

"Is that a *bed* thing?"

"Not the way you mean," I said. "No guy ever hurt me, no."

Inside

She sipped the water like it was Highland

166

Park, forty years old, rolling it round her mouth. She was good at making things last. So much counselling, so many hours of therapy, so good at tricking her own brain into choking off at the neck whatever her body was going through. So she sipped and savoured and delayed the precious moment when she would finish the first one. Great excitement then. Now she had a bottle she could use for something. Make something. Change something. And she had cardboard too. And the wrappers from the muesli bars. Oh, she had plenty to keep her busy. And she could do sit-ups and yoga. She could make up poetry and set it to music. She could think of fruits beginning . . . apple, banana, citron, damson. Dances beginning . . . American Smooth, Black Bottom, Cha-cha-cha, Dashing White Sergeant, Eightsome Reel, Foxtrot, Gay Gordons, Hesitation Waltz. And try to do the steps. Until she stumbled on the toilet and turned her ankle.

After that she curled up in a ball and cried for a while. Roared and screamed and wailed. That had a name in some kind of therapy too.

At six o'clock in the morning, he was flat on his back, covers at his waist, bare chest rising and falling, slow and steady. I turned away and swung my legs down, trying to make my movements as small as they could be. I had just transferred my weight to my feet, just clenched my bum to lift it off the bed, when he laid his warm hand on me.

"Don't go," he said.

"I need a pee." The hand was gone, but I could still feel the tingle of it, a perfect print of it, all five fingers and the palm, and it made me think of glitter scattered over glue. I scrabbled on the floor for the t-shirt and yesterday's knickers. "Plus the kids," I said. "D'you want a cup of tea?"

"Coffee," he said and turned over, until he was lying face down with his arms under his pillow. He had old acne scars on his back, flat purple patches all over his shoulder blades, a few down as far as the dip in his waist.

"I'm glad to see you don't have a hairy back," I said.

He grunted, could have been a laugh. "Yet," he said. "Dave was like a gorilla by the time he was seventy, and I take after him." I pulled the t-shirt on over my head. "Would you love me if I turned into a seventy-year-old gorilla?" Like it was really happening, not just a day dream at all.

"Sure," I said. "If you wax it." And I left the room before he said any more.

■ ■ ■ ■

"No school today, Ruby-duby-doo," he said when he finally appeared. I had the kids up, washed, and eating toast and jam in the kitchen. He was wearing those canvas trousers and a work shirt again, no tweedy suit today, but he'd shaved and his hair was pulled back from his forehead, the top half in a ponytail that hung down over the curtain of the bottom half. That hairdo that was just for girls until the Italian footballers started doing it. "Cheers for the coffee, Jessie," he said, putting the cup in the sink.

"Am I not getting back?" said Ruby in a tiny little voice.

"Hm?" said Gus. He'd forgotten, as much as he had on his mind.

"You're kidding," I said. "Miss Colquhoun said she'd miss you so much she might come out on Saturday and see you. She'll be sad every day until you're back again."

"But this is Jessie's day off," said Gus, "and you get to stay here with her."

"No," said Ruby.

"You've got to, Roobs," he said. "Daddy needs the car."

"Did Mummy take her car to heaven?"

she said. I glanced at Gus. Where *was* Becky's car? Still at the bottom of the drop? Police station? Junkyard?

"Yes," I said.

"Stupid," said Ruby. "In heaven, you can *fly.*"

"Do you want some toast?" I said to Gus. "Listen, if you tell me where the van keys are, I'll do some bits of shopping or whatever."

"The van's not really . . . you can't get both kids' seats in it."

"Could you use it and I'll take the car?" I asked him.

"Does Mummy need her car to come and visit us?" said Ruby.

"Mummy coming!" Dillon said.

"Do we actually need any shopping?" said Gus.

"Fine," I said. "No problem. I'll stay here till you're back. Be great fun, eh kids? You can show me the best bits of the beach."

"When the shop's open's the best bit," said Ruby. She gave her toast crust a look of distilled hatred and dropped it on the floor. "Mummy cuts them off, by the way."

"Bet Mummy doesn't drop them on the floor, though," I said.

"Didn't," said Gus. "Mummy's gone, Roobs."

"A puppy would eat them up," Ruby said.

"Yeay!" said Dillon. "Puppy-dog! Woof-woof."

"Can we get one, Dad? Can you look in the paper at the resky dogs? Maybe there's a resky dog?"

"I'm off," said Gus. "See you tonight."

I followed him from the kitchen through the living room to the front door.

"Tonight?" I said. "You think it'll take all day?" I could have chewed off my tongue when I saw the look on his face, everything falling blank.

"How long should I give it?" he said. "Persuading them to do a post-mortem, I mean. Before I call it quits?"

"I'm sorry. I just hope they're okay with me as long as that. I hope nothing happens that I can't handle. Cos I don't think they could take more bad stuff, you know."

He smiled. "Them?" he said. "They'll be fine. I hope *you're* okay. Don't let Ruby walk all over you."

"Okay." I leaned in to the hug he was offering. Easy, affectionate, not a trace of new, awkward feelings. I might as well have been handing him his packed lunch and reminding him we were having the Joneses over for bridge that night. Christ, I was even holding a tea towel.

171

"What's a resky dog?" I said.

"Rescue," said Gus. "For God's sake, don't read the adverts out the paper to her."

I nodded. "How does she even know about them?" I asked.

"God knows," said Gus and was gone. I wandered back through to the kitchen and put the tea towel over the rack. I'd babysit. I'd have another go at the milk stain on the couch — I'd noticed the sour smell, even stronger, as I passed through — but I wasn't giving it Calamity Jane's cabin all day long. Suddenly, playing houses — playing mummies and daddies — didn't sit that easy. It was like I was in a dream and I kept waking up for a minute and seeing that it made no sense at all, but before I could shake it off I was asleep again.

"So who told you about rescue puppies, Ruby-two-shoes?" I said.

She narrowed her eyes as she looked at me. "Mummy," she said. "Come on, Dill. Let's go and play."

I unstrapped Dillon and set him down, let them wander off with jammy hands and crumbs in the folds of their clothes. I wiped the table and the high-chair tray, shook the crumbs out the back door for the birds, thinking about a woman who would tend a garden and look for a puppy while she was planning to kill herself. A woman who would let herself get pregnant two more times after a depression that crushed her. Someone who would end her life instead of getting out of a marriage she was sick of.

But she'd left a note.

And who knows how it would feel to be married to someone that didn't love you. Even a great guy like Gus. Or a moody bastard like Gus, who hated you asking anything he wasn't ready to tell you. Which one was he, when you got right down to it, really?

I stared out of the kitchen window, thinking of how he had told me he didn't want to bring the novelty pen through the room, even in a bag. That's who he was. And how could living with a guy like that be bad? I could just see one corner of the grey plastic lid. It was still in there. I felt a pulse starting to thump in my neck. *Stupid bi—*

Then I stopped myself. Instead of that, I told myself: *it's hidden away and it can't float out. It can't hurt you. And for the first time in your life, you've got someone to help you. Someone even willing to give his kids a talking-to about it. So don't waste his efforts and freak yourself out, eh?*

But I could feel the misery unrolling over me like fog. Gus *had* been great, but it wouldn't last. He'd get sick of me like everyone always did. There'd be some day, some advert on the telly, or some fancy-dress costume, some daft comedy that suddenly had a slow-motion pillow fight where you could see them hit people's face and they'd have them stuck to their eyelashes and be spitting them out of their mouths, and I'd lose it. And Gus would have had a long day or a bit of bad news or be stressed like last night (*Did you switch that bloody monitor off when you were touching it?*) and he'd wish that just for once I would give it a rest, and he'd roll his eyes or crack a joke and this lovely, impossible bubble would burst and then there'd be nothing.

Unless. I could feel the blood draining out of my face and my hands turned cold. Unless I made the most of this miracle — having someone who cared — and tried again. There was a novelty pen, in a bag, in the wheeliebin, ten feet from where I was standing. I could open the lid and find out if the bag was see-through. If it was, I could look at what was inside and count to a hundred. And then tonight I could tell Gus what I'd done, and instead of *so what* I'd get a great big cheer.

And if the bag wasn't see-through, then at least I tried.

I'd walk on the beach and I wouldn't avoid the sticks and seaweed at the high tide line, which is where they always were. I wouldn't look at them, like some OCD freak, and I wouldn't look away from them either. I'd act like a normal person. And I'd tell Gus later how brave I'd been.

"I'm just nipping out the back, kids," I shouted. My voice was warbly with adrenalin; I sounded like a pigeon. There was no answer. I stepped outside into the porch and then outside again to where the wheelie stood against the wall, next to the wood store. I gripped the lip with both hands and breathed in and out.

"Gus King cares about you," I said out loud. "Sick timing, but it's true. You're not alone anymore. It's all going to be okay."

I lifted the lid with my eyes screwed tight shut, then leaned over the rim and opened them.

TWELVE

It was empty. No bag, see-through or otherwise. Nothing. Not so much as a sweetie
wrapper. I let the lid fall again and rolled
around to lean against the porch wall until
my breathing settled.

He had taken it away. I smiled at the
thought of it, and a warm feeling started
low in my stomach. Not one in a million
people would know I'd be freaked out at
the thought of it being there and take it
away. Not even folk with problems of their
own. Not even my sister-in-law, who was
dead scared of heights. Especially not her,
actually.

"But the thing about" — she pointed
upwards but couldn't say the word — "is
that you can . . ." She pointed downwards
and gave me a patient smile. "See? Whereas
feathers" — oh, she could say that word
okay — "can't harm you at all. That's just
silly."

I had swivelled in my chair to stare at my mother. We were all sitting round the table having Sunday lunch together, for the benefit of Allan's suitable new fiancée.

"Yes, they can," I said.

Penny blinked and smiled, a flash of her eyes and a flash of her teeth for each one of us round the table, one after the other. My mother managed a bit of a smile back. My brother dropped his eyes. I kept up my hard look.

"In a roundabout way, right enough," I said. "But they caused me quite a lot of harm once, didn't they Mum?"

"They can't have," Penny said, patiently. "What do you mean?"

"Oh, Jessie likes nothing better than to spoil nice things," my mother said. "She'll never learn, no matter what lessons are sent to her. Take no notice, Penny. It's not worth worrying about."

"True," I said. "Not worth a worry. Not like dropping from a great height and going splat and crunching all your bones to rubble."

I got sent away from the table. Twenty-two I was, and I got sent to my room. I could hear my mother saying sorry and assuring Penny that she wouldn't have to put up with me again. That poor Allan was too kind for his own good, but I just spoiled everything, been the same since I was a child. "Takes after my late husband," my mother said. She always called him that. *Late.* Maybe she even believed it herself by now.

"Jessie?"

I looked down. Dillon was standing in the porch doorway, one foot on top of the other so that only one of his socks would get wet. "Done a poo," he said. "A big one."

"Good!" I said. "Let's see if it's big enough to win a prize!"

He giggled and held up his hands for me to lift him. I took a deep breath and held it, but it wasn't so bad. Just kind of warm smelling, really.

"I don't even know where your changing box is," I told him, carrying him inside. "Or if there's a special bucket." I stopped. Dillon was winding his fist into my hair, tugging it. "In fact, the bins must need emptied something chronic, eh?" I said. "Here's the deal, Dill. I'll change your bum and then you help me empty the buckets out to the wheelie, eh?"

"Can I help too?" Ruby was standing in her bedroom doorway with her hairbrush in her hand. "If you do my bobbles?"

"Deal, squeal, spit, and seal," I said.

178

"Squeal, squeal, squeal," said Dillon, wriggling and releasing quite a lot more smell.

"Dill's got a wet sock, by the way," Ruby said. "I'll get some dry ones."

Turned out there were nappies in bags all over the house. It must have been a pretty powerful deodorant on them, not to mention airtight twist-ties, but still I was ashamed to think that I hadn't gone round and cleared them before now, that they'd been piling up since Tuesday. In the basket in Ruby's bedroom, in the tin bin in the living room, in the kitchen flip-top, in the white plastic bucket in the bathroom. Everywhere except Gus's bedroom, in fact, and since the baby's cot was in there it took me a while to believe it. I searched down the sides of the furniture and even in the bottom of the wardrobe (which was nuts), then I carted them out one by one and tipped them into the wheelie.

"What day do the men come, Ruby?" I asked. "Do you know? Don't want to miss them."

Ruby shook her head and held out her hairbrush and bobbles. "Wash your hands and do my bunches," she said.

"What's the magic word?" It popped out automatically like I was a slot machine.

"Now," said Ruby. Then her small eyes filled up with tears. "You're supposed to laugh. It's a joke. It's funny."

"Is that your joke with Mummy?" I asked. She nodded. Tears were falling down her cheeks, one after the other, faster and faster, and when I went and put my hand on the back of her head, she pressed her face against me and howled. Which started Dillon off too.

"I'm sorry, hunny-bunny," I said. I opened my mouth to say more, but what was there to say? She didn't know me, and even I didn't know what I was doing here. I didn't understand how asking about a post-mortem and organising a funeral could take Gus all day, even if he had to buy a suit to wear to it. But his face that morning when I had questioned him? I didn't want to see that again. I stood holding them against me as they wept, looking down at the whorls of their hair, identical patterns on their little heads.

"We need some chocolate," I said. Not from being some kind of stupid Bridget Jones bimbo, but from remembering what totally mental, off-the-scale shit sweeties could sort for you when you were five. Me? I was well past the age when chocolate could help, but being the big one with the money who could buy it for the wee ones? That was pretty great too.

The M&Ms were finished and the best the fridge had to offer was Babybel cheese. I checked inside the big pans, the butter bit in the fridge, the backs of the high cupboards — everywhere I'd have stashed it if it was me — and only found cream of tartar and mace, tins of Carnation milk and Devon custard, tangerine segments and packets of lemon jelly. I could make a sell-by-date trifle, I thought, sure that some of this stuff had to have been here since Granddad Dave was on the go. Why would Becky not have cleaned out the cupboards? She grew her own veg but didn't chuck out the old stuff in the larder?

Dillon's coat was a solid wodge of padded nylon, and once he was trussed, I had no worries about him. Ruby's was trimmed with fur and shiny pink and only reached the top of her thighs.

"Have you got a pair of waterproof trousers?" I asked her. "I think it's going to bucket."

"Wellies!" said Dillon.

"You betcha," I said. "You too, Ruby. And hats on, hoods up. No discussion." That had worked when Gus had said it.

The rain started when we were just about

as far from the cottage as we were from the shop, no point turning back, since if we were going to get drenched we might as well get drenched for treats. Dillon was walking at forty-five degrees into the wind with his fringe plastered back over the outside of his anorak hood and his eyes watering. Ruby put her head down like a little bull and bar-relled forward. I checked ahead of her for obstacles, but the beach was clear; she'd be okay. I took Dillon's hand, cold and pink, and tried to tuck my hair inside my hood to stop it whipping across my face.

"Hot baths when we get back," I said. "Hot chocolate, jammies on, telly on, fire lit, cosy socks."

The children said nothing, just kept fight-ing their way into the wind towards the sweeties. I felt an enormous rush of what felt a lot like love for them both. Little kids doing what little kids do. No one telling them they were devils for wanting to do it. That wasn't what she had said, not exactly. "Something devilish about you, Jessica," is how she had put it. "From your father."

"What does that make you then?" I'd said. "You slept with him, not me."

And then she'd go on and on about how I was a test — my mother was big on tests and lessons; nothing just *happened* — and that she embraced God's plan no matter what he sent her.

"Look!" said Dillon. He had pulled back and was pointing at something on the ground. I turned my back on the wind — relief! — and crouched down. I thought it was a rat, drowned, or maybe a mouse. But then I saw the beak and the claws and knew. A starling. Black and sodden. Not scary when it was wet, no chance of anything floating towards me.

"It's a dead bird," said Ruby. "Dirty." She started to kick sand over it and then stopped. "It's dead," she said. It wasn't a question, but I could see her thoughts turning and I knew what was coming next.

"Ditty!" said Dillon.

"Mummy's dead," said Ruby. Still not a question. Her cross wee face was tied up tight. "Dead like that?" She kicked the bird, and it shifted a bit into the slush that the rain had built up behind it. I winced. "Not gone to heaven?" said Ruby. She kicked the bird harder. "Dead like that?"

"Poor buddy," said Dillon. "Dop it, Ruby. No kicking!" It was the most I'd ever heard him say. Wee darling, feeling sorry for a dead bird even if he had to be brave and stand up to his sister.

"Listen," I said. I grabbed Ruby's hand

and tugged her away from the thing. "Keep walking and I'll tell you."

And I did. About how our body is just an earthly shell to hold our soul, and how our soul flies out of our body when we die and lives forever. In heaven.

"What's a soul but?" said Ruby.

"Soul but," said Dillon, back to normal.

"Your soul is . . ." I said. No point in giving them the holy spirit living inside each one of us routine. I never even met a minister who had a bloody clue what the holy spirit was. "Okay, your soul is . . . your essence." Silence. "Or, your spirit, your vital spark."

"That bird was dead," said Ruby.

"Your soul," I said, louder, "is the bit that the Blue Fairy gave to Pinocchio to turn him into a real boy." Both faces turned up to me, just for a second, until the rain hitting their cheeks turned them down again. "And Sleeping Beauty? Her whole body except for her soul was asleep until the Prince kissed her. And the wicked Queen poisoned every single bit of Snow White *except* her soul, and that's how come she was okay. You know Babe?"

"Babe the Pig?" said Ruby.

"He was a pig with a person's soul," I said.

"And your body dies," said Ruby, "but

your soul lives forever and it can fly."

"You've got it," I told her. "Close enough, anyway." I steered them towards the low dunes at the top of the beach and the path that cut through to the campsite shop, then stopped, tugging on their hoods to hold them. At the corner of the nearest caravan, a figure was huddled under the shelter of the overhang. Must really want a ciggie, I thought, hoping it was true. But I knew who it was even before he came shuffling over to stand in front of us.

"Please, jess?" he said.

"Yeah, hiya," I said. "Didn't recognise you . . ." *dripping wet with another two days' muck.*

"Where she is?" he said. "Jaroslawa. You tell, jess?" He was hunched inside a soaking wet worky's jacket that was only making things worse, chuting the rain down onto the thighs of his jeans. There's nothing worse than wet jeans, unless it's wet trainers and he had them too.

"Okay, I'm sorry to be telling you this," I said, "especially if you had a fight and maybe you said things you didn't mean. Cos you are going to be sorry for the rest of your life." He didn't understand a word of it. I tried again. "She died. On Tuesday. I'm sorry. She died."

"But her soul will live forever in heaven," said Ruby.

My mother would be proud of me.

"Dead?" He crossed himself. I nodded. "Jaroslawa," he said, like he always did. "Sick?"

"Car crash," I said. "She . . . listen, I'm sorry, but she . . ." I didn't want to use the simple words he would understand in case the kids understood them too. "She committed suicide," I told him, talking quite loud that way you do to help foreigners decipher it.

"No," he said. He had stopped hunching against the rain, and the way he stood there with the water streaming down his face, over his eyebrows and through his scrubby beard, made me think of the starling. "Not ever. No way. Jaroslawa! Jaroslawa!"

"I know," I said. "It's tough to take. But you need to stop hanging around us, right? If Gus sees you, it'll make it harder for him. So you have to just leave us alone." The kids were huddled in beside me, sheltering, but a strong gust blew a good soak of rain against us and made Dillon start to grizzle. "Listen, I need to get going," I said. "You should go back inside. Get in out the rain."

But he was still standing there when I reached the corner of the track and turned.

I looked back twice, and he was still just standing there.

At least the shop was open. The door dinged and we fell in, dripping and shaking like dogs.

"Stay on the cardboard!" It was the same woman as yesterday, Princess Charming herself, in jeans and a fleece now instead of her kaftan, barking at us like a sergeant major. "Get that kid off my clean floor!" The lino was newly mopped and she'd laid flattened boxes on top to walk on, but she hadn't wiped it off or let it dry, and the cardboard was soggy round the edges. She'd find out later about the ink coming off when she saw inside-out *Walkers Crisps* and *Borders Biscuit Co* all over.

"Why the heck would you clean a floor on a day like this?" I said.

"No dafter than going out for a walk," said the woman. She was poring over a ring-binder full of dockets and a pile of loose papers, but she still had an eye for the kids, watching them like she could hear them ticking and see the fuse fizzing down. "What do *you* lot want anyway?"

"Treats," I said. "Sweeties, chocolate, fizzy juice, bubblegum." She frowned and heaved a sigh up from under the floor. "You are open, right?" I said. The kids were off up the sweetie aisle already, hunkered down, concentrating hard.

"Not really," she said. "I'm open for deliveries. Half-term next week. There's a big order coming in, only God knows what's in it." She lifted a handful of papers and let them fall.

"You seem a bit flustered," I said.

"Aye well," said the woman. "I've been let down. Wee madam was just supposed to clean the weekly vans for change-over day. Don't ask me how she ended up ordering stock and booking in. And now she's upped and left."

"When was this?" I said, wondering if she meant Becky.

"Haven't seen her since Saturday," the woman said. "My friend in Gatehouse that has a B&B said, 'Get yourself a Pole, Gizzy. They work like black slaves and there's never a word of complaint from them.' So I got myself a Pole and look at me!"

Light dawned, better late than never. "Ros," I said.

"Aye!" Gizzy barked, loud enough to make Ruby raise her head and look over. "Where's she skipped off to? Do you know?"

"Home to Poland," I said. "She left a job?" As well as a friend in need.

"A good job. Flexible hours and accommodation. And my friend in Gatehouse had the cheek to say they were grateful. *Grateful!* Even when it's all on the books and contracts to your armpits, they're not to be trusted."

"So you've got an opening?" I said. "Flexible hours?" Because here's what I was thinking: I couldn't stay at Gus's. Couldn't just move in. Couldn't live with myself if I did. But I'd love an excuse to be nearby every day. For him and the kids. Let it happen more naturally, on less of a sick timescale sort of thing. Plus, four days at the Project and the odd night behind the bar at the leisure club wasn't exactly keeping me in fox furs.

Gizzy looked me up and down. "I'm not interested in a mum," she said.

"I think that's illegal," I told her. "But I'm not their mum. I'm just babysitting today."

"Our mummy's dead in heaven," said Ruby, coming up and putting an armload of crap on the counter. She turned to go back for more. "Her earthy body is dead, but her soul has flied to heaven."

"Here!" said Gizzy. "Is this the King kids from the end house?" I nodded. "I heard on the news. What experience do you have?" She didn't even take a breath in between. It couldn't really have been much clearer: she wanted the dirt dished even if she had to give me a job to get it.

"I run the D&G Free Clothing Project for St. Vincent de Paul Church in Dumfries," I said. "Cash handling, stock control, cleaning and organizing, all that. Supervising other staff. But it's only four days a week — I'm off on Thursday, Saturday, and Sunday."

"I need Friday, Saturday, Sunday," she said. "But we can work it round. References?"

"Father Whelan and Sister Avril Kennedy do you?"

"Well, I'm not much of a one for Catholics," said Gizzy. "At least you're Scottish." She was giving me a good look up and down, appraising, and so she might have noticed me starting to breathe faster, might have seen me rub my hands on my thighs. I knew I had to ask her.

"The upholstery," I said. "In the vans. Is it foam? Mostly? Is it microfibre?"

"Don't tell me you're allergic?" she said, with her lip curling.

"Not to microfibre," I said. Deep breath. "Aretherefeathercushionsinthevans?" The only way I could say it was so quickly that chances were, I'd have to say it again.

"Oh! La-di-dah!" she said. "Twenty featherbeds, eh? Goose-down pillows in satin cases! Eiderdowns to spare! No there bloody aren't, and if you paid the cleaning bills, you'd know why."

"Good!" I said. Too loud, trying to shut her up before she thought of any more names for them.

"You can start tomorrow on a two-week trial," she said. "Eight sharp and bring your references." Dillon came up and tried to heave his own armload up beside Ruby's. I bent to help him. "There's no discount, mind."

"I can't start tomorrow," I said. "Not till after four anyway. But I'll work on till it's done." I stood up and held out my hand. "Jessie Constable."

"Gisele MacInstry," she said. "Gizzy."

"That's us set then," I said. "Can you put me in the tick-book for this lot and take it off my first week's wage? *I'm kidding,*" I added before she could blow a blood vessel. Slowly, she went back to her usual colour: the deep purplish brown of someone who runs a good seasonal business and spends the winter somewhere warm with cheap drink.

"Aye, well," she said, "I suppose. Butter wouldn't melt in that Ros's mouth and she's turned out useless." She cracked open a plastic bag with a flick of her wrist and started ringing up the junk on the register. "Yes to everything. 'Jess, Gizzy' this and 'jess, Gizzy' that and then upped and walked. What's wrong with *you*?" Because I was standing staring at her.

"Polish accent," I said.

"Oh, don't go all offended on me," said Gizzy, rolling her eyes. "*She* was bad enough. I called her Rosalind once and got an earful. As if I could pronounce what Ros was short for! I meant no harm."

"Ja*ros*lawa," I said. Gizzy blinked at me. "He's Ros's friend," I said. Ruby squinted up at me. "*Ros's* friend," I said again. "He's nothing to do with Becky. He's looking for *Ros*. Which . . ." I looked into their three faces and then settled on Ruby. "Which . . . makes tons more sense. Why would you be worried enough to come looking for someone after an hour or two? But Ros left on —"

"Saturday," said Gizzy. "And this *friend* needn't come looking round here for her. I'm sick to the back teeth with the lot of them."

"I wish I could remember his name," I said to Ruby and Dillon as we sailed back down the path with the wind at our backs. I could feel the rain soaking through the neck of my coat, but it was a holiday compared with the outward journey.

"Wanna sweetie," said Dillon.

"Mister!" I shouted. "Kaaaaz? Mr. Wet Man! Mr. Kaaaaaz!" I would have probably shouted *Mr. Polish Guy* if it hadn't been for Gizzy. "Help me shout, kids." I swung their arms with a one and a two and a one-two-three.

"Mr. Kaaaaaz!" Ruby and me shouted.

"Wanna sweetieeeee!" Dillon shouted louder than both of us.

"Dillsky," I said. "It's pouring with rain if you haven't noticed. You need to wait till we get home."

"There he is," said Ruby. She pointed to the row of cabins and bungalows at the edge of the sand and then pelted off, pumping her arms so hard that her whole body twisted with each step. I could just hear her shouts — "Mr. Wet Guy!" — being torn out of her mouth and hooked away by the wind. I took a tighter hold of Dillon and followed her.

She ran right up to the middle house, the big one, and under the awning thing, halfway between a real garage and a carport.

"Mr. Kaz!" she shouted, and it was suddenly deafening under the roof. I hissed at her to come out.

"There's nobody here, Ruby-doo," I said. "Come on. This is someone's house, you know." And they were in too; the tumble drier was going.

"I saw him," said Ruby. She was standing like Zorro in the middle of the floor, just on the oil stain where the car would be if it was parked there. "He was peeking at us. He was *here.*"

"Aye well, he's not here now," I said. "And Dillon's shivering. Come on."

"Mr. Wet Guy," said Ruby in a come out, come out wherever you are voice, high and wheedling. At the back of the garage, where the canoes were bundled, someone laughed and smothered it.

"Kaz?" I said.

"Kazek," he said. "Jess." He stood up from where he'd been hiding behind the canoes and sidled out. He was wrapped in a sheet of bright blue crackling plastic, like for covering a boat or something.

"Right," I said. "Kazek. Yeah. Good. Okay. Jaroslawa is not dead."

"Alive?" he said.

"Yes," I said.

"Where *is* Ros?" said Ruby.

"Where she gone?" said Dillon.

"Why you said is dead?" said Kazek. He

194

came shuffling out from among the canoes. His trainers were so wet I could hear them squelching.

"Misunderstanding," I told him. "Is this your house?"

"Is here?" he said. "Is back?"

"She's away home to Poland," I told him. "Why are you wrapped up in that tarpaulin?" What were the chances he'd understand that? He was shaking his head, moving forward all the time, right up close to me.

"No," he said. "No way. Not go home."

"Sorry," I said. I was staring at the space between the edge of the tarp and his neck, the way it stood out from being so stiff. I could see quite a bit of his collarbone, almost out to his shoulder, and I didn't think he was wearing anything under there. I stepped back.

"You good woman," he said.

I took another step backwards. "Roobs," I said. "Goan, go back out to the beach, eh? Go on." She scuttled outside. He must have been pinging her radar too — no way she'd go just because I told her.

"You make me happy, jess?" Kazek said. "Jaroslawa is no dead. You make no cry, jess?"

"No way!" I said, and Dillon flinched

195

against my neck at the sudden loudness. I hadn't even realised he was drowsing. "You're seriously weird, pal." I hutched Dillon over so I could hold him with just one hand and I stretched the other out, pointed my finger. Jabbed it really. "Just stay out of my way." Then I turned tail and ran. All the way along the beach, over the rocks and up to the cottage, locked the door, checked the back door was locked too, and still couldn't help looking out the window for any sign of a blue plastic cloak coming our way.

THIRTEEN

There's a noise the computer makes at work when you fire it up for the day. It's a bit like the start of *Rhapsody in Blue* from that film, and a bit like a fire alarm that doesn't quite get going. There's silence and then there's a whooshing noise lifting up and then the computer sort of hums all day, except you don't really notice until you switch it off at night. That's what happened to me when Gus came home, eventually, at nearly six o'clock, when it was dark outside again. I thought I was awake and firing on all cylinders until he opened the door and walked through. Then I went *whoosh* and started humming, and it felt like I'd had about half as much again blood pumped into me. I felt the smile break out over my face and couldn't help it. The same daft look spread over his and his neck went red. He picked the kids up, both together, and blew on their necks, but he was looking at me.

It wasn't till after dinner that it all went wrong, and I had no idea what had happened or how to make it stop, put it back again. I was washing dishes. He was sitting at the table, drinking up the last of the water from the jug I'd put there. No wine tonight. Family tea. And he was watching me.

"What?" I said.

He smiled, but a miserable smile like you'd never believe. "Nothing," he said. And we were silent again. He was tracing a pattern in the water Dillon had spilled on the plastic tablecloth, pulling lines of it out from the puddle like spider's legs. It was another five minutes before he cleared his throat and spoke. "So you went for a walk, eh?" he said. The wet clothes were hanging on the pulley, still dripping every now and then. "Meet anyone?"

The obvious thing was to tell him about Kazek. He'd had a flakey when I'd mentioned the guy last time, but that was because he thought Kazek was Becky's boyfriend. And it was the day she died. Now I knew he was Ros's creepy friend and it was two days later.

"Not a soul," I said. I'd keep Ruby and Dillon away from that house with the

198

awning, and I'd steer pretty clear too. "Apart from the woman in the shop. Oh, by the way —"

"I didn't get any joy about the post-mortem," he said, interrupting me.

I caught my lip. Couldn't believe I hadn't asked him. That must be why he'd been sitting there silent, waiting for me to remember. "They did the basic examination. But I didn't find anything out. Nobody came to speak to me at all."

"Isn't it detectives they come and talk to?" I said.

Gus laughed and rubbed his face. Just like that, we were friends again.

"God, yeah, you're right," he said. "Bloody *CSI* strikes again. Me sitting there for hours!" He stood up and whirled a gob of kitchen roll off the holder, wiped the table, went to the bin, and then froze there with the lid pushed open.

"Gus?" I said. He said nothing and didn't move. It was like that bit in science fiction when the world stops and you can skip about without anyone seeing you. "Gus?"

He cleared his throat. "Did you empty this?" he said.

"Ahhh, yeah?" I said. "I emptied all of them. Dillon did the nappy from hell and it went from there."

He walked to the back window and looked out. If anyone had asked, I'd have said he was staring at the wheeliebin, but that was crazy.

"Gus?" I said, a third time. "Did I do something wrong?"

He spun round so fast that I had stepped back before I could help it. "Did I say you did?" he said.

I took another step back.

He sat back down at the table and wrapped his arms around his shoulders. Then he started rocking, side to side, like he had one time before. "It can't. God, it can't. It can't be happening again."

"Hey," I said, flinging the dishcloth into the sink. "What's wrong? What did I do?"

Slowly he let his arms go, straightened up, and looked at me. "You're not angry," he said. It was a statement, not a question.

"Oh, I'm fuming," I said. "I'll turn green and burst out of my clothes any minute as soon as you tell me what I'm supposed to be angry about."

He held out both his hands and took hold of mine. "That I didn't do it before you had to," he said. "That I left it for you. Took you for granted. Treated you like a skivvy. Expected you to run about after me, wait on me hand and foot, while I treated the place like a hotel."

I nodded, understanding like. But the truth was it didn't make sense, not really. He'd lain in his bed while I brought him coffee and gave the kids their breakfast. And he'd lain in the bath while I cleared the lunch and took them out too. So why would shifting a couple of nappies freak him out this way?

"Sometimes," I began.

"What?"

But I thought the better of it. *You're like two different people,* was what I was going to say.

He was quiet after that, moving through to the living room, lighting the fire, putting the telly on. He didn't watch it, though. I could tell from the way the screen was reflected off the whites of his eyes that he wasn't really looking there. I sat down in the other chair, watched the end of some cooking programme and the start of some dieting one, feeling like I hadn't felt since I was fifteen and Steve Preston took me to see *Pleasantville* and grabbed my hand twenty minutes in. We were paralysed then, the pair of us, our hands warming and sliding so we had to grip even harder on to the other's fingers to keep a hold. Neither one of us knew how to stop it, like someone who's learned how to take off in a plane but had no lessons on landing. And I couldn't help thinking about the pocket of space in between our palms filling up with sweat like a chicken kiev and what would happen when we burst it open.

It was over an hour before Gus spoke again, and I had to ask him to repeat it. I had been back with Steve Preston's sister Sandra, who was my friend, who I'd told all about that very first therapist (what was her name?). And Sandra Preston had told everyone in our class, and the guidance teacher called my mum up and I got hell for it.

Literally. Got hell described, had the best verses of the Bible read out where they talked about it, had it explained why I was going there and why that was what I deserved.

"That's not hell, Mum," I'd said after a really mad bit. "That's the earth after Armageddon. Get it right, eh?"

"Therefore shall her plagues come in one day, death and mourning and famine," said my mother. *"And she shall be utterly burned with fire: for strong is the Lord God who judgeth her."*

"There you go again," I'd said. "That's Armageddon too."

"I was asking about the bathroom bin," said Gus.

I turned and stared at him.

"Sorry," I said. "Miles away." I smiled. "Nice to be back, though. What about it?"

"I don't suppose you happened to notice what was in it?" he said. "When you put it in the bin bag?"

"I just tipped it right into the wheelie," I said. "No bag." He was quiet long enough for me to half turn back to the telly. Some poor cow was weeping in a front of a wrap-around mirror in her underwear, her belly jiggling up and down.

"I was going to save the stick," he said. "If it was in there. The test stick, you know." He was staring at the telly too now.

"I didn't notice."

"Only . . . that's all there is of that wee baby now," said Gus. "That's all there ever will be. No photos, no footprint, nothing. Just one blue line."

"God, I'm sorry," I said.

"We could tip it out and look through."

"I suppose so."

At last, he turned and looked at me. Beamed at me. "Thanks," he said.

"Thanks?" I said. "You want me to do it?"

"I'm not bothered," said Gus. "You do it if you'd rather." He turned back to the telly again and it felt weird looking at the side of his head, so I did too. The poor cow had her clothes back on now, really bad ones, and they were starting on how dry her hair was and what crap teeth she had.

"Will I get you a torch?" said Gus. I looked up at the centre light of the living room, one of those cloudy glass bowls that hangs down on three chains that flies always die in. I seriously thought he was asking me if I needed some extra light for watching the telly by. Then I twigged.

"You want me to get it tonight?"

"Of course not," said Gus. "I thought *you* meant tonight."

I turned and looked out of the window — the curtains weren't drawn — at the perfect square of black out there. "Thought I meant tonight when?" I asked him. "I didn't say anything."

"Okay," he said, and his voice was that kind of extra patient that's covering up being dead annoyed.

"I'll get it first thing in the morning," I said. "Easier in the daylight."

"Smellier the longer you leave it, though," said Gus. "I'll get the torch and get it now."

I stood up and he stood up, and we just looked at each other.

"I'm confused," I said. He dropped back

into his chair like someone had cut his strings. His head went down. His arms came up. I knelt down beside him. "I'm sorry," I said. "I don't know what's happening."

"It's me," he said, his voice thick and low. "I just assumed you meant right now when you said you'd do it. It doesn't matter."

But that was wrong. It does matter. The order things happen in makes all the difference in the world. I said I'd do it *after* he assumed I was going to. Totally different from the other way round. And if I started messing with what came first and what came second, I'd be right back at square one again.

"Jessie?"

I blinked and there he was, closer than he'd been a minute ago. He leaned closer still until he was resting against me, forehead to forehead, and it was like a Geiger counter. As soon as he touched me, something unrolled inside me like ink in water and I had to take a big breath.

Then he turned at looked at the telly screen. "Local news," he said. "There might be a bit about Becky."

So we sat through the speed-trap budget scandal — hypocrisy and cronyism — and the even bigger Peter Pan scandal — embezzlement and corruption — and all I

205

learned was that someone in the newsroom at *Look North* had a thesaurus. We watched the same grainy film of the cops and divers at the Nith as they'd shown the night before — dead, drowned, body; no dressing that up — and then the bit where a senior copper stood in front of the railings saying the man was unidentified and calling for witnesses. Then, right at the end, just before the weather, suddenly there was a shot of the Wanlockhead road and the newsreader's voice was saying mother of two, Rebecca King, inquiry on Tuesday, post-mortem completed, and police "not seeking any individual in connection with the incident."

"That means they're sure it's suicide," said Gus, sitting back in his chair and looking straight up at the ceiling. "They'll never investigate now."

"I don't believe it," I said.

"What?" said Gus, rolling his head forward slowly to look at me. His face was drained and grey.

"I just *can't* believe it," I said. "You're lovely. And the kids are great. This house is gorgeous and the beach and everything. And your work . . . that pram . . . and the garden and the cabbages . . ."

"What the hell are you talking about, Jessie?" said Gus. "What cabbages?"

"In the garden," I said. "In rows. Weeded and everything. I can't believe there was any reason for her to kill herself. It's insane. There's abortion and divorce and Prozac. Even if the perfect life wasn't good enough for her, how could she think she wanted no life at all?"

"I really need to stop talking about this," Gus said. "Stop thinking about it, if I can. I need to go to bed."

No arguing with any of that. So he went to bed and I went to bed. It wasn't a decision. More like, we'd done it the night before, and what was different now? And things happened, like they had the night before, and why not again? Except it *was* different. It was worse. It wasn't shock and raw grief and living in a dream this time. Tonight there was no excuse for it at all.

And it was different other ways too. It was better. I don't know what kind of cold bitch I had been the night before, rating him, thinking to myself how he measured up. Bloody miracle he was still in one piece at all, was what I thought that second night. And anyway, it was more like therapy, really. Afterwards he was totally different, slumped half over me half under me like a . . . what it made me think of was a deflated dinghy, a tent with the guy-ropes down. I didn't tell him. Couldn't make that sound like sweet nothings, but it was the best thing I'd ever known.

"Hey?" I said. "Are you asleep?" He shook his head against my neck. "I meant to say earlier. I've got a job."

"I know," he said. "At the Free Clothing Project."

"No, another one," I said. "Here, actually."

"Where?" He was still holding me, but he didn't weigh so much now.

"Campsite," I said. "Becky's old job. With Gizzy. The hours suit — more or less — and I was needing something else as well." Now it felt as if he was a tree and I was climbing him. Arms and legs rigid around mine. Head up off the pillow on his stiff neck, and I could tell he was staring at me. Even through the dark, I knew he was staring hard.

"Ros," he said. "Not Becky."

"Oh Jesus Christ," I said. "I am so sorry. That's the second time I've done that today." Then I remembered that the first time was talking to Kazek, who Gus didn't want to think about (and who could blame him?), or who I didn't want to talk about (although I couldn't have said why to save my life), so I bit off my words and hoped he

208

wouldn't ask me.

He didn't. He just softened against me and lay back down, shifting me right into the hollow of his body, all four limbs wrapping me.

"Brilliant," he said. "That's perfect."

We breathed in time with each other for a while. Drifting. Only I didn't like where I was drifting to.

Love needs trust, and trust needs honesty. I can't remember which one of the therapists told me that, but I believed her. Kazek wasn't Becky's other guy, and there was no excuse for keeping quiet about him. If I got it in the neck for putting Ruby and Dillon in danger, it was no more than I deserved. I opened my mouth to start speaking, but he beat me to it.

"Can I ask you a great big favour?" he said. I nodded. "I know it's a lie, but could you not tell Gizzy we only met on Tuesday? Tell her we're friends from Dumfries. Or tell her we've been seeing each other for months. Whatever. Tell her something she'll understand, though eh?"

"It *would* be quite hard to explain," I said. "I'm having a bit of trouble with it myself."

"I'm not," said Gus. He shifted his weight on top of me again, pushing my knees open with one of his. "I don't care. I don't even

209

really care what Gizzy MacInstry thinks either." He lifted himself up away from me and manoeuvred to the right spot. "Nobody else had to live with *Becky* but me." And as he said Becky, he pushed inside me, all the way in, slick as I was from last time, and my stomach turned at the same time as everything south of it melted. "This would have happened whenever I met you. Just because I met you on the worst day of my life, it makes no difference."

I wrapped my legs around his back and my arms around his neck, and I didn't ask why he wanted me to lie to Gizzy if he didn't care what she thought of him. Just enjoyed the feeling of his skin against mine — I'd never done it without a condom before. And thinking about that, imagining what was happening inside me, looking forward to him crying out, looking forward so much to that moment when I was the most important thing in the world to another person, one split second when you can be sure they wouldn't be without you, no matter what came after, and then remembering that it wasn't a split second — Gus cared and even the worst day of his life didn't get in the way — and I felt everything that had melted start to burn, and then I was shaking and making a noise like a camping kettle and Gus was laughing and shushing me and my whole body bulged and then burst like a boil (except nice, though) and I yelled, and Ruby shouted "Dad?" from her room, and Gus shouted back "Wait a minute!" and then I started laughing and we stopped. Breathing like bulls, the pair of us, giggling like kids.

"Ruby?" Gus called softly. There was silence except for our breaths. "She's dropped right off again," he said and settled his head into the crook of my neck.

"That's the first time that's ever happened," I told him.

"Ever ever?"

"Ever . . . like that." I hoped he wouldn't need details. I was shy now and I had a bit of a feeling I'd farted.

"Me too," he said. "First time I've ever done it . . ." He was shy too. "Without any . . ."

"Fiddling," I said, making him laugh again.

"We're meant to be, Jessie C." And then he said it. That word. "Love at first sight," he said.

And so even though I knew it was love at fourth sight, really — he hadn't thought much of me at all the day of the Disney cakes, and he had barely noticed me in the

Project and the library — I didn't tell him. And I told myself that word only counted when it was a verb and it came between *I* and *you*. What he'd just said was just something people say.

"Night-night, Gus," I said.

"Night-night, Jessie-cakes. Sweet dreams."

Fourteen

Friday, 7 October

Needless to say, they were anything but sweet dreams. But I kept on top of it all. I'm good at staying in control of my dreams, even though the one time I told someone about it, which was Steve at work, he looked at me like I was green with purple spots.

"Your dreams are your *sub*conscious, Jessie," he'd said, like he'd just invented the word. "Out of your *conscious* control."

"Fair enough," I'd answered. "Maybe it's my sub-subconscious that controls them. I'm just saying that I don't dream about stuff I don't want to."

"The problem with positive thinking as a therapeutic device," said Steve, "is that it's so depoliticized that it, in effect, privatises misfortune and translates it into blame." Which was a very typical Steve kind of thing to say and ended the conversation like only Steve can.

And it's only that one thing anyway. I can't stop myself dreaming about being late and naked and legs like putty. I certainly would have put the stoppers on that one sex dream I had about Steve after I'd broken up with Mike Finlayson and Steve had been really kind about me crying in the laundry room and hadn't brought politics or ethics or anything into for once (just went and got me a bacon and egg roll and a hot chocolate with hazelnut).

But if I find my dreams veering towards a metal framed bed, I can turn right round and walk out the door. And if my dream self walks up to a pile of something on the ground and it's waving a bit and the light's shining through it, it always ends up being bubbles or an anemone or something, and no matter how hard the wee sneaky poltergeist that lives in my head tries to turn it into a big pile of them, it never quite gets there.

Thursday night in Gus's bed was a close thing, though. In the dream, we were in his workshop and I was looking around at all the light bulbs, except they weren't light bulbs anymore (you know the way it goes); they were pencils with big bulbs on the ends. And my mother was there (as usual), and she was saying what a shocking state

214

things had got to and where were the . . . then her voice would get fuzzy and I couldn't hear. *Imagine having all these pencils all over the place,* she said, *and their big glowing ends and no . . . on them.* So the symbolism wasn't exactly a puzzle. Because my dear mother would drop dead if she knew what Gus and I had just done, and she'd no more say the word *condom* than she would blow one up and draw a face on it at a party.

But as well as the sex thing (thank you Dr. Freud), it was novelty pen ends too, and Gus was saying they were all next door and he'd finished them. But if he opened the door of this workshop bit and then opened the door of the storage place too, they would probably catch a draught and blow right in.

So he opened the door and I was punching the buttons on the baby monitor to tell him to stop, except the monitor was a phone and I didn't know how to work it. A Fisher Price phone that played tapes too, and Ruby said *the battery's dead,* and I woke up.

Another night survived. Good old sub-subconscious. Well done. Have a drink on me. Have two.

And even if it had failed and I'd dreamed about them, breakfast with Ruby and Dil-lon was enough to drive any other thoughts out of my head. Most of the problem was Gus being so determined to get Ruby back to nursery for the day.

"Break her in gently," he said. "Otherwise she'll start on Monday with five days straight."

"But why?" I whispered. We were standing in the bathroom with the door pulled. The kids were in the hall putting their boots and coats on. "She could have another week off. Do mornings only, day about. Gus, think about it. Her mum's just died."

"Miss Colquhoun seems to think she should be at school."

"She never said that!"

"She threatened to come out here checking up on us if Ruby wasn't at school."

"No, she didn't!" I could have shaken him. How could anyone misunderstand a simple conversation so badly? *Well, maybe if their wife had just driven off a cliff, Jessie.* So I took a big breath, counted to ten, and let it go. "I'll take her in," I said. "But if she doesn't make it, you'll have to get her on the bus."

"If she wants to leave early, I'll get her in the van," he said, kissed my head and left me standing there.

"The same van I couldn't put the kids in yesterday?" I said, following him. *Jesus,*

Jessie, give it a rest, I told myself, but I kept following all the way through to the kitchen, stepping over the children on the hall floor.

"You can't put *both* kids in the van," said Gus. He was on his knees at the cupboard beside the door, rummaging in amongst the Tupperware and ice-cream tubs. "It's fine with just Ruby."

"What are you looking for?" I asked.

He was stirring the tubs round, collapsing the neat towers and sending lids wheeling over the floor. "Flask," he said, finding it. "It'll be brass monkeys in the workshop today."

"What'll you do with Dillon?" I said. I bent to pick up a couple of the lids and got close enough for him to grab my legs and pull me towards him, holding my bum in his hands.

"He'll be fine in his snowsuit." He put his mouth against the front of my jeans and breathed out hard, like when you're trying to melt ice on a window. I could feel the heat right through my clothes. "And he runs about a lot anyway," he added, looking up. "It's me that gets freezing, sitting hunched over at the table all day like . . ."

"Like who?" I said, smiling down, melted away to nothing again. "What are you making just now anyway, hunched over your table? I thought it was something huge."

"Gepetto," he said. "Bob Cratchett. One of them. Man, I need to see something that's not Disney one of these days."

"Dickens, though," I said, running my hands through his hair. "I'm impressed."

"Muppets' Christmas Carol," he admitted and got to his feet with the flask in his hand, went to the kettle.

It wasn't until Ruby and me were in the car bumping over the track through the caravan site that I realised he'd misled me. Or misunderstood me, anyway. I hadn't meant how would Dillon keep warm, I'd meant who was going to look after Dillon if Gus went to town in the van? But I shook the worry away. What did I know about their arrangements, really? Neighbours and baby-sitters and friends to turn to in a pinch? Except on Tuesday it hadn't seemed like there was anyone. And nobody had come round with a pan of soup or a bunch of flowers since the news broke about Becky. Funny that. How could a family be so all alone?

I swung round towards the shower block and shop and there was Gizzy, standing at the open gate of the enclosure where the big Calor tanks were. She had her jeans and fleece on, Crocs on her feet, but she had a look of bed about her, her hair flat on one side, pale pink fluffy socks.

I rolled the window down. "See you about four," I called over.

"Four on the dot," she shouted back, her voice croaky, definitely pre-breakfast. "And don't come dragging any weans."

"If she didn't sell sweeties," said Ruby, twisting round to watch Gizzy out of the back window, "she'd be rubbish."

"You have got your head screwed on tight, Tootie," I said.

"Is that good?" said Ruby. "Sounds ouchy."

"It's very good," I said. "Now, listen, Roobs. Don't take any crap today. If anyone does anything that makes you feel crummy, you go and tell Miss Colquhoun, okay?"

"Like if Jay McVitie shows me his scab he's pulled off?"

"More like . . . yeah, why not?" I said. Could she really have bounced right back already? Was she really not scared to be going back into school? Even the wet pants, never mind the dead mum, should still have been bothering her today.

Or maybe it was me. Maybe I had an aura around me that was strong enough to help a wee girl like Ruby going through what she was going through. When I got into work, I'd have believed it.

"Oh-ho!" said Dot. "Who is he?" I had done no more than come round the corner and take my keys out of my bag to open the door. She was waiting in the doorway, standing there in her good maroon moccasins and her good matching maroon coat buttoned to the neck and belted too. She always looked so trim. I hated to see her having to wait with chip bags blowing round her feet and nothing to read but graffiti. But dropping off Ruby and finding a place to park had slowed me down some.

"What? Who?" I said, blushing.

"Who me? Says you," said Dot, mocking.

"What's this?" said Steve coming up behind me.

"Couldn't have been! Then who?" Dot sang. "Jessie's got a boyfriend," she said to Steve.

"Is that his car you came in?" said Steve. "I saw you parking at Whitesands when I was coming over the footbridge."

"God almighty!" I said. "Who needs security cams?"

"Oh, he might be a keeper if he's letting you borrow his car, Jessie," said Dot as I got the door open and we all hustled in. "But it's a right old waste of money driving in from Catherine Street and paying to park

220

all day."

Not to mention stopping off for more new socks and knickers on the way, I thought. In Dot's world, where your shoes match your coat, there's nothing about a new boyfriend that would make you come to work from anywhere but home, where all your clothes were. I slung my coat and bag behind the desk and went round putting the lights on for the day, took a duster with me, gave the shirt shelves a flick as I passed them. They were black enamelled metal, from a bankrupt art supply shop, looked great when they were clean (spotless, as Dot would say) but drew the dust like iron filings on a magnet. The pipes were starting to warm up, creaking and popping like old men's knees at mass, and I carried on round past the kids' section, the stands we'd scrounged from the garden centre in Castle Douglas when it closed down, meant for trays of annuals but perfect for babies' tiny clothes, rolled pairs of socks like sugar bonbons, sets of vests tied together with ribbon — that was Dot — looking like those potpourri cushions you get in the useless tat department on the ground floor of Barbour's — every posh department store probably, only I'd not been in enough of them to know. I stopped and ran my hand over a pair of

Thomas the Tank dungarees and a matching jersey. Dillon would look cute in those. He'd suit blue with that white-blond hair of his. Then I heard Dot coming with the coffees and walked away before temptation got me.

"Everything okay in the Layette section, Jessie?" she said, putting down a mug with a jumbo scone balanced over the top of it, warm scones a la flour in your coffee — a Dot special.

"*Layette* is looking lovely, Dotty."

"Dot," she said. "Think I don't know when you're laughing at me, you young ones that know everything and what you don't know isn't worth knowing."

But I wasn't laughing. She hated being called Dotty as much as I hated being called Jess. Her brothers had called her Spotty Dotty when she was fifteen and only got to wash her hair once a week and it hung on her face, she'd told me. But why was that story that Dot had repeated a hundred times making me feel so freaked out now?

"Soooooo." Dot had a way of nestling her folded arms in under her bosom that made me think of broody hens. "You've got yourself a nice lad at last."

"He's just a friend," I told her, but I could feel myself blushing again, and she didn't believe me.

"Another one!" said Dot. Steve wandered up with a bale of shirts that had been tried on and needed refolding now. Needed sniff-checked and then refolding. I could feel my heart hammering. I had promised to keep it quiet and had made Gus promise the same, but I had to tell someone.

"The same one," I blurted out at last. Dot's powdery face clouded. "Gus King. The sculptor. The one that's wife just died."

Dot's face changed the way it does. Her eyebrows went up in the middle and down at the ends and her eyes went diamond-shaped and shiny. And it looked like her mouth had a drawstring round it, a tiny rosette of a mouth. A dot of a mouth.

Steve was standing with a shirt collar tucked under his chin, ready to fold the sleeves in and, with his mouth open and his eyebrows raised, he looked like a cartoon of surprise.

"What?" I said.

"Oh Jessie!" said Dot. "That poor girl!"

"No!" I said. "*She* didn't know! God sake, that's not how it was at all."

"How can you be sure?" said Dot. "She killed herself. Oh Jessie!"

"Because —" I stopped. Because she was already dead when I met him, of course.

But I couldn't say that after telling them yesterday that he was my friend. "Because —" I tried again. "Because even though they weren't happy, Gus loved his kids and he'd never have left them like his dad did, and he tried to make it work."

"Can't have tried that hard," said Dot. "The poor girl flung herself off a cliff."

"Drove off the road, and not because of anything Gus did," I said. "It was finding out she was pregnant again that did it. She didn't want to have another baby."

"She was *pregnant?*" Dot whispered the last word. She always did. She whispered *cancer* and *asylum seeker* too.

"It's actually more common than you'd think," said Steve, back on social statistics where he was happy, back out of the mess of the heart. "Women are more likely to commit suicide while they're pregnant than at any other time. More likely to be the victims of domestic violence too."

"Thanks, Steve," I said. "That's a cheery thought to take through the day."

"How could anyone take her own life and the life of an innocent baby?" said Dot.

"And her friend had left," I said. "Her only real friend. Took off back to Poland without saying good-bye." Of course, I had no idea if that was true; Ros might have come round with farewell balloons and a teddy bear that played "Goodnight Sweetheart" when you pressed its tummy. I was just trying to stop them thinking Gus had driven her to it.

"But what kind of woman kills herself over a friend when she's got a husband and wee ones?" said Dot.

"Ah," said Steve. We both turned to hear the words of wisdom, but he just nodded with a really full-on Steve look smarmed over his face.

"Ah, what?" I said.

"Loveless marriage, inability to fulfill traditional female roles, intense friendship with another woman, loss of friendship causing despair. I see."

"I don't," said Dot.

I did. It was another one of Steve's favourite themes. Practically everybody was gay in Steve's world, but nobody was just getting on with it. Everyone was *sublimating* and *repressing* and *suffering.* Everyone from Billy Bunter to Jimmy Krankie. Anne of Green Gables and Henry the Eighth. Everyone you could think of — except, of course, Steve, who was just interested in the subject in an objective way. And was single. And hung out with a load of women in a clothes shop all day.

"No way," I said. She'd been with a different bloke before Dillon was born and then a different one again to get knocked up this last time. "Becky was as straight as a . . ." And then I wondered. What about the fact that Gus had never managed to —

I felt myself blushing.

"I'm right!" said Steve.

"About what?" Dot asked him.

"Steve," I said, "do women who've not come to terms with their . . . selves" — this was for Dot; there was no whisper quiet enough for the words I needed to say — "ever act promiscuous with men?"

Dot squeaked and started clearing the coffee cups away. *Promiscuous* had done it for her.

"Oh yes," said Steve. "The Goldilocks Syndrome — looking for some individual in the societally acceptable gender who's just right. That's very common."

"Well, in that case," I told him, "I think, for once, you might be right, then."

Should I tell him?

Would it make it worse, or would it make everything clear so he could grieve and recover and be free? Would it help him not feel guilty that things never worked between them? Or would he feel humiliated and worse than ever? He was a guy, even if he was a good one, and guys can be funny that way. So, even though I had thought that the worst bit of my new job at Sandsea would be the loneliness, when four o'clock came round, I was dying to leave Gus and the kids in the cottage and head out to the first van to scrub it down and think things over.

Not that getting rid of Gizzy was easy. You'd think cleaning a caravan was the kind of thing you could just crack on with, but I wouldn't have hit on the Gizzy system in a million years. First, she told me, you Hoover everything, for the sand. Even when you can't see it, there's always sand. She'd never been able to get them told that they couldn't fill the caravans with sand.

"Well, on a beach holiday . . ." I said.

Then — she ignored me — you turn the water off at the outside valve.

"So you're not tempted," she said.

"Tempted to . . . ?" I climbed up the metal steps after her and went inside.

I've always liked caravans. They make me think of Wendy houses, Polly Pocket and pop-up books, playing at life instead of slogging at it like you do in a house. And then they're so totally, comprehensively, unrelentingly *plastic.* I'd checked with Gizzy because I'm paranoid, but I'd have dropped dead to come across them in here. Foam inside polyester, microfibre inside acetate, polymer inside viscose, all wrapped up in plastic walls with plastic windows and plastic cupboards full of melamine. A caravan was like a shrine to the by-products of the petroleum industry, like a spaceship from a world where no one had ever thought of ripping the coats off of poultry and stuffing them in bags for keeping warm. They were my kind of place, and this one was a classic. Every shade of brown, orange, gold, tan, beige, yellow, and cream that had ever been turned into dye and used to colour polyester was in here. It looked like a big bag of smashed toffee popcorn and, what with the crackle of the nylon carpet and the gritty squeak of the sand down the sides of the Crimplene cushions, it sounded not far off it too.

"Tempted," said Gizzy, "to use water to clean." She set down her bucket on the floor and took out three Spontex cloths and three bottles of cleaner. "Lemon in the kitchen, pine in the bathroom, lavender in the living room," she said. "You soak a cloth" — she showed me — "and wipe it round and if the muck doesn't come off, that's special cleaning and they lose their deposit. Any questions?"

"How d'you clean the toilet seat?"

She stared hard over my shoulder. "Pine in the bathroom," she said.

"Same cloth as a the sink and shower?"

"Doused in this stuff," she said, shifting her gaze. "You could eat raw pork that's been soaked in this, you know."

I swallowed and smiled. "What about the bedrooms?" I said.

"Duster," said Gizzy. "It's in the rules there's no food or drink allowed in the bedrooms. There shouldn't be any need for wet cleaning in there. And if there is —"

"They lose their deposit."

"You'll go far," she said and almost smiled. *Unless I stay in one of your vans and contract C. difficile and a side of E. Coli,* I thought but said nothing.

"And," she said as she turned, sloshing lavender Flash over her cloth, "don't think you can go maverick on me and I'll not know. The water metre's right by my desk, and it's broken down van by van."

"But wouldn't it be cheaper to use soap and water?" I asked, following her past the breakfast bar to where the fitted orange and yellow bench ran round the end wall under the window.

"Water," said Gizzy, wheeling round and gripping her cloth so tight that drops of purple cleaner fell on the laminate floor, "is the enemy. Our septic system is our biggest single expense. Bigger than gas. Bigger than the electric. Bigger than the two-stroke for the mowers and the batteries for the solar glows put together."

"I thought it was the . . . other stuff that buggers your septic," I said.

"It's both," said Gizzy. She had wiped the big table and the fitted shelves and now she was backing across the floor, swiping the cloth over the laminate. I had to say, it was pretty shiny and smelled fantastic too. "We've eighty-five vans here, Jessica. Eighty-five families of eight in high season — and more than eight often enough; they can't fool me! — all drinking too much and not letting their barbecues heat up before they sling the chicken legs on. Have you any idea the strain that food poisoning puts a septic system under? Not to mention the chip oil down the sinks, nappies down the bogs, biological washing powder glugging down my drains like there's no tomorrow. I see them. Kids soaked in cola from head to toe at bedtime one day and then the self-same clothes sparkling white again by the next day's tea. Try and tell me they get that done on septic-friendly soap flakes! I tell you what — those dry toilets in Portugal? If I thought I could get away with it, I'd have a good go."

"Don't they stink?"

"Honk to hell," said Gizzy, "so I'm stuck with it."

She stood showed me the face of the cloth she'd been holding against the floor. It was the dark grey of a drowned mouse.

"Pigs," she said. "Filthy pigs." Then she turned the cloth over to the clean side and started on the nooks and crannies of the fireplace wall.

It wasn't so bad. Bit of bog roll for the toilet seat instead of the cloth of horrors and I could just about believe that I was really cleaning. And it was nice to think of the families rolling up here next week for half-term, kids hitting the beach with their buckets and spades, grannies and grand-dads sitting on the benches in ten layers of fleece, watching them. And nothing that any of the last lot had left behind made them out to be filthy pigs, as far as I could see. I found shells and dried seaweed (nothing worse, thank God) in the bedside drawer in one van. Cleared them away and hoovered the sand out, but I lined them up on the outside sill of the big end window. Only wished there was a starfish to prop there too. I took the soy sauce sachets and half-empty ketchup bottles out of the cupboards like Gizzy had told me — "no one wants secondhand cup-a-soups," she'd said. I laid out the trays with the two shortbread biscuits, two teabags, two nondairy creamers, and three paper straws of sugar: the Warm Scottish Welcome, it was called in the leaflet, and I folded the ends of the toilet rolls into points and stuck them with gold labels embossed W*here the sand meets the sea,* which was bound to make you start thinking about where the sewage emptied every time you unpeeled one.

Then I came to Moormist, one of the vans up the back near the trees. The living room was neat and bare, but there was a stack of short-bread, creamer, and teabags in the fruit bowl on the breakfast bar. There was a toothbrush and razor in a cup in the bathroom, and a pyramid of nearly finished bog rolls on the cistern. And though the main bedroom was empty — beds smooth, blinds down — in the tiny room at the end of the passage, like quarters on a submarine, one of the four bunks was being slept in.

It was heaped with blankets, piled high with pillows, and on the floor at its side was a book — a diary, it looked like with its black vinyl cover — and a necklace. Except the diary wasn't a diary at all, it turned out when I went back for a closer look. It was a printed book, old-fashioned, thin paper, tiny wee writing — not English — and it had a bookmark in it.

When I saw what the bookmark was, I turned to stone. A strip of photo-booth pictures, just the same as the ones I'd seen before. The two of them, arms around each other, eyes shining, big grins. It looked like love to me.

But what did it mean? If this was Ros's book and necklace, if this was her hideaway, why had she not cleaned up after herself before she left? And why did she need a hideaway at all, if she had accommodation? I thought of an answer immediately. If Steve was right, it was easy: she needed some-where to meet Becky. But why would they not use a bigger bed than that bunk then?

I cleaned and straightened, dished the nest back out between all four bunks, put the cup back in the kitchen and the razor and toothbrush (for her to sweeten her breath and shave her legs?) in the black bag I was dragging round with me.

I stuffed the three cloths — reeking now — back in the bucket, hefted it and the Hoover down onto the grass and then, with the bin bag over my arm and Ros's book and necklace in my other hand, I stepped into the darkness.

I was crouched over between the Calor bottle and the rubbish bin, turning the water back on, when I heard someone running towards me, heavy footsteps and ragged breathing coming through the dark. I thought it was Gus, looking for me. My mind leapt to the kids, the cops, some new disaster, but the outline of the figure was wrong. I crouched lower, pulling myself into the shadows, and heard him jump up on the metal step to pound on the door.

"Jaroslawa!" he whispered. "Jaroslawa!" And then a stream of words. Polish words. It was Kazek. Maybe he knew that this was Ros's hangout, and when he'd seen the lights on, he thought she was back again. I kept as still as a corpse, scared to move in case the bin bag crackled.

"*Jestes tam?*" he was saying, weeping and raging at the closed door, his voice a rasp. Maybe he was the reason she went away. Maybe he was off his head or his meds and he drove her away from her job with the flexible hours and her friend who needed her. He was sure as hell frightening me.

He had stopped talking, stopped pounding. I think he turned and slid down the door; I heard his trainers squeak on the metal grid of the step anyway. He was less than five feet away. If I put my eye to the gap between the gas bottle and the van wall, I could see him. Then I thought — if I could see him, he could see me! And I dropped my head, letting my hair fall forward to hide my face.

But still something was gleaming, shining bright and pale on the ground beside me. I reached for it and pulled it into my lap. Ros's book. The pages were edges with silver and suddenly I couldn't believe that I hadn't known as soon as I clapped eyes on it at her bedside. A soft black leatherette book with silver-edged pages? It was a Bible. And not a necklace either, but a rosary.

I stood, without thinking.

"Kazek?" I said.

He started and his boots scraped loud on the steps. "Jaroslawa?" he said, standing.

"No, sorry, it's me." I walked towards him. "But you're right, you know. She didn't go home. Look." I held the book and the beads out towards him and he snatched them from me, kissing them and speaking hurried, wretched words.

"You," he said at last, raising his head. "Help me?"

FIFTEEN

Which shows what a Sherlock I am. I'd got just about everything wrong that I could have so far. But I was right about one thing: Kazek was scared shitless, and scared people aren't scary.

"Jaroslawa?" he said, like a cracked record. "Dead, jess. You try make happy not cry. Good woman."

And just like that, it made sense. He hadn't meant to say, *Hey, my girlfriend's gone, but you could take over, sweet cheeks.* He meant, *It was kind of you to say she wasn't dead and stop me grieving. Thank you.*

"It's too complicated," I told him. "I thought you meant Becky. She's dead. I never meant that Ros was. I'm sorry." But, of course, he didn't understand me. Anyway, he had moved on.

"You?" he said and pointed to the bucket and the Hoover, both lying on their sides on the grass, I could smell the stink of the pine cleaner; the lid must have been loose and now it was seeping away. "Key?" he asked, miming, pointing at the door.

I opened it. If he needed to see for himself, that was all right by me. But he didn't go round calling her name and searching for her. He went straight to the kitchen, dragging a chair, climbed up and felt along the top of the cabinet, down behind the cornicing and pulled out a packet wrapped in a Morrison's bag with the bunny-ear handles tied together to keep it secure. He kissed this too, like the Bible, and held it against his chest for a minute; then he climbed down and put the chair away.

"Oh, right!" I said. This wasn't Ros's place after all! I opened the bin bag and fished about until I found the toothbrush.

"Thank you," said Kazek and put out his hand.

"No!" I pulled it back and dropped it in the bag again. "God, that's vile."

"*Jednorazowka?*" he said, scraping a finger down his face, through the beard.

"Yeah, but it's filthy," I told him. "You'd get germs."

He was still staring at the bag, like he really wanted that manky old toothbrush and Bic back.

"Where's the rest of your stuff?" I said. I

pointed to his coat and trousers, mimed folding clothes. He shrugged and held out the legs of his jeans showing them to me. "That's it?" I said.

He held out his arm to me, slapping the thick fabric of his jacket sleeve. It was sturdy, right enough, solid in fact, but it had shrunk and buckled, and it was too tight across his back to button closed. Not really that warm then. And not waterproof either: the fake leather bit across the shoulders was cracked and flaking, as if it had been . . .

"Oh Jesus!" I said. "You borrowed that tumble drier in the carport down there?"

"Jess," he said. "Tumble dry!" He swept an imaginary cloak — tarpaulin, in fact — around himself with a crackling noise. Then he shrugged and smiled at me. *"Nie chce znowu zmoknac?"* he said, and even though he didn't mime I knew what he was asking from the look on his face, sheepish and hopeful. He wanted to stay in the caravan, like Ros used to let him do. But Ros did the books and she knew when the vans were free. For all I knew, Moormist would be full of kids in wetsuits by tomorrow.

"I'm sorry," I said. "But here." I took out my wallet and gave him a twenty.

"Thank you, jess," he said.

"Jessie," I said, pointing at my chest.

He laughed again. "Jessie-Pleasie!" Then he took a last look round the van and headed towards the black square where the door stood open onto the night.

"Hang on," I told him. I was 85 percent sure this was okay. "You can come back to the house." It took a bit of miming, but he got it eventually. Started shaking his head as soon as he understood what I was trying to say.

"No way," he said. "No tell Gus King. No way, José."

"Why not?" I said.

And he treated me to another long splurge of slow, loud Polish that might as well have been whale song. But I had another plan anyway.

"Wait here then. Ten minutes." I held up both my hands. "I'll see what I can do."

"Any problems?" said Gizzy. She was at her desk in the office, and it might have been my imagination, but it looked like her desk lamp was turned so the light hit the water metre square on. She'd have seen that I hadn't been tempted then.

"No, fine," I replied. "Do I chuck these cloths now or wash them?" One look at her face told me all. "I'll just rinse them then."

I planned what to say while I stood at the sink, wiping the bucket, squeezing the cloths. "It's lovely here," I said when I returned. "I suppose you're full up for half-term next week, though?"

"All but one," she said. "How?"

"My friend from work was talking about getting away with her grandkids. Not far, just a break. A view of the sea, she said."

Gizzy was clicking through screens on her laptop. She spoke absentmindedly. "Sea views are the first to go," she said. "The one that's left's a woodland setting." There were a few trees up the back near Moormist right enough, but a woodland setting was stretching it.

"Is it you who thinks up the names?" I said. "That's lovely: *woodland setting.*"

She looked over the tops of her specs. "That's not the name of the *van.* The van's called Foxleap. You should have been checking the list by name. Oh my God, I might have known it was too good to be true, you waltzing in just when I . . ."

"Aye, aye," I said. "Sundown, Cliffview, Moormist, I know. So I'll see you tomorrow, eh? I'll just head off home then." I scuttled away before she could tell me to leave the master key.

He was right where I'd left him, waiting huddled in his shrunk jacket, still holding his Bible and rosary. He followed me as I crept about with my torch, peering at the van signs, trying to stay on the quiet velvety grass and keep off the gravel where our footsteps crunched loud enough to drown out the sound of the sea. Foxleap, when we finally found it, was nicely tucked away — I suppose that's why it was empty — and I was pretty sure no one heard me turn the key and ease the door open. Inside, it was the usual monument to beige, but Kazek looked around it like he'd just checked into the Ritz. Then he turned to me and spoke really slow and quite loud, as if maybe I'd understand Polish if I just would give it a go. He raised the Bible and waved it in my face, holding it so tight that it bent into a curve, trying so hard to tell me something he wanted so much for me to know.

"Wasting your time with me, pal," I said. "I've had it shoved so far down my throat I could shit it. Didn't work then, won't work now."

"English," he said. "I try. Jaroslawa no leave me. Never. No way. Wojtek no leave

241

me. Never no way."

"Who?" I said.

Kazek opened the Bible at the front cover and showed me the two words printed there. *Wozciech Zajac.*

"Gone," he said. "Bad man. Frighten."

I looked at the words and back at his face.

"Let me get this right," I said. I pointed to the Bible and then to Kazek, raising my eyebrows. He shook his head, pulling faces. Then he did a mime that that would have made my mother drop dead if she'd seen him. He put his hands out to the sides and let his head loll, pretty good crucifixion pose, then he rolled his eyes and blew a raspberry. I laughed. I couldn't help it. He jabbed his finger at the two words and then held his hands together in prayer.

"Right," I said. "This is somebody else's? That's his name written there? Wozzy . . ."

"Wojtek."

"Got it. Where is he?"

"Gone," said Kazek. "Bad man." Then he gave up and broke into Polish again.

"But you kissed it," I said. "I'm confused."

"Confused," said Kazek. "No shit, Jessie-Pleasie." I laughed again. He was weird, filthy, stank like a dead dog, had scared me badly twice, and was probably going to lose me my job in the next day or so — but I liked him. Even when nothing made any sense at all, I felt like I knew where I was with him.

"So, Ros?" I said. "Jaroslawa? And you?" I made a kissy noise and fluttered my eyes.

"No!" said Kazek. "No way. Friend, jess? Friends."

"So tell me this then." I took the photo of Ros and Becky back out of the Bible. "Ros and Becky?" More kissy noises.

He raised his eyebrows, thinking about it, then shrugged. *"Nie wiem,"* he said. "Maybe. She is dead? Dead, Becky, jess?"

"She is," I said. "She killed herself. Ros went away and Becky killed herself. And now you need to move on, right? Find a new place. You can have a couple of nights here, but then you have to go."

He shook his head. "No way Jaroslawa leave me. Friend, Jessie-Pleasie. No way."

"Why are you talking like Tarzan and Jane?" said Gus. It was gone nine by the time I got home. *Home!* Back to the cottage, finding him in the kitchen, polishing shoes, newspaper spread all over the table. Paolo Nutini on the Fisher Price tape deck. I'd said: "Hiya. Missed you. Tea? Hungry?" Now I laughed.

"Yeah, you're right," I said to him. "I will

243

speak in whole sentences from now on, like I'm sitting an oral English exam."

"Aye, whole sentences of total mince," he said. "How'd it go?"

Obviously the thing to mention was finding the Bible and meeting the crazy guy, sneaking him into an empty van, and lying to my boss. That was the headline news of my first day. But I couldn't forget the definite sound in Kazek's voice. *No tell Gus King. No way.* And I couldn't imagine how Gus would take it, anyway. Would it be like the bathroom bin? Like the baby monitor? One more way to piss him off and have him tell me I hadn't and change the subject and play the Becky card until I couldn't tell up from down? I shook myself. Where the hell had all that come from? What I meant was I was probably going to piss him off anyway when I started in on Ros and Becky, so why piss him off for no reason too.

Instead, I told him about Gizzy and the water-free cleaning, about the woodland setting and the warm hospitality and he listened and smiled, still working away at Dillon's shoes with a toothbrush, cleaning right into the stitching.

"Sorry," I said, in the end. "You must have heard this before. From Ros, I mean. Or passed on from Becky."

He kept on scrubbing, but his smile fell away. "Ros didn't hang out with me," he said. "And Becky didn't tell me anything. I was a spare leg with that pair, Jess."

Which was a brilliant opener to what I wanted to say. The kettle was nearly boiling, and I took the chance to steel myself, have a quiet pep talk, plan how to deal with him going bananas if it turned that way.

"This is just a thought," I said. "It wasn't even mine. It was Steve at work." He looked up. "Is there any chance that Becky and Ros were more than just friends?" The red started under his sweatshirt collar and climbed his neck in splotches. I couldn't drag my eyes away from it. "Cos," I went on, "I know things weren't great between you and that might explain why Ros would take off — a breakup, you now — and that might explain why Becky could get so bothered about her leaving too. And maybe the reason she . . . ran around — sorry; that's not a very nice thing to say — was because she didn't want to think she was what she was, and maybe the reason she didn't take the pill or whatever was like some kind of denial too? And Steve even said that she might have had trouble with the idea of babies and it might explain the depression."

There was a long silence. The toothbrush moved slower and slower until it stopped. He put Dillon's shoe down beside the other one and lined them up like for inspection in the army.

"Who's Steve?" he said, at last.

"Oh God, nobody really," I said. "Done tons of Open University and thinks he's Einstein."

"I'll try again," said Gus and his voice was very steady, like he was talking someone down from a high ledge. "Who the fuck is Steve? And why the fuck were you talking to him about Becky?"

I blinked a couple of times. Well, at least there was no denying I'd pissed him off this time.

"Steve," I said, "is my pal from work and of course he knows about Becky, because for one it was on the news, and for two I had to explain why I was driving in from out of town in a strange car and where I went on Wednesday. Which was, in case you've forgotten, to pick up your daughter at school and bring her home, even after I had said she wouldn't be able to cope, which she couldn't. And after I'd said I couldn't do it because I'm no good with kids and I shouldn't be left with them. So shove that up your arse, Gus King."

There was an even longer silence after that. Hardly surprising. But when he spoke again he was a different person. Well, in a different mood, anyway.

"It's just . . . what you said." His voice was quiet and kind of wondering, like he was trying to wrap his head round it. "It's quite a lot to take in. All at once."

"Well, while you're taking it in then," I said, "I think I'll get the torch and go and get the pee-stick out the bin like I should have done last night. I'm sorry I went off at you."

He had picked up Dillon's shoe again and was staring down at it, turning it over and over in his hands, and he only nodded sort of half-listening and half off in his own wee world kind of way. No chance of him apologising too, it didn't look like.

Outside, with the torch balanced on the kitchen windowsill, I lowered the wheelie-bin onto its back and shook it until all the nappy bags and banana skins and other crap were up near the top, then I got down on my hands and knees and peered inside. The stuff from the bathroom was a long way down; I could see two bog roll middles and a plaster. I was looking about for a long stick when I heard the back door.

"Don't do that," said Gus. He held me by

247

the waist and dragged me backwards. My knees scraped on the hard ground through my jeans leg.

"Hey!" I said, wriggling out of his reach. "I can't keep up. *Do it. Do it now. Do it tomorrow. Don't do it at all.*"

"Don't do it at all," Gus said. "It doesn't matter now. I'm sorry, Jessie."

"Yeah, what the hell *was* that in there?" I said.

"I was jealous," he said. "And I was just saying what was in my head, cos with you, I can."

So I put my hands in his and let him pull me to my feet.

"I get it," I said. "Flexing your muscles, kind of thing? Well, news-flash, Gus: you overshot."

"Yeah, I know," but he was still smiling. "But it's not brought the sky down, has it? I pissed you off and you straightened me out, and it's over. It's brilliant." He kissed me, and it seemed kind of rotten to carp.

So I changed the subject. Or changed it back again anyway. "Why doesn't it matter now?"

He put his arm around me, tucking me in against him, and led me around the house to stand in the garden and look out at the black sea.

"Don't know," he said. "It just seems like that baby isn't really real anymore. I only heard about it on Tuesday and by the end of Tuesday, it was all over. Seems daft now. Keeping something to remember it by." We stood side by side listening to the rush and sweep of the tide, smelling the chimney smoke, snatched by the wind and sent gusting past us. I shivered.

"Come on," said Gus, rubbing my back hard, trying to warm me. "Let's crack open a bottle of wine and sit in front of the telly like a pair of old farts, eh?"

"What's on?" I said, turning and following him back inside.

"Oh, bugger all," he said. "I'll let you loose on the video collection and you can choose."

But the first three films I spotted were *Forrest Gump, The Witches of Eastwick,* and *Dances with Wolves* and my heart fell into my guts and died there.

"We could just listen to music," I said.

"What's up?" He ran his hand along the shelf of boxes. *Chicago, Chicken Run, St. Trinian's.* "Jessie, what's wrong?"

I went to one of the armchairs and sat down, hugging myself, feeling colder now than when I was standing in the dark of the garden.

"I know they're all pretty ancient," he

said. He pulled a box out of the row. "Have you seen *Crouching Tiger*?" I shook my head. "Give it a go?" I shook my head again. There had been too much stress already, no room for more. If I couldn't get myself together, I would just sit through whatever he chose and hope he didn't see my eyes screwed shut.

"Jessie?" he came and crouched in front of me, cupping my face in his hands. "Tell me."

So I did.

"Forrest sits on a bench and a — shit! — a feather floats down and it keeps coming back all the way through. *The Witches of Eastwick* has a storm of feathers all over the road and they get stuck to him. The Indians in *Dances with Wolves* wear headdresses. So do the dancers in *Chicago*. *Chicken Run* — clue in the name. And *St. Trinian's* has a pillow fight. Probably. I've never plucked up the courage to watch it."

"There's absolutely no feathers in *Crouching Tiger, Hidden Dragon*," he said.

"Yeah, except there probably is," I said, and I knew I hadn't managed to keep even a drop of the misery out of my voice.

"There really isn't," he said.

"Okay," I nodded. "What about *Robin*

Hood, Prince of Thieves? Any feathers in that?"

He sat back and thought hard for a minute. "Not a single one," he said.

"Except for a hundred and fifty million arrows," I said. "So who the hell knows about *Crouching Tiger* either, eh?" I was angry. So hurt and sick of it and so disappointed that I'd spoiled everything again. I wished he would just get on with it, laugh or shout or sneer or do whatever he was going to do, but do it soon and get it over.

"You poor sweetheart," he said. "You poor wee darling. You know what you need?" I looked at him, half laughing, pretty sure he'd suggest the last thing I could even think of doing right then. "You need to sit on my knee and let me tell you a story," he said. "Like Ruby when she's sodded something up and wants to punch somebody."

I laughed then. "Exactly!" I said. "That's exactly how I feel."

"You're just like her," he said squeezing in beside me and lifting me into his lap. "In a few years people are going to be saying. 'Oh, Ruby's just Jessie over the back.' You wait and see."

I curled my feet up and stuck them down the side of the chair between the arm and the cushion, then I tucked my head under his chin.

"Your hair smells nice," he said. "Covers the smell of whatever that smell is in here."

"It's milk," I said. "I spilled some on Tuesday night. I'll have another go at it in the morning."

"So what's your favourite story from when you were wee?" he asked, beginning to rock me.

I laughed so loud and sharp that he jerked his head away, saving his eardrums.

"You're kidding, right? My mum used to pray for me when I made a 'nuisance of myself with my nonsense'. Do you want to hear the prayer?"

"Something tells me I'm not going to like it," he said.

"He shall defend thee under his wings and thou shalt be safe in his feathers."

"What a prize bitch," said Gus.

"A few years ago, I'd have thought you meant I was one for telling tales on her," I said. "But I'm getting better."

"And you'll get even more better now I'm helping," said Gus. "So here's where we'll start. Tell me what happened."

I was wedged in tight to the chair and his arms were wrapped right round me, but I stiffened and tried to wriggle away. He held me tighter.

"You're as safe as a baby in your mother's bell— Bad example. You're as safe as a bunny in a burrow. Tell me and I'll make it better. I'll take care of you."

"You're not angry with me for saying that about Becky and Ros?"

I thought I felt him flinch and I turned to see his face, but he was smiling by the time I could see him.

"I'm angry about whatever happened to you to make you think I could be angry," he said. I was too tired to follow. Too tired to do anything except give in, really.

"My granny had a quilt," I said. "I've never told anyone this before. Except therapists and them. I tried to tell Dot just the other day, but I crapped out in the end. Okay, so my granny had a quilt. It was plain mustard-coloured silky stuff on one side and green and pink patterned on the other side. Flowers and kind of bandstand things. She'd had it since she got married.

"And it fitted perfectly onto the three-quarters bed in her spare room. My bed when I stayed there. With a bolster pillow and a pillowcase that had lace at the end like the pantaloon legs of the girls in my book of nursery rhymes.

"But it was jaggy. It wasn't so bad on the

inside where there was a sheet and a blanket under it, but if you put your arms outside the covers, it jagged you to bits."

Looking back with my adult brain I can see that it was wearing out, washed too many times, getting threadbare, and the feathers were poking through. Back then, five years old, all I knew was that one night I found if I pulled the jags they came out, and it was soft and comfy. So I did. I pulled and pulled, my little hands roving all over the patterned top, finding the spikes and pulling them out. Every time I thought I had finished I found another one. Then I started on the inside, through the mustard backing. And there were just as many there.

"So I pulled the feathers out," I went on. "I've never bitten my nails so I could get a hold of every last one. I must have been awake for hours doing it. And then in the morning I woke up again, dead early too. Something had made me sneeze."

No prizes for guessing what, although it had been years later with a therapist called Moira that I had worked it out: in the night, more feather ends had worked their way to the surface and there were more jaggy spikes for me to pick at.

"So by the time granny came to wake me, the bloody thing was practically empty. Well, not really, but there was feathers absolutely effing everywhere. She opened the door and they all blew up in a big storm like a snow globe and I could hardly see her through them. It was quite a small room."

"And was she angry?" said Gus.

Granny had stood at the door with her mouth wide open as the feathers settled. She had blown one off her lip and then she had started —

"She was furious," I said. "I got the worst row I'd ever had in my life."

— she had started laughing. She kicked the feathers up like she was walking through autumn leaves in the park and she said —

"She said I was an evil wicked child and I'd spoiled something precious that couldn't be replaced."

— she said, *Eh, dear, Jessie my darling. I didn't know how thin that old thing had got. I think it's time it went in the bin now, eh?*

"I don't believe you," said Gus. "What's that got to do with looking after kids?"

"Eh?"

"Why would that make you say you're not good with kids?"

"Because if a bad thing happens I won't be able to cope. They won't be safe with me."

"There must be more to it than that."

"I've told you everything," I said. "Swear to God." That same therapist, Moira, had taught me how to put things in a box and put the box in a room and lock the door. So there was nothing more to say.

"What's wrong with your face?" he said.

I put my hand down in my lap like he'd caught me picking my nose. I hadn't even realised I'd been touching it. That little puncture mark in my cheekbone, so faded now you couldn't see it unless I had a suntan. So small that only I knew it was there. I didn't even know if I could really feel it anymore or if I just touched the place I knew it had been.

"Nothing," I told him. "My face is fine. And that's the whole story of my pteronophobia. You think it's going to be something that makes sense and it doesn't. I can't watch a film I've never seen before because my granny gave me a row for wrecking her quilt. I'm an idiot."

He just looked at me. "You'll trust me enough one of these days to tell me it all," he said.

And a flash of anger blazed through me. He didn't believe me? Look at what I'd swallowed from him in the last three days, and he had the nerve not to believe a perfectly sensible story from me? Maybe not

256

true, but sensible for sure.

Except under the anger was something else, I knew. Down the stairs into the garden, over the lawn, and into the lift — the therapists never tell you what a lift's doing in a garden, by the way — down and down and down, past the panic and the memories and past the room with the box (locked tight) right down to the basement. And then out again at the beach. This is *some* lift, from a beach to a garden — and the beach is the *safe place.* Annabel — another one — told me that nearly half of the folk she spoke to chose that same lame beach. Or they chose their own bed or their armchair. And some chose a mountain. And one she told me about chose Harvey Nick's food hall, but I reckon that was for show and probably in her head she had a wee beach there, one floor down in a lift maybe.

But the thing is this: in all my imagining of that safe place, I never expected someone to meet me when the lift opened its doors. Now it seemed like if I went down, past the anger and panic and memories, Gus would be there. And the beach had a name: Sandsea Bay.

"Now what kind of story d'you want *me* to tell *you*?" he said.

257

"Tell me about something you've made," I answered. I knew how big a thing I was asking. "Like the pram. Or something you want to make. A plan."

He knew how big it was too.

"Okay," he said, at last. "You might think this is daft. It's a shed. It was a shed. A garden shed. And I dismantled it and used the planks to turn it into a boat. Or like a raft. And I floated it down the river — that was the only way I could think of to move it — right down the Dee, and when I got it to the workshop, I rebuilt it."

I waited for a while and then I asked him: "What's it called?"

"Shed Boat Shed," he said.

"So . . ."

"And," he said. "I put a video camera in the middle of the floor while I was taking it down, revolving. So it was making a film of the all the planks coming off and you could see the allotments outside and the sky and everything, and I filmed the journey on the raft, and then I put the camera back in the middle of the floor and filmed it going back up. So when the last plank goes on the roof, it's completely dark again and that's the end."

"Wow," I said. "Can I see it?"

He shook his head. "It's sold."

"Hey!"

"Yeah. You can't see it but until Tuesday, you could have driven around in it. I sold it and bought Becky a car."

"Did she like it?"

"She thought it was an okay shed. She didn't think much of the raft, and she thought it took up a lot space in the workshop when it was a shed again. She'd have a fit if she saw what's in there now."

"Jesus," I said. I had felt sorry for Becky, angry at her, jealous of her, puzzled by her. But that was the first moment I just felt nothing for her. If she didn't get Shed Boat Shed, she wasn't worth the bother.

"I bet the kids loved it," I said.

"Dillon was too wee to know, but Ruby thought it was brilliant," he said.

"Have you got a copy of the film?" I asked. It took him a long time to answer.

"The film's part of the piece," he said. "It's sold too."

I felt like I'd asked if I could get a painting in cream to match my couch. Felt like I'd had no business looking down my nose at Becky. Poor, miserable Becky.

"Bed?" said Gus.

And he carried me all the way.

Sixteen

Saturday, 8 October

I had thought that I was in a love story, a sad one, with a happy ending for lucky me. Ros was selfish — broke Becky's heart, left Kazek in the lurch. Becky was selfish — ruined her husband's life, broke her kids' hearts. Then I came along, not deserving what I got but holding on to it anyway.

Then came the weekend that changed everything.

At the end of every summer when I was a kid, my mum used to say she'd be glad to get back to work for a rest. Now, I couldn't see what could have tired her out on a caravan holiday, because this lot that stayed at Sandsea never did a hand's turn. Gizzy, God rot her, had forwarded the customer services line to my mobile and all day Saturday folk were phoning to say they'd run out of bog roll or couldn't work the shower, or there was a spider, mouse, or funny smell somewhere there shouldn't be.

And that was on top of the actual jobs she gave me. Plus Gus was working, locked in his studio, so I had the kids too, even though I told him Gizzy would sack me on the spot if she found out. They were fine. Ruby was a big help, pulling the bed sheets off and stuffing them in a black sack for me. She made it too heavy for her to lift, so Dillon and her rolled it along the floor and shoved it out onto the grass like a pair of dung beetles. That was as helpful as Dillon got, really. Except that he happened to be looking out the window, so he was the one who spotted Kazek coming.

It was as soon as we went into the first really tucked-away van. He must have been watching for me.

"Mr. Kaz!" Dillon shouted.

"Kazek!" said Ruby, looking too.

I opened the door and stood back, shut it after him, just a quick peek to see if anyone was watching, but with all those net curtains who could say.

"Hiya," I said. "Have you come to say good-bye? Have you sorted something out for yourself? Moving on?"

"Trouble, Jess," he said. "Friend?"

"Listen pal," I told him. "I'm sure you've got a hard luck story. Who doesn't? And I've heard them all. But Ros is gone, you've got your friend's beads and Bible, and there's not much more I can do."

That was the moment I found out it wasn't a love story after all. He took the Morry's carrier bag that was tied shut with its own handles out from inside his jacket and started undoing it. I was wiping the kitchen cupboards, but I kept half an eye on him. Ruby and Dillon went back to the bedroom for Dill to bounce on the bunks while Ruby stripped the pillow cases for me.

Kazek unfolded the bag so slow and careful it was maddening. It looked like a book. Another Bible? Wrong shape. Then he tipped it up and what was inside fell out onto the breakfast bar. The Queen's face looked up at us from the top note of a bundle. He shook the bag again. Another bundle just the same. Two neat, solid blocks of fifty-pound notes. Or maybe they were fake. I wouldn't know.

"I'll have my twenty back then," I said, picking up the nearest and flipping through it. They crackled, new and crisp, and gave off a smell you wouldn't mind smelling, not like the stink of money at all. "Are they real?" I asked him. "Real, Kazek?"

He nodded, picked up the other bundle, and showed me the number on the top one, then the next number on the next one. Then he made the farting noise again like when he'd told me he wasn't a good Catholic boy and he threw them over his shoulder, like so much dross.

"Got it," I said. "Real but stolen."

"Jessie-Pleasie," he said, and he took my hands in his. "I am a good. I am not a bad. Believe me."

"But you're in big trouble."

"In Little China," said Kazek. He wrapped the money up again, tied the handles, and returned it to its hiding place. Then he turned to me. "I phone?"

He had tens of thousands of pounds and he was living off stale shortbread in an empty caravan. If he was a villain, he was a really shit one. I handed him my mobile.

"Two minutes," I said. "And it better not be Poland, pal."

The only word I understood was *Jaro-slawa.* Other bits sounded like English — *powered zinnias, jamboree* — but Ros's name was the only thing I knew for sure he was saying. He said that plenty times, talking very slowly, explaining something to someone, then talking faster, interrupting, getting interrupted, then almost weeping, nodding his head and shaking it — saying what sounded like *shuprasham* over and over again. He finished up with saying something slow and clear, sounded like a number from the tune of it and the *zero-*sounding word — *zero jeden szesc cztery cztery, cztery dwa, zero dwa, jeden trzy* — and then he hung up, wiped the phone on his jeans, and gave it back to me.

Ruby and Dillon had rolled the dung-ball bin bag as far as the living room and were standing staring at us.

"Cztery," said Ruby.

"Cze cze," said Dillon.

"Mówisz po polsku?" said Kazek to Ruby, bending down.

"Czy Ros umarl?" said Ruby. "Dead? *Tak jak Mama?"*

Kazek sat back on his heels on the toxic orange carpet and began to cry.

So I gave him the rolls and margarine that the folk in the Spindrift van had left in the fridge and let him use the tin opener to open the tin of tuna they'd left in the cupboard and told him I'd see him tomorrow.

"Forgive me," he said. "Has to be."

The phone was ringing when I opened the cottage door and let the kids run in. No sign of Gus, and so I thought it was probably him on the line, telling me he'd be late.

Again. *God's sake, Jessie.* I told myself I should be glad he phoned at all and didn't just turn up at midnight. But still I let it ring. So the answer machine clicked on. I should have seen it coming but I didn't, of course.

"Hiya!" it said in a woman's voice. A girl's voice, young as my own. "This is the Kings, but we're at the beach. Leave a message!" I hit the button and played it again. "Hiya!" She didn't sound like someone speaking into a machine. She sounded like someone calling out when they've just spotted a friend. "This is the Kings, but we're at the beach." A bit of a sing-song lilt to it. *This is the Kings, but we're at the beach. To Market, to market, to buy a fat pig. The corn is as high as an elephant's eye.* She must have recorded it when they'd just moved in. When it seemed like a novelty. When she'd got over feeling low after Dillon and thought she'd never go through it again? Except Gus had said she'd only just got over Dillon. So maybe she'd just met Ros when she recorded it. Maybe Ros was the one she thought would be phoning her. "Leave a message!" And that was why she sounded the way she did. There was no reason for her to sound like that if she was depressed and missing the town and stuck in a mar-

265

riage with someone she'd never loved, not brave enough to live her real life.

I hit the button and listened one more time, looking at my reflection in the hall-stand mirror. I couldn't help smiling at her voice. She sounded so happy.

So that's why I was still standing there when Gus came in. I turned and smiled even wider, but all he did was that flick-flick look that makes me think of a camera taking snapshots. Blink and he's looking down at the phone. Blink and he's looking at me again. Flick-flick.

"Don't let me stop you," he said. I shook my head, still smiling. "Whoever you're phoning," he went on. "Don't mind me." He came and stood right behind me to hang his coat on one of the pegs, reached round me to put his keys down but he didn't touch me. "You never talk about anyone," he said. "Friends. I've never heard you mention a single one. It'd do you good to have a good natter with a pal."

His face was unreadable, not scowling, not smiling exactly, although he had a twinkle in his eye. He looked . . . smooth. He looked like you would look if you had a black widow spider crawling on your cheek and you didn't want to get it angry. I shuddered. *Where the hell did that thought come from?*

"I have so," I said. "I've mentioned Steve. How could you forget him coming up, eh?"

"Oh yeah, that's right," said Gus. Finally, he put his arms round me, hooked his head over my shoulder, still looking at me in the mirror. "Go ahead and phone him."

"I wasn't phoning Steve!" I said. "I wasn't phoning anyone."

"What's wrong with Steve?" His eyes were dancing now and I smiled at him, crinkling my nose. I couldn't follow what was going on here.

"Nothing," I said. "He's a nice bloke."

"So why don't you phone him?" said Gus.

I turned. Maybe I could see him more clearly face-to-face. Maybe the mirror was twisting things.

"Gus," I said. "I wasn't phoning Steve. I never mentioned Steve."

"Yeah, you did. Where are the kids?"

"Kitchen. Okay, yeah, I did, but only after you accused me of —"

"I didn't accuse you of anything. I said go ahead and phone him."

It was happening again. It happened one way round and Gus said it happened the other.

"You said I never mentioned anyone from

work. I said I did, I mentioned Steve. But I never mentioned phoning him."

"It doesn't matter," he said. "Keep your voice down. I don't want the kids to hear you shouting."

"I'm not shouting," I said.

He raised his hand like in some kind of surrender. "Okayyyy," he said. "Whatever you —"

Then we both flinched, in formation, when the phone rang. I put my hand out to answer, but Gus grabbed my arm.

"I can't face the cops tonight if it's them again," he said.

"I'll tell them you're out," I said. I didn't try to get my arm free. I didn't want to find out how hard he would grip if I pulled away. I didn't want to know.

"Don't you want me to hear his message?" he said. "I'm not the jealous type, Jessie. I was just trying it on for size yesterday. It's really not me. If I come and visit the Project tomorrow, it'll just be to see where you work. It won't be to check him out."

The ringing stopped and the machine kicked in. He didn't even register Becky's voice, just kept smiling at me. I kissed the end of his nose.

"No need," I said. "You know Steve. Or he knows you anyway. He was in the Scouts with your brother."

"Hello?" said the voice on the answering machine. "Yes, hello. My name is Eva Czerwinska. Kazek has given me this number. I am trying to find Jaroslawa. I hope you can help me. My number is 0048 32 413 5857. Thank you very much. Good-bye."

"Who the hell was that?" said Gus.

"No idea," I said.

"But you knew they were going to phone," he said. "You were waiting."

I shook my head. "I'm just in the door. I was looking in the mirror. I was listening to the message. Becky's voice, you know."

"How did they get this number?" said Gus. "Who *was* that?"

They got the number from a homeless guy with a wad of money. And he got it from me.

I said nothing.

"I'm not phoning Poland," he said. "Cost a fortune. Not just to tell them she's gone home."

"You could report her missing," I said.

"Again?" said Gus. "You don't think they'd think that was a bit much? Two in one week? Different with Becky — she left a note."

"She'll phone back, probably," I said.

"Who?" He spun me round and held my arms tight enough to make the flesh squeeze out between his fingers.

"Gus, God's sake, you're hurting me."

"Did you say you'd been listening to Becky?" he said. "Christ, I just got that. Who'll phone back? What are you trying to say?"

"Her," I said. "That Polish woman right there. Let me go! I was listening to Becky's recording — *leave a message we're all at the beach.* Let me go!"

He dropped his hands and stared at me. Then he turned and banged the answering machine so hard it bounced on the table.

"Message deleted," said the voice. He banged it again, twice. "Outgoing message deleted."

"No!" I said. "That was Becky's voice. You wiped Becky's voice!"

"Why the fuck would I want Becky's voice answering my phone?"

"Not on the phone," I said. I was scrabbling at it, punching buttons. "Just the tape or whatever it is. For the *kids.* Her voice sounding so happy. For the wee ones."

And there they were, summoned by the raised voices, sidling round the living room door. Dillon solemn and soft like he always got when he was tired, his mouth hanging open and blue smudges under his eyes. And Ruby like a sitcom housewife, arms folded, mouth set. "What's all this then?" her little face seemed to say, and I smiled at the sight of her.

"What's for tea?" she asked. "We're starving, by the way. Mummy always used to give us a snack when we came in even if it was nearly teatime, eh Dill?"

"Mummy?" said Dillon.

Gus turned away to face the hall stand mirror. He bent his head until it was pressed against the glass. The stand rocked back on its little ball feet and creaked with the strain. He wasn't knocking, but he was pushing so hard it might splinter the wood or break through the plaster. And he was whispering. I leaned close.

"I'm sorry, I'm sorry, I'm sorry," he was saying. But it wasn't an apology. It was a mantra. It was *stupid bitch* with different words. And now he was saying something else. His voice was strangled from keeping it quiet. "Please, Becky. Please, don't. I can't take it again. I can't take it anymore."

"What did she do to you?" I whispered. Slowly, the pressure of his head on the mirror lessened. The glass creaked in its frame, the front legs came down onto the floor again.

"Kids," I said, "I'll make you sugar fingers if you wait in the kitchen."

"Wot dat?" said Dillon. But Ruby knew sugar anything was great and she dragged him away.

"Gus," I murmured to him, smoothing his hair back. "Go through and wait in the bedroom, eh? I'll be as quick as I can."

Sugar fingers was only buttered toast, dipped in brown sugar and cut into strips, but Dave had some cinnamon in his cupboard and I sprinkled that on. I left them trying to work out whether they liked it or not and hurried back through.

He was sitting on the edge of the bed with his head in his hands. I went over to him, eased his hands away, and let him rest it on my shoulder instead.

"What did she do?" I said again.

"She hit me," said Gus. "Go on and laugh."

"Why would I laugh?"

"Size of her," he said. "Size of me."

"Did you hit her back?"

He shook his head. "I was getting there, though. I was so angry. I'm so . . ." he pulled away a little and turned so he could look at me. "I'm so angry, Jessie. I'm scared of how angry I am. I'm cracking up."

"No, you're not," I told him. "But of course you're angry." Angry enough to pound the answering machine, grab me by the arms.

"I'm acting like she did!" said Gus, as if he had mind-read me. "I feel as if she's inside me. I feel like, when I speak, it's her voice — sniping and sneering."

"You never hit her back," I told him, slow and sure. Was I trying to make him hear me or was I telling myself? Assuring myself it was all going to be okay?

"And she called me a wimp for it," he said. "She told me I was a coward and a joke."

"And now," I said, "she's gone. But she's left a big echo. You're not turning into her. And I'm not going to turn out to be like her. It's just an echo. It'll fade." I was soothing both of us now.

"I can't believe she's gone," he said. "You said you were listening to her — I thought she was back. I can't believe she's gone to stay."

And it was at that moment that we both heard the car, trundling along the track, turning in, stopping. Gus's eyes flared and I felt my breath come quicker. Crazy. I don't believe in ghosts — certainly don't believe in ghosts that can drive, anyway. But if the ghost of Becky King *was* here, it would feel my boot up its arse for what she'd done to this guy and those kids, and for all the

273

nicey-nicey stories she'd shovelled at everyone else. Miss Colquhoun, I meant, but I bet there was more of them.

It wasn't, of course, the ghost of anyone. It was the cops. Again. The sergeant and the woman one called Gail.

They sat with Gus in the living room and I went to take whatever was coming when Ruby and Dillon sussed the sugar fingers recipe. Of course, I took a tray of tea through, so I got to hear some of it. I was all ready to weigh in. Pretty clear I didn't need to though.

"The Fiscal himself is satisfied," said the sergeant. "Since there was a note and after what you've told us about your wife's . . . lifestyle. But we want you to understand that if you yourself have any doubts, Mr. King, any doubts at all, you're quite within your rights to request a full PM and inquiry." He stopped and looked at me, standing there like a frozen idiot with the tray. I came back to life and put it down on the coffee table.

"If I thought there was any chance of the inquest coming back with 'accident'," Gus said. "Jesus, 'murder', even — I'd say go for it. But that wouldn't happen, eh no?"

"Fatal accident inquiry," said Gail. "No, there's no chance of that, Mr. King."

"No inquest?" I said.

"Fatal accident inquiry," she said again. Her partner made some kind of movement. My guess is she said it ten times a day and it drove him mental. "Not when the case is as clear as this one."

"Unless the family requests it," the sergeant said. "Same with the full post-mortem. Just tell us, Mr. King."

"Gus?" I said, looking down at him. He was staring into the fire. He'd lit it, as usual, on auto, and it was just beginning to glow. I'd thought he would snatch at any chance at all, no matter how slim. The way he'd been talking. And now, when it came to the crunch, he was going to let the record say suicide after all?

"I forgot the milk," I said and went back to the kitchen. Ruby and Dillon had sugar fingers hanging out their mouths like dogs' tongues. They were sucking and giggling. Surely soon they'd be choking. "Nice, eh?" I said.

"Yummy yummy in my tummy," said Dillon.

"Except they're really just toast, though," said Ruby.

Becky grew cabbages and had her own car and these two kids and a cottage by the seaside and she *looked* happy in the pictures with Ros. And if she loved Ros she could follow her, and if she didn't want a baby she didn't have to have one. Maybe she *was* turning the car. Maybe it *was* an accident. How could Gus not want an inquest? What had changed since he was wild for one, desperate to try anything to keep that word away from the children? The door opened behind me and the WPC appeared, as if she'd heard what I was thinking and had come to tell me it was *fatal accident inquiry.*

"A word," she said. "We'd better step outside." All right for her in her coat and shoes, but I followed anyway. The back of the cottage was a different world from the front. It was sheltered, what with the trees and the rise of the land, but somehow the endless wind — too strong in October to call it a breeze — at the front made it feel alive. That and the sparkle off the sea, the gulls, the long high sweep of the sky. Back here, the dark was darker and, despite the shelter, the cold was colder. The ground felt damp instead of whipped dry and there was no salt in the air. Just that rotten leaves smell and the soft moss underfoot. I had taken a dislike to the back of the house the night of the wheeliebin and nothing would change my mind.

"You're surprised," the copper told me,

once the door was closed at our backs, and I thought again that for someone who was hoping to get people to talk, she didn't half make a lot of statements and ask hardly any questions.

"I am," I said.

"You don't think Mrs. King was suicidal," she didn't ask.

"I never knew her," I said. "Don't look like that. I told you I didn't know her the first night you were here."

"But you're surprised anyway," she didn't ask again.

"I'm . . ." I could feel her watching me, even though it was full dark with not a single star and no gleam of moon through the thickness of the cloud. "I'm surprised Gus wants to leave it," I said. "He's so . . . troubled. I thought he'd want everything investigated right to the last little thing. He's in such a mess, you know? I'm just surprised he's ready to let it go."

"Troubled and in a mess," she repeated. "Of course he is."

"Of course," I agreed.

"He said as much to us," she said. "Can't believe she's gone. Can't believe she's really dead. It's the funeral'll sort that out for him. Not an inquiry. That just keeps things in the air, hanging on."

"I suppose so," I agreed.

"So you don't really know anything," she told me. "You don't actually have any information you need to share."

"No," I said. "You're right. Can I ask you something?"

"It's very common," she told me.

"I haven't asked you yet."

"To be unable to accept that someone has died, I mean," she told me. "If you love them."

"Oh yes, of course. I know. Like Elvis and Diana." I could feel her staring at me. But it's true. There's never a conspiracy about someone nobody cares two hoots for. A worldwide belief that some daytime soap star who died at ninety actually didn't die till ninety-three. And of course I hadn't said the other name to the copper, the big one. *Jesus*, Diana, and Elvis, I really meant, like I'd tried to tell my mother once too. "They didn't want him to be dead, so they just said he wasn't," I had explained. It hadn't gone well, and the more I tried to convince her that I didn't mean any harm the worse it got.

"It's like the ultimate good review!" I'd said. "Hung from a cross? So what! Holes all over you? Granted. Starved? I'll give you starved. Bled white? Since you mention it, yes. Bunged in a cave with a great big boulder over the door? I believe so. But *dead* — no way. Or if he was, he's alive again now. Glory Hallelujah! I'm not calling them stupid. He was their friend and they loved him, but come off it, Mum! If you got like that about one of your friends, I think two thousand years later people should be ready to let it go."

And then she'd started in with the prophecies and the sure and certain hope and the life everlasting — which was why we'd been talking about it in the first place, her going on about how her mum died and who was to blame, and me asking why it was *blame* if death was the start of the good bit. Why not credit? If the Bible was true, then death was great and murder was a helping hand.

I blinked and peered through the dark to the faint gleam of the woman copper's face.

And what about suicide? It wasn't throwing away God's greatest gift at all, was it? Not if the greatest gift came after. It was just kind of . . . impatient and sort of greedy. Except not even the happiest of the clappiest actually saw it that way. And those cults that off themselves by the thousands? Even the Brethren think they're nutters as well as sinners. Which they shouldn't, actually.

"So," said the copper, "ask me."

I blinked and refocussed on her. "Do pregnant women really kill themselves a lot?" She breathed in sharply. "My friend at work said yes, but it's just so horrible."

"Mrs. King wasn't pregnant, was she?" said the cop. "Was she?" An actual question.

"Gus didn't tell you?"

"I can't discuss Mr. King's statement with you," she said, back in charge of herself again.

"Isn't that a reason to do a full PM?"

"It's Mr. King's decision."

But then what had they meant by *her lifestyle*? I thought they meant her running around and getting knocked up.

"Can I ask you another question?" I said.

"I really can't discuss it with you."

"No," I said. "This is something completely else. You know Becky's friend, who went away?"

"No."

I kept my sigh really quiet. I didn't want to piss her off; she wasn't exactly helpful to begin with. "Gus didn't mention her? Okay. Well, how do you try to find a missing person is what I wanted to ask."

"Is she over twenty-one? Any reason to suspect foul play?"

Did wads of sequential notes and the most

terrified person I'd ever seen in my life count as reasons? "As far as I know, she's over twenty-one."

"You don't know her all that well then," the cop informed me.

"I don't know her at all," I said. "Never met her. Gus does, though. Can a friend report a friend missing? It doesn't have to be family?"

"Mr. King's got enough on his plate," she said. "He wants to get in touch with the hill walker that found his wife, you know. Say thank you. Not everyone would do that." She sounded less cold and blank when she spoke about "Mr. King." Could Gus have charmed her? Well, I suppose he'd charmed me.

"I just thought it would help if we could find Ros," I said. "She could fill in the blanks. Closure, you know."

"Blanks?" she said. "Mr. King has said very clearly he's satisfied with what we've done. And there's nothing like a funeral for closure, anyway."

Which is total guff. The funeral keeps you busy and it's basically a party, and it's not till afterwards that you realise the guest of honour is really and truly dead. Or it's afterwards, anyway, that you start to get that dead means gone, and gone means forever.

And that's when heaven and angels and life eternal count for nothing, and the holiest get just as sad as the rest of us, and that says a lot, if you ask me.

Maybe the copper was right, though. Gus was better after they'd gone away. He made pancakes for us, tossing them and catching nearly all of them, and he shut the bathroom door and got in the bath with the kids while I cleared it all away.

When he came back through in his dressing gown with his wet hair in a towel, he sat down in his armchair by the fire and stretched like a cat. "That's that then," he said. "Done and dusted. Just the funeral to go."

"You didn't tell the cops she was pregnant," I said, just like that.

"Eh?" He sat forward and unwrapped his hair, started rubbing it hard. It would frizz like hell unless he had some pretty posh conditioner on it. Which didn't seem likely.

"So why aren't the police wondering why she did it?" I said. "What did they mean about *her lifestyle*?"

"Yeah," he said. "No, that's all fine. I told them about her and Ros."

"You *what*?" I knew I was gaping at him, couldn't help it. "That's not — That was just Steve at work!"

He was raking his fingers through his wet hair. It stretched and snapped, and when he had finished there was a cat's cradle of hairs caught in his fingers. So much hair, his scalp must be throbbing.

"I had to say something," he said. "They knew it wasn't an accident. They saw the note." He rubbed his hands together and made a ball of hair, threw it in the fire. It hissed and there was sudden stink, like witchcraft. "You showed them the note, Jessie. They were never going to think it was an accident after that."

And I dropped my eyes. That was true. It was my fault.

"Well, there's one good thing then," I said. "Surely if they think Ros leaving is why Becky . . . they'll be willing to try to find her. I asked that Gail — outside — but it has to be someone who knows her. It would have to be you."

His hair in the fire was still fizzing. I had to breathe through my mouth to stop smelling it and feeling sick.

"You asked the cops to look for Ros," he said. And it was like he'd been taking lessons from Gail, because it wasn't a question at all.

"Maybe I should go home for a bit." I hadn't planned to say it. It just formed in my mouth and was out before I knew.

"But they told you it would have to be me." Like he hadn't heard me.

"Or her sister, I suppose," I said. Maybe he *hadn't* heard me. "If she phones again, we could tell her. Or we could phone her back and tell her."

"Please don't go." He *had* heard me, then. He leaned forward and picked up the poker, shoved the ball of hair deep into the heart of the fire. The crackling stopped and the smell faded away. "Please stay, Jessie. I'm sorry it's so tough for you, but please stay."

I nodded, relieved. I didn't know what I'd done wrong, but I wanted to make up for it. Even though that felt like ten steps back. It felt like I was sixteen again, like a shit-load of grunt work on Caroline's couch had been blown completely away.

"They wouldn't give me the hill walker's address," he was saying. "Can you believe that? They said I could write to him, and if he wanted to he could write back to me. A letter! Not even an e-mail."

"Will you?" I said.

He nodded. "I really want to pay him back. Try to anyway. And one day," he reached out towards me, "one day soon, I'll find a way to pay you back for everything

you've done too. Everything you're doing.
I'll find a way."

Seventeen

Monday, 10 October

I really needed space to think it through. To try to sort out Ros and the money and Kazek and Gus and the pregnancy and postmortem and inquest and what anything meant. A long walk along the beach on Sunday would have done it, but Sunday was worse than Saturday for kids and caravans, so I held out for Monday and the prospect of shutting the office door. Dot, though, was in a talkative mood, like a budgie on my shoulder all morning.

"Father Tommy said there was something wrong right from the start," she opened with. She had set up her ironing board across the doorway, trapping me in the office so she could talk it all out to me. The corruption poisoning the fairies at the bottom of the magic garden had got into the *Scotsman*.

"Monsig just didn't want to spend our

money where it wasn't needed," I said. "He's not psychic. What's happened anyway?"

"What hasn't?" she said. "Embezzlement, backhanders, bribes, gangsters." She was ironing, and as she pressed down hard on a coat collar, a cloud of steam billowed up and hid her face. If she'd cackled, she could have got cast in *Macbeth*.

"In other words, you've no idea," I said. "Gangsters? In Dumfries?"

"*Master* gangsters, it said in the paper," Dot insisted. "I'll cut it out and bring it in to show you. Investors are leaving like rats from a sinking ship. Of course, Father will never go back on his word. We'll lose out in the end, just you see. It's like the end of days in Dumfries this last while."

I was trying to compose an e-mail.

"The end of days," I repeated. My mother was a big one for the end of days.

"Two suicides," said Dot. "Two deaths anyway. Disappearances . . ." she trailed off.

"Who's disappeared?" I said, wondering if the world was small enough for Dot to know Ros. But she was staring out of the front window. "The end of days," she said again softly as the door opened and a pair of police in uniform walked in. I girded my loins, squeezed past the ironing board, and went to face them.

"We are a confidential service, officers," I said, smiling but speaking very firmly. "You'll need to speak to Father Tommy Whelan over at St. Vince's and just between you and me, he'll make you get a warrant. But since you're here, what am I saying no to, today?"

Because it wasn't the first time — or the tenth either — that the cops would be looking for someone right down hard on their luck and think we'd love to help them. I suppose, to give them their due, one of the reasons to suddenly need new clothes and shoes in a hurry is if you've got blood or whatever all over your old ones, but it would take a brass neck to walk into some drop-in clinic dripping with murder blood and ask for a clothing project voucher.

They took their hats off — trying to signal that they were staying? — and that's when I recognised the sergeant who'd been in Gus's house last night. He'd already recognised me. Cops are quick that way.

"Miss . . . Constable, isn't it?" he said. "Long time, no see."

The other one — just a youngster, the look of a farmer's boy round him, red cheeks and gold hair — gave him a sharp look. He hadn't missed the twist in the voice any more than I had.

"Unless you're donating," I said. I had spied the black plastic bag in the farmboy's hand. "Not uniforms, I hope. Ho-ho. That could cause some mix-ups."

"I wonder if you would cast your eyes over these gents' clothes," said the sergeant.

"What's your name?" I asked him. "I don't think I ever caught it." I didn't really care, but asking questions and getting people to answer them was something my therapist Eilish had taught me for if I was feeling flustered, and I'd got into the habit.

"Sergeant McDowall, and this is Constable Anderson."

He had put the bin bag up on the table where the belts and bags were laid out and he pulled out, first, a big sheet of thick polythene and then an armload of dark fabric, smelling of mould and damp and something worse than either. He started spreading them out.

"What's this in connection with?" Dot said.

"A gentleman met with an unfortunate situation," said McDowall, "and we're trying to identify him. We wondered if maybe he was one of yours. He looked your sort."

I turned over the trousers. Jeans. Fancy stitching on the pockets but no logo. Impossible to say. Same with the jersey — hand-knitted, no labels. The t-shirt was from Primark, so it could be. The underpants were brown and cream nylon y-fronts, definitely nothing to do with me. The young copper was hauling another item out of the bag and this did look familiar. Thick and sturdy, the fake leather shoulder patches flaking. My mind flashed on the memory of Kazek flapping his arms to say how warm his coat was, and I didn't hide it quick enough, felt my face turning pale.

"What?" said Anderson. "You recognise this, do you?"

"Oh Jessie," said Dot. "Do you?"

"No," I said. "Not really." But his words were echoing in me — *an unfortunate situation.* If ever anyone looked like meeting with one of them, it was Kazek. I had to know. "How long have you had these then?"

All three of them were staring at me.

"Why do you ask?" said McDowall.

"Just . . ." I scrabbled for an answer. "They don't smell too good." It was true; they didn't.

"Nearly a week," said Constable Anderson, getting a dirty look from the sergeant for his trouble. "River water, you know."

A week. Not Kazek then. I let my breath go and felt the colour come back to my face.

McDowall was glaring at the constable, but Dot was still watching me.

"River water?" she said. "A week? Is this the poor soul that came out of the Nith at the Whitesands?"

"Poor sod," I said. "Maybe if he hadn't been wearing such a big thick coat he wouldn't have sunk."

"That's an odd word to use," said McDowall. "Why not say drowned? If you know something about this, Miss Constable . . ."

"I really don't," I said. I was watching Anderson's hands. He was rootling about in a plastic bag he'd had in his pocket. He took out a crucifix and half a dozen of those rubber charity bangles and laid them down.

"We don't do accessories," I told him. I lifted one of the bangles, a pink one.

"It's not in English," said McDowall.

"Polish." I didn't mean to say it out loud, but when I looked up again all three were staring at me.

"Are you sure you've nothing you want to tell us, Miss Constable?" said McDowall.

"There's this," I said, praying it was the right thing. If only Dot had left me alone to think, I might know. "I tried to tell what's her name, Gail, last night. There's a Polish person missing. Her name is Jaroslawa

Czerwinska; she was Becky King's best friend and she disappeared a week past Saturday. She hasn't gone home and no one knows where she is."

"Saturday," he repeated, frowning at me. "*This* incident took place on Tuesday."

"It *was* the drowning!" said Dot. "Oh, the poor man."

"So it's hard to see how they're connected," McDowall went on.

"I never said they were," I told him.

"Except we have connected them, haven't we?" said McDowall. "Mrs. King went in the Nith on Tuesday and this man came out, and you know both of them, it seems to me."

"I didn't know this guy," I said. "First I knew was watching the frogmen like everyone else."

"You're sure of that?" said McDowall. Anderson was putting the clothes away again.

There's a crucifix on the wall. I went over and put my hand on it. "I didn't know the man who died in these clothes," I said. "Never met him, don't know anything about him."

"Well, there you are," said Dot. It seemed to be good enough for young Anderson too. Only McDowall looked unimpressed, like he knew how many times I'd lied on Bibles to save my neck when I was wee.

"Again, I can't help noticing that you said *died,* Miss Constable, while your colleague here said *drowned.*"

"And it's a small town," I said. "I bet loads of people know Becky King as well as this guy."

"If anyone knows him, they're keeping quiet about it," said McDowall. "Thank you for your time, ladies." He followed Anderson back to the front door then turned. "Czerwinska, eh?"

And now, too late, I saw that I had really blown it. I had given the coppers Ros's name. Ros, who worked on the caravan site where a guy was hiding who had the same coat as the guy in the river and had the guy's Bible and his rosary too and a ton of dodgy money, and I had hidden him. And if the cops asked me why, I'd have nothing to say.

I had to find Kazek and get rid of him before they came round to interview Gizzy or one of the proper caravan people saw him and freaked. And now I had to tell him that, as well as Ros taking off, his other friend had drowned. Unless he knew? Was that why he had come to Becky's house looking for Ros that Tuesday evening? Was that why he was so scared?

But if I sent Kazek away, I'd never find him again, and he was the link to Ros, and Ros was the link to Becky, and Becky was the thing I couldn't let go. Who she really was, why she really died.

And then I thought of the answer and couldn't believe it had taken so long. Stupid me.

The day couldn't go quick enough after that. Dot listened to the local news at noon and came back to the office with her eyes out on stops.

"He didn't drown," she said. "I've just heard it on the radio. Oh Jessie, his throat was cut. He was dead before he ever went in."

I sat back and stared at her.

"They've just released the information," she said.

She looked down and when she looked up again there were pink spots in the middle of her cheeks. "Jessie," she said. "Why didn't you say he had drowned?"

"You're kidding?" I said. "You think I *knew* him?"

"You don't know Polish," she said.

"I said *died* because — you'd know this if you ever listened to Steve — it's more respectful. Death is equal, whether you slip away in your own bed or misjudge your auto-erotic asphyxiation."

"Jessie!"

"You asked."

We glared at each other for a bit.

"How would it be with you if I left early?" I said. "The cops were right about one thing, Dot. My friend's wife really did die last week and he really does need me."

She turned and left again and I just barely heard the words as she was leaving. "The end of days."

Gus was in the cottage when I got there. Only three o'clock but the fire was lit and there was a beer on the arm of his chair and a *Daily Record* open on the coffee table. Dillon was asleep on the couch and Ruby was colouring in at the table.

He had met me at the door. He'd almost seemed to block my way for a minute, but it was probably my imagination.

"I thought you'd still be at the workshop," I said. He rubbed a finger along his jaw and then I got it. He was embarrassed at me catching him. "Good to see you taking it easy," I said and I gave him a quick squeeze. "And what are you making pictures of, sweetie?" I asked Ruby, leaning over her.

"Mummy in heaven," said Ruby. Becky had wings and a long white dress; only her dark hair — two strips of black crayon down each side of her head — stopped her looking like a standard-issue angel. "Only but how do you draw a white cloud on white paper, Jessie?" Becky in the picture was suspended in the middle of empty space like those daft pictures of the ascension. I turned to Gus.

"Daddy's the artist," I said. He looked back at me, unsmiling. Was that another insult, thinking he could paint angel pictures? Or was it just thoughtless to imagine him drawing his dead wife? I turned back to Ruby. "Here's how," I said. "I'll do a cloud shape and you colour outside it with blue to make the sky."

She frowned at the picture and then at me. So I showed her. Drawing the puffy cushion for Becky to balance on, then filling in round it. I made another cloud in the background.

"Who's that for?" said Ruby.

"Granddad?" I said.

"Mummy doesn't like Granddad," Ruby told me. "Ros could live there." It was only a picture. So I said nothing, but I didn't dare catch Gus's eye. I went into the kitchen and called to him from there.

"I need to check in with Gizzy," I said. "Then I might need to run into town for her. Is it okay if I use the car? Oh!" He was right there beside me.

"I can't face the workshop," he said. "It feels like it's all gone . . . it just doesn't feel right anymore." I nodded, but I couldn't stop the thought: *Good, you thought of a way to account for just lolling about in the middle of the day.* He sat down at the table. He had this way of sitting that was a sort of a collapse but with a real force behind it so the chair legs grated over the lino. I could see from the marks on the floor that he must do it all the time.

"Can I talk to you?" he said. I looked at my watch and out of the window at the failing light. Even if the police decided to follow up on Ros and they got onto to Gizzy tonight, why would they go searching round caravans in the dark? If one of the holiday people was going to see Kazek, it would be in the daytime when they were out and about, not at night once they were huddled round their eight-inch tellies or their Scrabble boards.

"Of course," I said.

"I can't face working on the piece," he said. "But I can't face the thought of all the work that's wasted if I don't finish it either."

"Just take a break," I told him. "Of course you don't feel like working just now. You've

297

not even had the funeral."

"But I'll go mad if I sit and do nothing."

"Okay, well how about this?" I said. "That woman copper didn't agree, but I think you need to track down Ros. You need to ask her if she knows why Becky did what she did. If she wasn't pregnant, why did she tell you she was? And here's another thing — maybe Ros would want to come to her funeral."

He didn't speak.

"I'm pretty sure the cops aren't going to lift a finger even though I've given them her name twice now. But maybe there's something here in the house — something with some information about her. She was Becky's best friend." And then I had a brainwave. "Or maybe she left something behind in her digs. I'll ask Gizzy."

"You gave the cops her full name?" said Gus.

"Not that they were bothered."

"How did you know her full name?"

I must have looked like a goldfish, mouth opening and shutting, nothing coming out. "I don't know," I said, slowly. "How did I find out her second name? You know how that can happen? You know something but you can't remember how you learned it?"

He stood up suddenly, came over, and put

his arms around me. "It's doesn't matter," he said. "You're right. I need to forget work for a while, and maybe finding Ros would be a good idea. She's bound to know something."

"Ruby told me," I said, too late to be any good. "She knows her name. She knows quite a lot of Polish, as it happens."

Gus swung me back and forward, still smiling down at me. "God, you've really fallen for Ruby's routine? What makes you think it's Polish she's talking and not just mince?"

I knew it was really Polish, I thought, because Kazek understood it, but I didn't tell that to Gus. I just repeated my story about running into town and went on my way.

How the hell was I going to tell Kazek the news about the Bible guy? The drowned guy, I would have to remember to stop calling him, now I knew. I still hadn't come up with an opener by the time I got to Foxleap, but I knocked anyway. Kazek opened the door a crack.

"Jaroslawa?" he said.

"I'm bloody sick of being a stand-in for Becky with Gus and a stand-in for Ros with you," I said.

"Jessie-Pleasie," he answered, opening wide enough to let me in.

"Okay, Kazek?" I said, taking his hands in mine. He sobered and his eyes were alive with worry. "Your friend." I pointed to the Bible that was lying on the coffee table.

"Wojtek?"

"He's dead."

He shut his eyes and let his breath go very slowly, then he shook his head once and opened his eyes again to look at me. There were tears there, but he wasn't reeling. He could take more.

"Murdered," I said. I drew a finger across my neck and made the sound. "And then," I had to let go of his hands completely to mime heaving a body into a water — *"Splash!"* — and I showed him the paper I had brought with me. The picture of the frogmen hunting in the river said it all.

He nodded. The tears didn't fall, no more following to push them down his cheeks. He wiped them away.

"I know," he said. "I know."

"Now," I said. "The police?"

"No!" Even with the windows shut, it was too loud a sound to come from an empty caravan. We both winced.

"Okay, okay," I said. "But I need to get you out of here. Pack up your stuff and come with me." I mimed walking away, both of us, with my fingers.

"Police?" he said, hanging back.

"No. I promise." For the second time that day, I did something I never thought I'd do again after I left my mother's house. This time, it was a Bible. I put my hand flat on the cover. "No police," I told him. So he hopped up on the kitchen worktop, got his packet of money down from its hidey-place, and we went on our way.

In the car I explained it, even though I knew he wouldn't understand.

"Gus needs to understand why Becky died," I said. He nodded. He knew two of those names, and he knew what *died* was. "I think Ros knows something. It's too much of a coincidence that Ros left and then days later Becky was dead. Right?" Another nod, but I knew I'd lost him. "You can help us find people who know Ros. Ros was taking care of you, and I don't think she'd have left you high and dry. You are in big trouble."

"In Little China," Kazek said again.

"You didn't kill your friend, though," I said, "because if you've killed someone you don't worry about them, and you were really worried about Wojtek. The money looks bad, but on the other hand, if you've

301

stolen money, you spend it. So whatever trouble you're in, it's not because you're a thief, right? Even though you really really really don't want to go to the police."

"No, no police," said Kazek. "Bible, Jessie-Pleasie."

"Yes, I know," I put my hand on his and squeezed it. "For a wee while anyway." He caught my tone and relaxed again. "But still you've got to ask yourself this question, Kazek," I said. "Why do I trust you? Why am I taking you where I'm taking you? It doesn't make any sense to me. You've done nothing that isn't dodgy since the first minute I clapped eyes on you and yet I'm acting as if you're my long-lost brother."

Which didn't mean much. Gus had a long-lost brother and I doubt if he'd do for him what I'd done for Kazek since I'd met him.

Gus.

Gus had been kind, more understanding than anyone I'd ever met, great to his kids, give you a lump in your throat to see them together, said he'd fallen in love with me, acted it too, wanted me, seemed to need me, made me laugh. But was it really true that I wanted to find out what had happened with Becky and Ros just to put his mind at rest, or was there a question I needed answered just for me? Did I trust that sweet, good, kind, sad man as much as I trusted this filthy, half-crazy scrap of trouble sitting beside me?

"You know my problem, Kazek?" I said. "I can't handle good things happening. Gus looks to good to be true, so obviously I'm going to find something to worry about. That's just me." And I ignored the voice inside me — Dot's voice, as it goes — saying, *Too good to be true, eh? And why would that be?*

We were turning off the bypass now, heading towards town and it seemed to me that the closer we got, the less easy Kazek grew. He was sitting forward, staring out of the windscreen. Maybe Dot was right and there really was something rotten in this place now.

Dumfries is a dead town at night, even without a murder in the news. A couple of clubs, a handful of pubs, no restaurants to speak of really, so once the evening classes chuck out, the suburbs are dead. I wound my way in on empty streets, houses with their curtains drawn, parked cars lining each side of the roads like barricades. I'd never tried to park outside my flat before. It hadn't occurred to me how there was never a space. And the barrier at the library car

park was down, which wasn't very neigh-
bourly when it was closed for the night
anyway. But maybe, I told myself, as we
walked back from where we'd had to leave
the car, that was a good thing. The road was
quiet and the stairway to my flat was quieter
still; maybe better that we were quiet too.

Kazek hesitated at the door, peering into
the dark mouth of the passageway.

"It's okay," I said. I held out my hand.
"Follow me."

Upstairs I opened my door and shoved
him in ahead of me. I don't go in for plants,
so it didn't matter that it was six days since
I'd been here. No harm done beyond a
scummy tea cup in the sink and a load of
wet washing growing black mould in the
basket where I'd left it.

Kazek walked around. The living room
cum kitchen was on one side, the bedroom
and the bathroom on the other. All tidy
enough. Poor-looking though. None of the
curtains were the right size for the windows
or the right colour for the carpets. And none
of the carpets were any colour I'd have
chosen. And throws. Throws look great until
you sit on them, then they're just blankets
hiding your manky chairs. And you can't
put throws over everything — tables and
chests of drawers and that — so they just

have to sit there looking like what they are. I looked at the place with visitors' eyes and with the eyes of someone who'd been in Dave's House of Vintage Charm for a week, looking out at the sea, looking down at the perfect faces of little children. There was nothing here that looked even half as good as Ruby's face, not even when it was covered in brown sauce and tripping her. Then, following him round, I looked at it with Kazek's eyes instead. And all I saw was the double bed and the proper-sized shower. The radiators and the big fridge. The washing machine and the telly.

"Loads of channels," I said, showing him the remote. "And you can eat anything you can find. Thank God for super-dooper pasteurised, eh? Milk keeps for months now." I went back to the bedroom and started putting clothes in a bag. At last! If I never wore this pair of jeans again, it would be soon enough.

"Your home?" said Kazek from the doorway.

I nodded. "And here's the best bit," I said. I held the phone out to him. "Call Poland. Call anyone. Get it sorted out. Call Ros's sister, what was her name?"

He took the phone out of my hand and for a moment I thought he might kiss it or kiss me.

"And I'll see you tomorrow," I said. I tapped my watch. "Five o'clock," I told him. "Got it? Five."

Gus hadn't asked me why I needed to go back to town. Maybe he thought I meant Gatehouse, didn't think of Dumfries. He'd know now, from the time and the petrol. But I had my bag of clothes as a cover story. There it was again. I couldn't tell him about Kazek, and I couldn't tell myself why that might be.

He didn't ask me where I'd been anyway. What he did say drove my troubled thoughts far away.

"You're right!" He had opened the door when he heard me. He took the bag out of my hand and put it inside the bedroom doorway then drew me into the living room, to the fireside. "You're dead right about Ros," he said. "I called the cops and they're not interested. But we need to find her."

"How can they say they're not interested?"

"She took her stuff," said Gus. "Some of it anyway."

"How do they know that? They checked with Gizzy?"

He shrugged. "Must have. So as far as they're concerned, she's an adult doing what she wants and there's no problem." I wasn't really listening, couldn't get past the news that the cops had been onto Gizzy so quickly. That they might so easily have decided to check around, and if they'd found me skulking about the caravan site — if it had been Sergeant McDowall anyway — I'd have been done for.

"So we need to wait for her sister to phone again," Gus said, "and then put our heads together."

"Agreed," I said. "And don't tell her the news from Dumfries."

He frowned.

"You didn't watch the local news today?"

He shook his head.

"That drowned guy didn't drown — his throat was cut. And he was Polish too."

"How'd they know that?" said Gus. He seemed to have paled. Why would that be? Well, he'd stood there and watched the frogmen that day. Or maybe he was squeamish about blood and guts and things.

"It must have been pretty obvious. From the body."

"I mean, how'd they know he was Polish? Is he like something to do with Ros or something? Some connection?" He really was a white as a sheet.

"Charity bangles with Polish writing," I

told him. "The cops came to work with the guy's clothes to see if maybe we'd provided them. 'Looked like one of yours,' the sergeant said. He seemed okay when he was here, eh? But he was dead sour today."

"The same cop?" said Gus.

"Small town."

"The same cop that came here brought that drowned guy's stuff to show you, and you told him Ros was missing?" He seemed really struck by it, like I'd been. Only I knew about Kazek being a link between them. Gus didn't, so what was his problem?

"Are you okay?" I said.

"There's a lot of Polish folk about," he said. "There's no reason at all the cops would connect them."

"Why would that matter?" I asked him. "Why would you care if they did or not?"

He watched me for a long time before he answered. And, when he spoke, it was slow and soft, as if he was trying to hypnotise me.

"Like you said. So's they don't worry Ros's sister. So they don't tell her about him and make her scared for Ros. Just like you said to me."

That made perfect sense and I smiled at him.

"I need to ask you something." His voice

was back to normal. "I need you to tell me something."

"Okay," I said. He slid out of his chair and came shuffling over on his knees to just in front of me. He reached out and put the flats of his first two fingers on my cheek, right on top of the old dot where the puncture mark used to be.

"I saw it when you were sleeping," he said. "And I want you to tell me what really happened when you pulled the feathers out of your granny's quilt. Tell me the truth, eh?"

Inside

She was filthy now. She could smell herself with every breath, even over the stench from the dry toilet. She had tied a biscuit wrapper up into a jagged little ball of knots and spiky edges and she chewed it, like those dry toothbrushes you get in machines at motorway services. It kind of worked. But she stank. God, she stank. So she wasted some water and the sleeve of her t-shirt. Bit a hole in the seam at the shoulder and unpicked the stitching. Ripped the sleeve into two. One she kept, carefully folded inside her cardboard pillow. The other she wet with a glug of precious water, pouring it like anointing oils in some holy temple. She kneaded the cotton until the water was all the way through it, damp and cool, and then she washed herself, her face and ears. Her neck, under her arms, scrubbing hard, the stubble giving her some friction. She took off her jeans and pants and wept at the smell of herself. She turned the cloth and washed gently, lovingly, like a nurse would cool a patient after a fever. She turned the cloth and wiped her feet. It was nearly dry now. More water? A little. And her feet tingled as she scrubbed them.

She waited until she was dry before she put her clothes back on. Inside out. And tried to imagine she felt refreshed. She picked up the cloth with part of a wrapper over her hand and dropped it down the drain hole. And she made herself not touch her hair, not scratch her scalp. Keep her clean hands clean as long as she could. She would save the other part of the sleeve until the water bottle after next was nearly empty. She was good at making things last. It was her way. Good at distracting her thoughts too. Try countries: India, Kuala Lumpur, Laos, Malaya, Nepal, Oman, Poland. She curled herself into the shape of a nut — the lozenge shape of a child inside its mother — and wept the pain back into something she could bear. Try animals: rat, snake, tarantula.

It could be worse, see?

EIGHTEEN

He put the lamp off and we sat in the firelight, side by side on the couch. It still had a bit of a creamy smell when you shifted.

"Okay. Well, first, my granny wasn't angry," I said.

"No?"

"But my mother was furious with me."

"What for? For upsetting your gran?"

"My granny wasn't upset. She laughed. She thought it was funny."

"Really? She wasn't pissed off?"

"Look, I'm sorry I lied before. I'll tell you the truth this time."

"Okay," he said.

"Okay." A log shifted and fell and the flames burned brighter. "So my mum, right? One of her favourite bits of the Bible is, *He who spareth the rod spoileth the child.*"

He reached out and touched my cheek again. "What did she hit you with to leave a wee hole like that in your face?" he said. "I can't understand parents who hit their kids."

"Really?" I said. "You've never lashed out?" I remembered the day with the cakes and how angry he'd been.

"At the babies?" He sounded shocked. "Ruby's the size of a button."

"Did Becky?"

He was silent. "You're telling the story," he said at last, which was my answer in a way.

"Okay, so, my granny should have known better probably, but she told my mum the funny story of little Jessie making a snowstorm in the spare bedroom, and my mum went ballistic. She asked what punishment I'd had and my granny said none. Ballistic squared. Granny had been going to chuck the quilt but my mum stopped her."

"Christ, she never made you stuff them all back in again."

"I'm telling the story," I said, nudging him. "And a bit of hard work wouldn't have screwed me up as badly as I am."

"You're not screwed up," said Gus. "You invented a phobia to *stop* yourself getting screwed up. Clever girl."

"How come you know about phobias? You said to me the very first night you didn't know anyone else —"

"I looked it up yesterday," said Gus. "And a wee bit today. 'A mistake in adaptive learning', isn't it? And not even that much of a mistake. You're dead right to be scared of feathers after what feathers did to you."

He sounded like every self-help book and website and first appointment in the world.

"After what feathers did to me," I agreed.

"Which was what, exactly?" said Gus. "Go on with the story."

"Yeah, okay, so, my mum, right? She put the quilt — dead thin now — on my bed and made me sleep on top of it. And to make me not pick at it . . . she tied my wrists to the bed."

A log settled in the fireplace. Gus reached out and took my hand.

"How old were you?"

"Five," I said

"And how many times did she do it?"

"Just once."

He was stroking my hand very softly now, like that game we used to play in school where you tried to tell when someone's tickling finger reached your elbow and you never could. Just like that game used to do to me, his fingers tracing my skin made me pop out in goosebumps and I had to make myself not pull my hand away. He'd said something.

"What?" I asked him.

"Your cheek?"

"A feather end was sticking in it," I said. "It made a hole. Made me bleed, cos of leaning on it for hours and hours."

"Why didn't you turn the other way?"

I remembered it with the kind of sharp crystal-clear remembering you only get after hours and hours of regressive hypnosis. I'd looked at that bloody room from every angle: the bed, the floor, the ceiling, close up and far away, in colour, in black and white. Play the tape forward, play the tape backwards, double-speed, triple-speed, shrink it down, fold it up, put it in a box, and lock it away.

"I didn't want to," I said.

"Jessie?"

"Stubborn," I explained. "There was a" — think fast, think fast — "a picture of Mum and Dad and me on my dressing table, from before he'd left, and I didn't want to see it. So I kept my face turned the other way even though there was a feather end sticking in my cheek."

"All night?" said Gus. I nodded. "But wasn't it dark?"

I was stupid enough to try to remember. And then of course, it was the *real* room that came back to me. The real thing I didn't want to see.

"Not very," I said. "There was a street light right outside her house and just a cotton blind."

"Whose house?" said Gus.

"Mine. My mum's, I meant."

"And a photo of your dad from before he'd left?"

"Yeah. Yep."

"And you were five?"

I saw the mistake I'd made. Because Dad didn't leave until I was seven. But did Gus know that? Had I told him?

"I'm sorry," I said. "That's all I can tell you."

"That's plenty," he answered. "She tied you to your bed when you were five, even though your granny wasn't angry. Even though your granny was absolutely fine."

"Don't," I said. "Please."

"Jessie," said Gus, "you are the bravest, best little girl there could ever be. You worked out a way to handle things that hurts no one else in the world. But you know what?" I shook my head. "It takes too much out of you. It's time to let go."

"Not really," I said. "It's a case of being careful."

"You love children, don't you?" he said. I felt a sob bulge up inside me. "Why don't you have one of your own?"

It burst out of me like a shout. And the pain. Christ, it felt like he'd cracked my ribs open and squeezed my heart in his fist.

"So it's time to lay it down," he went on.

"How do you know what to *say*?" That was a translation of what I was thinking. What I was thinking was that for someone who'd only looked it all up on a computer that day, he certainly talked a good game.

"Because I care about you," he told me.

"Someone else cared about me once. And he didn't get the first thing about it. Couldn't stand it."

"Becky said she loved the kids, but she didn't love feeding them or changing them or bathing them or singing to them or playing with them. So what did she love? Babies need you to do stuff. That's what babies are. And you're fucking terrified of feathers even if you won't tell me why. Loving Jessie King means getting that."

"Jessie Constable," I said. But even though I was correcting him I didn't mind really. He'd nearly said *I love you,* and I knew it was true.

"Big excitement yesterday then," said Steve when I arrived the next day.

I straddled one of the black bags piled in

316

the doorway and started on the many locks. We have locks and alarms and deadbolts so that folk won't break in and steal the free clothes, but nobody ever takes the black sacks of crap that people dump on us when we're closed. The sign with the donation hours is two feet square and written in red and the note along the bottom — do not leave donations in doorway when shop is closed — is outlined in waves of orange and yellow highlighter, but it's still an obstacle course every damn day.

"You said it," I agreed, thinking about Kazek and then stopped and turned. "What do you mean?"

"The cops bringing those clothes," Steve said. "Of course. Why, what else happened?"

"How did you know about that?" I asked him. I was booting the bin bags inside. I didn't want to have to take my gloves off and touch them — it was that special kind of cheerless cold this morning, the river fog seeping up the side streets, beading our hair and clothes, dripping down the windows.

"Dot told me when she phoned to check the shifts," he said.

I kicked a bag that didn't have clothes inside and hopped about a bit until my toe stopped throbbing.

"That better be boots," I said. But it felt

like metal and my guess was pots and pans. The Free Clothing Project has a massive clue in the name, but when folk get to clearing out their cupboards they just think "charity shop" and if we're the nearest to where they live, we get whatever they're clearing. I usually bung it all in a supermarket trolley and trundle it up to Oxfam, who're never that happy to see it either, but they can't say no until they've at least checked it through.

"She said you might have recognised the jacket," said Steve. "But you denied it. Quite right. You need to ask Management where we stand, confidentiality-wise. I'd have done the same."

"God's sake, Steve," I said. The neck of the heavy bag looked clean enough actually — even though a doorway in St. Vincent Street is nowhere to leave anything overnight if you want it fresh in the morning, between the dogs, the drunks, and the gulls — so I squatted and untied the handles. "Think I'd give a stuff about line management when some poor bloke got slashed and chucked in the Nith? I didn't recognise the coat. It was a work jacket with plastic shoulders. A donkey jacket."

"Oh."

"Yeah." Steve had a problem with donkey

jackets. First, we weren't allowed to call them that. And then he vetoed them altogether, along with army surplus, those silvery marathon blankets, and terry-towelling nappies. I reckoned the jackets and blankets were warm and practical, but Steve thinks they're humiliating and one step up from asking tramps to stuff their clothes with newspapers. (He was all for the towelling nappies, mind you, and vouchers for the launderette, until I pointed out that you're not allowed to wash nappies in a launderette, which he wouldn't know because he's never had to use one. And since nothing makes Steve madder than someone making out he's clueless — or "insinuating that he's out of touch with the reality of our clients' lives" as he put it — that meeting ended on a sour note.)

"So how's Gus?" he said, changing the subject. "Have you heard from him again?" This was very innocent-sounding, but I was sure Dot had told him I'd come to work in Gus's car.

"Gus is great," I answered, and I couldn't help smiling. I looked down to hide it. "Wow. Cake tins," I said. "Yeah, that's the thing about destitution. It can play havoc with your home baking." I retied the bag handles and took it through to the Oxfam trolley.

"When I say 'great', mind you," I added coming back again, "I mean he's doing really well for the kids. And he's a great guy. He's not so hot in himself, obviously. And he beats himself up like you wouldn't believe."

Steve was raking through the rest of the bags now. Holding up a shirt with an appraising look in his eye. He put it down quickly when he saw me watching. "For what?" he said. "Survivor guilt? He needs counselling."

"Not exactly. Coffee? Tea? He doesn't even think he should take time off work, if you can believe it," I said. "He was freaked out because he couldn't crack on with what he's meant to be doing."

"Sculptor's block," said Steve. "I never thought of that. Coffee."

Sister Avril phoned then to tell me there was a volunteer care-worker coming in today to pick up some women's clothing and take them to her client's house for trying on.

"Why can't the client come and choose her own?" I said. You hear about those care homes where they don't even try to make sure the old dears get their own clothes back from the laundry. I heard once about a place where they washed the teeth in one great big bowl and just dished them out again. "The whole point of the Project is that it's supposed to be a shopping experience. Not a —"

Sister Avril cut me off. "Size twenty-eight," she said.

"Ah," I said. Not much dignity for the client if we had to move the racks back against the wall to wheel her in. "Twenty-eight. Wow. I'll see what we've got."

"God be with you," said Avril, like she always did, making it sound as if he'd phone her at the end of the shift to tell her what I'd been up to. She and my mother would have got on like a house on fire, if only each of them didn't sum up the other one's hunch that Satan still walked among us.

I took Steve his coffee and switched the computer on.

"So what's he working on?" he said. "It wasn't like a statue of her or anything, was it?"

So I told him about Dave's House and was pleased to see the frown growing. *Hah!* I thought. *You might have done a hundred and fifty Open University courses, but you're still one of us. You don't get it, do you?*

"Have you seen it?" he said.

"No. Why?"

"Just . . . it sounds . . ." He couldn't seem to finish.

So I told him all about Shed Boat Shed, laying it on thick. His frown deepened.

"Yeah, that too," he said. "Did you see that one?"

"No, it's sold. That too what?"

"They sound . . . familiar," said Steve. I could feel myself blushing. Not only did Steve get Gus's kind of weird sculpture, but he'd heard of them, read about them in the kind of Sunday papers they'd get mentioned in. Maybe he'd even been to a gallery and seen them.

"There must have been publicity when Shed Boat Shed got sold," I said. "I know it went for a bundle."

Steve shook his head and sipped his coffee. His wee round glasses steamed up and when they cleared, he was staring at me. "But the one you say he's doing *now* sounds dead familiar too," he said. "And you haven't actually seen either of them."

"What are you saying, Steve?"

"Just . . . sounds like he talks a good game," Steve said, and I don't think I managed to hide how I felt to hear my own thoughts come back at me.

"But I have seen something he made," I

said. "Listen to this, eh?" I might have made it sound better than it was. "Lights and like . . . landscapes inside, like a grotto. You can't really see it. It's a bit of a nightmare to be honest, and you wouldn't want it in your house if you lived alone. But it's totally brilliant and it's right there in the workshop. I saw it with my own eyes."

Steve had finished his coffee and he fiddled with the cup, not looking at me.

"You didn't see him make it," he said. "He might have bought it."

"He couldn't afford it! God's sake, Steve. He's got a workshop full of bits and bobs and a half-finished sculpture and a finished sculpture and he says he's a sculptor, and you knew he was an artist from knowing his family, but you still can't work out how all that fits together? What's your problem?" I knew, of course. It was just like the disciples, except for the other way on. You believe what you want to believe, and you don't believe what you don't want to believe. Steve didn't want to believe in Gus, so it didn't matter what I said, he'd find a way to make it seem dodgy.

"I don't trust him," said Steve, right on cue. "It's been a week, Jessie, and he's . . . it's like he's put a spell on you. He's got his hooks right in you, and I can't see why."

"Thanks a bunch!"

"I didn't mean that. God, hardly. Just, you're usually so careful with people. Even with . . . us."

He'd been going to say *me.*

"I just don't trust him."

"You don't have to," I said. "I trust him." I felt a flicker, but it was small enough to ignore. "I'm glad I was careful with people all these years, so nobody else managed to get their hooks into me and I was free when Gus came along." I didn't care if I was hurting him. He didn't look hurt, though. He looked puzzled.

"You make it sound as if you've only just met him," he said. "I thought you were friends."

The shop door dinged before I could answer and I turned, gratefully, away. I didn't recognise the man who stood there. Definitely not a client. He was in his fifties, dressed in jeans and Timberland boots, with a Gore-Tex fleece on top and a Gore-Tex shoulder harness on top of that with a phone velcroed on. He smiled at me.

"Miss Constable," he said. "I'm here about the clothes."

I blinked. Then I got it. This was the volunteer care worker, and I hadn't started searching for what we might have in a twenty-eight. I smiled back. A few years ago I'd have said he didn't look like a typical volunteer, back when they were all church ladies. But it was getting hard to tell now. Folk were getting nervous about their jobs and rounding out their CVs. And some of the big companies in town had cottoned on to giving time instead of money too, all those middle managers taking an afternoon to streamline some charity into efficiency and sending the little old church ladies packing with the new rules and the computing system.

Father Tommy was sick of the lot of them. "Say it with cash" was one of his slogans. He'd tried to tell that to the Peter Pan steering group. But he'd said a lot of other stuff too. "Hierarchy, a line of command, central control of resources. It's not a quilting bee." And someone at the meeting had piped up — I knew because Dot had told me — "Would His Holiness be interested, Father?" and there'd been a lot of tittering and a few jokes about Bishoprics and Presbyteries, which didn't sound all that funny and Father Tommy resigned from the committee saying that it would all end in tears.

And hadn't it just! Poor old house was lying there with the roof off and the blue polythene sheet flapping and a bulldozer sitting chained up in the garden, because the plant hire company wouldn't let the volunteer building crew use it and wouldn't send a driver (or even come and pick it up) until they got paid. A fiasco, just like Father Tommy had said, and who could blame him for sounding a bit chuffed about it.

I was on my way to the outsize section when I turned.

"Women's clothes?" I asked. How could a male volunteer help a woman try clothes on?

"Men's clothes, Miss Constable," he said. And that was another thing. Volunteers were *Miz* users all the way. Only the little old church ladies ever *Miss*'ed me.

"Size twenty-eight is a woman's size, though," I said.

He stared at me. I stared back. Steve cleared his throat and disappeared through the back. When he had gone, the man moved forward, pretty fast, between the rails and tables.

"I hear you didn't want to say where you'd seen them," he said. He spoke without moving his bottom lip, as if his teeth were clenched. Made him look like a ventriloquist's dummy.

"I have no idea what you're talking about."

"Bit late for that," he said. "You did better

than that yesterday. 'If only he hadn't been wearing a donkey jacket, he might not have drowned.' " He said in a high, mincing voice, mocking me.

"*Those* clothes!" I blurted. I started back, but he grabbed my arm.

"Hey!" I said. "Steve?" I heard the toilet flushing and shouted louder. "Steve!"

"Where is he?" he said. "What do you know?"

He was gripping my arm really hard just below the elbow and he started turning it back, like you do when you're taking a drumstick off a roasted chicken, until it snaps. But I'd been well trained in getting out of someone's grip who was bigger and stronger and thought they could bully you. I looked quickly to check my aim and then stamped down on his boot. My foot bounced back, aching. Steel-toe caps? But I'd distracted him long enough to let me knee him hard in the groin. *Then* I felt his grip slacken, and I twisted my arm away. I got myself behind the counter and yelled again.

"Steve!"

He was limping badly, but he made his way to the door.

"Hey, pal," I said. He looked up, just for an instant, and I had him. *Click!* We always keep a camera behind the desk in case there's trouble.

"I haven't finished with you," he said, pointing at me, jabbing the air with his finger. His other hand was cupped over his crotch.

"Oh, you're a big scary man that's holding his willie," I said. If someone really goes for me, I always turn lippy. And it worked on this guy. He left without another word.

"Were you shouting?" said Steve. "I was in the loo."

"Yeah, sorry," I said. "Listen, Steve, what exactly did Dot tell you happened yesterday?" Because *someone* had told that guy everything, down to the very words. So either Dot or Steve, whether deliberately or accidentally, had said far too much to someone.

"What I said," said Steve. "Why?"

"Trust me," I told him.

"Dot said the police thought you recognised the coat."

"Did Dot say whether *she* thought I did too?"

"No," said Steve.

"Did you tell anyone?"

"Tell them what? What's going on, Jessie?"

"I'm not sure," I said. "I need to think. So if you didn't mind looking out some twenty-eights, I'm going to slip away."

There was an idea growing inside me, like some kind of toxic toadstool, but I couldn't root it out. Dot had said something to me and when I called her on it, she'd toughed it out, counting on me not asking her to follow through. She'd slipped and she knew it. Then I shook myself. *Dot?* Dittery Dot? Dot lived in a bungalow in Thornhill with a Corgi. But still.

I took the camera with me. Round to Catherine Street, into the library. I didn't have time to check for myself, so I went to the reference desk and asked the librarian there.

"Hi," I said. "Listen, am I right in thinking that you keep press clippings?" He nodded. "So does that mean you go through the papers every day?" Another nod. "So if something had been in the news about Dumfries, you'd know, right?"

"If it was memorable enough," he said. "I'm not the oracle."

"Oh, you'd remember this," I assured him. "Are there gangsters in town? Known gangsters?"

He laughed. He must have wondered why I couldn't join him. "No, not that I can recall," he said, clearing his throat.

"So there's not been anything in the paper

about real proper master gangsters?"

"Not in the *Standard*," he told me. "Maybe the *Marvel*." And he laughed again, at his own joke this time.

I thanked him and left, my head fizzing. However Dot knew about gangsters in town, it wasn't from the paper like she'd said. She was in this. She had to be.

I hurried across the road to my flat. I'd told Kazek I'd be back in the evening, so I hoped I wouldn't surprise him in the shower. But it was better to do it now. If the Timberland boot man was going to have me followed, he'd do it at four when the Project closed. This might be my last chance to drop in on Kazek safely, for a while anyway. Thinking that, I changed direction, went to the corner shop, and stocked up on milk, rolls, chocolate bars, big bags of crisps, some bacon and eggs. The girl behind the counter stared at me and couldn't help her lip curling. *I know, I know,* I wanted to say. *Only stoners buy bags and bags of junk food in corner shops in the middle of the day. But where would your business be without them?*

Kazek *was* in the shower, but fully dressed, with the shower head in pieces on the floor of the bath. "Jessie-Pleasie?" he called.

"It's me!" I called back.

"Broke. Fix," said Kazek. "Come in."

And then he explained very fast, with lots of pointing at the shower head, what I already knew: that the water only came out of one side and the hot and cold didn't mix together properly. "Fix," he said. He had my pathetic little collection of tools laid out on the slip mat. An adjustable spanner, a set of screwdrivers from out of a Christmas cracker, and a hammer and measuring tape in matching purple flowers that I'd got at work in the Secret Santa.

"Thank you," I said. I held up the carrier bags and then went to the kitchen to put them away. He'd been busy in there too. The cheap cabinet doors that had slipped down on their hinges until they were all hanging crooked were all hanging straight again. And — was this even possible? — the wrinkles were gone from the vinyl flooring. I bent down and squinted along the length of it. There should have been ripples like in the mouth of a whale, but there was nothing.

"Fix," he said, coming up behind me.

"How?" I asked him. He reached into the swing bin and pulled out a rolled-up strip of vinyl, then he showed me the line of tacks along the far end holding it down, screwing his face up in apology for the shoddy workmanship.

"I'll let you off," I said. "You lifted and relaid my lino?" I turned round and checked out the living room. "Haven't hemmed the curtains yet, I see. Free-loader." He caught my tone and smiled.

"Okayyyyyyy," I said.

"Okayyyyyyy," said Kazek.

I pulled the camera out of my bag, found the picture of the Timberland boot guy, and handed it over. I should have seen it coming. Kazek dropped it. Good hands though; he caught it before it hit the floor.

"Bad man," he said. "Jamboree."

"Let's phone Ros's sister." I had to mime before he got me, but he got me in the end. I handed him the phone and watched while he punched in the number.

"Hello?" she said, when he passed the phone to me.

"Eva?" I said. "Hello. My name is Jessie Constable and I'm a friend of Kazek's."

"He told me," she said. "He gave me a different number for you but no one answered, and then he called me yesterday. Thank you so much for taking care of him."

"How do you know Kazek?" I asked, but she had her own priorities.

"Do you know where my sister is?"

"I don't. I hoped you could tell me something that might help me find her. She left the place she was staying on Saturday."

"She would never leave Kazek and Wojtek. Or worry me this way. Why has she not phoned me?"

"I don't know," I told her. "I really can't say. But here's a good thing. She took her stuff with her. Some of it anyway. She left deliberately. Packed and made plans."

"She would not leave Kazek," Eva repeated. "Why would she do that, eh?"

Now this was a problem. I didn't know what her sister knew about Ros's life, the possible Becky connection, the money, the kind of people Ros hung around with if Timberland Guy was one of them.

"Listen," I said. "I showed Kazek a photo of someone," I said. "I'm going to pass you over and I want you to ask the name. Okay? Ask who it is." It only took a moment until I had her back again.

"Gary," she said "Gang man. Does *he* know where Ros is?" Here she broke down into dry heaving sobs. I put my hand over the phone.

"Gary?" I said to Kazek, pointing at the camera. He nodded and crossed himself. "But who is he?" I said into the phone. Gary the Gangster? Didn't seem likely. Thomas the Tank Engine. Larry the Lamb. And if

Ros's sister knew there was a gang mixed up in this, did she know about the money too?

"How does Ros know him?" I asked.

"She doesn't," the sister said. "Why would she know such a person?"

"Look," I said, "I don't want to worry you, but Wojtek is dead." Her gasp made the line crackle. "And Kazek is terrified for his life. It's true, even if he hasn't told you. I can't actually believe this is happening — and if you knew Dot, you'd know I'm not kidding — but Ros is involved somehow. A young woman killed herself. Not Ros, for God's sake! Her friend Becky. So I really need to find Ros, because she's the one who's skipped and left all this behind her. She must know something."

"You are looking for my sister to answer questions?" said Eva. "Not to make sure she is safe and okay?"

"Where did Kazek get the money?" I asked her.

"What money?" she said.

"Ask him." I passed the phone over and listened to them. I was beginning to think I could understand Polish by now. I could get the gist of the intonation anyway, and I couldn't believe what I was hearing. I grabbed the phone back.

"Well?" I said.

"He doesn't know what money you mean," Eva said.

"He bloody does," I said. "God, if we had Skype, I could show you." Except of course I didn't know where he'd stashed it this time. "Okay, listen. Can you think of anyone Ros would go to? Any town she's got friends in, any particular reason she'd have to go somewhere instead of somewhere else?"

"I think I don't trust you," she said. "I don't know how you know all these dead people. Or why you are looking for Ros. What is the real true reason you want to find her, eh?"

"Oh, great," I said.

"I think I will call the police," she said.

"Yes, good! I agree," I told her.

"Let me speak to Kazek," she demanded.

"To tell him not to trust me? Why should I?" But I handed the phone over anyway, because she could just as easy call back after I'd gone. I gave him the hard stare with my arms folded all the time he was talking. *Policja* was the only thing I understood out of the whole endless stream of it. He talked her round too. "*Nie dzwon po policja.* No police. Okay," was the last thing he said before *Czesc* and hanging up. He raised his hands, surrendering. Hung his head too.

335

"Sorry, Jessie-Pleasie," he said.

"Okay," I said. "I will find something, either in the cottage or at Gizzy's, in Ros's old gaff or in the office or something somehow, or something she said to Gizzy or Gus or Ruby or *something* for God's sake that'll help us work out where she's gone — and then we can find her."

He nodded. He walked over to the kettle and held it up, questioning, for all the world like we were just two pals hanging out in my flat, like you do.

"Only what's that going to change?" I said, sort of to him but more to myself, really. "She might be able to tell me why Becky killed herself, but how can she get Gary the Gangster off your back?"

"Jaroslawa jest prawnikiem," said Kazek. *"Prawnikiem,* Jessie-Pleasie."

"Write it down," I said. I gave him a scrap of paper from beside my phone and once he had scribbled on it, I put it in my pocket and sat back. I was exhausted. Then I hauled myself to my feet, opened the fridge, and showed him the shopping.

"Stay here," I told him. "Don't answer the door."

NINETEEN

I stayed exhausted too. Four o'clock came crawling round, and I had to drive back to the cottage with the car windows open to keep myself awake. One good thing about living down a farm track and through a caravan site, though — especially when you had to take it at five miles an hour behind the bin lorry — was I could be sure Gary or one of his minions wasn't following me. I stepped out onto the turf and let the sea breeze blow my hair back. Minions! Could someone be a friend of Dot and have minions? Henchmen, heavies, muscle. A week ago I thought I knew what my worries were, and they were bad enough. I turned and looked towards the cottage. Then, in the time-honoured way, it all went tits up because I met a guy.

I could see him through the living room window. He was sitting at the table, bent over something. Reading, maybe, or writing. And I could hear the sound of the kids, squealing and thrashing about with something. Would I go back? Undo it if I could? I pushed my sleeve up and looked at the red mark where Gary had grabbed me. Thought about Kazek in my flat and Ros's sister. Gus lifted his head and waved. I waved back and trotted up the path.

"Hiya!" I shouted.

"Jessieeeeee!" squealed Ruby.

"Mummmmeeeeee," said Dillon coming along at her heels. He put his head against my legs and hugged me.

"He doesn't mean it," Ruby told me. "He calls everybody that babysits Mummy."

"I know," I said, playing it cool, but my heart had filled my chest until I thought my coat would pop open. "So what are you doing?"

"Playing at funerals," said Ruby. "Come on, Dill. You be the dead body and I'll be the angel."

I took off my coat and scarf and fluffed my hair in the mirror, stopped just short of biting my lips and pinching my cheeks. Got close though.

"Did you hear that?" I asked Gus. He *was* writing — a proper letter on a pad of writing paper with a lined sheet underneath to keep it straight.

"Yeah," he said, laughing. "Wee toe rags. I told them about Becky's funeral, and Ruby took to it. Hey, guess what?"

"Who're you writing to? Relations?" I said. "What?"

"What relations?" he said. "I thought I'd told you. I'm writing to that hill walker. See if he wants to come to the funeral maybe." I couldn't keep the frown off my face. He raised his eyebrows, silently asking.

"Ohhhh, I don't know," I said. "Just. Okay, that's a nice idea. He might. Best to give him the choice. But what about your mum and your dad? And why not try to reach your brother? And surely Becky must have some family. Why not let them all know on the off-chance some of them might want to come too? That's all. I'll butt out. That's all I'm going to say."

"Guess who phoned today," he answered. I think it was an answer anyway.

"Your brother," I tried. "Becky's mum? Who?"

"Try again, Jess," he said. "Who have we been waiting to hear from?"

"Who?" I said. "Oh! Ros's sister?" *Shit!* Did she phone here after we spoke to her at the flat? Had she dropped me in it? Can't have, the way he was smiling at me.

"Close but no banana," he said. "Ros called."

I flumped down into one of the armchairs. I could feel my mouth hanging open but couldn't close it.

"Seriously?" I said. "She called here?"

"It's not that much of a shocker, is it?" he said. "She doesn't want her job back, if that's what's worrying you. Yeah, she phoned and said she'd just decided to make a clean break. She met someone else, got a chance of a job up north, took it."

"Someone else as opposed to who?" I said.

"Becky," said Gus. "You were right about that. Don't know why I didn't see it for myself. Years ago."

I nodded. "What did she say when you told her Becky died?" I asked. Gus whistled and shook his head again. A big reaction, he seemed to be saying. But what a weird way to signal it, far too lighthearted for how it must have been.

"She took it pretty hard," he said. "Obviously. I told her she wasn't responsible. If she didn't know Becky was feeling that bad, how could she have guessed? But Ros is one of those people, you know. Takes care of everyone. Really — what's the word? — conscientious."

I nodded slowly. The sort of person who

wouldn't leave a friend from home stranded in an empty caravan when she knew he was in trouble. None of this made sense to me.

"Well," I said. "That's that then. That's one mystery solved."

He had bent his head to carry on writing, but he looked up at me now.

"That's all the mysteries solved," he corrected. "Unless you're talking about the thing you've still got to tell me." I tried not to let my eyes grow wide. "Did you ever think, Jessie, that if you let it all go, tell me everything, the whole pteronophobia might just blow away like a . . ."

"Feather?" I said. Just like that. I was amazed at how much easier it was than even a week ago.

"I was going to say puff of smoke, but okay. Come here," he said. I hauled myself to my feet and went to sit on his knee. He squeezed me so hard my bra squeaked. "I heard what Dill called you. And Ruby's talking rubbish, you know. He doesn't call babysitters that. Just you."

I stood up, stretching — he really had squeezed me quite tight — and he ran his hands up and down my body. Big strong hands. Safe hands. I remembered Kazek catching the camera before it hit the floor.

"It's not called rubbish now," I said.

"Ruby's talking *recycling.*"

He laughed again even though it wasn't really funny. "So, what do you fancy for tea?" he said. "T-bone steak or Lobster Thermidor."

"Oh, I don't know," I said. "Not sure I'm hungry enough to do justice to a T-bone. And I had lobster for lunch . . ."

"In that case, then, maybe I can interest you in some tuna, pasta, and sweet corn?"

"Perfect!" I said. "As served in The Ivy. I think I'll just take a wee stroll along the beach first, mind you. Cooped up all day, you know."

"Want company?" said Gus.

"You finish your letter," I said. "But can I ask you a question?" He nodded. "Why aren't you typing it? Is it to make it more personal?" To me, letters on writing paper were so unusual that they seemed kind of weird now. Like only stalkers would send them.

"Haven't got a word processor," said Gus.

"You haven't got Word on your computer?" I said.

"What makes you think I've got a computer?" said Gus, looking around as if he expected to see one magically appear. Right enough, I hadn't seen it around, but I knew he had one.

"You said you looked stuff up," I reminded him.

"It's in the workshop," he told me. "I use it for graphics. No need for Word."

"Right," I said. I thought Ruby would feel left out if she was the only one at nursery who didn't use a computer, but then maybe she got a shot when she chummed him to work — when he *was* working, that is, when he didn't have sculptor's block. I thought of what Steve had said and put it out of my mind again as quickly as it had come in there. I said no more. Dill might be calling me Mummy, but they were Gus's kids and if he didn't think they needed a computer yet, I wasn't going to argue.

It was nearly completely dark outside, too dark to walk on the track with its tufts and potholes, but okay down on the beach with the long sweep of empty sand. I put my hands deep in the pockets of the coat I'd borrowed — it had looked so much warmer than mine — and with my head down against the wind, I took off along the bay.

So Ros had phoned. If no one else had called since and I went back now and dialled 1471, I could probably get right on to her. Tell her to call her sister, ask her what she was planning to do to help Kazek. How could I explain it to Gus, though? Say I wanted to get some cleaning tips? But she wasn't really much of a cleaner, was she? Gizzy had said as much. What was that word Kazek had used — the magic word that described her powers? It was written down on the scrap of paper tucked in my jeans, but too dark to read it now.

Well, I'd try the phone later if I got the chance, when Gus was out of the way. And even if I never got through to her, I could tell her sister she was okay. I'd as good as told her anyway — that she had packed her stuff and taken it with her — but it wouldn't hurt to follow up with some actual news. Via Gus. Like the news about her taking her things had come via Gus.

And that's why I was out on this walk, even if I didn't want to think the thoughts out loud. Maybe Ros had phoned Gizzy too, and I could ask her. I could check that the cops had really been on to Gizzy about Ros's things. I was just making sure. As I turned up the rise towards the office and shop, I was glad to see a light still shining. I knocked on the door and tried the handle.

"We're closed," she bawled. "Ring the emergency number and leave a message."

"It's Jessie," I bawled back. I could hear her sigh right along the passageway and through the closed door.

"What do you want?" she said, opening up on the chain.

"Has Ros called you?" I asked. "Oh, gonny let me in, Giz. I'm freezing."

"Ros?" she said. "What makes you think that?"

"She phoned Becky's house," I said. "Got the bad news." Gizzy sat back down at the computer and pushed her hair back with her hands. Whatever she was trying to do, it wasn't going well by the look of her. "Do you think we should tell the police?" I went on. "I know they weren't going to pursue it but . . ."

"Eh?" said Gizzy. She was only half-listening, looking between a manual cracked open flat by her keyboard and whatever mysteries were on the screen. "Tell them what?"

"Since they took the trouble to phone," I said.

"Did they? What did you tell them? Oh bloody hell, I *have*! I *did*! I just did that!" She stuck her middle finger up at the screen and picked up the manual to give it a closer look. I was glad she wasn't looking at me. I'm sure my face fell.

"The police didn't call here to ask about Ros disappearing?" I said.

"Who told you that?" she said. "They'll

say anything to shut you up."

The strict truth was that no one had told me that. Gus had told me that police had said Ros took her things, and when I asked him if they'd heard it from Gizzy, he said they must have. Maybe they were "just saying anything" to shut Gus up too.

"I tell you what," said Gizzy. She pushed her glasses up onto her head and rubbed the bridge of her nose. "If she'd phoned here today, I'd have reached down the line and dragged back by her scrawny wee Polish neck. She's left me in total bleeding chaos."

"Can I have a go on the computer, Giz?" I said. I was feeling in the pocket of my jeans for the scrap of paper.

"Can you do spreadsheets?"

"No," I said. "I just want to Google something."

Gizzy rolled backwards in her chair. "Be my guest. See if you can pick up a virus that'll melt the whole thing down so I'll never have to look at it again."

I Googled translation devices, picked the first one, hit Polish to English and copied in *prawnikiem* from the note. *Lawyer,* it told me. Ros was a lawyer? Working as cleaner in a caravan site? Jesus, Kazek might be a brain surgeon working as a . . . it occurred to me then that I didn't know what Kazek and Wojtek had come here to do.

"Cheers," I said. "See you Friday."

"Get ready for Armageddon," said Gizzy. "After the October half-term break's the worst clean of the year. Site's full and the weather's so crap that they're all in their vans mucking them up. I'm just warning you."

"In your own special way," I said, but she was back to the manual again and didn't hear me.

Ros was a lawyer. I could sort of see how that would help Kazek, although if Gary the Gangster was the sort to cut someone's throat, he didn't seem to have much respect for the law. And if Ros *did* respect the law, then how did she square the wads of fifties away? And why did she leave? Why didn't Gus ask her? Nothing he had told me made any kind of sense at all.

But I had to trust Gus. He had turned my life around, made me hope that it was going to be something worth living. Damn Steve for making me doubt him! I shoved my hands even deeper into the coat's pockets, and that's when I felt something I hadn't noticed before. Right deep down in the lining, there was the unmistakable cold jagged shape of a bunch of keys.

My heart beat harder at the very thought of it. He was so secretive. He'd been so weird that night when he took me there. But I just wanted to see the pram again, maybe take a look at the replica house in the workshop next door, just to set my mind at rest. I wasn't checking to see if there really was a computer in there. Why would he lie to me about that anyway?

I hunched into the collar of the coat as I passed the cottage, sure that if he looked out the window he would see me and know where I was going. Know that I was spying on him. Then he'd ask me to leave and I'd be back to my lonely wee flat — with Kazek, of course. I shouldn't be snooping round after Gus. I should be 1471-ing Ros and telling her to get her arse in gear and help her friend. But since I was here . . .

Which side would I look in? Pram was in one and House was in the other. I'd seen Pram. I hunched over the padlock on the other door and started searching for the right key. It took a while, and then once the door was open, it took me a while to find the string that pulled the light on too. At last my fingers fastened round it and I tugged. Blinked, stepped back, nearly stumbling. The wall was right in front of my face, less than two feet away. A breezeblock wall right to the ceiling and all the way to both sides. It filled the space completely. How would he ever get it out? And where were the windows? The door? It was supposed to be a copy of the cottage, but it was just a block. It made me think of a tumor, sitting there inside the byre. Solid and ugly. No wonder he didn't want me to see. And no bloody wonder he couldn't face coming here and working on it. It was monstrous. It made me feel queasy. Or it and the smell of the cattle drain combined. I wanted to lock the door again and run away.

But, I told myself, *on the other hand, here it is.* Okay, he'd embellished a bit about how far he'd got. He hadn't skimmed over the blocks or done the windows, but still. There it totally was. And no wonder the other room was such a mess. There was no room in here for anything else besides this. Nothing in the two-foot-wide passageway between the front of House and the byre wall. Nothing, that is, except for a sack — an old-fashioned hessian sack, tied shut with string, leaning against the corner. I couldn't help myself. I tiptoed towards it. There was a bit of a smell coming off it, hard to say what kind of smell, but it stirred some kind of troubled feeling in me. I bent over and touched it. It gave and resisted both. It was squashy but there were wiry little points too. I knew I'd felt that before, the give and resist. What the hell was it? I pulled a bit at the string around the neck and peered inside.

Then I was out, banging off the stone and the breezeblock, ricocheting like a pinball, back out into the dark of the field.

A sack of them. A whole brown sackcloth bag of them and I had felt them. Put my hand right on them and felt the curled ends give and the spike ends squeak and prickle. I retched and bent over, but my heart was thumping too fast and my throat was too tight. I had touched them! I had pulled the string. And it might have come loose and they'd all have burst out and I'd have been trapped in there with them flying around me. I'd never have got them back into the bag and Gus would know and —

Gus.

I was drenched in sweat but as cold as a corpse as I stumbled back, pulled the light switch, and closed the door. I locked up and dropped the keys back into the pocket of my borrowed coat.

Why would Gus have nothing at all in the same workshop as the piece except for a sack full of *them*? How could that be innocent? How could that just happen to be?

It couldn't. He must have collected them and put them there deliberately. He must be keeping them there as a way of scaring me if I ever stepped out of line. He'd tie me up in there with them, or he'd go to the workshop in the night and get them and empty them all round the room while I was sleeping and tie me down and . . .

I could hear a voice, and it was Lauren's voice, telling me to breathe in and breathe out. In for four and out for five. In for five and out for seven. In for six and out for nine and catch a hold of my racing thoughts and start to fold them up and put them away.

Of course he collected them. He didn't want me to walk on the beach and see them. It was just the kind of thing Gus would do. And they were in a sack in his workshop because . . . he didn't want to put them in the wheeliebin and upset me. He'd even taken the very first one — off the end of the novelty pen — he'd taken it out of the wheeliebin, taken it right away. That was last Tuesday night. A week ago today. I stopped short. Why did that thought bother me?

Or. Maybe he had a sack of them like he had all that other stuff lying around. Maybe he'd had it for years, lying about with the light bulbs and lamps, but last week when

351

he knew I was coming, he moved the sack to the other room in case I saw it. And that was why he didn't want me to follow him through when he went to get Pram. Maybe that was the whole reason why he was so peculiar that night. Poor Gus. Worrying about me. I was glad I'd had that fright before I could look for a computer; he didn't deserve me spying after all he'd done for me.

I let myself in at the cottage door and went to find him. He was in the kitchen eating pasta with the children. He looked like he hadn't a care in the world. The same way he'd looked in Marks and Sparks with Ruby that day, before he smashed his phone. I smiled at him.

"I was just going to send out a search party for you," he said. "You okay?"

"Party!" said Dillon. "Happy Birthday!"

"Your pasta's cold," said Ruby. "And we ate all the top bit with the crispy cheese." She waved her fork at the dish in the middle of the table, a wodge of pasta and, right enough, no top bit at all.

"I don't mind," I said, sitting down. "I'm just happy to be here. I'd eat anything so long as I could eat it with here with you."

Gus screwed up his nose and laughed. "Oh, kids," he said. "This is too good to be true. What will we give Jessie if she'll eat anything, eh?"

"Liver," said Ruby.

"Yum, yum," I said.

"Rice pudding and gooseberries," said Gus.

"Rice pudding and bogies!" said Ruby.

"Bogies," said Dillon. And then he went straight for the big one. "POO!"

"No, no, don't make me eat poo," I said. Gus leapt to his feet and went rummaging in the larder, came out with a jar of Nutella. He opened it, put in a finger, and then came towards me waving the brown goo like a snake's head, to and fro.

"Jessie eats POO!" said Ruby. I took a tiny nibble, no way I was going to suck his finger in front of the kids.

"Yum, yum," I said.

"Not poo, not really," said Dillon, troubled now by the thought of how often he'd had toast and Nutella maybe.

"Not really, baby," I said.

"I'm a baby too," said Ruby. "Dillon's the second baby. I'm the first one."

"You're a beautiful baby, baby," I said.

"But I'm a big girl," said Ruby. "Bigger than Dillon."

"Oh Ruby, I love you," I said. "You're just brilliant."

"I am actually," said Ruby. "That's okay for you to say that. That's actually true." Under the table Gus had reached out both his feet and grabbed one of mine between them. The pasta was lukewarm and under-salted — for the kids, probably. But I'd never tasted anything so good in my life. And when we bathed the kids together, me washing Ruby's hair and Gus playing subs with Dillon, I felt as if my heart had steel bands round it, it ached so much from wanting this to be my future. It was the happiest night of my life. Before or since. It was the best, most hopeful, most innocent moment I've ever had or ever will.

It lasted about half an hour. And it was my own fault. I pulled it to pieces single-handed.

"My turn," said Gus, once the kids were in bed. "If you don't mind." He had his coat on, the same one I'd borrowed, and his wellies too.

"You going to the workshop?"

His face clouded. "My turn for a walk," he said. "I told you — I can't face the workshop just now."

"I don't blame you," I said. "Know the truth? That night we were there, I thought it was kind of creepy." I thought he looked amused, and I even thought I knew why. How creepy would I have found it if he hadn't hidden that sack away?

As soon as he was out of the house and I'd followed the bobbing spot of yellow torchlight until it was far away down by the water's edge, I made for the phone in the hall and dialled 1471. There were so many clicks and buzzes I thought for sure it wasn't working, and the ring sounded funny too, but after a minute a woman answered.

"*Czesc?*" she said.

I punched the air. "Ros?"

"*Masz jakies wiadomosci o mojej siostrze?*"

"This is Jessie Constable, I'm a friend of Gus King and I —"

"You?" she said. "What is it you *want* from me?"

"Eva?" I said. "Oh, shit! You phoned back?"

"What are you talking about?" she said "You called me."

"Sorry, sorry," I said. "When did you phone? Did you leave a message? Did you talk to Gus? Did he tell you Ros phoned?"

"What? Why did you not tell me this earlier when I spoke to you?"

"No, no, no." God, as soon as I talked to this woman it was instant confusion. I don't know whether it was her or me, but I had more luck talking to Kazek with the sound effects and the miming.

"Ros phoned *after* I called you today," I said. "What time did you call here?"

"I called the number Kazek gave me yesterday and I left a message. I do not know what you are asking me."

"I'll work it out and get back," I said. I hung up the phone, desperate to get it out of my hands, like it was a wasp that had just stung me. If she had phoned yesterday and her number was the one in the memory, then how did Ros talk to Gus today? I thought it through very calmly and of course it wasn't that difficult. In less than a minute I knew.

There must be another mobile somewhere. There had to be. Gus had stamped on his, Becky had taken hers with her — she'd used it to call Gus, call his voice-mail anyway. But somewhere in this house, there must a phone that Ros had called to tell him she was okay.

It wasn't in his coat pocket. And it wasn't in his trouser pocket. (I'd put my hands in his pockets when we were standing looking down at the kids in their beds; there was only some change in there.) I looked in the hallstand drawer, with the gloves and spare keys. There was a charger but no phone.

Nothing in the sideboard drawers in the living room. Nothing in the kitchen junk drawer. Nothing in the top drawer of Gus's dresser in the bedroom or in his bedside cabinet either. In Becky's bedside cabinet — this was the first time I'd opened it; I'd just been putting my glass of water on the top and ignoring the drawer and cupboard bit — there was a lot of photos. Ros and the kids, Ros and Becky and the kids, just the kids (where was Gus?). And a diary. It sat there in my hand like a grenade with the pin out. I poked a finger in and nudged the pages open. *I can't stand this anymore,* it said at the top of the page. *Life doesn't feel worth —*

I snapped it closed. I wasn't going to read any more than I had to, but I wished I had read it days ago. He was right to be satisfied, not to want the Fiscal making a song and dance of it. Even her writing was screwed up smaller than an ant with cramp. Tiny, tiny little writing — nothing like the scrawl she'd left in the suicide note, once she'd given up and decided to let it all go.

Where else could I check?

There was a basket in the back porch, where stuff got put that came out of pockets before the clothes went in the machine. That was a likely spot for a mobile to end up. I let myself out the back door, tipped the basket towards the light, picked out a few purple ponies whose pink manes and tails were hiding everything and . . . bingo! A phone.

With no charge. I tipped the basket again and threw it back in.

And that's when I saw the thing I'd missed before.

I reached in and pulled it out, feeling it stretch and then snap and sting my hand as the end of it came free.

Ja jestem Droga, Prawda i Zycie, it read. Polish. It was broken, the rough ends of the rubber pale and crumbling, like it had been ripped off. I turned it over in my hands. It had to be Ros's. Not as good as a phone with a number in it, but . . . if I knew what charity this was, maybe it would give me some clues. Like if I wore an RSPB one, people might find out I'd worked in the shop and then they could ask my old work-mates and find out my mother lived in San-quhar and go and ask her for my number. Or something. Worth a try. I took my mobile out and phoned the flat. Would he answer? He was being careful, letting the machine get it, but he picked up when heard me say, "Kazek, it's Jessie."

"Jessie-Pleasie," he said. "You okay?"

"Face hurts from grinning," I said. "Listen." And I read the words on the bracelet to him.

"Ya yestem droga pravda ee zeekie," I said.

"Oh," he said. A soft cry like he'd turned and seen a sunset. He said the words back to me, pronouncing them better. "How, Jessie?" he said. "What?"

"What does it mean?" I asked him. What were the chances he'd be able to put it into English, over the phone, without miming?

"Is Bible," he said. "I am path and truth."

"I am the way, the truth, and the life?" I said.

"You read Polish Bible, Jessie-Pleasie?"

"It's a . . . oh, shit," I said. "It's a rubber bangle, Kazek. Arm, right? Hand? Charity?" There was silence. "Listen." I held the bracelet up to the phone and snapped the rubber.

"Opaska!" he said. *"Bransoletka-cegielka?* Brad Pitt. Save fish. Save planet."

"Yes!" I said. "We're getting better at this. It was Ros's."

"No," he said. "No way, Jessie-Pleasie. Not Bible. Not Ros. *Ja jestem Droga, Prawda i Zycie?* Was Wojtek."

"It can't be," I said.

"Police give?"

I turned the bracelet round in my hand

again. The crumbling rubber on the broken ends, like it had been snatched off. Like in a struggle. Then I whipped my head up as a noise came over the turf, from the track, a hollow scraping, rumbling sound. It was Gus dragging the wheelies.

"I've got to go," I said to Kazek. "Go to sleep, let Jesus keep." Fuck sake, I was quoting my mother.

I shoved the bracelet in my pocket and slipped inside again. I didn't want to see Gus right now. I needed to get my head straight. It wasn't Wojtek's bracelet, couldn't be. It had to be Ros's. Maybe her mum sent it, and she snorted and gave it to Ruby, who wouldn't understand the words. And Ruby used it for a catapult and burst it, and Becky left it in the basket when she washed Ruby's jeans. There was a simple explanation for everything, really. Gus was a good man. And I was going to prove it. I was going to tell him the worst thing anyone could hear and he was going to love me anyway. And then I'd tell him I'd love him even if he told me the worst thing he could tell me. And he would. And it wouldn't really be bad, like my worst stuff wasn't either. He would explain it all. He would make sense of everything.

I heard him nudging the wheelie into its

space on the porch and coming in the door.

"I love your kids," I said to him, when he came into the living room.

"Me too," he said laughing. "Have they been up, running about, being lovable like?"

"No, I'm just saying. I love kids and I'm sick of keeping away from them. I need to speak to you."

He held up a finger to tell me to wait, went out into the hall, and came back without his coat. He dropped down into his armchair and started unlacing his boots.

"I thought I should steer clear cos I'd never be able to cope if something happened. And you have to cope. If there's little kids around. You just absolutely have to. Because if you don't, then everyone's stuffed, aren't they?"

He sat waiting for me to go on, holding both ends of his laces tight, making me think of a cartoon of a bird pulling a worm I'd seen in a book when I was wee and hated.

"Something happened. More than I've told you."

"I know," he said.

"About my granny's quilt."

He said it again. "I know."

"But I want to trust you," I said. "I'm going to tell you. Even though it's the worst thing I've ever done in my life. Unless you want to go first and tell me?"

He went back to his boots again then, finished taking them off, set them at the fireside to dry out — he must have been on the beach — and rubbed his socks together.

"I'm all ears, Jess," he said.

"Please, please, *please* call me Jessie," I said. "My mother calls me Jess. I can't stand thinking about my mother when I'm here with you."

"So tell me the rest of the story just one time," he said, "and you never have to think about her again."

Like he knew it was my mother all along and not my granny at all. Like he knew already what I was going to say.

The rest of the story. Where was I starting from? What had I said before? I pulled the stuffing out of the quilt and my mother tied me down. I'd told him it was in my room at home, but he'd seen through that. He knew it was my granny's house. And he knew I couldn't turn my face, but he didn't know why. Could I tell him? I could try.

"My mother was going to some . . . jamboree," I began. Gus laughed and I joined him. Where had that expression sprung from? Oh, yes, Kazek had said it to Ros's sister on the phone. What a weird

English word for him to know. Or maybe it was the same in Polish, like polka. But why was he talking about it anyway? "Yeah, sorry," I said. "My mother was off to a jamboree. All weekend. But Friday was my granny's whist night. So my mum bedded me down and my granny came in to check me before she went to bed."

I remember the door opening, the look of the flowery landing wallpaper in the lamp-light and Granny's head, done up in rollers and shining with cream, coming slowly round the door. I squeezed my eyes shut. So ashamed for her to see me tied up like a dog in a yard. *Suffer the little children,* my mother had said to me and, *a child is known by its doings.* As well as the line about the rod and the spoiling, of course. She just loved that one.

"She'd carped on and on at me about the quilt — showing her up, how she had to sit through a lecture from Granny about how children were children and you couldn't knock it out of them, shouldn't even try. She was so angry. I couldn't bear that I'd made her so angry. I couldn't stand the thought of Granny seeing what a bad girl I was that my mum had to tie me."

"Wait a minute," Gus said. "This isn't the night you pulled the stuffing out?"

"No, this was after. My mum tied me up so I wouldn't do it again."

"Was your gran still angry with you?"

"No, I was telling the truth when I said she thought it was funny. But she didn't think it was funny when she saw me tied."

"What did she say?"

"She didn't say anything. She just made this noise."

She had walked over to my bed and bent down low to kiss me. Then she froze and slowly she pulled back the covers, showing my wrists and the ropes. She made a whistling, whooping noise and turned away. Couldn't she bear me in her sight? Then she made a noise that was like a dragon in a cave, a horrible roaring, choking sound. Was this the wrath that my mum was always warning me I would bring raining down?

"I heard a crash and I opened my eyes. Granny was lying on the floor, rolling from side to side. And she was in brown puddle. Probably not brown, but it was dark in there. She'd thrown up. God, her hair and her shiny face with the face cream. And she was clutching at herself and making this noise."

That *noise.*

"It was like a kind of gobbling," I told Gus. He was right forward in his chair, right on the edge, holding his knees, staring at me with his mouth hanging open. "Wet and choked and just the most horrible thing I'd ever heard. I didn't understand what I'd done."

"What *you'd* done?"

"I know, I know, I know now," I said. "But I didn't know that night."

"What happened?" he asked.

"I turned and faced the other way. Even though there was a feather end sticking in me. I kept facing the wall. And eventually she was quiet. She passed out. That's what I know now, grownup me. Little me thought she'd fallen asleep."

And I fell asleep too, the way kids do. I slept until her crying woke me. Her sobbing and the way she was calling my name. *Jess, help Granny. Help Granny, there's a good girl. Dehhh, hehhh Gannnn, goohh guuhhh.* But I wasn't a good girl. I was a bad girl and my mother had tied me up, so I couldn't help Granny like a good girl would do.

"She wet herself," I told him. "And she shit herself. There's nothing dignified about dying, you know."

"She — fuck sake, Jessie. She *died*? When you were tied up and couldn't —"

"Eventually. It got light and I was hungry. Then I wet myself too. And I slept and so

365

did she, then it was dark again and she was moving, thrashing about, and her head knocked against the floor and, God, the smell. The smell of the pair of us in there."

When it got light again and I looked at her, it wasn't Granny anymore. It was this purple thing. Lying there, crusted and twisted. I didn't understand. I heard her talking to me a lot after that, but I know now I was dreaming. Or hallucinating.

"I was there another night and day after the day she died. One more and it would have been me too. But my mother came back and found me."

Only that was a memory I wasn't going to touch with a ten-foot pole. I wrapped it up, shrank it down, and threw it out to sea. So far out that it went over the horizon and hit the setting sun and it hissed as it shrivelled and disappeared.

"And so that's why I thought to myself I should stay away from kids because I can't handle feathers, and you've to handle things with little kids because they can't cope on their own."

Gus had put his head down in his hands and now he rubbed his face hard, but he hadn't rubbed away all the tears when he looked up again.

"That doesn't make any sense," he said.

"You were five and you were tied to your bed. How could you cope with that? How could anyone?"

"I know," I said. "It makes no sense at all. Sometimes things just don't." Like Wojtek's bracelet in Becky's junk basket. But I wasn't going to think about that now.

"Is that really really really what happened?" he said.

"Gus," I said, "don't even. It took me twenty years to get that night straight. Twenty years to sort out what was what."

"How come? It sounds pretty clear to me. Hellish, like, but clear. And it's no bloody wonder you can't forgive your mother, by the way."

I said nothing. I didn't want to milk the sympathy. I didn't want him to know that for twenty years and counting my beloved mother hadn't managed to forgive me.

TWENTY

Wednesday, 12 October
Which is why I ended up phoning her the next day. I only ever phone my mother when I'm dead angry and dead clear and there's no chance she'll gaslight me. As to *why* I phone her, I'm just keeping the lines open, just in case the day ever comes. And, she's my mum. Caroline with the couch told me about these baby monkeys that get taken away from their mothers and put in a cage with a fur-covered box. It's pretty useless, hard and hollow and that, but it's all they know. And the thing is, if you take it away from them, they pine for it. Even if you take it away and replace it with an actual female monkey who cuddles them back, they pine for the fur-covered box cos it's what they know. So I don't beat myself up anymore about phoning my mum sometimes. I'm a monkey.

"Jess," she said when she answered. I

wasn't holding my breath to hear what followed, not really. "Long time, no hear."

"Things must be bad, Mum, if you've had to put your phone to incoming calls only." Two sentences — one each — and we were fighting. I took a deep breath and tried again. "How's Allan and Penny?"

"Fine, as you'd know if you ever called them."

"Oh, they're feeling the pinch too, are they? Can't afford to call me?"

"Penny's busy with the children," said Mum. "It's all right for you."

"Yeah, lucky me. Okay, now you ask me a question and before you know, it'll be a conversation."

"Any man among you who bridleth not his tongue," said my mother.

"James, Chapter 1, I forget the verse," I said. "I'm rusty."

"Well, I suppose you've no call for it, in your everyday life," she said. "Just pick a saint and light a candle."

"Actually, Mother, what I do is sort clothes and wash them and help people who really need them to choose what's best and try not to make them feel too crap for being there. What have you done for anyone except yourself lately?"

"My prayer group —"

"Exactly," I said. "Well, it was lovely to catch up, as always."

"That's it?" She almost shrieked it. "Not a word for months —"

"From either one of us," I said. "Not until I phoned you."

"I shouldn't have to phone you," she said. "I'm your mother."

"How often do you phone Allan?" I said.

"Penny's busy with the little ones," she said again. "That's different."

"If I was busy with kids, would you phone me?" I asked.

"Don't tell me you've disgraced yourself on top of everything," she said. "I'm not stepping in, Jess, if the social workers take it off you. I can't start all that at my age."

"You are unbelievable," I said. "No, I haven't disgraced myself. I'm still single and childless and living alone in my thirties. Is that what you want to hear? Is that what you want for me?"

"Well, that's a mercy," she said. "But don't try to make me feel guilty because you set your face against everyone. I didn't train you to turn people away. I've done my best to help you make friends. If you were part of a community . . ."

"I'm not joining the church, Mother. I don't believe any of it. Why don't you join a mosque first and tell me how it's done when you don't actually buy a single word?"

"Oh, Jess," she said. "You push people away. You don't keep in touch. You ignore people who're trying to be in touch with you."

"Give my love to Allan. And Penny as well if she's not too busy with the children to take it."

"I try to help," she said. "I suppose nothing came of it?"

"And remember where I am, every weekday except Thursday. Don't pass the door."

"I'm not in the habit of going into such places, Jess," said my mother. "You know how easily upset I am by . . . unpleasantness."

"Yeah, beggars and lepers can whistle as far as you're concerned."

"I don't share your taste for long-haired layabouts, Jess. That's no need to —"

"Just as well there's plenty of folk who don't mind them. Like Jesus and me."

"Do not take the Lord's name —"

"I didn't. I was referring to him in a completely normal —"

"— in vain, if you'll let me finish."

"— way. As opposed to Jesus motherfucking Christ in a" — the phone went dead in my hand — "cummerbund."

"What's a cumblebund?" said Ruby. She was right beside me, standing on the cold lino in her bare feet, her toes white. Her circulation must be as bad her daddy's. I peeled off my bed socks and put them on her.

"You're a cumblebund," I said. "You're the best little bundle of cumbles I've seen today, anyway."

"Can I keep these socks?" she said, sliding them up the lino at the edge of the carpet strip towards the living room. She turned. "Dillon's got a minging nappy, by the way." She smiled and disappeared through the doorway.

It was long gone eight before Gus got up. He came into the kitchen wearing the old hairy suit and a white shirt and tie. His hair was in a ponytail. He had his everyday black work boots on.

"I know," he told me. "It's the best I can do."

"You look daft, Dad," said Ruby.

"Thank you, my sweetheart," he said.

"But where are you going?" I asked him. He opened his eyes very wide and then glanced between both the kids.

"Quick word in the living room, Jess?" he said. I followed him. "Have you forgotten? I know you were upset last night, but . . . do you have black-outs?"

"What are you talking about?"

"It's Becky's funeral today. You're watching the kids."

"I have absolutely no memory of this," I said.

"You said days ago you would watch them whenever it was," he told me. "I said I was taking them, and you said no. So I asked if you would watch them."

"Yeah, yeah, I know," I said. "I remember that."

"You just said you didn't."

"No — yes. Oh, shit. Look. What I meant was I didn't remember that it was *today.*"

"But I just told you last night."

"I forgot."

"You just said you remembered."

I turned away and walked towards the front window. There must be a way to work this out; there had to be. I was freaking out at Gus because my mother had just scrambled me. That was all. Then I froze.

It was caught in a cobweb in the corner of the frame. Four inches long, grey and white, with a weird brown streak through it. It was kind of separating, like greasy hair combed away from a parting, and it blew gently back and forward.

"What's up?" said Gus.

"Nothing," I told him. I couldn't drag my eyes away from it. The sheen on the curve of it, where it all held together; the little gaps on the straight bit where it spiked into points like the teeth of a comb. And the brown bit that didn't belong. "Look, I was really upset last night, like you said. And I think you're more upset than you know this morning. So I'll phone in sick, you go to the funeral. I'll see you tonight. I'll get a hold of myself, I promise. Stop . . . fretting about things that don't matter."

"What things?" he said.

At last, I managed to turn my head. I turned my whole body, faced him.

He was looking at me in one of his many special, creepy ways. I had the thought before I could block it. *Not creepy,* I told myself. Just really alert, with his head on one side, slightly off to the side, like a bird with a worm. That bloody bird with a worm again.

"Stupid things," I answered. "Like why Becky put the bins out last Tuesday before she drove away."

"What?" There were two spots of colour high up on his cheeks.

"Things like that," I said. I couldn't stop thinking about it, right there behind me. What if a gust of wind blew it free? Was the window closed all the way? Could it blow in through a gap and land on my neck? I could feel my skin crawling.

"Tidying up," said Gus. "Putting her affairs in order, they call it. Seems about right to me."

"Okay," I said. "But she must have waited for the binmen to come and then brought them back over too," I said. "And that's bothering me. Fine, I agree, she'd clear out the nappies, but why would she wait until the men came and then wheel them back? This week it was dead late before they showed up."

"And what makes you so sure she did?" said Gus.

"They were here," I said. "I met you in Marks, we came back here, you went away with the cops and came back with them. And then you got the pen from Ruby's bedroom and went outside with it. The wheeliebin was there on the porch, and I don't see how it got there." He said nothing. Didn't move a muscle. Didn't even blink. "Stupid things like that," I told him.

"Maybe the men were early that day," he said at last.

"But she drove away through the farmyard so no one would see her," I said. "Would she really risk bumping into someone when she was doing the bins?"

"Or maybe someone else brought them back," he said. "For a favour."

"Who, though? When I asked if there was someone who could come and stay with the kids, you said there wasn't. And why wouldn't they do the favour this week again when they knew what a time you were having?"

"Jessie," he said. "Are you sure nothing's upset you?" And I swear he glanced at the corner of the window. Unless I was going crazy. Unless my mother had really messed me up again.

"Noth—" I said, but he cut me off.

"It was probably Gizzy," he said. "She hates our wheelies at the end of the path making her site look untidy. That'll have been it."

I nodded. It made sense. But I knew I would never ask Gizzy. I didn't want to know.

"So," he said, sounding like someone who was off on a picnic, not heading to where he was headed today, "you're sure you can face the kids? Last night must have kicked up some dust."

I went back to him and put my arms around him then. He was leaving his children with me. And I knew how much he loved them. And yet it was me he was worried about.

"We're both knackered," I said. "I'm going to ask for some time off once everything's settled."

"What everything?"

Kazek and the money and Ros and Gary the Gangster, was what I couldn't say.

"This everything, of course," I said flipping his tie. "The funeral."

He tipped my face up and kissed my cheek. I waited until he was out of sight before I wiped the trace of the kiss away.

And I *would* be okay with the kids. I was in charge of whatever I chose to do. I wasn't in charge of how I felt, but I didn't have to let how I felt run the show. "Thanks a bunch, Stacey!" I whispered to myself. Nothing like a bit of cognitive behaviourism to strip you of any comfort and make you feel like crap. I went into the kitchen — "All right for a minute, kids?" — and put on a pair of rubber gloves.

"Another nap-py!" Ruby sang. "Cos of all the gra-hapes!" I wondered if it had ever occurred to her she used to wear them too. I didn't tell her. I went through the living room, into the hall, out the front door. Since Ruby had my bed socks, my feet shrank and stung when they hit the cold brick of the path, beaded with melting frost, and reaching in towards the living room windowsill I stood on a thistle too.

I couldn't have said why, but while I stretched my hand out towards it I thought of my granny's face, wooden and purple, pebble-dashed with the dark vomit that she'd died in, teeth dry in her mouth, eyes clouding over like eggs slowly poaching.

And bugger me if it didn't help. Or maybe Gus trusting me had helped. Or my mother giving me something to push against. Maybe all three. For whatever reason, I grabbed it, pulled it free of the spider's web — it had stuck itself in there quite tightly — and brought it towards me, holding it up in front of my face for a good long look.

My heart was going *gub-gub-gub,* right up in my throat, and I knew I was shaking, and not just from the cold seeping up my legs and through my thin nightie. But I stared at it, the quill, like nail parings, like dead skin, like claws; and the grey part, stiff with grease, waxy; the softer white part, plump, plush, and gleaming. It was disgusting. It was horrific. And there was something else too. That funny brown streak running through it. I brought it closer still. Did they all have that? Did I just not know because I'd never looked before?

No. Definitely not. Not all feathers had that patch of stiffer brown in them, because it was a thread from a hessian sack. I pinched together two yellow rubber fingers and plucked it out, watching the waxy, gleaming length of it cleave to let it go and then fold in on itself again. I opened my fingers and let the strand of hessian fly away.

I dressed the children in warm clothes and wellie boots, did their teeth, brushed Ruby's hair and tied it in bunches, then set out with them across the turf to the workshop. I had to know.

"Oh, Daddy'll kill you," said Ruby, when she knew where we were going.

"I'll chance it," I said. "Did Daddy not like Mummy coming here?"

"Mummy," said Dillon.

"Mummy's dead and living on a cloud in heaven," said Ruby.

Yeah, I thought, as I dragged them along. Even though she wasn't pregnant after all. Because she couldn't stand it anymore. Even if she was gay, she wasn't from the fifties (or the Brethren). She loved her kids and her garden and she had a friend. So what exactly was it that she couldn't stand anymore? What else was there apart from the one thing in her life I hadn't even looked at until now, because it was the best thing I'd ever had? A dream come true.

All any girl really wants is a guy who can get over his wife dying before the sun goes down. A guy who understands and understands, and then sets little hoops for you to jump through. Saves up a great big sackfuls of little hoops without even telling you and starts the training the very next morning after you've told him how bad it was — worse, surely, than he could have dreamed of. Or I wouldn't want his dreams if not, anyway.

If it was true. Maybe it was just a feather, with a bit of brown crud stuck in it. Once I saw the workshop, I'd surely know. The picture of that sack was burned onto my eyeballs. If he'd moved it, it would look different.

He'd moved it right enough. I left the kids playing outside — they'd found a muddy puddle and couldn't believe their luck — and opened up the House side of the workshop. It didn't seem nearly so bad in the light of day with the children squabbling and giggling. Or maybe it didn't seem so creepy without the sack lying all alone on the little bit of space between the stone wall and the breeze-block wall. It was gone. I walked to the corner and looked along the length of the room to the back. It wasn't there either, just another passageway between the breeze block and the stone. A window in the stone on this wall. I walked along and looked round the next corner. Breeze block and stone. A door in the stone, wooden, barred shut and padlocked. And the fourth wall. Breeze block and the other wall this time was plaster, dividing this side of the workshop from the one where Gus had taken me. No sign of the sack anywhere.

I closed up again, padlocked the door, and opened the other one. The smell of the old drain was worse in here. Gus couldn't have worked in it even if he'd wanted to. He'd definitely been here for a visit though, because there was the sack. Just inside the door, the neck tied tighter shut than I'd left it.

Still. Still I couldn't bring myself to face it all. Still I was telling myself that his ploy with the feather in the spider's web had worked. I had touched it and stayed standing. I hadn't curled in a ball and squeezed my head. I had dressed the kids and come looking for more. Come looking for answers.

I let my gaze move around the crazy jumble of the workshop, over the shelves and tables, over the bags and boxes and parcels. The answers had to be here. He was a mystery to me, this man I'd fallen for like a rock off a cliff, and here was his secret place. Even if I couldn't bring myself to ask the questions, the answers were here.

Only, once I'd been looking round for five minutes, I wondered how secretive he was really. Ruby — I lifted my head and looked out the door at them: muddy but happy — had said Mummy didn't come here, but there were notes in Becky's handwriting everywhere. That loose loopy script I remembered so well: *I'm sorry, I can't go through it again. I can't go on.* So she didn't just scrawl in her suicide note. She scrawled all the time. Except in her diary. Which didn't make sense at all.

Until all of a sudden it did. That diary wasn't in Becky's writing. That book in her bedside table belonged to Ros. Because Gus would know if Becky had kept one, and he'd have read it after she'd killed herself. So it wasn't Becky's. It was Ros's, and she'd given it to Becky before she went away. Or Becky had taken it. And what else might she have taken? I remembered the phone in the basket on the porch. Ros's phone? Becky's mobile gone with her and Gus's destroyed. Was that Ros's phone?

Was this the answer at last? The police thought Ros had taken her things because her things were gone. But if Becky'd had Ros's diary and her mobile, then she could have had her passport and clothes and everything.

I started searching in earnest then, because wherever Ros's stuff was, it wasn't at the house. I tore into boxes of nails and bolts, tore open sacks and bin bags, rummaged through piles of canvas and tarpaulin, peered into drums of wire and plumbing parts and finally found it right at the back of the room, a black sack, another bloody black bin bag, that felt — who knew it better than me, who booted them over the floor every day and rooted through them? — like clothes and shoes.

"Oh shit," I said, dragging it into the middle of the floor where there was some space to open it and some light to see. "She killed her friend and then herself and Gus knows it. *That's* what he's hiding. That's why he freaked when Ros's sister phoned." A tingle went through me and I knew what had been niggling away at the back of my brain. If Becky killed Ros, then Ros hadn't phoned to say she was fine. Gus lied. Gus knew. Oh God, if only he'd told me last night when I asked him about the worst thing he'd ever done. I didn't even think — not really — that covering up a crime by his

children's mother when she was dead anyway was all that bad. Understandable anyway.

If, I reminded myself, catching hold of the
runaway train of my thoughts. If this is
Ros's stuff in here. I stuck my fingernails
into the plastic and pulled open a hole.

Jesus God! I reeled backwards at the
smell. Mould and mud and something foul
like a bunch of flowers left in the water too
long if you breathe in deep when you pour
it away. Rot and slime and decay.

But not death. Not animal. If it had been,
I'd never have been able to turn the hole
into a tear and see what I'd found. I closed
my eyes, opened them again, looked down,
and let my breath go in a rush of disap-
pointment and foolishness. It was just a load
of Gus's old clothes. Soaking wet. Shoved
away in a bin bag like only a guy would do,
but Gus's clothes. Not Ros's. My lovely,
horrendous solution wisped off like the
smell that was clearing from the bag now
that it was open again. I raked through the
things: a coat, one of those khaki ones with
a long tail that kids used to paint the
Anarchy sign on the back of; a jersey,
ruined; a pair of tweedy trousers, totally
ruined; black dress shoes, well-ruined. He
could have worn them to the funeral if they

hadn't been, instead of going along like some lout in his work boots. A flicker of unease crossed me at the thought of it. The thought of what, though? I sat still and listened to myself.

How long had this lot been here? Not long, if they were still soaking. How could he not remember that he'd just ruined his black shoes, the day he put work boots on for his wife's funeral? When he remembered, why would he not come here and get the bin bag to start drying the stuff out again? Why didn't he dry it out straight away? So I started going through the pockets, thinking maybe a petrol receipt or a lottery ticket or something would tell me they'd been there longer than I thought.

There was nothing in the jacket pockets. Nothing in the trousers' back pocket. I pulled the front pockets inside out to look, and that was when I saw it. I stared. I reached my hand out and picked it up. It was tiny, the size of an apple pip. I'd never have seen it if it hadn't been so bright. So unbelievably fluorescent orange. It was a crumb of rubber from the broken end of a bracelet.

I was so calm. I locked up and got the kids, took them home, only using half my brain to fight the madness that was growing inside it. Gus might have waded into the sea to save a baby gosling that was getting swept away. (Except that was river water, and I knew it). And maybe when Ruby broke her bangle that Ros gave her, he put it in his pocket. (Except Kazek said it wasn't hers). I still had half my brain free for the kids.

"You are so having a bath when we get in. Yes, before lunch. You look like chocolate mice."

"Lot-lit," said Dillon.

"I'll bring you some treats to eat in the bubbles, but you're getting a bath and you're getting your hair washed. Ruby-licious, you're filthy!"

I dropped the torn bin bag into the wheelie. I'd tied the stuff back up again in a new one and hoped he'd not have memorised the knot he'd used the first time. Then I hurried inside. The phone was ringing.

"Hello?"

"It's Gus," he said. He sounded hoarse and far away.

"Hiya," I said.

"Becky?" I couldn't cope with what it might mean if he was asking what he seemed to be. So I pretended not to understand.

"What about her? Gus, are you okay?"

"It said in the online *Standard* her funeral

386

was today. What the hell's going on there?"

"I don't know what you're asking me. What do you mean it said in the *Standard*? Who picked the day?"

"What's happening?" said Gus. "Is Becky dead, or isn't she? Who are you?"

"What's this?" I said, "the start of an insanity defence? Where the hell are you anyway?"

"I'm closer than you think, and I'm coming home," he said. "It's way overdue."

"Was that Daddy?" said Ruby. I was staring at my reflection in the mirror, thinking about Granny laughing with the feather stuck to her lips, Granny twisted on the floor with her eyes clouding.

"It was," I told Ruby. I looked down at both of them, hair stiff with mud, dried mud cracking off their anoraks, cheeks daubed like war paint. "What are you like?" I said. "Well, here's the good news. You're not going in the bath. We're going on a trip. We're going to visit . . . can you guess?"

"Mummy?" said Dillon.

I kicked myself. "Kazek!" I said. "Yeay!"

"Yeay," said Ruby. "Mr. Wet Guy. *Dzieki*, Jessie."

"Deekeeeee," said Dillon.

I was reeling, but I still managed to notice

that there were two proper baby seats in the van. And that's when the anger arrived at last to take over from all the fear. He'd done nothing but lie to me since the minute I met him. What was the point of that one that day? To keep me at home with the kids while he . . . what? Was that the day he went to the morgue or was that the day he went to the cops? Becky wasn't pregnant and she probably wasn't gay either, and Gus had a piece of Wojtek's bangle in his pocket, a guy who ended up dead in a river. And Gus had river water all over his clothes. And — this filled me with such boiling rage I thought I'd have to pull over, like I wasn't safe to drive — nobody talks back to voice-mail messages. *Nobody!*

This time I got a parking space no bother, middle of the day, middle of the week, and I hustled the kids up the stairs into the flat.

"Mr. Wet Guy," said Ruby. *"Czesc!"*

"Czesc mala," said Kazek. He turned to Dillon. *"Czesc maly. Co dzis porabiasz?"*

"Eh?" said Ruby. "Is this your house? I thought you lived at the beach." She started wandering round looking the place over.

"This is my house, Roobs," I told her and was surprised to see her turn on her heel and shoot me a look of anguish.

"You live with us!" she said. "Daddy and

Dillon and me."

"This is my old house," I told her. "Kazek lives here now that I live with you, sweetie."

This satisfied her and she went back to her poking around. Dillon had found the remote and switched the telly on. Some programme about houses in the country. He held the handset up to me, the mud cracking off his cheeks as he stretched his pleading smile as wide as it would go.

"Cartoons, Jessie." I got my *Shrek* DVD out and put it on for them.

"I'll bring you some crisps," I told them, but Kazek pulled me out into the hall.

"Why babies here? Gary! Dangerous!"

"Gary doesn't know I live here."

"Gary find out."

"Maybe," I said. "Well, okay, at least *Gus* doesn't know I live here. Look, Kazek." I pulled the broken bracelet out of my pocket and put it in his hand. He groaned — such pain — and two tears fell onto the little curl of orange rubber in his palm.

"Wojtek," he said. "Where find?"

"Gus," I told him. "I think . . . I don't know what to think, but we have *got* to go to the police. We *have* to."

"No, Jessie-Pleasie," he said. "*Gary zna tego policjanta I sa dobrymi kumplami. Nic nie rozumiesz!* You no understand."

"No kidding!" I said. "Okay, well, what about this? What about a priest? A Father? I need to tell someone. What do you think of that then?"

Kazek blew his cheeks out and wrinkled his brow. Then he nodded. "Okay. Holy Father? Okay."

I dialled the number praying that it would be Father Tommy and not Sister Avril who answered.

"Good morning," said his voice. Was it really still morning?

"It's Jessie."

"Jessie, my child," he said. "How are things down on the catwalk?"

"I'm not at work, Father," I said. "I'm at home and I'm in trouble. I need you to come. I —" I was ready to plead and cajole, but I'd forgotten who I was talking to. He might not wear a cape or his pants outside his trousers, but Father Tommy was already in the chute to the Batmobile.

"God keep you, my child," he said. "I'm on my way."

It was less than ten minutes later when the pounding came on the door.

"Jesus, Father, cool it," I muttered, as I trotted along the corridor. He hammered on the door again, and I was on the point of taking the chain off when something stopped me.

"Who is it?" I said.

"Jessie, I know you're in there." Gus's voice was ragged, like he'd been running. Or crying. I could hardly hear him through the door.

"How?" I said. "How do you know this is my flat?"

"Just let me in and I'll explain."

My hand was on the chain when he thundered his fists against the panels again. Both fists, fast as anything, like in a cartoon when they go round and round and turn blurry. It sounded like insanity.

Kazek came out of the living room, pulling the door shut behind him.

"Is Gary!" he whispered. "Don't open, Jessie-Pleasie. Is Gary. He kill me. No open door."

"It's Gus," I whispered back. "Gus?" I said in a normal voice. "Please tell me what's going on. How did you find me?"

"Why did you run away? Where are the kids?"

"They're here, of course," I said. "Where else would they be? But Gus, you need to calm down if you want me to let you in. You're scaring me and you'll scare them too." Ruby had sidled round the living room door with her eyes like saucers.

"Is that Daddy?" she said.

He heard her. "Ruby!" he shouted. "Daddy's here, darling. Open the door."

Ruby sprang forward and when I held her back, she started to scream. Gus went back to pounding.

"Let me in or I'll call the cops, Jessie," he said. "You've no right to take my kids away."

He had a point. And how was he supposed to explain anything through a door?

"Just promise me you'll stay calm," I said. Kazek was shaking his head. He took Ruby and lifted her up into his arms, holding her tightly. I undid the chain and had my hand on the lock to turn it before Kazek understood what I was doing.

"No, Jessie-Pleasie!" The pounding stopped. There was silence.

"Gus?" I said. "Are you still there?"

I heard a whisper and put my ear close to the door.

"What did you say?"

"Bitch." He hissed it at me. "Who the fuck have you got in there?"

I felt my face drain. "Gus, no," I said. Even then, even then, I was looking for reasons not to believe what was happening.

"Fucking filthy bitch."

He was upset after the funeral.

"Fucking filthy wheedling whining bitch."

I'd taken his kids.

"Fucking moaning stinking filthy bitch."

He heard a man's voice in my flat.

"Gus, no," I said again.

There was an explanation for everything else. Somehow. And I'd listen to it too. If he just passed one test. There was a bag of clothes hidden in his workshop. Either it was innocent or it wasn't. I had to know.

"Gus," I said. "I've got something to tell you. I brought the kids here because I don't want them to see the cops at your place."

And here was my answer. His footsteps hammering on the concrete close, and ringing on the stairs as he ran away until there was silence apart from *Shrek* and Dillon eating crisps and Ruby still softly crying.

I went to the bathroom and got cool cloths for the children's faces to wipe away the muck and the tears in one go. I was numb. Hands cold, lips blue, but still my head was fizzing. How did he know where I lived? A week ago he hadn't known a thing about me. He hadn't even known my name. And then with a click, another piece of it fell into place. He *had* known my name. He thought it was Jess. And at long last I knew why.

I was coming back from the bathroom when I heard the sound of new footsteps on the stairs. Soft as it was, Kazek heard it too. And Ruby. He had put her down but he kept his arms around her.

"Daddy?" she said.

But I'd know those crepe soles anywhere.

"Father?" I asked, loud enough for him to hear me through the door. "Before I open up, is there anyone hanging around? Did you see anyone out on the street?"

"Oh, Jessie," he said. "What manner of mess are you in now? No, there's no one."

I opened the door and he took in the tableau. Kazek crouching on the floor, Ruby red-faced and sniffing, me white with shock and still shaky. It was Kazek he came back to.

"Kazimierz Czarnecki," he said. "We've all been looking for you."

TWENTY-ONE

"Are you a . . . what's it called?" asked Ruby, looking at his purple surplice and dog collar. "A Santa?"

"Close enough for rough work," said Father Tommy. "And who's this fine fellow?"

"Dillon King," said Dill, who had come to the living room door.

"So what's been going on here?" Father Tommy said. I gave one of the cloths to Kazek for Ruby and put the other one over Dillon's hot wee face myself.

"Mum," he said, miserably. Father Tommy raised his eyebrows.

"It's a long story," I said. "How do you know Kazek?"

"It's another one," said Father Tommy. "And I don't actually know him. But I'm very pleased to meet him." He spoke like a headmaster confiscating a catapult. His next words explained why. "Since some of that money you absconded with was mine, my son. Or St. Vincent's anyway."

"*Prosze ksiedza . . .*" said Kazek.

"*Nie tak oficjalnie,*" said Father Tommy.

"You speak Polish?" I asked him. He was as Irish as a peat bog.

"I was a great fan of his late beloved Holiness," he said. "I learned a bit in case I ever met him. And no, I never did. Not in this life anyway, plenty time later."

"Well, thank God for it," I said. "I'm in serious need of someone who can talk to Kazek and tell me what the — what's going on."

"I would dearly love to know what the — what's going on myself, Jessie," said Father Tommy. "But these children are out on their feet. Let's get them settled and then we can talk, eh?"

Which is how it came to pass that Ruby and Dill got the couch and Father Tommy, Kazek, and me sat in a row on my bed like the first line of a dirty joke.

"Absconded from where?" I said.

"JM Barrie House," said Father Tommy.

"That's it!" I said. "That's why he kept saying *jamboree.*"

"*Nie ukradlem zadnych pieniedzy,*" said Kazek. "*Nie jestem zlodziejem.*"

"Well you might not think taking fifty

thousand pounds makes you a thief, but we'll have to agree to differ."

"He's right," I said. "He's not a thief. Show him, Kazek."

Kazek stretched over to my nightstand and took out the Morry's bag. He untied the handles, just as he had before, and shook out the two blocks of notes.

"Well now," said Father Tommy. "That's excellent news. That makes things a sight more easy."

"Don't be so sure," I said. "The other one — Wojtek, Kazek's friend? — it's him they fished out of the Nith with his throat cut." Father Tommy crossed himself and asked Kazek a question. Kazek nodded and wiped a tear away.

"And we know who killed him," I said. "Or at least, I thought we did, until, maybe it was . . . Okay listen, Father." I stood and went to my dressing table, got the camera that I'd left there.

"What do you know about this guy?"

"Gary Boyes," said Father Tommy. "Hey! Is that the Project?"

"He's a gangster," I said. "He might have killed Wojtek. Or had him killed anyway. Oh! That's it. Gary ordered it and Gus did it?"

"What are you talking about, Jessie?" said

Father Tommy. "Gary Boyes isn't a gangster. He couldn't order a killing."

"Father, he *is.*"

"He's a gang master," said Father Tommy. "He's in charge of the boys — including this one — who're doing the roof."

I knew my mouth had dropped open. "A gang master," I said. "Not a master gangster. Bloody Dot!"

"Oh, Dot!" said Father Tommy. "I know about *Monsignature Whelan,* by the way."

Kazek spoke again then, and Father Tommy sobered and nodded.

"Quite right, child," he said. "It's no time for laughter." But Kazek wasn't done. He opened his jacket and took out Wojtek's rosary and Bible, the broken bracelet too. I caught Ros's name in the stream and watched Father Tommy's face grow more and more solemn.

"I can't believe it," he said, when Kazek finally stopped talking and flopped back to lie flat on the bed.

"What?" I asked him. "Tell me before I burst."

"The steering committee were told Gary Boyes was a licensed gang master. Kazek here tells me he took their passports, paid them nothing, made them sleep on the site. So they ran away." He turned to Kazek.

"Why did you take the money?" he said. Kazek answered without opening his eyes and Father Tommy laughed.

"It certainly got their attention all right," he said. He fanned the notes out from around their band. "And you haven't spent a penny of it, eh? A good Catholic boy. The blessings of the church in your early years, Jessie, never depart from you."

"Yes, okay, okay," I said. "A teachable moment, I know. But then what happened?"

"They had a lawyer — this Ros? — who was going to fight their case," Father Tommy said. "But she's gone, he tells me. So they drew straws to see who would go and confront Boyes. Wojtek lost the draw and arranged to meet him."

"At Abington services," I said. "Of course he did. And instead of giving him the passports back in return for the money, Boyes lured him away and killed him."

"Poor child, poor child. Another good Catholic boy too. And the lawyer? Where's she? In the Nith, are we thinking?"

"I wish I knew," I said. "And here's another thing. Why didn't Kazek let me call the police? Ask him that."

"I don't have to," said Father Tommy. "Oh, it's a wicked world. You know Sergeant McDowall? His wife's name was Boyes before they were married. I married them myself. He's Gary Boyes's brother-in-law. Best man at the wedding."

"Well, he's as bent as a boomerang," I told him. "He told Boyes I knew something and that's when Boyes came to the shop." I pushed my sleeve back and showed him the bruises, yellow but unmistakable. "No way past a bent copper. Close ranks, bury the bodies, business as usual. If Kazek spends a night in the cells, he'll be lucky to see morning."

But I had underestimated the surpliced avenger. Father Tommy's eyes flared, his nostrils flared. I think maybe even his moustache flared.

"Jessie," he said. "If there's one thing I've learned in the past decade of pure hell and damnation, it's this. Bugger the ranks, bugger the organisation. I don't care who it is — the police force, the Church that I love like my mother, the Boy Scouts — bugger them. It's not worth one hair on the head of the most miserable sinner born to save a police force or a church that's gone bad."

"You'll go with him to the cops?"

"And stay by his side."

"Well, thank God for you," I said. "Only, Father? A Catholic priest shouting 'bugger the Boy Scouts' is going to get some funny looks, you know."

"I forgive you for that, my child," he said. "I'm in a forgiving mood today." I flopped back, flopped right back just like Kazek, and stared up at the ceiling. Father Tommy turned and skewered me with one of his looks. "And how did you get yourself mixed up in all of this?" he said.

" 'All of this' is actually only half the story," I said. "Their dad," I nodded through towards the children, "is married to the best friend of Ros the lawyer. Only she killed herself last Tuesday. And Gus had Wojtek's bracelet. I still don't see how that could be."

"But how do you come to know them all, Jessie?" said Father Tommy. "How is it that those children are here? In the state they're in? If it's you who joins the two halves together, you must know."

"I thought it was pure chance, Father. Until I worked it out today." I sat up, leapt to my feet. "Can I go out for a bit? I'll take the children, if you want me to. You can't drag them round where you're going."

"Ah, I think we can all spend a quiet hour right here, until your return," he said. "I can practice my Polish with this fine young man, and it's been a while since I saw *Shrek*. I'll sit on the couch and eat a bag of crisps very happily. On you go, child, on you go."

How long had it been since I was here? I'd given up coming for Christmas the year my mum told me that my blaspheming was tainting the whole day for everyone, even Penny and Allan's daughter who was fourteen months old. My blaspheming. All I had done was point out that if God had sacrificed his only son to Herod when he was a toddler instead of waiting till he was in his thirties, it would have saved a lot of other little boys.

"But look on the bright side, eh?" I'd said. "It probably never happened."

"What do you mean 'never happened'?" said Penny. "It's in Scripture."

"But only according to Matthew. Not the other three. Matthew, you know, the only one that happened to mention — what was else it? — oh yeah, an earthquake on Good Friday. One out of four witnesses recalled a massacre of baby boys and an earthquake. Something wrong somewhere, if you ask me. I think if four people — or even just two should be enough, eh Mum? — if the same people were all at the same massacre and earthquake together, they should agree on what happened. Eh no?"

My mother had put her head into her hands by this time. Her paper hat fell off into her prawn cocktail.

"Sorry, Mother," I said. "You should have stuck to waving it at me and making me swear on it that I hadn't been smoking. It was when I *read* the damn thing that it all started to go so wrong. Reading what you told me was true and trying so hard to not remember the truth that you told me was false. It was a recipe for disaster, really."

So maybe calling their Bible a *damn thing* was a tiny little bit blasphemous, actually, I thought as I rang the doorbell. I'd really try to rein it in today. The doorbell playing "How Great Thou Art" didn't help, and the sight of my mother when she came to answer it made the little devil on my shoulder whisper things in my ear. She was wearing one of her midcalf, brown skirts and a cream shirt with a high, ruffled neck, fawn cardi, no jewelry, no makeup, modest in the sight of the Lord. But her hair was a bright copper red, not a single grey one anywhere. Some of the brightest hairs were kind of springy and coarse the way grey hair grows in, but the colour, well, the colour had to be a gift from God to reward her good life, right? Anything else would be unholy and shameful and not the Brethren way.

"Jess?" she said.

"Mum," I answered. "I just want to check out something you said to me. What would I not have followed up on? What were you doing to try to help me?"

She stood back to let me in and ushered me towards the living room. She had been sitting knitting with the radio on, a small, pale yellow jersey in a lacy design.

"Sale of work?" I said. "That's really lovely." I was determined to try.

"Idle hands," said my mother. "What are you asking me?"

She sat back down and picked up her needles. There was going to be no offer of tea then. But then she'd not long had one judging by the empty cup and the crumbs in the saucer — one of those squint saucers with a bulge for the biscuit; I had bought it for her for a birthday present and I wish I could say it meant nothing to see her using it.

"On the phone," I reminded her. "You said you supposed I wouldn't have followed up on something. Something about not keeping hold of my friends?"

"Oh yes. Someone was here looking for you," she said. "A rough sort, but a nice enough way with him."

"When was this?"

404

"Months back," said my mother. "Hasn't he phoned you yet? Maybe he's shy."

"Months," I repeated.

"He came once looking for you and then he came back for some leaflets I said I'd bring him. Came back a third time to talk them over too."

"Church leaflets?" I said, thinking I'd got it wrong after all.

"So I thought he might be a nice friend for you, appearances aside."

"Because he's a long-haired lout," I guessed. "And he said he knew me."

"Of course he knows you," my mother said. "You were at school together. I think, you know, that he liked you then. Carried a wee torch all these years. You could do worse. You could end up alone, Jess." She heaved a sigh and looked around at her neat living room. *Alone like me,* she was hinting. But she'd ended up alone because she beat her husband out the door with her Bible. I said nothing. "And just so you know," she went on, "he knows all about you. So you've nothing to fear on that score."

"Right," I said. "So. You told him everything, eh?"

"I had to, Jess," said my mother. "Tell the truth and shame the devil."

"You told him about the pteronophobia

and why I've got it."

"I told him you had mental troubles," she corrected me. "What you did when you were five."

"Yeah, that's right," I said. It was her version he was expecting. Granny collapsed when she saw the feathers. That's what he had been waiting for me to say.

"And if God has sent you the miracle of a good-hearted boy who can stomach you after that, you shouldn't set your face against it."

I fingered the little place on my cheek where the hole had formed in those long hours.

"There's nothing there," my mother said, her voice cold with scorn.

"I know," I told her. "It faded, years ago."

"You could still offer yourself to Jesus." She always said this, like it was good sound practical advice, and she always said it that way too. Like I was borderline even for him, but you never know — he *might* take me.

"Which one?" I replied. I was right back in my well-worn groove now, all the old favourites. My mother hissed like a serpent. She hated my multiple-Jesus theory. I hadn't meant it to be offensive. I just reckoned there was two at least. Actually, that was only because I'd had the idea first about Moses and it made a lot of sense there.

"One of the Moseses is all, 'Get back to Israel, get back to Israel,' that's what matters to him, right? And the other one is like, 'Okay, so the deal is we wander the earth but we stay off the seafood? That'll do me.' It's not the same guy, Mum! And whoever was writing the story must have known it because the only way it hangs together is make him live for five hundred years. It's worse than Bobby in the shower. It should have got fixed in the edit."

And as for Jesus? One of them was all poverty and humility and foot-washing and he was great. But the other one was *Son of God, get me! I'm eternal, I'm fantastic.* It wasn't the same guy. Couldn't be.

"It's just like Winston Churchill and Brangelina," I said to her. She stuck her needles back in her yellow knitting and folded her arms, ready to fight the good fight of faith. "If you hear a kind of bogus slogan about keeping secrets and eating nettles, you think, 'oh that was probably Churchill, eh?' I bet he never said half the stuff he gets the credit for. And if you hear some Hollywood couple's brought out a line of vegan cupcakes with a flavour named after each of their children and you want to tell someone, you're going to say it was Brad and Angie, aren't you? So any old tale about some preacher round about that time, round about that place . . . you know?"

"Tale?" she said. "Tale? Great is the truth, Jess, and mighty above all things."

"Finally," I said. "Something we agree on. Great is the truth, Mother. You're right there. So this friend of mine. Did you tell him the great mighty truth about what *you* did when I was five?"

"I?" said my mother. "I protected you. I kept quiet. Never breathed a word."

"You breathed plenty to me," I reminded her. "You basically stuck a knitting needle in my ear and scrambled my brains for me."

"Why do you say such ugly things?"

"Fair enough, I'll say it pretty. You kept quiet about how I wrecked granny's quilt and how she came in and saw and was so angry that she had a stroke and died on the floor right in front of me begging me for help and how I did nothing, for no reason at all. For two days."

"Jess, what is the point of going over it and over it?" she said.

"And how, worst of all, I concocted a crazy story about how I was tied to the bed, and you tied me."

"I was punishing you for killing my

408

mother! I was following God's teaching and training you up in his ways. That's how much I still loved you. After you killed my mother!"

"I was five," I said. Shouted really. "Even if she *had* dropped dead over a few fucking feathers, I was *five.* But she didn't, Mother. She died when she saw what you had done to me. She died of disgust when she saw what you were. You killed her. Not me. Because it matters what order things happen in. It *matters* what caused what and what came later."

"You broke my heart," my mother said. "You break my heart whenever I think about you."

"Got it," I said. "It's just a shame that none my therapists has managed to change my memory to what you prefer. None of them: Jennifer, Lauren, Caroline, Moira, Annabel, Eilish, Stacey. Have I forgotten anyone? Oh right, of course, you wouldn't know. You've never been. You don't need to because you've nothing on your conscience, and you won't come with me because you don't owe me a thing."

She didn't answer, just sat there praying, with her needles clicking away as fast as ever. I was summoning the courage to stamp all over my dreams.

"What was his name?" I asked her. "This old friend who came to you?"

"Gary?" said my mother. "Gavin? It started with a G, anyway."

"Gus," I said as the walls came down on me. He'd been to my mother months ago and asked about me.

"Could have been Gustav," my mother said. "Gus for short." Which didn't seem likely although, as she said it, something like a faint smell was beginning to distract me. A breath of an idea, far away.

I did my breathing. In for five out for six, in for six out for eight. So none of it had happened. Not really. We hadn't chanced on each other. He hadn't forgotten the day with the cakes. He'd tracked me down after that day and found my mother. Why? He hadn't understood, like some super hero, the first time I told him. He'd been mugging up on it for months. Of course he had. Where? Probably in the library. That's when he learned where my flat was too. I could feel the tears gathering. How many times had I told myself it was far too good to be true? But the kids were true, and what a great dad he was, and Pram was true even if House and Shed were . . . if Steve was right. And why? What was the point of it all? It wasn't as if it was random. He had set me up. He'd laid a plan and he'd put it in motion the day that Becky die—

I shook my head.

"What?" said my mother.

No way. Becky didn't kill herself. No way. Everything was coming clear now. The diary was hers but the writing on the note, like the writing in the workshop, was his. Gus had snagged me that day in Marks and Spencer's. I was part of the plan.

"What?" said my mother again.

"I can't believe it!" I burst out. "How can someone fool you so completely?" He was acting the whole time, pretending to understand, pretending to love and care and — He made some mistakes, though. No one could have got over Becky so quickly. That was sick. And no one would have let a stranger take his daughter to school the day after her mum died. No one would have *sent* his daughter to school. What was that all about? And he should have wanted to know where Ros had gone to. Where the hell *had* Ros gone to? And where exactly did I come in? What part of the plan *was* I? All of a sudden, I knew.

I was his alibi. I was to hear him talking to her, in the food hall, and I was to drive him home. He knew I was the type, after the day with cakes. He knew I was interfering (inappropriate, unprofessional). I was to drive him home and persuade him to call the police. And I was to find the note too. I was supposed to be with him from before Becky died until the police started searching. It was only when it all went wrong that he came up with that mad story about talking to a voice-mail. And that was only because the hill walker found the car so quick. Oh my God! The hill walker. Gus had asked him to come to the funeral. I leapt to my feet.

Then I sat down again. No, no, that was crazy. He only wrote last night. He told *me* he was asking him to the funeral. Actually he was just making contact. If he was going to "pay back" the hill walker, it would be another long slow plan he put together, like the one he'd put together for me.

I really needed to keep calm and try to see which bits of this hall of mirrors were real and which bits were Gus's stories, as borrowed and fake and stupid as the famous sculptures he said were his that only someone as dumb as me wouldn't have heard of, like Steve had.

So what was true? Gus killed his wife. Tricked me. Ros disappeared.

And all of a sudden I knew where she was.

Knew why Gus couldn't face the workshop too.

He wouldn't be there. He wouldn't dare. Not after we'd told him that the cops were onto him. I warned my mum not to let him in if he turned up at her door — it didn't take much persuasion: all I had to say was *drugs* and she couldn't get me out fast enough to get the chain on at the back of me. I took the farm track instead of the lane through the caravan site, stopped in the farmyard, and waited for the workers to come over and tell me I shouldn't be there.

"A week past Tuesday," I said. "A week yesterday. That was the day that really got you pissed off, eh?"

"Coming and going all bloody day, the pair of them," said the fat one. He hawked and spat the way men do. Some men.

"Were they really?" I said "Coming *and* going? Both directions?"

"You were there," he said. "What you asking me for?" He sniffed back hard again and then stopped before he spat.

I'd never get them to think carefully enough. Maybe the police would have more luck when it fell to them, but I'd bet anything that one car left and then another car left hours later and nobody came back in

413

between times. Not driving anyway. Because the only way that Gus could have done it would be to take his car to somewhere nearby and leave it there. Get a bus back and walk the footpath home. Then take Becky in her car, send it over the cliff, and come to town on his own to pick up Ruby, go to Marks and Spencer's, and meet me. And all the time Dillon was in his cot in his sodden nappy.

"Never mind," I said to the farm guy. "You better gob that out before it chokes you."

I trundled on down the track to the back of the house. My charger was in my bag. I got out at the back porch, unplugged the washing machine, plugged the charger in, and hooked up the dead phone from the basket. With my own mobile, I started to call Gizzy's number. I'd ask her for Ros's number and I'd ring it and then I'd know. But I didn't need to. Once the battery started charging, Ros's phone lit up like Christmas. Missed calls and voice-mails. Texts and e-mails. Gizzy's number was there. Her sister's number in Poland too. And so it was true.

I turned my feet towards the rough path over the turf that led to the workshop, and the brick grave he'd built inside, and to whatever was left of her in there. The sun was sinking in one of those mad splashes of pink and orange that would look hellish anywhere else but a sunset, and the sea was calm, just rippling in without a hint of foam. It was heaven here. Just heaven. And everything I'd asked myself about Becky — asking what was wrong, what did she want for, living like this? — was true of Gus now. All his talent and his wife and his kids and this beautiful place. What was wrong with him to carve out this evil from life and throw everything precious away?

I think I saw him out of the side of my eye quite a while before my mind took in what I was seeing. There was no jolt anyway, when I turned round and looked full on. He was sitting with his back against the workshop wall, facing out to sea. He'd changed his clothes again, long shorts with pockets on the legs and thick walking boots. Better boots than the ones he'd worn to the funeral. He had put on jewelry too, strands of coloured string and shells on leather round his neck. And Jesus, he'd cut off all his hair. It was sticking up like a brush. He watched me approach him without turning his head. I could see the glitter of reflected light as his eyes moved in their sockets.

I stood right in front of him, cutting out

the sunlight, and his skin that had seemed orange in the blast of light looked dark and dirty now.

"Gus," I said.

"Who the hell are you?" he said. "Was that you I spoke to on the phone?"

And it wasn't Gus's voice. It was similar, but not the same.

"Where's Gav?" he said. "Where's Becky? That was just Gav being Gav with the funeral crap, right? But where are the kids? Who *are* you?"

"Jessie Constable," I said. "And you're the sculptor who made that pram, aren't you? Jesus Christ, a *twin* pram. You're the other one. That's what Steve said. The other one. You're Gus King."

I turned and watched the sun slip down into the long ribbon of cloud on the horizon. It was easier to talk once the light was low.

"Where have you been?" I said at last.

"Thailand," he said. "Idiot. I couldn't stay here after Dave died. I thought 'Thailand for me!' Nothing but a load of wee girls on their gap year with their daddy's gold card. Still. Gave Gav and Becky a break, house-sitting for me."

"Oh Jesus," I said. "It was more than that. Gav's been life-sitting for you."

"Eh?"

"I met 'Gus King' a week ago. He even showed me round his studio."

Gus put his head in his hands and groaned. "He's harmless," he said. "Never going to win the husband of the year award, mind you. Poor Becks. But she loves him. She talks about leaving, but she'll never do it."

"Not now she won't," I said. "But I think she was going to. She had a friend, a lawyer, that was going to help. You might even know her. Ros, from the caravan site?" He shook his head. "Anyway, I'm sorry to have to tell you that Becky really did die last week. Car crash. It's down as suicide —"

"She'd never leave the kids."

"But — I'm really sorry to say this about your brother — I think he might have . . ."

"Yeah, it wouldn't surprise me," said Gus. "Jesus, wee Becky."

"You said he was harmless!"

"Harmless as long as Becky stayed, and I thought she'd never leave. I knew if she walked, anything could happen. He must have totally flipped."

I sat down beside him. Not too close. It was frightening to see that familiar face, tanned brick-red but otherwise just the same, and to hear that nearly identical voice.

"He didn't flip," I said. "He planned it for months." I saw him turn to stare at me. "He stalked me. He built that thing in there. At least, I'm assuming he built it. It wasn't you?"

"What thing?" said Gus.

"Breeze block," I said. "A . . . crypt, I suppose you'd call it. I think Ros's body's inside."

"In there?" He had sprung to his feet. "Seriously? There's a body in there?"

"I think so," I said. "I haven't got a key."

But it only took him a minute, four or five good kicks, to burst the hasp free of the wood and get the door open. He gazed at the wall in front of his face, looked from side to side.

"I've been right round," I said. "There's no way in."

Then he backed up, took a run at it, and scrambled until he had got the upper half of his body up on the top of it. He swung his legs up too and disappeared.

"Nothing," he called back. "Except there's a wire, there's a box or something. Like a . . ." I heard a snapping sound and he reappeared and threw a bright blue and yellow object down towards me.

"Oh, God," I said. "It's a booster — you know — a hub. It's for a baby monitor. I think she was alive when he put her in there."

He landed beside me, stumbled, and then was gone. He kicked down the door of the other workshop and I could hear him crashing and banging around, dragging something heavy, small things hitting the floor, smashing.

"Can I —"

But he was back, trailing a flex, plugging together the extension and the . . . it looked like a drill. Of course it was, and he fired it up and set it against the mortar between two bricks.

That was when the night descended to hell. The last of the glow was gone from the sky and the cold was seeping up from the ground and the noise of it, brutal and whining, the dust and the stink of the motor getting hotter and hotter and the look on his face, running with sweat and grit and I could only stand there, waiting and praying. *Please God, please God, please God.* Was there any chance?

"Go through and get the claw hammer," he shouted at me. I ran to the other workshop and stared around. A claw hammer? Where would it be? But I found it quickly enough, and a pick axe too, so I brought that with me, and when I was back by his side he threw down the drill and picked up the hammer and clawed a brick out of place, put his hand into the hole, and bellowed with rage and frustration. I shone my phone light and saw metal gleaming. He whacked it with the claw end of the hammer and grunted.

"Zinc," he said. "Not steel. We're back in business." And he was right. He got the drill through it, pulled with the hammer, pulled it into a hole, and drilled the second brick, the inner layer of this hellish thing Gus — no, Gav — Gav the bampot, Gav the black sheep, harmless Gav — had built.

And once there was a hole right through, the work went faster. He clawed a brick out and punched and drilled and pulled the metal away and clawed out another brick, and when there were four or five gone and the space was the size of a drain, he threw down the hammer and turned to me.

"Go in," he said, shoving me. "I'll keep working. In you go."

Of course it made sense. I was smaller, but for a just a minute I hung back, staring my horror at him. Then I shook myself into courage. *Remember your granny,* I thought. *Time to do good, Jessie. Time to go.*

I knelt down and put my hands through the hole into the darkness, breathing in the smell that plucked me back through time to that night on the quilt with the ropes round my wrists and the thing on the floor that wasn't Granny anymore. Then I closed my mind and pulled until my shoulders and head together were jammed into the tiny space, scraped by the jagged edge of the zinc and the rough cobbles of mortar. I twisted, one shoulder first, my face buried in my arm, and wriggled my chest forward, breathing out, compressing my ribs, trying to shrink myself. I had to get through now. I couldn't go back. I was stuck. I was jammed like a cork. Then I forced my arm to go behind my head, I heard my elbow pop but it made some room, and I inched myself farther and then I was through! My shoulders were through and my waist and hips and legs followed until I flopped down onto the floor. I sat up, looked back through the hole at Gus's filthy purple face, and then clicked my phone light on and turned away.

All I could see was bricks. Blocks and mortar and a concrete floor. I summoned the courage to roll the light around. A toilet. There were plastic bottles and bits of cardboard and packets ripped to shreds. A pile of cloth. Nothing else in there at all.

That pile of cloth. It had to be. I walked slowly over and saw it become, in the pin of light, two halves; denim and wool and a foot in a sock and a head of dark hair curled away from me. So still. I put out my hand, expecting the wooden shock of a corpse, but when I touched her shoulder, she was soft. And she was shaking.

I crouched.

"Ros?" I said. "It's all right. You're going to be okay."

She moved as slow as a tree growing, turned, showed me that round face and the dark eyes.

"Are you here?" she said. Her voice was a rasp. "Are you real? Where are they?"

"I'm really here," I told her. I put my hands on her cheeks and let her feel the warmth from my skin.

"I thought I was dreaming again," she said. "You're really here? Are they okay?"

"Jessie?" It was Gus's voice.

"She's alive!" I called back to him. "Keep working on the hole so we can get her out. She's very weak." I heard the motor start up again and felt the concrete floor begin to thrum under my knees as he put the drill to the wall. She started shaking, sobbing; that noise must have terrified her when it began. I put myself close behind her, drew her to me, and spoke softly into the cup of her ear.

"It's okay," I said. "Ros, it's okay. It won't

be long."

"I'm not Ros," she said. "Where are my babies? Tell me you got them away."

TWENTY-TWO

We carried her, between us, back to the cottage. Gus's arms were jelly from the drill or he'd have taken her, but I wanted to carry my share of the weight. I had been so blind and so desperate to stay blind, hanging on to my fairytale long after I should have seen the truth. I could have saved her at least a few days of the hell she'd been in.

She didn't seem to know how long it had been, though. That was a good thing, in a way. We sat her down on the couch and Gus laid a fire and lit it — another shiver as I saw that same body doing that same job in exactly the same way; I kept having to look at his hair to make it stay real that he wasn't the person I thought I knew. He was no one to fear. I was safe now.

Except . . .

"Where is he, do you think?" asked the other Gus. The real Gus. We were in the kitchen making food for Becky, making a hot bottle and a cup of sweet tea, a piece of toast with butter and honey, something easy to get her started on. I shook my head.

"And when do we call the police?" he said. "Why are we waiting?"

"When Becky's stronger," I told him. "When she can convince them she doesn't need hospital. She needs to stay with her children now."

She hadn't been able to take in what I had told her. "Where are they? *Where* are they?" she kept on asking. I went back through with a warm towel to wipe her face, and I tried again to explain.

"They're at my flat," I said. "They're with a priest — Father Tommy Whelan, from St. Vincent's? You must have heard of him." She nodded vaguely. Of course, she had. Everyone in Dumfries knew Father Tommy, and she was a Dumfries girl. I thought of something else. But first things first. "And Kazek's there."

"Who?" she said.

"Ros's friend from the Peter Pan project?"

Her face clouded, she was drifting. "The roofer?" she said. "One of those migrant worker guys that Ros . . . where is Ros? She was there and then she was gone. I was so out of it. What did he give me?"

I shook my head. Who knew what he gave

her? As to where Ros was, she'd been cremated just that day. The Fiscal was satisfied. There'd been a note. The next of kin ID'd her. No need for a post-mortem, no need for an inquiry.

"But they're safe?" she said. Gus came in with her tea, perched on the edge of the sofa, held it to her lips.

"Careful, it's hot," he said. How could she see him without flinching? Maybe when you really knew both of them they didn't look anything like each other, but every time he came close to me, my skin prickled. I remembered the feeling of being close to Gus, the other Gus, that other tingling, and my stomach heaved. I had slept with him, fucked him (tell the truth and shame the devil) while his wife was in that stinking cell. He'd left me here with his kids and gone there to — to what?

"What was the baby monitor for? Could he hear you?"

"God, I pulled it out!" said Gus. "I should have left it. Evidence."

I saw Becky look at him, just a flicker. "Other way round," she said. "I could hear *him*. He told me everyone thought I was dead. He told me he was going to kill the kids. He wouldn't tell me when. I was so scared."

"He'd never have killed the kids," I said.

"Men like him kill their kids all the time," she said. "Ros told me. They're fine as long the wife stays, and if she tries to get away they kill the kids to torture her. It happens every day." I nodded, Gus had said as much. The real Gus. Harmless as long as Becky stayed.

"He might have wanted to," I said. "But he'd never have got away with it. He'd have been caught."

"He's clever," said Becky. She had sipped half the cup of tea now and she reached out for the toast, took a bite, and chewed. "He found a . . . patsy. He told me. Through that wire. He'd found a girl with a history, screwed up about kids, you know. Childless but obsessed with them? He made her look weird. He made her tell people she knew him when she didn't. He'd phoned a help-line, he told me. Said this strange woman was moving in on him and the kids and he didn't know what to do. He's clever. Make you believe anything if he tried. He's clever that way."

I nodded, even managed to smile, but she saw through it. Her eyes flared and she shifted, spilling a bit of her tea.

"Oh my God," she said.

"Yep," I replied.

Gus looked from one to the other of us. "I'm going to heat you up some soup," he said. "If that toast's gone down okay. And then we're calling the cops. We can't leave it much longer."

He went to the kitchen. I knew my eyes had followed him; I didn't know why until Becky told me.

"It's okay," she said. "There's no phone in there." I turned, caught her look, knew that she knew what I was thinking. Knew she was thinking it too. She put out her hand and I took it.

"God, I'm filthy," she said. "Do I stink?" I screwed my nose, said nothing, and she managed a smile. "How are they?" she asked me. "Really and truly. Are they okay?"

"They missed you," I said. "Dillon doesn't really believe you're gone. Ruby just about roared the house down when Gus — damn it! — when Gav told her. She's been asking all sorts of questions about heaven and angels. But I'm sorry to tell you, they've been sort of okay. Gus — *Gav* is a fantastic dad. They love him, don't they?"

"They do," she said. "He is. Why do you think I stayed this long? When someone sets out to fool you and they're really good at it, it works like you wouldn't believe."

"Oh, wouldn't I?" I said. I could feel a

428

huge bale of sobs unravelling deep down inside me. It was good news. It was all good news. The best there could be anyway. Dead people couldn't come back to life, so what could be better than finding out that the dead one was single, no kids of her own, and the mum whose little ones needed her was back again, a miracle? What was wrong with me? Kazek was safe. Becky was safe. If I could be there when Ruby and Dillon saw her, I would treasure the memory all my life. So what was wrong with me?

As if I didn't know. What was wrong was that I'd had a weeklong dream, loved and loving, feeling the fear letting go, someone to listen, little hands holding mine, laughs at the tea table, someone who thought I was wonderful. I could still hear his voice saying "bravest and best little girl." I should have known — did know deep down — that it was all too good to be true.

"Oh, Jessie," said Becky, and she put her hand out to me. "What did he do to you?"

I shook my head, sending the tears out of the corners of my eyes. "Nothing," I said. "Nothing in comparison. You shouldn't even be thinking about anyone else except Dill and Ruby."

She squeezed my hand tight, shook it, made me look at her; her face was solemn, her eyes huge.

"You're wrong," she said. "I'm the one you talk to. I'm the only one who'll understand. He bricked me up in a cell for a week. Yeah, he did. But that's easy. Tell someone that and all you get is sympathy. It's the seven years before that really fucked me. Like the stuff he did to you. It's the stuff you can't tell anyone because they'll just say you're imagining it or it was your own look-out, or they'll laugh and tell you you're over-reacting." She leaned in close, her breath metallic on my face. "It's the stuff he made you believe you did to yourself. That's what kills you."

"Cup-a-soup," said Gus, coming back. "God bless Dave and his store cupboard. I remember this stuff from before I went away."

"So, Jessie," said Becky. "Will you make the call?"

"You're calling the cops?" said Gus.

Becky's face was a shadow as she looked at me. "Course," she said. "Gus, can I ask you a favour? Can you go to Jessie's and get the kids? Maybe keep them there for another hour or two. Give me a chance to get clean. Then bring them home? Here, I mean. I know we'll have to move out now you're back, but . . ."

"You've got it," he said, leaping up. Desperate to be doing something. He snatched the car keys I held out to him, repeated my address, and was gone.

"*He's* a good guy," said Becky. "He's the real deal."

"Will he work out why we wanted him to go right now if we don't want the kids back till later?" I said.

She shook her head. "01387 253 555," she said. "That's our flat at Caul View."

"Yeah, you're right," I said. "That's the only place he can be."

We didn't really make a detailed plan, no synchronised watches or anything. We just both knew what had to be done and we did it. I called the number and Gav answered.

"Gus," I said.

"How did you get this number?"

"Online," I said, crossing my fingers and hoping he'd swallow it.

"How did you know I'd be here?" he asked. My heart sank. If he was suspicious of even that, we didn't have a hope.

"I thought it was worth a try," I said, trying to sound breezy. There was a long silence before he spoke again.

"What do you want?" he said. That seemed like a bit of progress! I tried to keep

431

the tension out of my voice as I answered him.

"I'm sorry about earlier. I wanted to say sorry. And ask if you're okay." The next silence was even longer.

"I've been thinking," he said, at last. "I said I trusted you with the kids. If you wanted to take them to your flat and let them hang out with a friend of yours, that's fine." In other words, I thought, that was something else to tell the police after I'd killed them. Something else to make me sound unsafe for kids to be near.

"I lost it today," he said. "At the funeral. And you got the brunt of it. I can't believe I spoke to you like that."

"You know what I think it was?" I said. "You're just flexing your muscles again. You're only human. After what Becky did to you, it's only natural you'd see what it felt like to do it to someone else if you got the chance. But look! You're sorry already, aren't you? You're a good man, Gus." Becky was giving me thumbs up.

"I love you," Gus said.

"I love you too. Come home, eh? The kids are sleeping. Come home to me."

I held my breath. The only thing that didn't fit was that he shouldn't have known where my flat was. I should be asking him

432

how he knew where to come in Dumfries to find me. I wasn't asking, and I didn't want him to wonder why.

I was wrong. There were two things that didn't fit. And he hit me with the other one.

"Why did you say the cops were at my place?" he said. I hesitated, and I think my face turned pale because Becky was suddenly still and alert, staring hard at me.

"I didn't say that," I told him. "Or I didn't mean to. I meant that I was *going* to phone them and ask them to meet me at your place. I got the kids out of the way in advance, you know?"

"Why, though?" Gus said.

"I was going to tell them something. But I changed my mind."

"Tell them what?" said Gus.

"I think I know why Becky killed herself. Finally."

"Because Ros left," said Gus.

"No," I said. "Ros didn't leave. Becky killed her. I found Ros's phone at your house. In the basket by the washing machine." He was so silent now that I thought the called had dropped. He'd forgotten about the phone. And he didn't like making mistakes and people noticing them.

"Gus?" I said "Are you still there? I know it's a horrible idea, honey. I know she's the kids' mum. But I really think it makes sense of everything. Ros is dead and Becky couldn't live with the guilt."

"Where did she dump the body?" he asked.

"Probably in the sea," I answered. "I bet it turns up soon. Like that guy in the river." I could have bitten off my tongue, but how to resist it? One of the reasons for luring him here instead of calling the cops on him was that I was dying to know how Gus had the bracelet if Gary Boyes had killed Wojtek.

"You've really forgiven me for all those things I called you?" he said. He was so close to biting down on the bait. Inches away.

"Of course," I told him. "There's nothing you can say to me that could change how I feel. I know the real you."

"Okay, in that case," he said. His voice had changed. "Who was that guy in your flat?"

"No one!" I said "A guy from the Project I'm letting use it because I'm staying with you. No one at all. God, if you'd ever seen him, you wouldn't worry!"

There was another silence. And then I heard him let his breath go. "I'm on my way," he said.

"I'll see you soon. Drive safely, eh?"

"Christ," said Becky, when I hung up. "That was brilliant. Remind me never to start a head game with you!"

"Are we really going to do this?" I asked her.

"Yes," Becky said. "We really are."

She had a shower, with me sitting on the toilet seat, just in case. She was still pretty wobbly. And after it, she and I went to the kitchen and looked through the cupboards. We tried out a few things but both settled on the same big black frying pan. Took a length of washing rope from the junk drawer too.

"I wish I felt stronger," she said.

"Nah," I told her. "You get to see his face. That's the first prize. And you deserve it. Seven years to seven days? No contest."

So she sat in the armchair facing the living room door, and I stood behind it. We closed the curtains in case he looked in. We heard the car. I gripped the pan handle and tried to breathe deeply. She managed to sit back in the chair and keep her face calm. She was amazing. She wasn't even gripping the arms. The front door opened.

"Hiya," he shouted.

"Hi," I shouted back. Shit! I hadn't been

435

expecting to talk. I sounded —

"Jess?" he said. "You sound —"

He opened the living room door.

"Hello, Gavin," said Becky. *She* sounded perfect.

I was too slow. I thought he'd be pole-axed, but he sprang forward, grabbed her arms, brought her down. I jumped over the coffee table, swung the pan, he took his teeth out of Becky's neck — he'd bitten her! — and started to turn and so it was his face, not his head, that I hit. And I felt the soft collapse of a cheekbone. He grabbed the pan. He wasn't out. He was rearing up, standing, holding Becky up beside him. I heard a sound like a sword being drawn. He spun around as she lifted the poker from the brass stand and brought it whistling through the air to his skull.

And then he crumpled. He folded, knocking against the table and shifting the chair with a shriek of its casters on the floor as he went down. We stood over him, both of us gulping and panting. Then I blinked and peered closer at Becky's neck.

"He broke the skin," I said. "You're bleeding. I should —"

"There's no time," she told me. "Tie him. Quick!" I wound the rope round his ankles and his wrists, knotted it, got the brown tape from the sideboard drawer and covered his mouth — God, he bit her! — then I took his ankles and dragged him to the door and outside, and between us we dragged him over the turf, watching his head bumping on the tufts, seeing his hair knotting and ripping.

If he had come round before we got there, we would never have been able to stuff him through the hole. Even with just his dead weight, it was touch and go. Me inside hauling, Becky outside shoving. When he was in, I bent and looked through the opening at her.

"Are you sure you can stand being back in here?"

"I wouldn't miss this for the world," she said. "Shift over and let me through."

We took the tape off his mouth and propped him up on the far away side. We stayed close to the way out. Close together too.

"If he gets free or just if he starts moving too fast," I said, "you go first and I'm right behind you, okay?"

"Okay," said Becky. "Ssh — he's stirring."

He coughed and groaned, then he quieted as he remembered what had happened, remembered enough to wonder what was coming now.

"Hi, Gav," said Becky.

I switched on the torch I'd brought.

"Hi *Gav*," I said. "I hope your head's clear, because I'd really like to get a few things straightened out before we leave you here, and the cement we mixed up won't stay workable for long, so we'll have to talk fast."

"You didn't mix any cement," said Gavin.

"Okay, you've got me," I said. "I didn't mix any cement. And I didn't get Becky out of here either. And I certainly didn't keep you sweet and then take your children away. It's all a fantasy."

"Gus is home, by the way," Becky said. "So even if Jessie hadn't sussed you, you still would have failed when he saw this place."

"Can I ask you what came first, Gav?" I said. "Where did it start? You don't just one day say, 'I know: I'll kill my wife's friend and pretend it's her and brick my wife up and find someone to blame when I kill my kids and tell her I've done it'."

"*Tell* her?" said Gavin. "Fuck that, I was going to put their bodies in here with her. There's a plate in the roof that lifts off. The mortar's just skim there. I was going to drop in more supplies and two dead kids to keep her company."

"Why?" said Becky. Her voice was low, all the bravado gone.

"Because you had *no right* to leave me and take them away," he said.

"And why kill Ros?" said Becky. "Why fake my suicide? Why not just say I had left you?"

"Seemed like more fun," he said. "Nearly went wrong though!"

"Fun?" I said.

"He's lying," said Becky. "It wasn't for fun. He didn't want anyone to think his wife could leave him."

"Ros died for *that*?" I asked.

"Ros deserved it," said Gavin. "She thought she had the right to stick her nose in and help my wife to leave me. She had it coming. It was her fault how she ended up. Her choice all the way."

"Did *I* deserve it?" I asked.

"You humiliated me," he spat. "You deserved everything you got."

"When was this?" I said. I honestly didn't know.

"The cake," said Becky. "He came home and told me."

"And that fucking hellish guff in the living room too," said Gus. He didn't sound angry. He sounded . . . aggrieved.

"The smell of the spilled milk?" I said.

439

"You're not even kidding, are you? And Wojtek. What did he do?"

"Who?" said Gus.

"The Polish guy they found in the river," I said.

"Who?" said Becky.

"Him!" said Gus. "I didn't kill him. He nearly did for me, though. It was all going perfectly, a-okay. The car went over, right to the bottom, out of sight. Could have sat there for days. And I got back to the side road where I'd left my car without another soul seeing me. Perfect place it was. Too perfect. Totally deserted road with a motor-way junction at the top and an A-road with a bus route along the bottom. Why do you think I picked it? Turns out I wasn't the only one. Fifty yards from my car — a body! Slit from ear to ear, dumped at the side of the road, just lying there, laughing at me. Just one of those sick things. A total coincidence. So I moved him. Gently down the stream. Merrily, merrily, merrily, merrily —"

I asked a question just to stop him singing before I threw up from the sound of it. Becky was quiet too. It had gone too far for her now. She was drifting again, exhausted, and must be in pain from the place he bit her.

"You tore off one of his bracelets," I said.

"Oh yeah, he was dripping with that gay-boy shite," said Gus. "Yeah, I burst one off. Meant to fling it in after him. Didn't notice I'd forgotten till I was emptying my pockets."

"You ruined your clothes," I said. "You went in the water."

"I had to," said Gus. "But it was a coincidence. I didn't kill him."

"Yeah, you did," I said. "And you're wrong about the coincidence. If Ros hadn't disappeared on Saturday, he'd never had been there to get killed at all. Where was she from Saturday to Tuesday anyway?"

"She was here," he said. "I had to keep her alive until the drugs were out of her. But it gave her a chance to think too. About how sorry she was she'd poked her nose into my business. Should have heard her snivelling and begging. Should have heard the things she offered to do."

"I don't want to hear," Becky mumbled. "Jessie, please. I'm so tired. I don't want to hear any more."

"Yeah, okay," I said. "Come on."

"See you in your dreams, girls," said Gavin. "I know you'll never forget me!"

We stood. I helped Becky up and helped her through the hole in the wall too.

"You'll do time for this," he shouted after

441

us. "Gus'll shop you. The kids'll end up in a foster home, Becky. Ruby won't even be twelve before she learns to give a —"

"Shut up shut up shut up!" Becky screamed.

And after that all we could hear was his laughing, until I had heaped up the bricks and poured the bag of dry cement all over them. Would it hold him? It would have to.

Becky turned and started walking home.

"The kids'll be back soon," she said. "I can't wait to see. . . ." She stopped talking and then she stopped walking and then she sat down like someone in a frock at a picnic but kept sinking, folding over, and dropping until her face was on the grass. I sat down beside her.

I thought about what he'd said. It was rubbish. Becky wouldn't do time. Ruby would never be near a foster home. I thought about Gus, the real Gus. Would he go along with it once he knew? And at last I thought about Gav. Tied up and in the dark. No matter what he had done. Tied up in the dark and starving. I got my phone out and dialled.

"Yeah. Hello? Hi, yeah," I said when they had put me through. "Okayyyyy. Jessica Constable. It's not my address, actually. But I'll tell you where we are. And I know I asked for you guys, but we might need an ambulance too."

I lay down beside Becky, looked up at the stars, told the cops the address, told them we were in the field between the cottage and the bay.

"Sounds lovely, doesn't it?" I said. "Romantic? Sounds too good to be true."

"Are you all right, love?" asked the dispatcher.

I started to tell her I was fine but stopped myself. "Not really, no," I said. "Can you stay on the line, please?"

"I'm staying right with you, my darling," she said. "You stay here with me."

POST SCRIPT

Think Sandsea's grim in October? Try it in February, when it's rained every day for three weeks and the beach is covered in seaweed and lumps of sodden driftwood and the odd rotting seal. My stomach lifts and turns.

"It's dead," says Dillon. "It might come back, though." It's not a bad lesson to learn at two years old; bound to make him turn out optimistic about life in general. Ruby was the one who really bust a fuse.

"You lied!" she screamed. "You told me Mummy was dead! Where's my daddy? Where is he? Bring him back. Now! Now!"

But there was no children's visiting in the remand centre. They talked on the phone and he wrote to both of them, sent Dillon pictures and wrote Ruby poems. Becky saved everything for them.

"He's still their dad," she says.

"Don't you worry . . ." I want to ask her.

It's easiest to talk when we're walking on the beach, when we don't have to look at each other, when we can both watch the kids instead. "Don't you every worry that they'll —"

"Turn out just like him?" says Gus, the real Gus. "Why should they? He's not going to bring them up, and they've only got half his genes. I'm a clone of Gavin, Jessie, and I'm nothing like him."

"I suppose you're right," I say. And I hope it's true. Hope more than either of them could know, because I haven't told them.

"I'm going to miss this place," says Becky. "I do love it here."

"And as soon as the conversion's done, back you'll come," says Gus. He's making a loft — like a real artist would live in — in half of the bothy, keeping the other half for a studio, adding a wee bit on. He made a lot of money selling Pram to some ghoul. So Becky and the kids will have the cottage.

"Yeah," says Becky. "And I need to be with my mum and dad for a bit. I need to try to explain why I cut them off like that." She glances at me. "Think of something to say they'd believe. No point in trying to get the truth past them." I squeeze her arm. She's right about that. I heard the same thing from Dot. Sister Avril too. *Why did*

445

she stay? Not ever *Why did he take her away from her family, mess with her head, kill her friend, keep her prisoner?* No, it's always *Why did she stay?*, like it's love and hope and trust that are the puzzle. Not whatever's wrong with Gavin.

"Evil," said Father Tommy when I asked him. "There. A nice plain answer everyone can spell."

"It doesn't explain much," I said.

"Neither does sociopathy," Father Tommy pointed out. "It just gets a higher Scrabble score. Lust, sloth, gluttony, pride, envy, greed, and anger. Hit all seven and you're evil. Gavin King's well on his way."

"You could be right, Father," I told him.

"Ah, Jessie," he said. "Have you thought any more about what I asked you?"

"I have. Would it matter if I was turning Catholic partly to bug my mum? Could we 'God's mysterious moves' that one away?"

"You're a terrible girl," he told me.

"Well, I'll let you know," I said. "You'd have to carb up for my first confession, mind."

"And then I could say your wedding mass." He was chuckling, teasing me.

"You're quite a romantic for a celibate priest," I said. "Dream on."

Kazek's gone to Poland with Ros's ashes.

446

He'll be back in Dumfries for the trial. He might stay at my place. He phones me a lot. We get on quite well — even over the phone — for two people who basically don't share a language. I think about Gav and his silver tongue and wonder if it's better this way.

But I have to decide what to do. Would Kazek still be interested in me if he knew? Should that matter? Do I really believe the evil of Gavin King will come out in his children? Is it best not to chance it? But if I commit a mortal sin, can I still be a Catholic after? Or is this latest news just one more thing that's far too good to be true? Like Jesus.

Tell me the story of how I was born, Mum.

Well, I was immaculately conceived, my son. And you were the child of the holy ghost. Mm? Oh, don't worry about who he is. I'll tell you when you're older. And I was still a virgin and there was this census, see? And a stable, a star, and a donkey or two. Three wise men with the shittiest notion of presents for a baby. There were shepherds involved. Somehow. Just your usual boy meets girl, angels, kings, and farm workers, really.

What would I *say*? Well, Mummy was a headcase and couldn't trust herself to have a baby in case she couldn't take care of it and it killed its granny one day. And Daddy wanted to wipe out his other family and not have to go to jail for it.

Yeah, right.

But if it's a girl I could call it Ros, and if it's a boy I could call it Wojtek. And no matter what it was, if I gave it life then we'd be square, the universe and me.

As every single one of those endless bloody therapists used to say.

FACTS AND FICTIONS

The Dumfries Free Clothing Project is based only very loosely on the Edinburgh Clothing Store and all the personnel are fictitious.

St. Vincent's is imaginary and not connected either to St. Michael's or St. Joseph's in actual Dumfries.

It would be folly to suggest that JM Barrie House in the book has no connection to Moat Brae House in Dumfries. What I will say is that the fictional council, the fictional committee, the fictional Gary Boyes, and the goings-on in general are not in any way connected to the marvellous work of the Peter Pan Moat Brae House Trust and their blossoming vision of a children's literature centre at the site. I took Moat Brae House down a very different path and am delighted that fact is so much better, in this instance, than fiction. Details of the real project can be found at www.peterpanmoatbrae.org.

Shed Boat Shed in the book is closely based on the work of Turner Prize winner Simon Starling, and Gav's imaginary House is very similar to the extraordinary and moving Semi-Detached by Michael Landry. (Thanks to Erin Mitchell, who read a proof copy and reminded me what this piece was called.) I think Pram in the story sprang from my imagination. If it didn't and anyone recognises the idea, as Steve recognised "Gus's" borrowings, I'd be grateful if you'd let me know at catrionamcpherson@gmail.com.

ACKNOWLEDGEMENTS

I would like to thank: everyone at Midnight Ink, especially Terri Bischoff, Nicole Nugent, Amelia Narigon, and Bill Krause (look, Nicole, an Oxford comma!); my agent, Lisa Moylett; the real Jessies — Jess Lourey and Jessie Chandler; my sisters in crime, Sisters in Crime; my sisters in life — Sheila, Audrey, and Wendy; the other three — Catherine, Louise, and Nancy; the new three — Sarah, Spring, and Eileen (paging Dr. Freud!); the cast of thousands from Mystery Writers of America, Malice Domestic, Bouchercon, Left Coast Crime, Harrogate, Bloody Scotland, and the Crime Writers' Association of the UK (who said writing was a lonely pursuit?); and my sister-in-law Bogusia Gruszka McRoberts, without whom Kazek would have been silent.

ABOUT THE AUTHOR

Catriona McPherson was born in Scotland, where she lived until moving to California in 2010. She is the author of the award-winning Dandy Gilver historical mystery series and is a member of Mystery Writers of America and Sisters in Crime. *As She Left It* was her first modern standalone. You can visit Catriona online at www.catrionamcpherson.com.